G000123310

Property

A. O'Connor

POOLBEG

Published 2007
by Poolbeg Press Ltd
123 Grange Hill, Baldoyle
Dublin 13, Ireland
E-mail: poolbeg@poolbeg.com
www.poolbeg.com

© A.O' Connor 2007

Copyright for typesetting, layout, design
© Poolbeg Press Ltd

1 3 5 7 9 10 8 6 4 2

A catalogue record for this book is available from the British Library.

ISBN 978-1-84223 -277-4

Typeset by Type Design in Palatino 9.5/14
Printed by Litografia Rosés, S.A, Spain

About the author

A. O'Connor, a graduate of NUI Maynooth and Trinity College Dublin, has written two previous novels published by Poolbeg, *This Model Life* in 2005 and *Exclusive* in 2006, and after working in marketing for several years now works in property.

Acknowledgements

Mark Twain advised: "Buy land. They've stopped making it." As a country we've certainly taken on that mantra with our obsession with property over the past decade, and that's why I thought it would be good to set a novel amongst the movers and shakers of our property market.

Thank you to Poolbeg for their continued support and advice: Kieran, Niamh, Conor, David and Lynda. A special thanks to Paula Campbell, doyenne of the publishing world. And thanks to Gaye Shortland whose editing ability never ceases to impress. Thanks to Deirdre Heavey at RTÉ. Thanks to Laura. And Orla and Tomás for your help. A big thank-you to all the booksellers whose work is much appreciated. And to all the readers who enjoyed *This Model Life* and *Exclusive*, I hope you enjoy *Property* just as much.

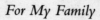

For My Family

1

They say the road to hell is paved with good intentions. As Denise Cunningham cast her eyes around the boardroom table of the charity Forward, she realised this to be true. The ten committee members were frantically brainstorming ideas for charity functions whose official goal was to raise funds for deprived children. But Denise knew the excuse for a glamorous and high-profile night out was of equal importance to everyone present. She sighed as she pushed her sunglasses further back into her hair, realising she was as guilty as any of them. Everyone on the committee was a particular type. They were mostly society wives, with too much time and money on their hands, interspersed with the occasional businessman who had made his money and now wanted the country to see him as an altruist, willing to give his time and money and be involved in good works. She knew all the secrets behind their careful images. The forty-year-old, immaculately groomed lady on her right, with an addiction to prescription drugs. The long-suffering blonde who sat across from her, whose husband slept with anybody, except his wife. The super-confident brunette, three seats down from her, who actually had had a major nervous breakdown four years ago. The handsome car dealer, whose hidden criminal record . . .

"Denise?" said Tony Higgins, the charity's chief, jolting her out of her private thoughts.

"Yes, Tony?" Denise sat forward and pretended to look interested.

"What do you think? We can usually rely on your judgement to decide an argument?"

Denise creased her forehead, pretending to think, a gesture that hid the fact she hadn't a clue what they had been talking about.

"I think we need to go away and sleep on this one for a couple of days before we decide," she said.

There was a general grumbling and nodding of heads around the table.

"You're right. I suggest we meet here on Friday afternoon before we decide where we have the ball," said Tony, closing over his folder.

People began to rummage for their bags and jackets as they stood up.

"Thank God you said that," whispered Denise's friend, Martha. "I couldn't listen to them scoring points any more."

"I know – the politics of it all," agreed Denise, standing up and swinging her oversized handbag over her shoulder.

Denise stood out from the rest of the women on the committee and from all her other acquaintances. It wasn't just her arrestingly pretty face, her tall, slim body or her long sleekly black hair. It was the way she carried herself. She had a natural air of cool confidence about her. Not arrogant or boastful, but just sure of herself. She was thirty-three years old, and more hip than all her friends. She could get away with any look, from ball-gown to combats and a T-shirt, and still look classy.

She and Martha waved and said goodbye to everybody, and left the boardroom. They walked through the headquarters of Forward, which was situated in a Victorian building behind Molesworth Street.

"So, are you all prepared for the big move?" questioned Martha.

Denise rolled her eyes. "Let's not go there. The new house is a mess. Cormac has employed two interior designers and all they seem to do is bicker and not get any work done. Meanwhile, Glenwood is still a construction site, and looks like it's going to be for some considerable time."

Martha looked at Denise, starry-eyed at the mention of Glenwood. It had been a word bandied around the press for a couple of years: a development of thirty-five palatial houses, built by Cunningham Homes, being marketed as an exclusive and gated community for the seriously rich and famous. The first of the houses were now due to come on the market, causing a frenzy of speculation as to who would be buying there and at what price.

"I can't wait to see it," said Martha truthfully.

"Neither can I!" Denise smiled, waving goodbye to Martha.

As she walked down the street towards her car, her mobile started ringing. She flicked it open and saw the caller was her husband.

"I've been trying to get you for the past hour," snapped Cormac Cunningham.

"I was in a meeting with Forward and had my phone off." She opened her sports BMW and stepped in, pressing a button to lower the convertible roof so she could take full advantage of the afternoon's sunshine.

"I always have my phone on no matter what meeting I'm in."

"Well, that's because you're special." Denise didn't try to hide the sarcasm in her voice, as she inserted an R&B CD into the player and switched it on. "What do you want anyway?"

"I want to know – have you started packing the stuff at the apartment yet?"

"No, and I'm not going to either. The house at Glenwood is nowhere near ready to move into yet and I'm not prepared to live in chaos for a long period of time with things half unpacked."

"These houses are going to be on the market in a month, and we have to be moved into No 1 by then."

"Ever the optimist," she said.

"Ever the pessimist," he shot back.

"Realist," she corrected.

"You wouldn't mind just helping me out here, would you? Our whole marketing strategy for Glenwood is based on a launch next month. And you know we have to be seen to be living there by then!"

She sighed, understanding where he was coming from.

Cormac and Denise Cunningham were trendsetters. Cunningham Homes had grown into one of the biggest construction firms in the country, and there was a great level of interest in them. The social pages of magazines rarely went to press without a photo of Denise in them. Denise had seen it all before. Cunningham Homes would use the fact that she and Cormac were living in No 1 Glenwood to attract the publicity needed in an industry where selling lifestyles was as important as selling homes. As first residents at Glenwood, they would set the tone for the rest of the site. It had been the same when they moved into the penthouse they had occupied now for three years. Cunningham Homes had built the apartment complex, The Pavilions, and had gained huge publicity because they lived there themselves. Denise was resigned to it: where she lived would always be dictated by where Cunningham Homes were building. As she thought of the grandeur of No 1 Glenwood, she knew she could live with it.

She switched on the ignition. "I'll start sorting through things today," she conceded, as she manoeuvred out of the parking space.

"Good." There was relief in Cormac's voice. "I'll see you later."

She turned off her mobile as she drove down the road.

A black car pulled out of a parking space across the road and followed her at a safe distance.

2

Cormac Cunningham put down the phone and massaged his temples.

"Well?" asked his sister, Lisa, drawing on a cigarette.

"She's going to start organising things."

Lisa looked cynical. "I know it must be hard for her to get anything done. She's so busy every day flitting between the hairdresser's and the boutiques."

Cormac shot her a warning look. "Can I remind you that you are breaking the law smoking in my office?"

"So report me." She sat back and inhaled deeply. "It's you who'll get the fine, not me."

Michael Farrell listened to the brother and sister sniping at each other without much concern. He had become well used to them over the years.

The three of them were sitting in the site office at Glenwood. As was customary on construction sites the office, a series of Portakabins, had been erected high, offering them a view across the site. Cormac stood up and went to one of the windows, looking down at the men busy working against tight deadlines. Across the site a series of spectacular houses, all with unique and individual designs, stood in various states of completion. The project was way behind schedule. When they had started Glenwood, they had envisaged the first of the homes coming on the market six months before now.

"No matter what, we release these houses on the market on the 18th of next month," said Cormac. "We've too much money out with these mausoleums – we need to start flogging them."

"Our whole marketing strategy is revolving around you two living at No 1," said Lisa. "If you're not in by then, it'll make the campaign look flat. I've got all the Property Editors from *The Independent* to *The Times* ready to do front-page features revolving around you and your lovely wife being the first residents of Glenwood."

"Well, tell them they should have those articles in their papers for the week of the 18th," said Cormac.

Lisa focused on her brother. "That means lots of photos of the interior of No 1."

"Yes," Cormac nodded.

"You need to get real, Cormac. I was in No 1 today and it looks like a – a – well, a building site!"

"Which is exactly what it is!" snapped Cormac.

"Look, we have everything under control," interrupted Michael. "Go ahead and arrange the press for the week of the 18th, Lisa. And it'll be all hands on deck to make No 1 ready by then."

"And if it isn't, it's me who ends up with egg on my

face," snapped Lisa.

Seeing Cormac about to explode Michael said quickly, "It'll be fine, Lisa."

Lisa looked in Michael's reassuring eyes and nodded.

No matter how highly strung Lisa became, and that happened a lot, a word from Michael could make her feel at ease. They were both in their mid-thirties and had known each other for twelve years since he had come to work in the sales office of Cunningham Homes. He had worked with Cunningham Homes for seven years and risen to the post of Sales Manager, proving himself an excellent estate agent and very popular with the Cunningham family. When he then made the decision that he wanted to go out on his own and open his own estate agents, Cormac had quickly offered to set him up in business. Cormac had very early on realised Michael's ability and didn't want to lose him. So they had come to an agreement. Cunningham Homes would set Michael up, and in return be the major shareholder of the company. The new estate agents, Farrell's, would represent them as their chief client. Lisa, by then a fully qualified estate agent had headed over to Farrell's and begun to work there in a senior position. There was no need for Cunningham Homes to have a Sales Office any more under the new arrangement, and she was only too delighted to continue working closely with Michael.

The Cunningham/Farrell partnership was renowned: quality homes sold with imaginative marketing campaigns.

"We'll let you get back to building." Michael stood up.

"Fine," Cormac said as he went to answer the phone.

Lisa and Michael walked out of Cormac's office. Cormac's secretary looked up from her typing to observe the two walk by. Lisa was a woman who stood out a mile. She had long dyed-blonde hair, which was matched with heavy make-up. She kept herself slim, and dressed loudly and often revealingly, and was guaranteed to be wearing the highest heels. Michael was a handsome man, full of energy and ideas. The press gave him a hard time, but the secretary had always found him polite enough. Unlike Lisa, who could switch from being full of fun to absolute bitch in a few seconds.

Michael and Lisa walked down the steps outside the office and got into his car.

"You mind if I do?" asked Lisa, lighting a cigarette.

"Would you stop if I said no?" he asked, smiling as he turned on the ignition.

"No." She shook her head and opened the window.

He drove from the makeshift carpark and through the site towards the entrance.

"They are some gaffs," remarked Michael as he drove past a couple of the houses.

"Hmmm, Denise is a lucky bitch moving into one – having said that, she has to live with Cormac, not so lucky. Are you still contemplating buying one?"

"I don't think so. Bit of a dream really, but I couldn't afford what we are asking for these."

"Cormac might do you a deal."

"What, like throw in a free dishwasher?"

"That would be about the size of it all right," she laughed. "But, well, you can't live in that townhouse all your life."

"And why not?"

"You're going to have to settle down and get married some day – you're getting on a bit now."

"Thanks!"

They both laughed.

"It's half four, that's me finished for the day," she said, yawning and sitting back in her seat.

"I'll drop you back to your car at the office, and then I'll just about make that showing in Sandymount for five thirty."

"Oh, don't bother with it. Ring Jayne and get her to do it instead. I need a drink – we can just go straight to the pub instead."

"We went to the pub last night," he reminded her.

"So what? We work hard and we play hard. That's always been my motto."

He sighed, and dialled Jayne's number at the office.

* * *

Denise looked around the duplex penthouse that had been their home for three years. Where to start packing? She walked into the kitchen and checked the pasta sauce which was bubbling away nicely, before going out and pacing the lounge again. Room by room was the only way to do it. She would start in the guest room and work her way up. Looking around the maple-floored lounge with its ultra-modern white furniture, she realised she would miss the place a lot. She walked over to the wall of glass and, opening it, went out onto the balcony. She enjoyed living close to the city centre. Everything was at hand for her. The development had been an overriding success for Cunningham Homes. The final phase was still being built but Cormac had put it on the back boiler as he concentrated on Glenwood. Although the space would be fantastic at Glenwood, being situated out in Kinsealy wouldn't be as convenient for her life. She had suggested to Cormac that they keep a small pad in town for convenience. He had just looked at her as if she had two heads, and firmly said no. Remembering that their help was off tomorrow, she decided it would be a good day to start sorting through things. The maid only ever got in the way.

The front door banged and she heard some rustling in the hallway. She went back into the kitchen and stirred the sauce.

"You home?" Cormac called.

"Just cooking dinner!"

"Nightmare of a day," he said, throwing himself on the couch and massaging his temples.

She wandered out into the lounge. He was eight years older than her but was ageing well. She figured that Cormac was one of those people whose presence was so strong you often forgot what they actually looked like. The power of his personality could literally sweep people away.

"Drink?" she asked, already knowing the answer.

"Whiskey."

She fixed for herself one too.

"What did you get up to today?" he asked, taking the drink and sitting up.

"You know what I did." She was irritated because she had told him of her Forward meeting over breakfast.

"No, I don't."

She nodded sarcastically. "I went to a knacker pub and drank with the locals all day long – as you can see I can hardly stand from the drink by now."

He glanced at her, slightly amused and slightly irritated. "Pity you didn't. It might have put some sort of a smile on your face."

She smiled broadly in a fake fashion. "But, my darling, every time I see you it makes me smile as my heart jumps for joy."

He smiled sarcastically back at her.

She got up and went into the kitchen.

"And before you start nagging, I'll make a start on packing things first thing in the morning," she called as she drained the pasta. "But I'm warning you, Cormac, come the 18th, if I arrive out there and the place isn't liveable, like it was when we moved in here, I'm just going to stay at the Four Seasons until it is."

She served up the food, then took the two filled plates into the lounge and down the corridor to the dining-room. He got up and followed her.

"I'm sure if Health and Safety knew the conditions we were living in here when we first moved in, they would have had a fit. Electrical wires hanging down from everywhere –"

"You're exaggerating –"

13

"Window missing from the bathroom –"

"It wasn't missing. It was broken."

"No railing around the balcony . . ." She placed the plates down on the table and sat down.

"Pity about you!" He opened a bottle of red from the wine rack and filled their glasses, "A couple of days of discomfort and you got to live in a place like this."

"I'm not doing it again, that's all . . . why the huge hurry anyway?"

"Because, my dear, we have a huge amount of money out in Glenwood, and we need to start getting it in."

She looked concerned. "Are we . . . stretched?"

"Not at the moment – but we're not in a position to go after anything else."

She nodded and smiled. She knew her husband. He wanted to go after something else.

"What is it?" she questioned.

"Huh?" He looked amused.

"Stop messing around? What have you your eye on?"

"You know about the Harbour Project?"

"Sure," she nodded. "That old industrial hole that they want to rejuvenate."

"Well, I've heard that it's about to get the go-ahead."

She smiled appreciatively. She knew the source of that information. Cormac's parents, Honey and Paul, were completely in with political forces.

"And I have my eye on some land there."

Denise sat back in her chair. "And you want to get in before the rush?"

"Yes," he nodded.

14

She felt a thrill going through her. He excited her when he spoke like that.

"In that case, you can rest assured I will be in residence at No 1 Glenwood by the 18th, even if my bedroom has no roof on it."

"That's my girl." He winked at her. He looked at his watch and began to eat quickly. "Better hurry. Meeting some of the boys at the Ice Bar at nine."

She raised her head. "Oh, you're heading out?"

"Yeah, forgot to mention it." He studied her face, "Do you mind?"

She laughed lightly as she continued to eat. "Not in the least!"

* * *

The Pembroke was packed with office workers. Michael manoeuvred his way through the crowd, trying not to spill the two pints of Heineken he had just got at the bar. He scanned the place looking for Lisa, confident that, as ever, she would have managed to find them seats. True to form, she was waving to him from a high stool at the other side of the bar.

"There we go." He placed the pints on the bar and sat up on the stool she had saved for him.

She grabbed her pint and took a large gulp. She tapped her long perfectly manicured fingernails on her packet of cigarettes. "This fucking smoking ban is driving me mad."

"Still?" He raised an eyebrow.

"It just pisses me off that they can tell us what we can

and can't do."

Michael looked at her and smiled. She hated anyone telling her what to do.

"You should have got Honey and Paul to put in a word with their friends."

"You kidding me? Mum actually supports the ban."

"Really?"

"She says she wished it was in force when she used to sing in the dance-halls. Her hair used to stink of smoke after every show."

"I'm sure she never complained though." There was a note of admiration in Michael's voice.

Lisa took another gulp of her drink and set it down on the beer mat. "Speaking of which, you're invited over for dinner on Sunday."

"I have a flying lesson booked for then." He was apologetic. He had just begun to take flying lessons, and Lisa knew he was really enjoying it and excited about them.

"But Honey insisted you come over." Lisa looked at him, her eyes full of concern. "She said she hadn't seen you for quite a while, and was going to get lamb in especially because it's your favourite –"

"All right, all right," he said half laughing, half irritated. "I'll reschedule my lesson."

Lisa looked thrilled. "You're nuts learning to fly anyway. It's too dangerous."

Michael just nodded and smiled, refusing to be drawn into another discussion with her about his flying.

"How did that showing for the house in Monkstown

go this morning?" he asked, quickly changing the conversation.

Lisa threw her eyes to heaven. "The idiot of an owner gave me totally wrong directions to get there, and I got lost, and when I finally found the house, it wasn't the least bit like he had described it to me over the phone – I mean, I've heard of shabby chic, but this was ridiculous. The place was falling apart. I would be embarrassed to show any of our buyers around it."

"It's a great area though. It would be snapped up in a minute."

Lisa shook her head. "The Farrell's name equals luxury. If you start diluting your message you're fucked."

He nodded in agreement. He hated turning away clients but Farrell's had placed themselves at the upper end of the estate-agency business, in both houses and apartments.

Lisa spotted a copy of *The Independent* lying on a table beside her.

"Do you mind if I have a look?" she asked the people at the table. They shook their heads and, taking the paper, she turned back to Michael and started riffling through it.

"What are you looking for?"

"Jayne rang me earlier and said that bitch Ali O'Mara had written something negative about us today."

"Again?" Michael looked annoyed.

"Here it is." Lisa folded over the paper, peered at the column and began to read. "'*I'm not sure if it's comforting or disturbing to discover that the rich are just as susceptible to being conned as the rest of us. There's been much talk about the launch of Glenwood recently. A cluster of houses that are monuments to bad taste, erected on the edge of the city, to be flogged to the rich and the unnecessary for huge sums. My opinions about the outrageous scam being pulled off by property developers, in their rush to put up the price of houses, are well documented. Although I discourage our participation in this ploy to make builders and estate agents richer, I can't blame Mr and Mrs Joe Soap who are forced to mortgage themselves to the ·hilt just to be able to afford a box, otherwise described as a semi in a glossy brochure. If they don't buy something, then they don't have a home. But what sense is there in a person, wealthy enough not to be out on the streets, buying in Glenwood? This is pure vanity buying, and a sad reflection on our society, as we chase the bigger, the better and in the case of Glenwood, the crasser. Of course the builders of this scheme, Cunningham Homes, are no strangers to pulling the wool over people's eyes. They've forty years of experience and along with their henchman, Michael Farrell, are laughing all the way to the bank. The joke's on you and me, mate.'"*

Lisa slammed the paper down on the bar.

"For fuck's sake!" Michael said, his face red from anger.

"That one's a bitter little bitch." Lisa took a gulp from her drink.

"Out of all the property developers, she seems to be the most bitter, and particularly nasty, about us."

"I know. Look, I'm old enough and ugly enough to take shit but she just really annoys me. It's like a personal vendetta or something."

"We're easy targets," said Lisa. "Honey and Paul have been fixtures for years, and now Denise has become well known in the society papers. And as for you, you put yourself out there a bit during marketing campaigns."

"Personal is good," said Michael. "When we launch a new site, I want to be seen."

"Well, a couple of your stunts might have got lots of publicity but backfired a little on you personally."

"Such as?"

"The time you paraglided onto the rooftop of The Pavilions?"

"Maybe I've overdone it a bit in the past." He seemed embarrassed.

"No, don't say that." She grasped his hand. "I love the way you put yourself out there like that, and most people really admire you for it, but you just have to be able to put up with the occasional bitterness as well, okay?"

"I guess so . . . I'm still going to go ahead with the clown idea though.'

"Clown idea?' Lisa was confused.

"Yeah, for the opening of Glenwood I'm going to dress up as a clown, and I've organised the zoo to lend us an elephant, and I'm going to arrive in on top of it –" He started to laugh as he saw the growing horror on Lisa's face.

Then she realised he was joking. "You bastard! I wouldn't put it past you though."

* * *

Three hours later they were the last to leave The Pembroke.

"Where are you going?' Michael asked, seeing Lisa start to walk in the direction of the office on Baggot Street.

"To get my car from the carpark."

"Oh, no." He grabbed her arm and stopped her. "You've had far too much to drink – it's taxi time for you."

"I'm fine." She tried to dismiss him, but didn't try to free herself from the grip on her arm.

"You're way over the limit!" He put out his hand to stop a passing taxi.

"You're such a fusspot!" She was enjoying his concern.

"See you in the morning." He opened the back door of the cab for her.

"Aren't you going to share the cab with me?"

"We're going in opposite directions," he reminded her.

"Oh yeah." She leaned forward and kissed him quickly on the lips, before sitting in.

As the taxi pulled off, he waved and then began to scout around looking for another cab.

3

Ali O'Mara enjoyed the feeling of being behind the scenes of a live television programme. There was an excitement in the thought that in just a little while, around the corner in the studio, she would be participating in a programme that everyone throughout the country would be watching. It was the same feeling she got from writing her columns in the press – that feeling of going beyond your own square yard, your own life, and reaching out to the rest of the country, saying something that might change people's thoughts and ideas, even if it was just for a moment. She was thirty-one and after ten years in journalism, it was a power that still awed her, and she was aware of the responsibility attached.

Now she was sitting in the lounge area of RTÉ with her charge for the night, a young woman who had come to her a couple of months ago with her story. And what a story it was.

Four years before, Jennifer Murray and her husband

Malcolm had been a young couple in their early twenties, very much in love, with a happy future taken for granted. That was until Jennifer arrived back from her first day of work and found her husband murdered in their home. It had become known as The Honeymoon Murder and had gripped the nation's attention for a couple of months in a blaze of headlines, before slipping away as another unsolved crime. Ali had been surprised when Jennifer had contacted her office and asked to meet with her. She instantly recognised her name. They had met in Bewleys and spent the afternoon there. Jennifer wanted to tell her story. She wanted to relive the pain of what had happened to her. She wanted to remind people that the case was unsolved. And most intriguingly for Ali she wanted to reveal a series of police blunders that she felt had hindered the finding of her husband's killer.

"Why do you want me to write about it?" Ali had asked.

"Because you're Ali O'Mara. You're the best investigative journalist in the country."

"Am I?" Ali had thought that night in her apartment as she pondered Jennifer's story. She had graduated from Dublin City University with a degree in journalism and a thirst to make a difference. And she had. Throughout her twenties, she had built up a fierce reputation as a journalist with a nose to sniff out a good story and had unveiled much corruption. She was lucky. Her editors liked her and gave her a free hand and also during the nineties there was a huge appetite amongst the public for exposing corruption. And Ali led the way. She was known as the woman who had brought down two ministers, a hospital board and a trade union. People had feared her, and she had loved it. Her unquenchable thirst to expose the truth drove her on. And then slowly she had stopped getting the big scoops. It wasn't as if she wasn't still looking – she was. Even a disastrous relationship that went on too long wasn't to blame. The scoops just stopped coming. She still wrote her columns, but had become more of a social commentator over the past three years. And then Jennifer Murray had contacted her, and Ali felt she was back on track. A shocking murder that stank of official incompetence and neglect, told from the victim's point of view. It was classic O'Mara, and Ali felt she was turning a corner from her dry spell. She would show them again.

"Go easy on that," advised Ali as she saw Jennifer hold up her glass for a refill from the hostess.

"My nerves are getting to me," said Jennifer, her pretty features obviously nervous.

"You've no reason to be nervous. I'll be sitting beside you through the whole interview, and if you don't feel comfortable about anything that is asked, just don't answer it, and I'll step in quickly."

"Thanks, Ali. You've been so good to me. You really have."

"Nonsense. It's my job."

"No, you really care."

The researcher came over to them, smiling.

"How are you feeling?" she asked.

"A bit intimidated," said Jennifer, "but I'm going to go on. I owe it to Malcolm that he's not forgotten and this case isn't forgotten about."

Ali put a reassuring hand on Jennifer's and pressed it.

"You're great!" gushed the researcher. "Listen, if you just want to follow me out to backstage, we'll fit you up with your mikes, okay?"

* * *

"Four years ago, a young woman came back just after her honeymoon to find her husband murdered in their new home," said the presenter. "Jennifer Murray is here with us tonight to talk about the murder of her husband and with her is Ali O'Mara, no stranger to this programme, who in a series of articles over the next four weeks, starting today, will be exposing a number of police errors during the investigation which Jennifer believes have stopped her husband's killer being found. Ladies and gentlemen, Ali O'Mara and Jennifer Murray."

The studio audience clapped as Ali and Jennifer walked onto the set and sat down in their awaiting chairs.

"Ali, if I can just start with you. Reading your article today, it seems that there was some serious neglect from the beginning of this case."

"That's right." Ali sat confidently with her legs crossed. "When Jennifer first approached me about covering what had happened, I was shocked that certain basic procedures were not followed."

"I want to talk to you in greater detail about that a little later on, but first, Jennifer, how are you coping now at this stage?"

"It's with me all the time. I can't get away from it, and because I loved Malcolm so much I don't want to get away from it, not until his killer is found."

"If I can take you back to that time. You and Malcolm had just returned from your honeymoon, and you had just returned to work."

"That's right," Jennifer's voice was nervous. "He was supposed to go back to work that day as well. But we had just moved into the new house, and he decided to take the day off to finish some painting he had been doing."

"What happened when you arrived home?"

"Well, I'd phoned him a couple of times and he hadn't answered the phone. But I hadn't thought anything of it."

A man in the front row of the audience began to shift uncomfortably.

"She was angry with him for not returning the calls," he whispered under his breath.

"I let myself into the house as I always do and called his name . . . there was no answer. I took off my coat and walked into the kitchen where I found him . . ." Jennifer broke off and, looking down at the floor, started to rub her forehead.

"Jennifer ran to a neighbour's house and they contacted the police at that point," intervened Ali, seeing Jennifer couldn't continue.

"No, she didn't!" shouted the man from the front row.

A muttering ran through the audience and Ali looked at the man, who had gone deathly pale and was now standing and walking to the centre of the studio. "She found him painting the kitchen and he had spilled paint all over the floor. She was angry with him for doing this. She was angry with him for flirting with the air stewardess on the flight home. She was angry over a lot of things. They started to row and she saw red and she picked up the knife and she . . . oh no . . . please no!" The man dropped to his knees and looked as if he was in pain as he began to shout, "I can see it all! She's killing him! He's in shock as she plunges the knife again! Uncontrollable! She can't stop herself!"

* * *

Denise looked on intrigued until the programme cut quickly to commercials. She pressed the remote control and turned off the set.

The man in the audience was obviously some kind of psychic. Either that or a nut, she reasoned. She casually wondered if there was any truth in it. She yawned, got up and looked around the lounge, where she had stacked a few boxes on beginning to pack. She walked over to the windows and looked out at the city lights and she felt protected. She was glad she hadn't gone out. It was a night for staying in and feeling secure. She looked at the time. It was late. No word from Cormac yet.

As if on cue, the phone rang.

"Where are you?' she asked.

"In the Ice Bar."

"Where else?" she yawned.

"Out with the boys."

She could hear a woman laugh beside him.

"Good for you."

"You could always come and join us."

"You sound half pissed already, as I'm sure all your comrades are. Not in the mood to be ogled by middle-aged businessmen, thanks very much."

"Suit yourself." He hung up.

She put down the phone. He would arrive in pissed in the early hours, waking her up.

4

Cormac turned off the shower, stepped out and wrapped the gigantic bath towel around him. He surveyed himself in the mirror. He was in good shape, but could do with losing a couple of pounds. He walked across the porcelain-tiled floor of the en suite and went into the bedroom. Denise was lying in the bed as, somewhere, the morning alarm on his mobile sounded loudly. He retrieved the mobile from his suit trousers, casually thrown on the floor the previous night.

"If I could find that blaring mobile of yours I'd have fucked it out the window," said Denise, not bothering to open her eyes.

"If you had done that, then I would have fucked you out after it," replied Cormac.

"Why do you set your alarm for a Sunday morning anyway? Come to think of it – why do you set the thing at all? You're always up before it starts going. All it manages to do is wake me."

"Maybe that's why I set it, to wake you. Otherwise you wouldn't bother getting out of bed at all."

"Oh sure." She sat up and stretched. "What time do we have to be at your parents'?"

"One o'clock."

"Any idea who's going to be there?"

"Not sure. You know Honey – whoever it took her fancy to invite during the week."

Denise stepped out of bed and he watched her tall slender figure cross the room and go into the bathroom.

As she turned on the shower, Denise was half looking forward to the afternoon. Whatever about Honey and Paul, their social gatherings were always interesting.

* * *

"We're going to be late – will you get a move on?" Cormac hollered to Denise before going to pour himself a quick whiskey.

A minute later Denise came into the room.

"Why do you always have to take so long?" His voice trailed off as he watched her walk across the room, fixing an earring on. Her long hair was casually swept back. Her light tan had been touched up with very light make-up. She was wearing a beige wraparound cocktail dress that came to just below the knee, with matching high heels. As he took it all in, he admired her, and thought she certainly deserved her title as one of the great beauties of Dublin.

"You're wearing so much make-up you'd think you were about to pose for the front cover of *Vogue* or something," he commented.

She gave a dismissive laugh. "And you're an expert on such matters, I suppose? I have never paid attention to your opinions on make-up or fashion, and I'm not going to start now. And you can put that whiskey down, because I'm not driving."

* * *

Cormac's Jaguar turned into the entrance of his parents' Shrewsbury Road home. There were quite a few cars in evidence.

"I see Lisa is already here," said Cormac, spotting his sister's car.

"Probably already half jarred." She stepped out of the car.

"What is it with you lately and drink? You'd swear you never touched a drop yourself."

"I can hold my drink and I know when to stop, unlike others!" she spat back.

They climbed the steps to the front door.

"You just don't know how to have a good time. You can be so . . ." he was frustrated as he searched for the right word, "boring sometimes."

"If I am, I suppose it's because we become the company we keep after a while." She rang the doorbell.

A few seconds later the door swung open and there stood Honey is all her bejewelled glory.

"Well, you two! It's about time! I thought you might be lost or something." She leaned forward, kissed Denise on the cheek and embraced her son. Honey still cut a glamorous figure for a woman in her mid-sixties. Her big coiffured hair was still the same honey colour that it was back in the early sixties when she was on the show-band circuit, and which gave her name. Her still attractive face was well made up. Her dress was low-cut and boasting an expensive label. And her diamonds were dripping from her ears, neck and wrists.

"Come on through," she said loudly and they followed her down the corridor into the parlour. Denise quickly scanned the room and noticed a couple of prominent politicians, a couple of captains of industry and a property mogul. As she circulated the room, effortlessly greeting everybody, she knew the politician to whom she was now speaking about his garden had been up before a tribunal a year back involved in a major bribery scandal. The captain of industry she was now speaking to about his daughter's recent engagement was under investigation for major tax fraud. The wife of a successful entrepreneur she had moved on to chat with about fashion had been found guilty of shareholding conspiracy ten years ago. She knew all their secrets. And it didn't matter here. Honey and Paul greeted old friends the same no matter what they had done. Rules were for others, not for these people.

Cormac watched his wife charm the guests, feeling irritated with himself for admiring the ease with which she did it. Nobody could do it better.

"Did you speak to Michael today?" Lisa sidled up beside him, cigarette in one hand and gin in the other.

"No – it's a Sunday morning. I wouldn't usually speak

to him on a Sunday morning."

"As if you ever observed the good manners of not ringing people at whatever time suited you. Your last Project Manager quit because you kept phoning him at three in the morning to discuss staff rotas."

"Maybe Michael got lucky last night, and is sleeping in with her this morning."

Lisa's face reddened. "Oh shut up, Cormac! He's probably slaving over projected sales figures that you demanded by today."

* * *

Michael rang the doorbell of the Cunningham home. He straightened his tie and shifted uncomfortably. He hated being late going into the Cunninghams'. Honey would lead him into the drawing-room like a prize bull, making a big fuss and forcing everyone to look at him. Not that he didn't enjoy his time there once he had settled in. The Cunninghams had always treated him like family. He owed them a lot.

"Hey – are you late or is everyone else early?" boomed Honey swinging the door open and kissing him on both cheeks.

"Sorry – I think I'm a little late."

"It's never a problem being late in this life," said Honey as he followed her in, "as long as you make sure you're not early for the next one. Look who's here, everybody! Michael, have you met Father Clancy before?"

*　*　*

Lisa pushed her half-eaten plate of lamb away.

"You not hungry?" questioned Michael, who had been strategically placed beside her at the dinner table.

"No, I had a big breakfast. When did you reschedule your flying lesson to?"

"Early this morning."

"I really wish you wouldn't do that. It's such a dangerous sport."

"Hey, that's why I like it!"

Honey clinked her fork against her glass.

"Hey, everyone, a bit of quiet! I was hoping that Father Clancy might say a little blessing over the dinner. Father Clancy?"

"I'd be delighted to." Father Clancy blessed himself as did everyone else at the table.

Denise looked at Honey as the prayer was spoken. Honey's eyes were closed, a look of piety on her face.

Honey had been a young show-band star when Paul had met her. She toured the country with her band and she was quite the celebrity. In fact, she was still well known, although that might now be more in connection with the construction company. Paul, as well as being involved in the building industry, had also run a couple of dance-halls back then. He had hired in Honey and her band for a few gigs, and romance had blossomed. When they had married, the press had shown a lot of interest in the entrepreneur and his singer wife. Then they had disappeared for a long time . . . slowly and discreetly building the business, raising the two kids, and developing powerful contacts and friendships, until they had become a force that couldn't be ignored any more.

"Amen," said Honey to the end of Father Clancy's prayer and fixed her gaze on Michael. "I have to say this is the best lamb I've ever tasted. Michael, we got it in especially for you, as I know it's your favourite."

"Thanks, Honey." Michael smiled at her appreciatively. Honey seemed to think every dish she served up was Michael's favourite.

* * *

Paul Cunningham stood after dinner with his son, Michael and the Minister Martin Quinn.

"You're not bullshitting me, are you?" Paul quizzed, his permanent sour-looking face looking extra grumpy.

"I'm telling you now, and I'm only telling you because you're close friends – the whole Harbour District is going to be announced as a rejuvenation project."

"Like they did with Temple Bar?" questioned Cormac.

"Like they did with Temple Bar, like they're doing with the Docklands. The next area for this kind of a programme is the Harbour area."

"Well, if that's the case, we need to get in there early, boys." Paul looked at Cormac and Michael.

"The earlier the better," agreed Cormac, thinking of the huge outlay at Glenwood, and how they were not in a good position at the moment to go anywhere.

"I took a drive down there during the week," said Michael. "It's just one big industrial wasteland at the moment. Full of crumbling rusty old buildings."

"Remember what Temple Bar was like before Temple Bar Properties was appointed to oversee the redevelopment of the area? You wouldn't walk down there at night."

"It's come full circle. You wouldn't walk down there now again in case you were accosted by stag parties and hen nights," said Cormac.

"But it's still an overriding success. As is the Docklands and as the Harbour District will be," said Martin.

"So who's going to oversee the redevelopment of the area?" asked Paul.

"Nobody knows yet. The government hasn't appointed any company or anyone."

"From what I could see when I went down there, the best site is the old Heavey's Mill," said Michael. "Just beside the water, and very central to the area."

"I'd agree with you," said Martin. "That's government property, so the sale of it will be arranged by the project management company in charge of the Harbour area rejuvenation."

* * *

"How's that charity you're involved with going?" a captain of industry asked Denise.

"Forward is going just fine. We've just completed the building of a new youth centre in Hartstown. In fact, we're going to be having a ball soon, and I was going to ask you to take a table."

"You never miss a chance, Denise!" The captain of industry laughed and put an arm around Denise's back, a little too low for her liking. "Sure. Give my secretary a call tomorrow and we'll take a table."

"They don't come cheap," Denise warned, as she expertly removed herself from his grip.

"I never thought you did." He winked at her.

* * *

"I have to say you get better looking each time I see you," said Honey, taking Denise's arm and leading her away from the group she had been speaking to.

"Thanks, Honey, you're looking great yourself."

Honey felt the soft material of Denise's dress. "The style! You're a credit to this family. You know, when Cormac brought you home to us all those years ago, I didn't know what to make of you . . ."

Denise smiled and braced herself. Honey had mastered the art of the back-handed compliment and Denise now waited for the insult to follow.

"I thought – who's this one and what's she about? But, you know, you've earned your badge. You've helped raise this family's profile and never let us down . . . in public." Her eyes glistened, looking for a reaction in Denise's face.

"Or in private," Denise said smiling.

"The figure on you! You're as slim." She gave Denise's stomach a hard tap. "Nothing stirring yet, no?"

Denise managed to keep smiling. "You've been asking

me that for twelve years, Honey, and no . . . nothing –
stirring – yet."

"Pity . . . a family needs new life to keep it going. It
doesn't matter how much money you have, it's children a
family needs." She looked over at Lisa, who was talking to
Michael and looking adoringly at him. "You're my only
hope at this stage. That one –" she nodded over at Lisa, "is
on the verge of the menopause and not a man in sight,
except that eejit," with a nod at Michael. "who won't lead
her up the aisle, or anywhere else for that matter."

Denise continued smiling but stepped back from
Honey. She really couldn't stand her when she was like
this. She felt she could say anything, and be as crude as she
wanted to be, and it was her God-given right.

* * *

Ali looked around her rented apartment and couldn't
believe she had been there five years. She loved her
apartment. It was just right for her. Just off Haddington
Road, it allowed her easy access to everywhere she needed
to be.

She checked the roast in the oven, and then continued
to stir the gravy in one of the pots on the cooker. She
enjoyed cooking and having people over to dinner.

The doorbell rang. She came out of the kitchen and
checked her appearance in the mirror in the hall. Her
brown shoulder-length hair was sleekly brushed back, and
her matching beige skirt and top fitted the bill perfectly.
She walked down the hall and opened the front door.

It was her brother James and his wife Úna.

"Hi!" greeted Úna, with a big smile, her blonde ringlets bouncing. She was carrying a bottle of wine.

Ali embraced her and kissed both her cheeks. "Oh, did you have to bring him!" Ali groaned and embraced her brother.

"I know – I tried to lose him, but you know what he's like."

"Hey!" objected James, handing Ali another bottle of wine.

"There was no need to bring all this booze," said Ali. "Sure you can't even drink, Úna."

"I am allowed a glass of wine," Úna insisted, taking off her coat and walking into the sitting room. She was four months pregnant with their first child. They had been together for years and both worked as graphic designers.

Ali went into the kitchen and opened the large serving hatch between the two rooms.

"That smells really good," said James, "and I haven't eaten all day."

"What were you doing?"

"We were trailing through department shops looking at prams – how boring are we?" said Úna.

"Well, you might as well get everything now. There's no point trying to run around getting things when you're very pregnant or after the baby is born, is there?"

"Exactly my thoughts on the subject," said James, getting up and taking the crackers and cheese from Ali through the serving hatch.

"You've had the place painted," observed Úna,

looking around.

"Yeah. I did it myself over the past couple of weeks."'

"Why bother?" James looked perplexed.

"Because it needed painting," said Ali. She measured her words as if she were speaking to an idiot.

"I mean just get the landlord to do it."

"Oh, I'm sick of asking him." She came in and handed glasses of red wine to her guests.

"So you did it yourself?" James was incredulous as he looked around the meticulously kept apartment. "You've done so much to this place, and all you're doing is adding value to somebody else's property."

"Pardon me for not wanting to live in a pigsty!"

"James!" Úna intervened, seeing Ali was getting irritated.

The doorbell rang.

"That'll be the others." Ali got up.

James and Úna threw each other a look and sighed.

Margaret, Brian and Tom had arrived together.

* * *

The evening was going well so far. Margaret worked in the Ombudsman's office, was married to Brian, a documentary producer, and they had one child. Tom worked in publishing and was going through a messy divorce. Everyone had met the others loads of times in the past and they all got on.

Ali cleared away the starters and brought the roast out of the kitchen.

"That looks scrumptious," said Úna, as her eyes lit up.

"Do you want a bit of coal on the side?" joked James.

"Oh shut up!" said Úna. "I've been having some strange cravings," she explained to the others.

"I was the very same when I was having Rory," consoled Margaret.

"I can put up with cravings," said Úna. "It's him making me feel like a freak that I can't stand!" She nodded at James. "And I'm only four months gone yet!"

"You've had the sweet, now taste the sour," Ali said.

"Isn't that a fact," said Margaret.

There was a lull in the conversation, then Tom looked at Ali.

"I was watching *The Late Late Show* last weekend," he ventured, looking sympathetic. Everyone looked nervous but also relieved that the subject had been brought up.

"What can I say? As a journalist, I have to believe a source when they approach me until it is otherwise proven. I ended up with egg on my face big time." Ali shrugged.

Úna placed a hand on hers. "Your record is so good that nobody will remember it."

"I don't know. I can hear them say it now. The woman who brought down two ministers, a union and a hospital board has lost her touch."

"They won't say that," said Tom

"Brian, did you buy that holiday home you were talking about last time we met?" asked James, deciding to change the subject.

"Yes, we finalised the sale last month," said Brian.

"In Leitrim, wasn't it?" asked Úna.

"Yeah, not too far from the Shannon," said Margaret. "Fantastic bolthole at the weekends, and such good value compared to anything you'd get nearer Dublin."

"I wonder what figure you're talking about when you say good value," said Ali. "And a bolthole is something you get to quickly, not something you have to queue for hours in traffic to get to on a Friday evening!"

"Well, we like it," said Margaret, feeling slightly hurt.

"We're going to have to trade up now the baby is on the way," said Úna. "I love our house at the moment, but we didn't have a baby in mind when we put it together. It's amazing that what you think is ultra-modern and trendy is actually a death-trap when you throw a baby into the equation. I mean we took away the railing from the stairs to give the house a more open look," she giggled. "Can you imagine how child-unfriendly that is?"

"Where are you thinking of buying?" asked Tom.

"We'd love Sandymount, but don't think we can afford it. But we have built up a lot of equity in the house, so we should be able to get something good."

"Do you hear yourself?" said Ali. "'Built up equity', as if it's something you've worked for. You've just bought into the fucking building scam! You've gained a little equity, and so that's given you the false confidence to throw yourself into further debt."

"Well, at least we have equity – what have you got?" said James. "You're making your landlord richer by painting his walls."

"No, I'm not. I'm just not putting a huge debt around

my neck for the next thirty years so the likes of Cormac Cunningham can get richer."

"Look, I know you're the nation's conscience and everything, and you've been lecturing us all for years that we're being duped, but it's you that's been left behind, Ali. You're thirty-three and what have you got? Nothing. The landlord could throw you out of here tomorrow and you've nothing that's your own."

"Look, you may buy your second homes in Leitrim, or eat beans on toast for the rest of your life because you want to buy in Sandymount, but I'm not making some builder richer."

"Well, you're a fool!" snapped James. "Because everyone is getting settled and secure, and you'll have nothing. But when you're the conscience of the nation maybe that doesn't matter!"

"He's kind of right," Úna said gently. "In fact, I brought some brochures over tonight for you to look at –"

"Brochures!" said Ali, now feeling under attack. "Am I hearing you right? I'm not going to fall for some drivel in a brochure about improving my lifestyle by buying a shoebox for an exorbitant amount of money!"

"Well, you should," advised James. "You're in an insecure career and you should have some security behind you as you get older. What happened on *The Late Late* should have brought that home to you. You're as good as your last gig in your business."

"Well, thank you very much!" Ali's cheeks burned red.

"I'll tell you something," said Tom. "Since me and Niamh broke up – do you know what we're fighting about? The house. Who owns how much of it and what we're entitled to. And in the meantime, until we reach an agreement and sell the house, I have to rent. And I'll tell you this, I can't wait to buy my own place again – whatever the cost!"

Ali kept her eyes on her plate and didn't respond. She was grateful when Margaret diplomatically changed the subject.

* * *

Her guests gone, the plates and cutlery all tidied away into the dishwasher, Ali poured herself a large glass of wine and sat by the Georgian window to think.

It had really been a bad few days. The psychic on *The Late Late Show* had set off a chain of events that she still found hard to accept. The programme had cut to commercials quickly once the psychic had started with his vision. But not quick enough for the whole nation to share it. Security had rushed in and taken him away. Ali had quickly turned to Jennifer to console her. But one look in her eyes and she had gone cold. She had known what the psychic had said was true. She sat back in her chair, for the first time in her life not knowing what to do. As it turned out, she didn't have to do anything. Jennifer had calmly got up and walked out of the studio without another word. The following day there was a media furore over what had happened. Answers were needed, and the police gave a very cautious statement. But suddenly people were talking and it transpired that Jennifer Murray had been the chief suspect in The Honeymoon Murder for quite a while. And the supposed examples of police incompetence, which Jennifer had referred to, were in fact carefully orchestrated manoeuvres to try and find some evidence on her. It was the biggest mistake of Ali's career. She had failed to check with her police contacts before she'd written the first article and so was completely in the dark. For their part, the police had been happy to sit back and observe Jennifer Murray going public with Ali to see if she would slip up. Nobody had foreseen the presence of a psychic and now the whole undercover operation was ruined.

Ali's editor, Barry, had been away for a week and she dreaded what he would say on Monday.

She took another sip from her drink. She felt like such a fool. All her critics had laughed openly at her. Anyone she had criticised in the past had delighted in her misfortune. Competitor newspapers had written about irresponsible journalism.

Ali casually picked up the brochures Úna had left for her. Maybe they were all right. Maybe she should start thinking about her own future and security, instead of trying to put the country to right all the time. She looked through the slickly marketed developments and felt nauseous at the marketing speech used: spacious, unique, quality, architecturally designed, urban chic.

And yet she suddenly felt the need for some of that security in her own life. She looked around her rented apartment and she genuinely loved it. It had been her haven, as she had taken on the world and her lovers . . .

well, she'd had a few casual affairs that didn't amount to anything long-term. And then there had been Richard. A relationship that had gone on for too long and caused far too much pain. She had met him when she was twenty-five and on top of the world. He was a playwright, a few years older than her. They had got on like a house on fire. He completely admired her work and what she was trying to achieve. He encouraged her fully. He at the same time was having some success with his plays. Then he'd had a breakthrough with one of his scripts being adapted for television. The success had gone to his head very quickly, and he became very arrogant. His next script was bought by the BBC and turned into a series. She was so delighted when he picked up his first Bafta. Not so delighted when he picked up his first mistress. When she heard of the affair, she confronted him and there were tears, accusations, recriminations and finally forgiveness. There were rumours of other dalliances and he denied them. Then they were out for a night in Renards. There was a young actress there who had flirted with Richard all night. At the end of the night he turned to Ali and said: "If it wasn't for you, I could be going home with her tonight." She stood there hurt and then she wondered what she was doing. She was on top of the world, bright, highly intelligent, not bad-looking . . . and putting up with a comment like that. She would not allow herself to become one of those victims she wrote about.

"I'll tell you what, Richard. Go home with her, because I never want to see your sorry face again." With that, she stormed out.

He had tried to call her again, but she didn't want to know. She threw herself further into her job, and the awards kept coming for her.

Now she opened a brochure for The Pavilions. It was the only development that was close to the area she was living in now. And she did want to stay local, if she moved. She cringed as she saw the development was by Cunningham Homes.

"Buying into the property scam, O'Mara?" she smiled wryly to herself and took a sip of wine as she started to read what the development offered.

* * *

"Come on, Honey, give us a song!" called one of the guests in the Cunningham living-room.

"Yes, Honey, do!" called another voice.

"My God, no!" Fake horror was written all across Honey's face as the room of guests were all now calling for her to sing. "No way! Uh – huh!" She shook her head vigorously. "My singing days ended forty years ago. I couldn't sing now if my life depended on it!"

"Sure you can!"

Denise looked on at the familiar charade being played out. No matter what event Honey was at, there always came a time in the evening when the crowd would start calling on her to sing. And Honey, secretly delighted, would refuse until it was insisted she took the floor and relived her golden show-band days.

A man sitting at the piano was messing with the keys

in anticipation of Honey starting to sing soon.

"C'mon, Honey!" came a pleading voice.

"Well . . . I . . ." Honey carefully stood up and, looking ever so slightly nervous, walked over to the fireplace. "You're all so terrible!" she remarked, looking around the room. "You know I don't sing any more!" She smoothed her golden hair. "But if you insist . . ."

"We do!"

She looked at the piano player. "OK, I will sing – just one number – a song I used to sing in the sixties." She looked over at the piano player, nodded and closed her eyes meaningfully. The piano player knew exactly the song she meant and began to play. Honey then opened her eyes and her powerful vocals filled the room with "And, Honey, I Miss You".

Denise glanced at her Rolex, and saw it was nearly ten. The Sunday had seemed to drag and as she glanced over at Cormac, deep in conversation with his father and a politician, she knew there would be no early escape for her that night. She stood discreetly at the back of the room, leaning against a doorframe. As she watched Honey giving everything to the song, she knew the rest of the evening would be occupied with her going through her repertoire, and loving every minute of it.

Everyone clapped as she finished the first song.

"And how are you?" asked a voice behind Denise. She looked around as Michael came in from the hall and stood beside her.

"Fine." She took a drink from her gin and nodded over at Honey. "You're after missing raw emotion."

"I could feel it from the bathroom." He pulled a face. "Do you think anyone would notice if I slipped off?"

"Er, yes," said Denise with a discreet nod in Lisa's direction. Even as she did, Lisa turned her head and smiled at Michael. "Anyway, if I have to suffer another couple of hours of this, then I see no reason why you shouldn't either."

Honey launched into a high-pitched "Stand By Your Man".

"After all, they pay all our wages," said Denise.

"Excuse me; the name of my company is Farrell's. It's my surname over the door."

"True," she grinned at him, "and my name is Mrs Cunningham. That's my surname in Cunningham Homes. But neither of us is going to leave early, are we?"

"No," he smiled. He always enjoyed Denise. They understood what the other was saying without having to spell it out.

She took a tumbler from the table beside her and handed it to him.

"So in that case –" she took the decanter of gin and held it up, "will I fill you up?"

Honey hit a high note.

"To the top!" He held out his glass and grimaced.

5

Going into her dressing room, Denise selected a suit for the charity lunch she was about to attend and changed into it. Looking into the mirror, she began to rehearse the speech she was to give at the lunch.

"Ladies and gentlemen, it is an honour for me to have been invited by Forward to address you this afternoon." She shook her head. "Ladies and gentlemen, Forward has granted me the honour of speaking to you this afternoon about the calendar of events we have planned for the next six months . . ."

She trailed off as she gazed at herself.

She approached the mirror closely and stared at her face intensely, unaware of the minutes passing by.

* * *

"My office – now!"

Ali looked up to see the speaker was her editor, Barry,

back from holiday.

She stood up from her desk and followed him, aware all her colleagues were watching.

Barry was glowering at her from his chair. "What the hell has been going on with this Honeymoon Murder?"

She sat down opposite him and ran her fingers through her hair. "A bad judgment call on my part."

"Is that all you can say!" he exploded. "We have been made to look a laughing-stock over this. Manipulated by the chief suspect on national television! And then, let me get this right, there's a psychic in the audience who starts jumping around the place making it obvious that we've been duped?"

Ali looked up from the floor and sighed loudly. "That's about the sum of it, yeah."

"When you came to me with this story, I thought you had checked it out cast-iron. Did you check with your police contacts beforehand?"

She sighed. "No."

"You're a fucking eejit!"

"I know."

"And I'm a fucking eejit to trust you! It's been a valuable lesson to me. Just because you're Ali O'Mara I thought you knew what you were doing."

"If you had met Jennifer Murray there was no way that you'd have suspected anything or doubted anything she said either. She came across as so honest, so truthful, so in love with her husband –"

"She murdered him in the kitchen, just back from the honeymoon! The old Ali O'Mara would have sussed her out. *She* wouldn't have fallen for her bullshit for a second!"

Ali began to get annoyed. "What's with all this 'the old Ali O'Mara' shit? As if we're two different people or something."

"Well, hate to tell ya, girl, but you are!" Barry, seeing Ali was getting upset, softened his tone. "Look, it's like anything in life – we start, we peak and then we go downhill. Such is the law of science. All those stories you broke were amazing journalism, and your name will always be respected because of it. But let's face it, it's been a few years since you had any good scoops. And in your pursuit of capturing a headline again, your judgment has become clouded, as has just happened with The Honeymoon Murder."

"It was a mistake, Barry, a simple mistake."

"You might think I'm being hard on you, love, but it's you who's been hard on yourself, always trying to match up to a brilliant past. Let it go and stick to what you've been doing over the past three years. Writing social commentaries about the state of the health service and property market."

"No! Do you know what the problem here is?" Ali stood up, her face angry. "It's the state of the media. I've always taken risks and that's why I got the reputation I did. If I was an unknown journalist who'd fucked up, you'd throw me out on my arse. You want to have the kudos of me working here, but none of the risks. Well, I didn't enter journalism for an easy life. I'm going to keep on looking over the shoulder of every corrupt businessman and politician and lawbreaker in this country!"

She turned and stormed out.

Barry shook his head. He'd seen it so many times before. Hacks in a race against themselves and running out of time.

Ali slammed her office door after her and pulled down the blind on the door window. She paced up and down. She picked up one of her awards from the shelf and read the caption: *'Journalist Of the Year 1998.'* She held it tightly before tossing it into the bin.

She was not beyond her peak. She was just going through a dry patch. Anyone who had met Jennifer Murray would have fallen for her sweet heartbroken act and never in their wildest dreams have thought she was capable of what she had seemingly done. Was there really anything so wrong with wanting to expose corruption and crime?

Was she the only person who didn't care about making more money these days and had a genuine interest in a just society? Why was it that, at every dinner party she went to, the main conversation dominating the night was how much everyone's house was worth? It was crude and vulgar and unimportant in a world as corrupt as theirs. She picked up the brochure for The Pavilions from her desk that her sister-in-law had given her.

* * *

"She's beautiful, isn't she?" said the woman on Lisa's left.

There was a huge turn-out for the lunch at Brown's restaurant on Stephen's Green. All proceeds going to Forward.

Lisa stifled a yawn as she listened to Denise drone on about helping underprivileged kids.

"She's so elegant and stylish," the woman on her right gushed.

Lisa wished Denise would hurry up so she could go out and have a cigarette and get back to work.

She had only come because Farrell's was just down the road on Baggot Street and even she realised it would have looked rude not to show up once she had been invited.

"Thank God!" she said as Denise finished up and stepped down from the podium.

"I'm sorry?" said the woman on her left.

"Thank God we have such a beautiful and elegant patron as Denise." Lisa smiled falsely at the woman, quickly got up and hurried over to Denise to say goodbye.

Denise was posing for a couple of photographers for the social pages of magazines when Lisa carelessly walked in front of them and announced: "I'm off."

"Oh, so soon?" Denise said.

"Hey!" said one of the photographers, annoyed his photo was ruined.

"Stuff it!" Lisa snapped at him.

"Er . . ." began Denise, "we're announcing the winners of the competitions soon. Won't you stay for that?"

"No. If I win the crate of champagne, keep it for me. Anything else and you can give it back to the charity. See you." Lisa walked off.

"Thanks for coming!" Denise called after her before turning her attention back to the photographers and posing again. "Sorry, guys!"

Lisa searched in her bag for her cigarettes as she stormed down Baggot Street, found them and hungrily lit up. A waste of a couple of hours, she thought to herself. She'd had to re-schedule a couple of showings because of it. She stopped off in a newsagent's to buy some more cigarettes and then went into Farrell's.

"Any messages?" she asked the receptionist.

"Just your brother asked you to call him."

Lisa walked up the stairs and through the main room where five estate agents were busy on the phones. She walked past her office and straight into Michael's.

He was on the phone.

He smiled up at her as she sat on his desk and crossed her legs.

"Let's face it, properties don't come on the market in that area often. So when they do, you have to act quick . . . sure . . . I know the last offer is well in excess of the asking price but the market is dictating the price, not me . . . yes, you can think about it for a day or two, but I'm not guaranteeing the house won't be sold when you get back to me . . . okay, so you want to put an extra fifty thousand on the last offer? That means you're offering 950,000. Thank you, I'll inform the vendors, and get back to you shortly." Michael hung up the phone and shouted' *"Yes!"*

"What's happening?"

"The house on Richmond Road. It's just jumping up in fifty thousands. I never thought it would be so sought after."

"Great. Is that the end of it?"

"You kidding me? I've got four interested parties nipping at my heels and all of them have big dosh. It ain't over until the fat lady sings." He nearly added something humorous about Honey linked to his last remark, but thought better of it. "How was Brown's?"

"Pure shite. Denise was doing her 'Diana, Grace and Jackie all rolled into one' act. I dropped some cash into their coffers and off I ran." She got off his desk. "You've got something on your face."' She started rubbing his cheek hard.

"Ouch! Watch it!" He pulled back.

She moved to the door as she said, "We need to sit down over the next couple of days and start work on those brochures for Glenwood."

"Why not tomorrow?"

"Suits me," she said. "Right. I'm off to do a showing now – oh, I had an interesting enquiry this morning."

"From who?"

"Ali O'Mara."

Michael sat back in his chair and folded his arms. "Really, and what did she want?'

"She was enquiring about buying in The Pavilions. I'm meeting the bitch there at four thirty tomorrow."

Michael was smiling. "I might take care of that appointment for you. I think I'd like to meet Ms O'Mara after all the things she's written about me over the years."

"Sure, you're welcome to her. Drinks after work?"

"Of course. See you in The Pembroke."

She winked at him. "It's a date."

* * *

"Another wonderful success," Tony Higgins said to Denise as most of the people left Brown's. "We raised much more than we expected and it was a great press turn-out."

"That's good," Denise smiled.

"And it's all thanks to you."

"Hardly, Tony." She laughed.

"I mean it. The hard work you put in and the wonderful image you provide for us. We're very lucky to have you on our board."

"Not at all." She bent forward and kissed his cheek. "I'll see you at tomorrow's meeting."

She walked out of the restaurant and was heading towards Brown Thomas when she decided to drive out to Harvey Nichols instead. She walked around the Green to her car and let herself in.

As she pulled out of her parking space, the black car pulled out several cars down and followed her discreetly.

6

It was evening and the city lay spread out under the reddening sky. Cormac was sitting on the patio, scrutinising his wife's photo in *Image*. It was a feature on leading society women in Dublin and Denise was to the forefront of them.

He got up and went into the bedroom where Denise was sorting clothes into a 'to keep' pile and a 'to give away' pile.

"How's it going?" he asked.

"It's a nightmare. I never realised I had collected so much stuff."

He picked up a dress from the 'to give away' pile and looked at it. "And wasted so much money?"

"I'm not even going to go there," she said and shot him a warning look. "Me looking good equals me in the social columns which equals press for Cunningham Homes. QED. Any time you don't want me to put a show on any more, please inform me. I'd only be too happy to hang up my socialite shoes and stay in and watch some good soaps."

He pointed to her photo in the magazine. "Sure – like you could ever stop wanting the attention."

"I don't go out to get it. It just comes to me, and if ever it doesn't come any more, so be it and I'll live with it." She continued to sort through her clothes while she spoke. "Moving is a fucking nightmare!"

"Why don't you just get Honey to help you?"

"Are you kidding me? She would put every stitch I owned into the 'to give away' pile on purpose . . . I'm starting on your clothes tomorrow and to warn you – I'm going to be ruthless."

"Aren't you always?"

"I think you're getting me mixed up with yourself."

He moved over behind her. "You looked pretty good in that magazine."

"A compliment! I'm in shock!" She continued to sort through the clothes.

He put his hands on her hips and then slid his arms around her waist.

She stopped what she was doing and put her head back as he nuzzled her neck.

"You're looking pretty damned good now," he said.

"Do I?" she asked, turning around to face him.

They kissed and he began to caress her back, his hand working on her zip. He began to kiss her neck. "Any more thoughts on the baby thing?"

"Baby thing?" She froze.

He continued to kiss her neck. "Yes . . . us having a baby."

She pulled back abruptly from him.

His face grew red with anger. "You still won't talk about this issue. Why won't you have a baby?"

"What? And lose this schoolgirl figure? I don't think so."

"So you're trying to tell me you're not going to have a baby because of vanity?"

She walked briskly to her clothes and began to sort them out again.

"You really know how to kill a moment," she said.

"So do you! I want to have a baby."

"Well, go have one then," she said breezily. "I'm not stopping you from having one. Just don't include me in the equation."

"We need to talk about this. You're not getting any younger."

"Good! I'm going to welcome the menopause with open arms, happy in the fact it will put childbearing years behind me."

He came over and grabbed her arms. "You can make me so mad!"

"You can get as mad as you like. You'll never get a child from me. It was never part of the deal."

"Deal! You talk about our marriage as if it's a business arrangement."

She pulled free of his arms and continued to sort through her clothes.

"Don't turn away from me when I'm speaking to you!" he shouted at her.

She turned to face him. "You can shout all you want,

Cormac. You don't frighten me like you do everyone else, and you never will. And you know it. You'll never break me."

"Ah, you're not worth it!"

"I think you'll see from my credit-card bills – I am."

"I'm going out and don't bother waiting up."

"I won't!" She turned and started sifting through the clothes again.

* * *

Ali looked up at the glass-dominated buildings which were The Pavilions. Dramatic-looking she had to admit, ultra-modern. She wasn't a fan of ultra-modern. She had always lived in and pictured living in period homes. Get over it, love, she told herself. You'll never afford period around this area. In fact, you can barely afford this.

She walked up to Building 3 and went through the glass doors. In spite of herself she started to get excited when she saw the high-spec interiors. She saw a sign that said *"Show apartments – 5th floor"*, got into the lift and pressed '5'. The elevator doors opened and she followed the sign that pointed to the show apartments. Her appointment was for four and she realised she was a little early. She wondered what the estate agent from Farrell's would be like. Probably some young glamorous blonde with an attitude. She imagined Michael Farrell liked to be surrounded by that type. She reached the door and, admiring the solid oak door that went from floor to ceiling, rang the doorbell. There was no answer for a minute and she thought the agent probably hadn't arrived yet. She tried the bell once more and was just about to leave and go to have a quick cup of coffee somewhere when the door opened.

"Hi, I know I'm early, I thought you might not have arrived . . ." She trailed off as she saw it was Michael Farrell standing in the doorway.

Michael stood there stone-faced. He registered her shock at seeing him and was enjoying it immensely, but refused to let the smile that threatened show on his face.

"Yes, Ms –" He looked down at the sheet of paper he was holding. "O'Mara, isn't it?"

"Er . . . yes." Don't you dare blush, she shouted at herself.

Michael stretched out his hand. "I'm Michael Farrell, from Farrell's Auctioneers."

I know who the fuck you are – haven't I been writing about you for years, she thought as she shook his hand.

"Do come in." Michael stepped out of the way. "Which apartment were you interested in, Ms O'Mara? We still have one-bedroomed and two-bedroomed available. All the three-bedroomed are sold. But I am able to say that the penthouse is due to be vacated next month and that is coming on the market if you are interested."

As if – she thought. "It's the one-bedroom I'm interested in at the moment."

"Oh – is it for investment purposes?" Bastard, he chuckled to himself.

"No. It's for myself." He obviously hasn't a clue who you are, she thought, which is just as well considering the stuff you've written about him.

He studied her intently. It was interesting seeing somebody whom he had only seen in photos over her column or on television before. She certainly wasn't what he expected. Much more attractive, he had to admit. Of course, when the only time he had read her was when she was writing something derogatory about himself or Cormac, he had naturally deemed her unattractive before.

"It's very high spec," she said as she walked down the hall and into the living-room. Yes, Ali, it would be great if you could concentrate on what you're here for – to view an apartment – she told herself.

"Well, it is a Cunningham Homes development." He said it in a sing-song voice. "As you know, Cunningham Homes have the best reputation." No thanks to you, he thought.

"Hmm." She took in the glass wall which offered good views. The kitchen which was ultra-modern. "You're near completion on this development?"

"Yes – on this phase. There is one final phase which is still being constructed – though most apartments in that have already been bought." He handed her over a sheet of paper. "The price list of what's available."

She scanned through the list and whistled. "It's very steep."

"I think you'll find they are very good value." He adopted a sympathetic look. "If you had bought here six months or a year ago, you might have saved yourself a hundred grand."

Great, she thought.

He shifted to an earnest look. "You know, I find with some people that they are so busy speculating about the price of property and giving out about the property market that they often miss the boat for themselves. Don't you find that? Follow me through to the bedroom." He turned and walked into the hall.

He *is* the smug bastard you had him down as, she thought. Having said that, she was taken aback that he was as attractive as he was.

"It's a good-sized bedroom," she conceded, "and I like the floor-to-ceiling windows."

"It's the attention to detail that makes Cunningham Homes what they are. Can I ask why you're thinking of buying in The Pavilions?"

"I've lived in this area for a long time and I want to stay local."

"You work locally?" You're enjoying this too much, Farrell.

"Er . . . not that far . . . just in town." Despite everything, she found herself slightly annoyed that he didn't know who she was.

"Well, there really isn't anything else new in this area. And if you go for a second-hand property, you're going into stamp duty."

"I know," she said, walking back into the living room. "Look, I do like it a lot, so I'm going to go and think about it for a few days and get back to you."

"That's perfectly fine." He pulled an apologetic expression. "Of course, I can't guarantee that there will be any left."

"What?" She was incredulous.

"Well, as I said, there are only a last few remaining in the final phase . . . and even that price list might go up in a week."

She rolled her eyes to heaven. "You're trying to tell me if I want it I have to take it now?"

"A five-thousand booking deposit will secure your apartment. A further ten per cent of the full amount is due on signing of contracts."

Don't fall for these bully-boy selling tactics, she told herself. But what if it's gone up by the time you've thought about it? She looked around the apartment. It was what she wanted.

"Okay." She took her cheque-book out of her handbag. "Who do I make the cheque payable to?"

"Cunningham Homes." He smiled broadly.

She leaned over the table and began to write the cheque. Did you ever think you'd be putting money into Cormac Cunningham's pocket, Ali O'Mara?

She handed over the cheque. Her head was bewildered with the whole experience.

"What exactly am I buying?" She couldn't keep the despair out of her voice.

"Take a look at these plans." He walked over to the table that had a development plan laid out on.

"You're buying No 49. Which is a third-floor south-facing apartment – 600 sq foot"

"Is there a view of the marina?"

"No. All the apartments with views of the marina are gone. But there is a small glimpse of the Dublin Mountains

– if you stand on the balcony at a certain angle."

"Great!" She didn't bother to hide her sarcasm. "It's a pity there's none left with a marina view."

He looked at her in a patronising manner. "This is a very sought-after development and you are lucky you have managed to buy here at all."

Unbelievable, she thought. I'm about to give them a huge amount of money and he's letting me think he's doing me a huge favour.

"So what happens now?" she ventured.

"Contracts will be signed within the next couple of weeks. Your apartment is ready to be snagged now, if you want to arrange that.'

"It's all so fast."

He nodded happily. "It's a fast business." He led her out to the hallway. "What business did you say you were in again?"

"Oh, eh, just the media"

"That sounds like fun."

She nodded. He locked the door behind him and they walked down the hallway to the lift.

"Are you parked outside?" Michael asked.

"No, I walked down."

They reached the lift. They inadvertently both went to press the lift button at the same time and touched each other's hand as they did so. They both pulled back as if they had been burned.

The lift door opened. "Eh, after you," said Michael, anxious to avoid any more body contact. She walked in and, as he followed, he pressed the button for ground floor.

They stood in uncomfortable silence until the lift door opened.

"Do I contact a foreman on the site to organise the snag?"

He reached into his pocket and gave her his card. "You can contact me directly to organise it. I have your number here, so I'll phone you over the next couple of days to organise a sales invoice to be sent out to you and get your solicitor's details etc."

They walked down the street until he stopped at his car.

"A pleasure meeting you, Ms O'Mara." He grinned as he put out his hand.

Ali felt she was in a surreal state of high confusion, excitement, fear and joy.

"Likewise."

She shook his hand and continued to walk down the street.

Michael sat into his car and watched her walk confidently away. He laughed to himself. He had enjoyed every moment of it. And he would have a lot more fun with Ali O'Mara before this sale went through. He took out her cheque and kissed it.

7

Denise looked at her mobile expectantly. She hadn't spoken to Cormac all day. It was now nearly eight in the evening and she was very anxious to find out if he was coming home soon. She picked up the phone and dialled his number.

"Yeah?" he sounded hassled.

"Where are you?"

"Still on site. Major hassle with some engineering here. Don't know what time I'll be home."

"This side of ten?" she enquired.

"Doubt it –" He broke off and started shouting at somebody on site. "Will you watch where you're driving that fucking thing – you nearly backed it into the fucking wall!"

"Okay, well, I've left some dinner in the microwave for you. I think I'll head over to Martha's for a while."

"Will you move those fucking pipes out of the way!" he roared at someone before saying down the phone, "Okay, whatever."

"You know how when me and Martha get together over a bottle of wine we natter for hours, so don't bother waiting up for me."

"Right. Talk to you later." He hung up on her.

A wave of excitement came over her as she put her phone down.

He had been very sour with her since their last baby conversation. He would get over it. They usually had that row every six months or so. Compared to every other row they had every second day, the baby one sent Cormac into a sulk. He would have to live with it. She had meant every word she'd said. She got up, walked into their bedroom and drew the curtains on the patio windows. Why the hell would she want a baby? Pain and agony and then as soon as it was born it would be taken over by Honey and Paul et al.

She didn't need a baby to be happy. She was happy. All around her she saw people who seemed to be unhappy. Who made up reasons to be unhappy. She didn't feel the need to invent imaginary needs.

She walked into the dressing-room and took a glance at herself, looking the height of elegance in her Chanel suit. Her heart started to beat a little faster as she stripped off her clothes. She then went into the en suite and began to run a hot shower. She got under the needles of water and let the water cascade through her hair and over her body. Finally, she emerged from the shower and wrapped herself in a bathrobe. She padded out to the kitchen, opened a bottle of wine and took the full bottle and a glass into the bedroom with her. Looking through a selection of tapes, she selected The Killers and put them on loudly. Looking at her watch, she saw it was fast approaching nine. She had plenty of time to get ready and could chill out having a couple of drinks and listening to the music in the meantime. She bent over and shook her still wet hair wildly before swinging it back up. Then she went and sat at her dressing-table and took a sip of wine. Looking at herself in the mirror, she took out some brushes and started to do her hair in a totally different way from normal. She brushed it high on top and back off her face, and applied some temporary blonde streaks through it, before blow-drying it. Then she opened her bottom drawer. Ignoring all her expensive brands of make-up, she reached to the back and pulled out a silver make-up box. Opening it up, she looked through what was on offer. They were cheap brands and colours that she would never normally wear. She started to apply the make-up thickly on her face, taking her time, sipping her drink and enjoying the music at the same time. She was experimenting with the make-up, fascinated at seeing her face take on a different look from normal.

She took about an hour getting ready and then sat back from the mirror. She marvelled at the transformation. She hardly recognised herself. She stood up, threw off her bathrobe and walked across the beige carpet into her dressing-room. She pushed aside all her designer-labelled clothes along the front rails and exposed a different style of clothes hidden at the back. She riffled through them before spotting something she felt like wearing. She pulled out the garment and twirled it around, examining it. It was a gold-sequined Lyrca mini-dress. She slipped it on. Then she reached into the back of the wardrobe and took out a pair of very high stilettos with gold straps and put them on. She stood back from the mirror and examined herself. She looked nothing like her usual groomed-to-an-inch self. She hardly recognised herself. And she liked it. She strode out into the bedroom and opened her jewellery box. Pushing aside the expensive pieces, she took out some big garish cheap bracelets and a necklace and put them on. She finished off the effect by putting on hooped earrings. Then she overdosed herself in cheap perfume. She was tingling with excitement. She picked up an open copy of *Image* and studied herself in the graceful photo before throwing it back on the bed. She knocked back her glass of wine and, looking at the time, quickly went into her dressing-room and pulled on a long cashmere coat. Then she put on an oversized hat. She turned off the music and left the apartment.

She walked down the corridor, keeping her head down, and took the lift straight down to the carpark. Her high-heeled shoes clicked along the concrete as she made her way to her Mercedes. She got in and drove out into the night streets.

* * *

Denise found a parking space near Baggot Street and pulled in. She got out, took off her coat and hat and put them in the boot, just keeping her handbag with her. Walking along in the warm night air in just the Lycra mini-dress and high heels, she attracted a lot of second looks as she tried to flag down a taxi.

One pulled over and she sat into the back.

"Can you take me here, please," she said to the taxi driver, handing him an address.

He looked at the address and then back at her in surprise. Then, taking in her get-up, he nodded to himself and took off.

The taxi cab drove out from the city centre towards the north side. The feeling of excitement was growing within Denise as the car began to drive through derelict run-down industrial estates. She turned off her mobile and put it back inside her gold handbag. Taking out her compact mirror she inspected her face. The cab was now going into an area that was filled with high-rise tower blocks. Denise looked out at the boarded-up shops and houses. There were people drunk out on the street, the occasional fight.

"You can just leave me off at the bottom of the street, ta," said Denise.

"Are you sure?" The taxi driver looked at her, concerned, in the mirror.

"That'll be fine."

He glanced at her and shrugged. "Twenty," he said.

She pulled out a note from her handbag and got out. He watched her long legs stroll down the street.

She felt excited as she heard some screaming come from a bar as she passed it. She felt slightly nervous, but knew she didn't have far to go. She turned the corner and there was a big nightclub in an old warehouse with a red-neon sign saying Stevie's over the door. She crossed over the road to the entrance. There were two burly doormen standing outside.

"Hey, Denise."

"Hi, Jason, Vincent." She nodded to the two men.

"It's not Tuesday night, is it?" asked Vincent.

"Nah, I got caught up on Tuesday, so I came tonight instead. Big crowd tonight?"

"Fairly packed all right," said Jason.

"Well, I better go join the fun and games."

"See ya later, Denise." Jason stepped out of the way for her.

She walked inside and up to the admission desk.

"Hiya, Denise," said the tired-looking blonde behind the counter.

"You got your hair done – I like it," said Denise.

"Thanks, love."

Denise took out a tenner and paid it over. "I'll talk to you later," she said, walking down the steps and through the big double doors. True for Jason, the place was full.

She made her way through the crowd to the bar.

"Your usual, Denise?" asked the woman behind the bar.

"Yeah, please," Denise answered, swinging up on a stool at the bar.

The barwoman opened a bottle of Ritz and put it in front of Denise with a glass.

"I like your dress," said the barwoman, filling her glass.

"Nice, isn't it?' said Denise, crossing her legs.

She took her drink, swivelled around her chair and looked out at the crowd dancing to the blaring music. She spotted a lot of familiar faces in the crowd. The crowd was rough and she knew it. And she loved it.

A fracas broke out in the corner and she looked over in anticipation. Two guys began to fight. The crowd started to scream as tables began to be thrown around. Three security men were over in a flash, pulled the fighting men apart and marched them upstairs.

"It's going to be one of those nights," said barwoman.

"Sure is," said Denise, swigging her drink from the bottle.

"Can I buy you a drink?" asked a man.

Denise turned around to look at him. He was around her age and handsome. He was a big burly kind of guy and she guessed he was the type into a few dodgy deals.

"I'm fine, thanks. I've got a drink." She pointed to her Ritz.

"I could always get you another," he pushed.

"Nah, I'm fine. Thanks anyway."

He put his arm around her waist. "I kind of was hoping we could get to know each other."

She gently pushed his hand away. "Another time, hey?"

"What's wrong with now?" He touched her leg.

"I'm really not interested." She looked at him straight.

"So become interested." He leaned closer to her.

"She said she wasn't interested," said Jason, appearing out of nowhere and putting his hand on the man's shoulder.

"This is none of your business," said the man menacingly.

"I'm making it my business," said Jason.

"Fuck off!" The man turned his back on Jason again, and grabbed Denise's knee.

Jason grabbed the man's arm and twisted it behind his back.

"Get your fucking hands off me!" shouted the man.

The adrenaline ran through Denise as she pulled back from the scuffle.

"I'm fucking throwing you out." Jason grabbed the man in a headlock and pulled him out the front door.

Five minutes later Jason came back to Denise.

"You all right?" he asked.

"Yeah, fine," she smiled. "Thanks for that, Jason."

"Any time."

* * *

It was one thirty and everyone was dancing. Denise was on the dance floor, dancing freely. The music was blaring and she was losing herself in it.

There was a podium on the edge of the floor and she danced over to it, climbed the steps and started to dance on top of it, looking down on the crowd below. There was a huge cheer from the crowd as she started twirling and dancing in a provocative way. They started to clap as she continued to dance wildly. Half an hour later, she jumped down and, hot and exhilarated, resumed her position at the bar.

"Get me another Ritz, and plenty of ice in it," she said, as she fanned herself with a cocktail menu.

* * *

It was the end of the night and people were pouring out on to the street.

Denise stood at the admissions desk, waiting for her taxi.

"It's here," said Jason.

"Thanks, boys," said Denise as she walked out of the club past the doormen.

"See you next week!" called Jason.

"Yeah, see you next week," said Denise as she closed the taxi door and it took off.

"You can let me off in Stephen's Green," she informed the taxi driver. She put her head back against the seat and closed her eyes, feeling alive.

* * *

Denise took her coat and hat from the boot of her car and put them on before getting in and driving back to her home. She quietly opened the front door.

She looked at her watch to see it was nearly four in the morning.

She tiptoed through the apartment and saw that Cormac was fast asleep in their bed. She closed the bedroom door and went into the main bathroom. Locking the door behind her, she ran a hot bath and took off all her clothes. She washed off all her make-up and then got into the bath and lay back in the suds, reliving the whole night.

8

"Well, I have to say I was very surprised to get a sales invoice in from Farrell's Auctioneers with your name on it," said Timothy Dwyer, as he swivelled around in his chair.

"You know, I just don't understand people. Everybody has been telling me for years to buy and, now that I have, everyone is so shocked!" Ali sat back and crossed her legs.

Timothy had been Ali's solicitor for ten years. Whenever she was writing something contentious, Timothy was always her first port of call to check where she stood legally. He had also successfully defended her legally with several lawsuits that had been brought against her.

"And Cunningham Homes on top of it all!" He threw his head back and laughed.

"They are the only developers who are building in the area I want to live in," said Ali, "and I'll be damned if I'm going to pay the government stamp duty for a second-hand house."

"I think you're damned now anyway." He waved the sales invoice in the air. "Having done this deal with the devil!"

She sighed. "Tim, what's the point in having all those awards if I haven't got my own walls to hang them on. I can't wait around for Mr Right to come along and buy with him. I have to get on with my own life and buy my own place. You know what I mean. I thought me and Richard would be together for life, and we'd do all that house-buying and child-rearing stuff together and it was all taken care off."

"It's not as if you've been on your own since you and Richard broke up."

"I know, but – no one special. You know what I mean?"

"Ah well, maybe you're better off. Look at what happened with the Murrays – you don't want to be another Honeymoon Murder!"

"Don't mention the war – please! Listen, where do we go from here with this contract malarkey?"

"Get your snag done. Have you employed an engineer yet?"

"No."

He reached into his desk and gave her a card. "Give this fella a call and he'll do it for you. Mention my name and you'll get a good discount."

"Thanks."

He took up the contracts and passed them over to her. "Now if you could just sign on both of these – one's the original and the other is your copy."

She took up the pen and paused for a second, feeling the rush of adrenaline as she signed her name with a flourish.

"Good woman." Tim took back the contracts and signed his own signature to witness them.

"Just need you to get me a cheque for ten per cent of the price and we're in business."

"I'll get my bank to put it into your account today." She looked at her watch. "I'd better run – I have to be over at RTÉ in an hour. I'm a commentator on a public-affairs programme."

"What's it about?" he asked, closing over the contracts.

She smiled. "It's about the outrageous prices being charged by developers, if you must know!"

* * *

Denise pulled her car into the driveway of No 1 Glenwood and got out. She walked up the cobble-lock driveway, admiring the red-bricked dormer-style house.

The door was open and she walked through. Inside was a hive of activity with workmen hard at it. Stairs were being sanded, skirting varnished, windows replaced, and electricians were fitting switches and lights.

"Is Cormac here?" she asked a passing plumber.

"Yeah, he's in there." He nodded through the huge opening that led from the hall into the lounge.

She walked through, carefully stepping over wood and debris. She was conscious of the men trying not to stare at her, dressed in her full-length fur. The lounge was gigantic and full of light from numerous windows. Double doors led through to the equally big dining-room and she walked through them to find her husband conversing with a middle-aged woman.

"Ah, here she is!" said Cormac. "Denise, this is Susan."

Denise took the middle-aged blonde woman's hand and shook it. Susan Haughey was a well-known interior designer. Denise took in the immaculately groomed woman, with her blonde bobbed hair, inquisitive eyes and overly confident manner and decided she didn't like her. She would have preferred to use the interior designer firm who had done The Pavilions. But when Denise had suggested this, Cormac had said no and started muttering that they hadn't finished the job properly and there had been some dispute over money. Denise hadn't asked any more questions, figuring out that ignorance was bliss. As far as she was concerned they had done an excellent job. Reading between the lines, she realised Cormac had probably refused to pay them their full commission and, using solicitors and his own powerful personality, had somehow bullied them into giving a sizable reduction which meant there now existed bad feeling between them. So Susan Haughey it would have to be.

"The house is amazing; the estate is amazing; it will all look amazing!" gushed Susan as she gestured expansively around the room. "There's so much room and grounds around the houses. I was doing this show house for a new estate last week, all lovely big detached houses, but they were so close together! Let's put it this way, you wouldn't have to leave the house to have an affair with the man next door!" She started to laugh and Cormac roared with the laughter as well. "I'm thinking opulence, I'm thinking attention to detail, and I'm thinking rich strong vibrant colours – red, purples, blues. Big couches with embroidered cushions. Gold fabrics. I'm thinking four-poster beds upstairs. This house is palatial – let's give them something palatial!"

Cormac nodded happily. "That sounds great," he said, thinking of how impressive it would look for the magazine photos. "Can you have it all done in three weeks?" It was more of an order than a question.

"It's going to be hard – but I think I can." She flipped open her mobile phone and started to dial a number.

"Er, excuse me." Denise stepped forward. "I'm not sure if I like the sound of all that."

Susan and Cormac looked at her surprised.

"You don't like what exactly?" asked Cormac.

"Well, just the ideas that you're mentioning."

"What exactly don't you like about them?" asked a stony-faced Susan.

"I don't want the place looking like a maharajah's palace."

"I didn't think that was what I had in mind either." Susan was irritated.

"I'm picturing something more contemporary, more neutral. A modern cooler look. I had in mind just straightforward light-coloured sofas, with a modern square look, cream carpet. Maybe porcelain tiles in the hallway when you come in."

"That sounds very cold and impersonal," said Susan.

"A bit like herself," Cormac muttered just loud enough for Denise to hear.

"I'm sorry, but you know I'm the one who has to live here, and I have to feel comfortable in my surroundings." She threw her hands in the air.

"Well, there is really no accounting for taste, but I have to go with my clients' instructions." Susan looked at Denise disdainfully.

"Oh dear, please don't take this personally, Susan – me not liking that particular idea." Denise looked at her sympathetically.

Susan felt disarmed and quickly changed her attitude. "Not at all! What I'll do is sketch some ideas and have you look through them and also show you some colour schemes – we can come up with something between us."

'That would be lovely, Susan. Thank you."

"I'll just go and measure up all the rooms," said Susan, walking out.

"You had to be awkward, didn't you?" Cormac snapped at Denise.

"Oh, come on, Cormac. Did you actually listen to what she was advising? It would be too much and tacky."

"I did listen."

"No, you didn't. Couldn't see past her big talk and gestures. You'll be grateful to me when you see the finished product."

Cormac's phone rang and he saw Lisa's number coming up. "Yeah?"

"Cormac, I've just been speaking to the property editor at the Times and he's going to give us the front page of the property supplement for the launch of Glenwood – on condition that you and Denise are photographed at home there, of course."

"Excellent! Well done!" He closed over the phone. "That was Lisa, she –"

"I heard," Denise interrupted. "The way she talks, I could hear her a mile away."

"We'd better get this show moving quickly. Let's find Susan."

They walked out into the lounge where a carpenter was working on some skirting.

"Will you watch what you're doing with that?" Cormac roared at him. "That's fucking American ash you're hacking away at, not the cheap plywood you're used to!"

The carpenter looked up, embarrassed, at Denise. "Sorry – I –"

"I've seen your handiwork before and it's fucking shit. Shape up or fucking ship out!" Cormac stormed off and followed Denise through to the expansive kitchen.

Denise closed the door. "Why did you have to speak to him like that while I was there?" she hissed.

"What difference does it make? He's a fucking eejit."

"I don't care what you do or how you treat people, Cormac, but don't do it in front of me, okay?" Her cheeks burned red.

"You'd have him destroy the skirting, would you? Sure you would. Why don't you take care of your own business your own way and I'll take care of mine?"

"You know, I will. And that means you can forget about my doing the photo-shoot for *The Times Property Supplement.*"

And with that, she left.

9

"What do think of this?" asked Honey, holding up a giant doll to show Lisa. They were shopping in a toy store for a gift for Honey's niece who had just had a baby.

"I thought Andrea had a boy?" Lisa asked.

"Oh, yeah, she did." Honey put down the doll and made her way over to the teddy-bear section. "That's her third child." Honey looked at Lisa almost accusingly.

"I know – two girls and a boy."

Honey started to examine the teddies. "Her mother's delighted, of course."

"Of course," Lisa sighed.

"Asked me when my lot was going to contribute to the human race – and what could I say? I've one daughter-in-law more concerned with her figure than breeding and a daughter almost reached her sell-by date and climbing up on the shelf as we speak."

"Thank you, Mother."

"It has to be said."

"And you're the one who has to say it." Lisa looked annoyed.

"What the hell is the story between you and Michael Farrell? You've been hanging around that fella for years. It's time he either pissed or got off the pot. You know what your problem is?"

"Enlighten me."

"You just don't know how to handle men. Men are like bulls, Lisa, and should be treated the same way. Put a ring through their nose and pull them up the aisle."

"Is that what you did with Dad?"

Honey ran a hand through her still-luxuriant hair. "I didn't have to. Not the way I looked and the way I sang. All the bulls were after me."

"I'd say you were a prize cow all right."

Honey put down the teddy she was inspecting and gave Lisa a disapproving look. "You're dirt, Lisa, pure dirt." She moved over to an oversized panda. "This is cute, don't you think?"

"I guess so." Lisa wished Honey would hurry so they could go and have lunch and a drink.

Honey turned to a sales assistant. "Hi there, would it be possible to get this gift-wrapped?"

"No problem." The sales assistant moved over and took the teddy off the shelf.

"It's for my nephew." Honey informed the sales assistant and then she looked over at Lisa. "Third child in the family. Have you any kids yourself?"

"A little boy," the sales assistant answered.

"Good for you. Nothing can bring joy like a child."

The sales assistant smiled and took the teddy off to be wrapped.

Honey walked over to Lisa and whispered, "I think she recognised me. Always pays to be nice to people and then they won't badmouth you. By the way, how was the lunch that Denise organised for that charity group she's involved in?"

"It went okay. Slightly boring."

"A bit like herself," Honey laughed. "I never can get to the bottom of that girl. I just can't fathom her. Although when you think of Cormac's taste before he met Denise, I suppose we should give thanks for her." Honey went over to the shelf that the panda bear had been sitting on. "Now, Lisa, here's a space for you. Why don't you hop up now!"

"Give me strength! Do you want to go for lunch or not? I've a showing at three, so you'd better get a move on."

* * *

Cormac drove his Jaguar through the old industrial wasteland known as the Harbour District. His father sat beside him and Michael was in the back seat.

"It's fairly miserable-looking," said Paul.

Old factories and depots were boarded up everywhere.

"But remember the state Temple Bar was in before they transformed it," said Michael "Not to mention what they've done with the Docklands. You have to think what this area has going for it. It's very central; its location beside the sea is excellent; it's easily accessible from all areas of the city."

"I agree with Michael," said Cormac. "All this area needs is an injection of funds and some good planning and you could have one of the most desirable places in Dublin to live in."

"It'll be years before this place is transformed, even if the government announces it as a redevelopment as we've been tipped off."

"Well, we can wait until everyone else has got in and miss the boat or we can get in at the beginning and make a killing." Cormac pulled up outside a huge run-down old Victorian mill.

"This is it," he said as they got out of the car. "Heavey's Mill."

"The place looks ready to fall down," said Paul.

"This is the best real estate in the Harbour area," said Michael. "Its location alone is amazing. As you can see, it has the sea on three sides offering breathtaking views and it is right in the middle of the Harbour District."

They walked into the extensive grounds around the Mill which were strewn with rusty old machinery and debris. The building itself had been badly vandalised

"You'll see that it is classic Victorian that could be sensitively restored in a beautiful apartment complex," said Michael. "Look at what they've done with all those old mills in Yorkshire."

"And there's a lot of land around the Mill that new apartments could be built on with the restored Mill as the central showpiece," said Cormac.

"Who owns this land?" said Paul.

"The state owns it at the moment, so it will probably go to public tender once the rejuvenation project is announced," his son answered.

"If it is announced," cautioned Paul.

"Oh, it will be announced all right," smiled Cormac knowingly.

* * *

Ali walked into the Ice Bar in The Four Seasons. Dressed simply in jeans, boots and a T-shirt, she exuded confidence as her eyes scoured the area for Timothy. Seeing him wave from a seat at the bar, she made her way through the crowd and took the seat he was keeping beside him.

"You're late," he accused.

"Sorry, I was interviewing this woman and got delayed. Awful story. She had an accident at work a year ago and got no support or understanding from the company she worked for. She was fired for not returning to work and she's now bringing a law suit against them." She turned the waiter behind the bar. "A white wine, please."

"What exactly happened to her?"

"It's a bit of a strange one. She was photocopying and the machine fell on top of her."

"The machine fell on top of her?" Timothy looked sceptical. "What was she doing, dancing on it or something?"

"As I said, it was a freak accident."

"Are you going to print the interview?"

"Of course. Just another example of how Corporate Ireland cares more for profit than it does for people."

"Er . . . Ali, don't you think you should investigate the story a bit further before going to print?"

"Why, do you think there might be legal repercussions?"

"Eh – no – it just sounds silly."

"Silly?" Ali was enraged.

"'Woman Struck By Flying Photocopier'! Sounds a bit makey-uppy to me. She's probably just on an insurance scam."

"For God's sake, Tim, she was injured!"

"Has she any physical signs of injury now?"

"No. But she's been left with the mental scars of the lack of support shown to her by her bosses."

"As I thought, insurance scam." Timothy nodded and took a sip from his wine.

"I don't want to talk about it any-more." She wasn't in the mood for an argument.

"Fine. I got the signed contracts back for your apartment in The Pavilions."

"Really?" She was excited in spite of herself. "So where do we go from here?"

"Once you pass the snag, you pay your money and in you go."

"I actually can't wait. I know this might sound weird coming from me, but the idea of owning my own place is really exciting me. Something of my very own."

"I certainly thought an old commie like you would never be saying that."

"Human nature, I guess."

"And if you look over there at the corner table, there's the man who made it all possible – Mr Cormac Cunningham himself."

Ali quickly swung around and looked. Cormac was at a table with another two well-known businessmen and there were five women with them. She judged the women to be all in their thirties and all were very good-looking. There was great joviality and laughter coming from the table.

"Is that man never not here?" said Ali.

"He's a man-about-town all right."

"Which one of the lovely ladies is his wife?" she asked.

Timothy peered over of them. "None of them. Haven't you met her?"

"Oh, in passing at a couple of events, but I wouldn't recognise her if I saw her. We are on two different planets."

"I can imagine. She's supposed to be nice though."

"I've heard she's mega-ambitious under that nice exterior. Let's face it, why else would she put up with that ignorant bastard if it wasn't for the money?"

Ali focused on Cormac's group and listened in.

"What's your new helicopter like, Cormac?" asked the glamorous brunette beside him loudly.

"Still in the hangar. Only been in it once. Next site I start I'm putting a helipad in it so I can avoid the rush-hour traffic."

The group all roared with laughter.

"Doesn't his wife mind he's out with all those beautiful women?" asked Ali.

"She mustn't or he wouldn't be with them."

"Does he play away from home?"

"There are a lot of rumours."

"I bet there are. Anyway, what time are the others coming?"

"About ten."

"I'm just going to pop into the loo."

Ali was in the bathroom fixing her hair when three of the women who were at Cormac's table came in. They were laughing and in great form.

"Cormac's great, isn't he?" said one.

"The best!" answered the other and the three started laughing loudly.

Ali took out a lipstick from her bag and started to apply it.

"He was saying that Glenwood is being launched in a couple of weeks. He's going to give me a grand tour."

"I bet he will, Barbara!" laughed the other.

"Where are we going tonight anyway?"

"You never know with Cormac – we could end up anywhere – and I mean anywhere."

More laughter from the three.

"You don't have any . . .?" Barbara lowered her voice but Ali could see in the mirror the girl starting to rub her nose.

"Sure I do." She glanced over at Ali. "I'll give you some when the coast is clear."

"It gives me a bit of energy for the night."

"You'll need it!" the three roared with laughter again. As Ali put her lipstick back into her handbag and walked past them to the exit she stared at them. She felt they were laughing with such intensity that it was forced and that if they stopped they might cry.

10

Denise heard the front door of the apartment slam, but continued to pack away ornaments into boxes in the middle of the lounge, not looking up as her husband flung his brief-case onto the sofa and he went to pour himself a drink. He hadn't come home the previous night after their argument at Glenwood.

"I'm not going out tonight," he announced, pouring a whiskey.

"Oh good!" Her voice was fake excited. "We can get a good video out and curl up on the sofa together and watch it . . . one of those nice rom-coms."

He ignored her sarcasm and sat down. "Recovered from your little tantrum yesterday, have you?"

"I wasn't in the least upset." She continued to pack and not look at him. "I was just making myself clear. I've told you before, Cormac. I don't care how you treat people, just don't do it in front of me."

"In future, I should just go namby-pamby around the

workers and bring them in a packed lunch, should I?"

"As I said, I'm not interested in how you treat them, just not in front of me."

"It's not as if you object to the success or the money." He picked up her fur coat lying on the floor beside him and flung it over at her.

"Did you ever think to yourself that you don't have to treat people like shit to get the best out of them?"

"People only understand one thing – fear."

"Oh, your parents must be so proud of you!"

"Well, yeah, as a matter of fact that's exactly how Paul did business."

"And do you want to end up like him? A grumpy old man who hasn't smiled in thirty years? What am I saying? You're already a grumpy old man who hasn't smiled in thirty years."

"At least I don't go around with that fake smile of yours all the time."

"Well, you should be glad of my fake smile. Otherwise you wouldn't be getting the front page of *The Times Property Supplement*, would you?"

He was relieved to hear her talk about the photo shoot. He had been worried when she had stormed out of Glenwood saying she wouldn't do it. Having said that, when it came to the crunch, Denise had never let him down when he had needed her . . . in public.

"Fake smile or no fake smile, you'd be doing that front page for *The Times* or you'd find yourself out walking the streets. I'd have you replaced like that.' He clicked his fingers "With someone more than willing to be on the front of the newspapers and proud to be married to me."

"Ha!" she roared with the laughter. "Well, if we broke up I can assure you that I wouldn't be on my own for long. I'd have you replaced much quicker than you would replace me."

Cormac felt himself become agitated and sat forward in his seat. "Who are you talking about?"

"It's hypothetical."

"You must have somebody in mind or you wouldn't have said it."

"I didn't have anyone in mind. I was just pointing out a fact that I have a lot to offer."

"If I ever find out that you're seeing somebody . . ."

She stood up and walked over to him "You don't frighten me, Cormac," she said sweetly "and you can keep searching to see if I'm unfaithful to you . . . let me know if you ever find anything. Just going to put the dinner on." She padded out into the kitchen.

* * *

Ali looked at her watch, increasingly annoyed. She was standing outside the apartment she was buying with the engineer to do the snag and waiting for Michael Farrell. He was half an hour late.

"I'm sorry about this," she said again and tried dialling Michael's mobile for the tenth time. It was still off.

The elevator doors opened and Michael came out smiling broadly.

"Sorry I'm late," he said. "I tried phoning your mobile,

but couldn't get through."

"It's been on all the time." Ali didn't try to hide the irritation in her voice.

"Are you sure?" Michael looked perplexed. "Maybe you got a digit wrong when you gave me your number –"

"I don't think so," she said irritably.

"Not to worry, not to worry. I'm here now and that's all that matters." He blustered past them with a key-ring full of keys and started to try them in the lock.

Ali quickly overcame her irritation at the prospect of being in her new apartment for the first time, and she excitedly waited for Michael to find the right key to let her in.

"Oh dear!" sighed Michael.

"What is it?"

"I think I've brought the wrong bunch of keys with me."

"Oh, for goodness sake!" Ali was aghast.

"No, wait! Got it! Phew!" He opened the door and stepped out of the way. "After you."

Ali couldn't help smiling as she entered the apartment. She walked through the small hall and into the living area, followed by Michael and the engineer.

She immediately felt disappointed. It was smaller than she had expected.

"It's grand, isn't it?" said Michael standing beside her, legs apart and arms folded, and a proud smile on his face.

"It's compact," she said. She moved over to the wall of windows that certainly let in plenty of light. As the engineer started working, she opened the patio door and stepped out onto the balcony.

"I thought you said there was a mountain view," she said to Michael as he followed her out. Dismayed, she pointed to the buildings straight across from her.

"Well, there is. Look over there." He pointed.

"Is that what constitutes a mountain view these days? You have to stand on one foot, and lean over the balcony in an acrobatic pose to see that view."

"I warned you of that – I said you could see it at a certain angle."

He had, actually, she remembered.

"Come and take a look at the kitchen." He beckoned her in.

She followed him into the small kitchen off the living room.

She had to admit, although small, the apartment was very high-spec.

"Just look at the luxury finish to this place." He ran a finger down one of the kitchen units.

"It's nice all right," she acknowledged.

"Nice? That's an understatement. The quality of design when you buy a Cunningham Home is second-to-none. You can boast to everybody you know that you've made the centre of your life a Cunningham Home."

"Hmmm." She smiled weakly. She wondered if he was always so overpoweringly cringy. He was true to his image in the papers. One thing was for sure, she had no intention of telling anybody that the apartment was a Cunningham Home.

"And now, Ms O'Mara, may I lead you to the bedroom?" He looked at her flirtatiously, and she felt herself going red.

Stop it! she thought.

He held the door open for her. Again the room was small, but with a full wall of windows gave the illusion of light and space.

"Very nice," she said, examining the wardrobes.

"Let's hope you get plenty of action here." He smiled wickedly.

Startled, she looked up at him.

"Re-action, I mean, good reaction . . . to this fine apartment." His smile turned to innocence.

She half-smiled back, wondering if he really was flirting with her or if she was misreading the signs. Oh, he's the type who would flirt with anything, O'Mara, she told herself.

"So, where do we go from here?" she asked.

"Are you . . ." he looked at her, concerned, "are you asking me out on a date?"

"What – I – er – no!" She felt herself go red again.

"Because I make it a rule not to mix business with pleasure." He looked at her seriously.

"No – I meant with the apartment. I meant closing the sale. I didn't mean . . ." She broke off as she saw his face break out in a huge grin. "You're pulling my leg," she said, angry with herself for being fooled.

"No – I am not pulling your leg, Ms O'Mara. And as I have explained to you before, I will not pull your leg, or any other part of you. Any more of this and I will have to let one of my assistants deal with you in the future!"

"Will you stop!" She couldn't help laughing.

"I simply cannot tolerate this – this harassment from a customer. The sale just isn't worth it." He started to laugh as well.

The engineer came into the room and Ali felt irritated that he had.

"I'm finished now," explained the engineer. "I'll have the snag typed up and forward it on to you."

"Oh – thanks," said Ali.

"Okay, I'm off then."

"Fine!" said Ali.

With a smile, he turned and left the apartment.

"Thanks again," said Ali after him before turning to Michael.

"So, what were you asking me?" asked Michael, eyes wide and innocent.

"I'm afraid to say anything in case you put some innuendo into it."

He shrugged his shoulders. "I'm not saying anything you didn't imply!"

She smiled at him cautiously. "Hmmm. The bottom line is, when can I move in?"

He threw his hands into the air. "Aye, aye, aye! We barely know each other and she wants to move in with me!"

"You're impossible!" She laughed and hit him across the shoulder. Even as she did it, she wondered how she had become so familiar with this man so quickly. She glanced at her watch. "I'd better run. I've got an appointment."

He followed her out into the hall and locked the front

door after them.

"Am I safe being confined in a small space with you?" he asked as he pressed the button for the elevator.

"I'll try to keep my hands off you." She smiled at him wryly.

"You got an appointment at a hairdresser's or something?" he asked as the elevator arrived and they stepped in.

"No, with work."

The elevator doors closed.

"What do you do again?" He looked at her curiously.

She felt uncomfortable and guilty thinking of all the negative things she had written about him. If he knew!

She changed the topic quickly. "I'm hoping to be in the apartment by the end of the month."

"Well, as I think we've already established, Ms O'Mara, you're a quick mover."

11

Michael lived on Adelaide Road. On the outside his house was a normal Victorian end-of-terrace house. But inside was a totally different matter. When he had purchased the house six years previously he had got an architect friend of his to redesign the inside with the sole instruction: "Be adventurous". He had certainly been that. The whole back wall of the house had been removed and replaced with a glass wall extended into the back yard. Much of the house had been turned into open plan. A sweeping circular staircase led upstairs to an open-plan living area that now had a wall of glass looking out the back to the canal.

Michael heard the doorbell ring and quickly grabbed his coat and rushed down the stairs. He was late for meeting Lisa in The Burlington for drinks and hoped whoever was at the door wouldn't delay him too long.

"Surprise!" said Lisa as he opened the door. She stood there, dressed in a white coat, holding a bottle of champagne.

"Lisa! I thought we were meeting at The Burlington."

"We were." She walked past him, casually swinging the champagne. "But I've got some great news . . . I closed the sale on the house on Morehampton Road."

"Really?" He smiled broadly. "What did you get for it?"

"One point two."

"Well done!" he said excitedly.

"So you know what? I just didn't fancy being out in a bar and having to go outside for cigarette breaks all the time. Standing in the street smoking a fag like a prostitute! So I thought I'd grab us some champers and celebrate back at yours instead."

"Great idea." He tried to sound enthusiastic, but was annoyed as he saw her take out her full box of Benson & Hedges and knew she would have his house toxic with fumes. He would have to have all the windows open for days to try and get rid of the smell of smoke. But what could he do?

"How was your day?" she asked as she walked over the spotlights embedded in the tiles of the floor and walked up the staircase.

"Fine. Met with Ali O'Mara for her to do her snag." He followed her up the stairs.

"You're enjoying playing your little game with her, aren't you?" Lisa asked, going into the kitchen and grabbing two glasses.

In a way I never thought I would, thought Michael. "Yeah."

Lisa put her cigarette into her mouth and struggled to

open the bottle. The bottle popped and she quickly moved to avoid the spilling of the fizzy liquid.

"So how are we going to mess up the sale of her apartment?"

"Ah, that would be a bit mean, wouldn't it?"

"What the hell is wrong with you?" She sat down. "Since when did you give a shit about being mean? That bitch has written nothing but cruel things about you and my family from her sanctimonious pulpit. And after all she's done, she's buying one of our apartments?"

"I know all that. But hardly worth the hassle of fucking up her sale."

"Who gives a shit? Anyway I told Cormac she was buying and he said he'd leave it up to you to think up some nasty surprise for her."

"Ah, Lisa, what did you go and have to do that for?" He was annoyed.

"I didn't realise it was a state secret." She studied him. "Maybe just before we send her the contracts, we ring her to say it's gone up twenty grand?"

* * *

Three hours later and Michael was wondering about the wisdom of an open-plan house. The veil of smog from Lisa's succession of cigarettes had infiltrated everywhere.

He glanced at his watch. It was nearly ten. He then glanced at the empty bottle of champagne on the floor which had been joined by an empty bottle of wine. And now Lisa was in the kitchen, prising another bottle of wine from his wine rack.

"Where's your bottle opener?" she demanded, slamming drawers open and shut.

"It's in the drawer with the cutlery – where you left it," he said.

Lisa took out the drawer completely and emptied its contents on the kitchen top.

"For fuck's sake!" Michael muttered under his breath. "Do you really think we need any more wine?' he called.

"Of course, and why wouldn't we?" She came out of the kitchen area, bottle of wine in one hand and bottle opener in the other.

"It's just I've some early appointments and I want a clear head for them."

She stumbled slightly as she approached him. "I find drink is the best thing for an early morning start. You can say what you like to anybody and you honestly don't give a fuck what they think." She turned and plonked herself down beside him.

"Hmmm, well, I haven't got your recovery powers." He sat forward.

"Oh, don't be like that," she said sitting forward and starting to open the bottle of wine.

"Like what?"

"Like a party pooper." She continued to struggle with the bottle opener.

"Give it here." He took the bottle and opened it quickly, filling her glass, but leaving his own empty. He didn't like it when she got sloppy drunk.

"You never used to be a party pooper. You used to be

able to party better than anyone – including me." Reaching forward, she filled his glass.

"I don't want any," he said.

"Oh, yes, you do!" She raised his glass and forced it into his hand. "I remember when you started working in the sales office at Cunningham Homes. You were out partying every night and still in the office before everyone else."

He smiled and sat back. "I still made more sales than everyone else."

"You sure did." She clinked his glass. "I remember when you started and everyone said you couldn't cut it. They said you were too soft to make it. Remember?"

"No, because they said it behind my back. But I was lucky enough to have you to remind me ever since." He smiled sarcastically at her.

"That's what true friends do. Tell each other things. You know, you're my best friend in the whole world, Michael."

"You've lots of friends," he laughed.

"Yes, but that's my point. You're my very best one. How long have we been friends, Michael?" She rested her head on his shoulder.

"Since my first day at Cunningham Homes."

"We hit it off straight away, didn't we?"

He laughed lightly. "We all partied a lot."

"That's why when you were leaving to set up Farrell's, I had to come with you." She raised her head and looked at him.

"And I appreciated it. All the support then, and

through the years. You've been a good friend to me."

She thought of Honey's words of advice. She could just come out and say it or let this opportunity go by and always regret it. She felt sick in her stomach.

"And not just friends." She looked at him seriously.

He felt uncomfortable. "Yeah?"

"We weren't always just friends – were we?" Her eyes searched his face.

Oh no! Michael thought. But it was bound to happen at some stage.

"Ah, we've always been friends," he said good-humouredly. "We've never fallen out or anything –"

She put her finger up to his mouth to stop him from speaking. "You're misunderstanding me. I'm talking about that night about seven years ago – remember?"

Shit! What to do? thought Michael. You could always pretend that you don't remember. Oh yeah – she'll really believe that!

"Seven years ago?" he asked innocently.

"The night we launched Farrell's. We had the do at the offices in Baggot Street – we were the last ones there –"

"Ah yeah," he laughed. "We were pissed out of our heads."

"We went back to yours. You know, I had such strong feelings for you for so long before that night I was so happy when we ended up together."

"Yeah – it was a bit of a shock to me as well."

"I used to watch you go out with all these other girls and think why doesn't he ever come near me? I don't know why we let it go after that night. Why it never happened again. Why we didn't start going out with each other."

"Well, we were very busy at the time." He nodded slowly.

"But as they say it's never too late. We're older now." She put down her glass of wine. "Wiser." She took his glass of wine and put it on the coffee table.

She reached forward to kiss him.

"Ah . . . er . . ." He turned away. "I don't think this is such a good idea."

"I beg your pardon?"

"It's just we're such good friends."

She was stalled in a ridiculous pose of reaching out to kiss and be kissed. "And your point is?"

"Well, no other point than that. I don't want to ruin our friendship."

"Look on it as taking our friendship to a new level."

"No, it's too much of a risk."

Realising she must look ridiculous in her 'Kiss me quick' pose, she abruptly sat back. "I don't believe this. Do you know how long it has taken me to say this? How many years to build up the confidence to lay my cards on the table?"

"Well, I wish you'd kept them close to your chest."

"It wasn't cards I wanted close to my chest – it was you!"

He reached out, took her hands and looking at her sympathetically began. "Lisa –"

"Don't Lisa me!" She pulled back her hands. "You've been making a fool of me for years!"

"No, I haven't."

"You knew how I felt about you and you led me on."

"I never led you on!" But you did know how she felt about you, he thought.

"Why don't you feel the same way about me? I've seen a lot of the trogs you've gone out with and I'm much better-looking than them."

Cheers! he thought. "There's no reason – I just don't feel that way about you. And our friendship means too much to me to risk it."

"Friendship? Ha! You can kiss goodbye to that." She stood up abruptly.

"This was what I was afraid off." He rubbed his temples.

"You owe so much to me and my family." She began to pace up and down. "You were a nobody when we picked you up off the streets and gave you a position. We made you part of our family. We set you up in business. You owe us everything!"

"I've worked my ass off for your family over the years as well."

"*Worked* being the operative word. You *work* for us. And I should never have forgotten that simple rule. You don't socialise with employees, you don't be friends with them and you certainly don't sleep with them."

"So why did you want to then?"

"Don't get smart with me! You're welcome to your trogs!" Her voice was loud, and she looked in danger of starting to cry any second. "That's all you deserve." She grabbed her coat and put it on. "And you can fuck off!"

She stormed off down the staircase.

Michael stood up "Lisa!" But a few seconds later he heard the front door slam.

* * *

"You can just pull over here on the right," ordered Lisa to the taxi driver.

"All right, my love." He looked at her through the rear mirror. She had been sobbing since she got into the cab.

She fished in her purse, handed him money and got out.

"Mind how you go," said the taxi driver, pulling off.

She stood outside the gates of her parents' house and saw there were five cars parked in the driveway. She'd forgotten Honey and Paul were having a dinner party that night. But she hadn't wanted to go back to her lonely apartment after Michael's humiliating rejection of her. She opened her purse, took out her mirror and started to slap some make-up on, putting on plenty of blusher to hide her tears. She walked through the gates and up the drive to the house. She steadied herself at the front door, took out her key and let herself in.

She could hear much laughter come from the dining-room. Her mother's the loudest of all.

She walked through the open doors.

"Well, Tommy, every joke you tell is funnier than the last!" Honey laughed again. "You're dirt, pure dirt. I just –" Honey broke off mid-sentence as she spotted her daughter in the doorway. "Hi, Lisa, we weren't expecting you tonight!"

"Neither was I!" Lisa walked in, smiling falsely, went straight to the drinks table and poured herself a vodka.

"Hi, Lisa," said a few of the familiar faces around the table.

Lisa turned around, smiled broadly and raised her glass. "Hi, all!"

"Why don't you pull up a chair and sit down?" Honey smiled, realising that Lisa had drunk too much.

Lisa got a chair, brought it over to the dining-table and sat down. "Unfortunately it looks like I've missed the main course," she said, reaching out to the roast in the centre of the table and taking a slice of meat.

"Maybe if you go out to the kitchen you can find something to eat in the fridge," urged Honey.

"Nah, I'll stay put. I was too late for the main course, but not too early for your singing. I'd hate to miss you murder 'You're Just Too Good To Be True'."

Honey cleared her voice and put her napkin down on her empty plate. "You might have missed the main course, but you haven't missed dessert. We're having lemon pie. You'll like that, being a bitter tart yourself."

Lisa smiled harshly. "I'll skip dessert. More for you. A prime example of wealth not equalling svelte."

Honey looked around the table "You'll have to excuse my daughter, everyone. She always goes like this when she hasn't had a boyfriend in ages. Lisa, why don't we go into the sitting-room and put on the television. Your favourite drama is on." Honey got up from the table and walked over to Lisa.

"What's that?" asked Lisa.

"You, my dear – you!" Honey grabbed Lisa under the arm and pulled her up.

Marching her across the hall and into the sitting-room, she closed the doors behind her.

"And what is all that about?" Honey asked, folding her arms.

"I took your stupid fucking advice and propositioned Michael." She walked over to the couch.

"And?"

"And he said he wasn't interested." Lisa threw herself onto the couch and started crying.

"Oh, get up off that couch and stop your crying. I raised an auctioneer not an actress," snapped Honey.

"It was the most humiliating event of my life. I've made a complete fool of myself. I'll never be able to see him again!"

"Oh, yes, you will. Your father has invested too much money into Farrell's for you to go swanning off from there. So you made a pass at him, he says no thanks – what happens then?"

"Well, I got upset and then I got angry and started yelling at him."

Honey raised her eyes to heaven. "I sometimes wonder what kind of a genetic by pass you are, because you certainly never got any of my brains. You couldn't have just discreetly and elegantly exited? No, you had to come across as a madwoman. So, not only has he said he's not interested, he's taken one look at you screaming and shouting, and definitely made up his mind he wants nothing to do with you."

"You're not helping me here!" Lisa nearly shouted.

"Oh, shut up and stop feeling sorry for yourself. You obviously played your cards all wrong, as per usual. Michael is in love with you – he just doesn't know it yet!"

"He doesn't and I never want to see him again."

"I'm not having a bitter spinster for a daughter, and, let's face it, they aren't exactly knocking at your door, are they, love?"

"Oh, I don't want to get married to him or anyone else!"

"You are getting married. A woman without a man is like a knife without a fork."

"Well, what can I do?" Lisa was exasperated.

"You go in to the office tomorrow as if nothing ever happened. You go in smiling and bright as a button and make no reference to it."

"And what if he brings it up?"

"He won't bring it up. He'll be just delighted to see you acting as normal. Pretend as if you can't remember anything. He'll put it down to the drink and you can go on as normal."

"But I don't think I can go on as normal."

"Yes, you can. You've got no choice."

12

Denise had to admit that when her husband wanted to achieve something, nothing got in his way of getting it. And as she walked around No 1 Glenwood, she could see the place was coming together nicely. Susan was there with her team of workers, busily putting up curtains, laying carpets, hanging pictures.

"What do you think?" asked Susan.

"It's excellent; it's shaping up really well. How long more do you think it will be?"

"Just another few days and we'll be out of your hair," smiled Susan.

Denise smiled back, thinking how only then the fun would start for Susan as she tried to get Cormac to pay for the full amount she quoted. Anyway, nothing to do with her, she reasoned.

The front door opened and in walked Cormac with a man called Niall Williams. Denise remembered him being a property editor with *The Times*.

Michael came in after them.

"Denise, do you remember Niall? He did the feature for us when we moved into The Pavilions."

"How could I forget?" Denise smiled at him warmly and approaching him shook his hand. "You wrote such a very flattering feature."

"All the truth, Mrs Cunningham." He walked into the lounge and took it all in.

"What do you make of Glenwood, Niall?" Denise asked, following him.

"What can I say? It's truly awe-inspiring. The size, the design, the scale of it, the attention to detail. It's certainly the best and most interesting development we've had in Dublin for quite a while."

"We're expecting it to be very popular," said Denise.

"Yeah, it will be very popular amongst millionaire noveau riche and pop aristocracy, that kind of thing."

"When were you hoping to do the photo shoot?" asked Cormac.

"Would Friday week be suitable?" asked Niall.

"Susan," Cormac called, "will you have everything finished by Friday week?"

"It's pushing it tight – but yeah, it'll be done," confirmed Susan.

The front door opened and Lisa came in with a batch of brochures.

Michael glanced at her and then quickly looked down at the ground. He was dreading seeing her again after their very embarrassing encounter. He had known it would only be a matter of time before such a situation would occur. He loved Lisa and her whole family. But he didn't love her in that way and never had. He had always regretted their drunken one-night stand as it had put their friendship on a different level. He had tried to ignore over the years the fact that Lisa was in love with him and went out of his way not to give her any false hope. But he had always known it would only be a matter of time before it would rear its ugly head.

"I'm just back from the printers and got the first batch of brochures for the estate," Lisa said, handing out the elaborate brochure to everyone.

"It looks great," said Michael, leafing through his copy.

"Doesn't it?" Lisa agreed, smiling broadly at him.

Michael returned her smile, grateful that she seemed to be over her anger at him. Maybe she couldn't remember anything – she had a lot to drink, he thought. Hopefully she couldn't.

"Fine job," agreed Niall.

"So everything is agreed for Friday week then?" asked Cormac.

"Agreed," said Niall.

"I'll have to try and get my husband to buy some nice new clothes for me for the shoot," said Denise.

"See it as an investment, Cormac," said Niall.

"Hmmm." Cormac looked at Denise and raised his eyes to heaven. "Oh, and while you're here, Niall, Michael has some news for you."

"Oh yeah, what's that?"

Michael frowned. He wished he hadn't said anything to Lisa about his idea of exposing Ali. She of course had to broadcast it to everyone. Now he'd got to know Ali a little, he found he didn't want to hurt her in that way.

"About Ali O'Mara," encouraged Cormac, as Michael continued to stand in silence.

"It's no big deal really," said Michael.

"Yes, it is," said Cormac. "Ali O'Mara has bought an apartment in The Pavilions."

Niall raised an eyebrow and looked at Michael. "Has she?"

Michael nodded. "Yeah, she bought a third-floor one-bedroom apartment there. She's due to move in next week."

"Well, isn't that something!" said Niall. "After all she wrote about Cunningham Homes! I wouldn't mind exposing that little truth in the least. She's been scathing about property editors as well, accusing us of fueling house prices."

"Well, now's your chance to hit back," said Lisa. "Come on – myself and Michael will give you a guided tour around the rest of the estate."

"Can't wait to see it all," said Niall.

"Are you coming, Michael?" Lisa smiled innocently.

"Eh, yeah." Michael nodded and walked with her to the front door. "You . . . eh . . . got home okay the other night?"

"Yeah – well, I woke up in my bed the next morning, so I must have!" Lisa laughed lightly.

"That's good," said Michael. "I don't know about you, but champagne always goes right to my head."

Lisa nodded as they walked down the driveway of the

house. "Right to my head," she giggled.

Michael felt hugely relieved that everything seemed to be all right between them.

Lisa kept smiling, thinking that Honey's advice wasn't that bad sometimes.

* * *

Cormac and Denise walked into the master bedroom of the house.

"We'll probably need a removal truck to remove all your clothes," said Cormac.

"You won't actually, because I'm making great progress with my plan to take this opportunity to have a sort out and give away a lot of stuff to charity."

"Excellent idea, that is!" Cormac's voice dripped sarcasm. "That's just what someone on the breadline needs – a designer dress. There will be a load of knackers going around in glittering cocktail dresses."

"So what? It's better than throwing them out."

"You could have saved me a fortune by only buying half of them in the first place."

"Sure, and you'd be the first to start making your snide comments if I wasn't turned out the best all the time."

It was Tuesday and Denise couldn't wait to head over to Stevie's nightclub that night. She had been yearning to go for the last few days.

"Where are you off to tonight?" she asked Cormac casually.

"Not me – we. We're going out for dinner with Peter

Fox and Steve Foyle."

Denise was alarmed. "You never said anything about this before."

"Well, I'm telling you now."

"You have to give me some notice for things, not last-minute like this. I've already made an arrangement to go over to Martha's."

"Well, cancel it. It's no big deal."

"It is a big deal to me. I can't stand Peter Fox or Steve Foyle. They are two sleaze-buckets who just stare at me, get drunk and then get leery."

"They are also important politicians who can give us the inside track on what's happening with the Harbour Project and help us get the old Heavey's Mill."

"Well, I've got another arrangement so you can bring one of your slappers for them to leer at tonight." She turned to walk away.

"Don't turn your back on me when I'm talking to you." He reached out and grabbed her arm, swinging her around.

Her eyes blazed with anger. "Oh, no, I couldn't do that. Not when I'm bought and paid for by you. I'm Cunningham Property and it's stamped across my ass!" She slapped her behind.

"Don't talk cheap," he shouted.

"Cheap! And if I did sell myself to you as Cunningham Property, the price you paid was far too low to put up with you."

"Well, you don't have to stick around if you don't want to. You know where the door is. You're so bloody hard."

"I have to be! If I wasn't I would have been swallowed by you and your awful family years ago and spat out."

Susan Haughey picked that unfortunate moment to walk into the room and find her employers shouting at each other and gripping each other's arms.

"Oh, my, I'm sorry. Do you mind if I come in?" she enquired nervously.

Cormac and Denise drew their eyes away from each other and looked at Susan and both shouted "Yes!" at the same time.

They then looked at each other, threw their heads back and burst out laughing.

Susan stood there, not knowing where to look.

Then, releasing their grip, Cormac and Denise put their arms around each other in a hug and kissed.

Then Denise smiled at Susan. "I'm sorry, Susan. Of course, come in. We're finished up here anyway."

Cormac and Denise walked past a very rattled Susan and down the stairs.

"What time is dinner and where?' asked Denise.

"Eight o'clock at the Unicorn," answered Cormac.

"I'd better head on home and choose what to wear then." She smiled at him and walked out.

* * *

The chink of glasses and chattering vibrated around the Unicorn.

"How are you enjoying your beef?" Denise asked Steve Foyle.

"Excellent!" answered Steve.

When he answered he stared straight at Denise's breasts as opposed to her face. But then she had purposely worn a very low-cut dress.

"This is what I enjoy most, being out with old friends," said Cormac, filling Steve's and Peter's glasses with rich red Bordeaux.

"Me too," smiled Peter and winked at Denise.

"So you think then that the Harbour Project will definitely be given the go-ahead?" Cormac pushed again.

"It's been given the official seal of approval – they'll be making the announcement very shortly," Steve confirmed.

"Myself and Michael Farrell were down there the other day. The place has lots of potential," Cormac said.

"Mark my words, the Harbour area is going to be the place where everyone will want to live and work in the not-too-distant future."

"I was quite taken with the old Heavey's Mill," said Cormac.

Steve roared with laughter. "Of course, you were. You're Cormac Cunningham. If you didn't realise what was the best real estate there then nobody would!"

"Who owns it now?" Cormac asked, already knowing the answer.

"It belongs to the state," said Peter.

"And if we were interested in buying it, what would the procedure be?" asked Denise, smiling.

Steve and Peter looked at each other.

"By that question, I take it you are interested in buying it?" said Steve.

"We don't want anyone knowing that . . . at this stage. We're just making enquiries," said Cormac. "From two old friends."

"Of course." Steve sat back in his chair. "The government is about to appoint a project management company to oversee the complete redevelopment of the Harbour area from beginning to end. Tenders will be invited for the different sites and projects and the project management company will decide who should get what."

"And I take it price will be the main factor in who buys Heavey's Mill?" said Cormac.

"Well, yes, price. But you know anything that the government is involved in also means that all aspects of the tender will be examined. In other words, the plan that you devise for Heavey's Mill will have to be seen to be beneficial to the area."

"And who do you think the project management company appointed will be?" questioned Denise.

"There have been a lot of companies going after this contract. But in the end it seems like it's been narrowed down to two. Projectrum – you know, the company run by Edel Garry – and O'Keefe Architects & Engineers."

"Simon O'Keefe?" asked Cormac.

"Yeah, Simon."

"I know Simon well."

"Might go in your favour then . . . if you decide to go after Heavey's Mill."

Denise reached over and lightly touched Steve's hand. "And could we rely on your support, if it went out to tender?"

"Of course," Steve put a hand over hers. "Isn't that

what old friends are for?"

Steve's other hand reached under the table and clasped Denise's knee.

She smiled sweetly at him, while discreetly reaching under the table and removing his hand.

13

Since Michael Farrell never seemed to be on time, Ali was surprised to see him waiting for her in The Pavilions foyer. The contracts for her apartment had been exchanged, monies paid, snag completed and she now had an overriding sense of excitement. For the first time in her life she would be a home-owner. For the first time, her home would completely and utterly belong to her and nobody else. It felt so good she couldn't help but wonder why she hadn't taken the step years ago. More unexpectedly, she found strange butterflies in her stomach at the thought of meeting Michael Farrell again. He seemed to have a strange effect on her.

"You're late!" he accused, as she swung through the tinted glass foyer doors.

"Don't you try and lecture me! I was only late because you are never on time, and I didn't feel like hanging around for you," she snapped.

His frown broke into a smile and she knew he was

joking her.

"Are you ever serious about anything?" she asked, irritated with herself that he always managed to undermine her coolness.

"Of course!" He took a bunch of keys from his pocket and held them up to her. "Now there's two copies of every key for the apartment – this one is for your letter box, and this," he handed over a gadget, "is the zapper for the carpark."

She couldn't help smiling as she reached over and took them off him.

"Thanks very much," she said.

"The best of luck with it," he said.

They stood looking at each other for a while. She expected him to say something stupid, but he didn't.

"Well, I suppose I'd better push off," said Michael and he began to move to the door.

"Yeah, me too. Thanks for all your help and everything."

"My pleasure." He began walking to the door.

She felt a little lonely watching him walk off and suddenly she called after him.

"Hey, smartass . . . fancy going for a drink?"

He turned, grinning. "I thought you'd never ask!"

They found a little pub down the road from The Pavilions.

"What do you want to drink?" Michael asked, as Ali took a seat beside a fire.

"A pint of Heineken, please."

"Hardly a lady's drink?" He smirked at her.

"I'm hardly a lady." She smiled back.

She watched him as he stood at the bar, talking to the barman. He certainly seemed to have the gift of the gab. What was she doing, asking him to go for a drink? Get over yourself, O'Mara; it's because you fancy him.

Michael took the two pints and walked across the pub, smiling at Ali. He was delighted she had asked him for a drink. As he put the drinks on the table, his mobile started to ring, and he reached into his pocket to grab it. Seeing it was Lisa phoning him, he let it ring into his voice mail, before quickly turning the phone off.

"Cheers!" He raised his drink and she chinked her glass against his.

"To your happy home!" he said.

"Where do you live yourself?"

"Adelaide Road."

"Nice." She raised an eyebrow. "Business must be good."

"It is." He nodded, putting down his pint. "What business are you in again?" he asked, staring her in the eyes.

She bit her lower lip. You'd better just be honest and tell the truth, she thought. If anything develops between you, it's better he knows from the start.

"I'm a – a journalist." She searched his face looking for any sign of recognition. Seeing there was none, she wondered if maybe he never read bad press about himself, so wouldn't have a clue who she was.

"That's interesting. Who do you work for?"

"I work for one of the broadsheets . . . I have my own

column . . . I do a lot of freelance as well and some broadcasting."

"Very interesting. You kind of write about fashion and make-up, that kind of thing?"

Now she felt herself becoming annoyed. Her dread of him finding out that she was one of his major critics was being obscured by the offensive fact he didn't know who she was. "Not exactly." She couldn't keep the sharpness out of her voice.

"Oh, what then? A gossip column?"

Now she flushed with annoyance. "No."

"Well, what? Cookery or something?"

That was the last straw. What an idiot he was! How could she think she fancied him, even for a moment?

"I'm a political commentator, if you must know," she said sharply. "I write about the corruption in this country and elsewhere. I'm often called upon to give my views –"

"Well, of course you would – being the woman who brought down three ministers, a hospital board and a union." He looked at her knowingly.

It was an effort to conceal her shock. "It was two ministers actually." She took a quick sip from her drink. "How long have you known?"

"Since the beginning."

"And you didn't think to say?"

"Did you?" he shot back.

"True," she acknowledged.

There was an uncomfortable silence.

She cleared her throat. "Have you ever read my column?"

"Oh yes!" He nodded in an exaggerated fashion.

"So you've read what I've written about you then?"

"Every last word. Nearly kept a scrap book of all your comments."

She sat back and crossed her legs, her heart sinking. "Well, you must hate me."

"That's a strong word." He sat back as well.

"Well, if I had read stuff like that about me then I would hate the person who wrote it."

"I do wonder how you can make such judgments of people without ever meeting them." He looked at her directly.

"It's my job. It's my job to comment on public figures. And you and the Cunninghams have become very public during the property boom."

"That's not our fault."

"Yes, it is. You've courted publicity wherever you can. I mean, how many gimmicks have you personally participated in to court publicity for developments you're selling?"

"What wrong with that?"

"Have you no shame? If you're not hang-gliding on top of an apartment block in front of an assembled group of press, you're arriving in a Santa outfit in a sleigh with reindeer."

"It all worked, didn't it? We managed to get untold publicity for all our developments."

"At the cost of making a clown of yourself!" She immediately regretted saying it, as his eyes lost their usual twinkle and he looked hurt. "I'm sorry," she apologised. "I didn't mean to be hurtful."

"You're only saying to my face what you've written about me countless times." He finished his drink.

"What do you want to drink?" she asked.

"Why do you want to have a drink with a clown?"

She studied him. "The same again, I take it?"

* * *

"What made you want to become a journalist anyway?" Michael asked.

"It was just always there. Ever since I was a kid."

It was ten o'clock and the two of them had been in the pub for five hours.

"My father was a solicitor, dealing in criminal law. He's retired now. I was always intrigued about how he used to work. I would stay up for hours, waiting for him to come home and tell me about the cases he was working on. I wanted to be in a similar line of things and I suppose that's when being an investigative journalist caught my imagination.'"

"He must be very proud of you?" asked Michael.

Her smile brightened. "Oh, he is. He thinks it's fantastic. He still meets up with all his barrister friends and he'd so proud of me. Or at least was."

"Was?"

"Come on, you must have heard about the fiasco that was the Honeymoon Murder?"

"Yeah, I did." He nodded.

"I used to be such a good investigative journalist.

Nothing came between me and a good story. But when I started winning the awards and getting all the praise, something happened. I lost my edge. I became frightened of failing and I kind of melted into social commentary instead of real hard-hitting stories. I took the coward's way out. I could live on all my former glory and still be in the limelight." She started to massage her temples. "I don't know where this is all coming from . . . I haven't even admitted this to myself before."

He reached over, took her hand and squeezed it. "Go on."

"But deep down I was so desperate for another national scoop that when the Honeymoon Murder presented itself to me, I lost all my training and instinct and just pursued the story without being thorough about it. The result was national shame. I'll never be given another chance now to prove myself. No editor would believe me if I came to them with a story."

He put his arm around her. "It will be fine."

"I hope so. But you know, after that happened I took a good look at my life and decided I needed something for me, for myself. And that's what brought me to The Pavilions that day to view the apartment."

*   *   *

Michael switched off the alarm as he entered his house

"Some place," she remarked as she walked across the beige tiles with their spotlights.

"The living area is upstairs," he said and she followed

him up the circular staircase.

"It's beautiful," she remarked, looking around.

"So are you," he said.

"That's a bit corny, even for you," she said.

He approached her and put his arms around her. The coat that was resting around her shoulders fell to the floor as they kissed.

14

"You did good the other night," Cormac said to his wife. "Steve Foyle is quite taken with you."

"Why thank you, kind sir!" Denise said sarcastically in a fake southern-states accent. "Any time you want me to dance for your guests, just clap your hands and I will oblige." She curtseyed in an exaggerated manner.

He ignored her sarcasm. "If we get Heavey's Mill, we'll be securing the most valuable real estate coming onto the market over the next three or four years."

"How much do you think it will go for?" She sat down on the couch opposite him.

"How long is a piece of string? That's why we need to get Glenwood sold quickly and off our hands so we are in funds to go the distance. Which will mean you parading your tush throughout any press we can get. Lisa is talking about organising an at-home feature with us for one of those celebrity magazines: *VIP* or *Hi Life*."

"Whatever it takes." She shrugged, knowing her role in

this operation. "Are you going out tonight?" she asked expectantly. Cormac had been in an anti-social mood over the past few days, staying in mostly. And she was getting huge withdrawal pains for her night out at Stevie's.

"Nah. Think I'll stay in."

"It would do you good to get –"

"Shhh!" said Cormac, spotting something on the news and turning up the television.

"After much speculation in recent months, the government today announced that the redevelopment over the Harbour District of Dublin is to get the go-ahead in a multi-million euro project," said the blonde newsreader. *"Details will be announced at a Press Conference to be held in The Westin Hotel next week."*

"That's great news –" began Denise.

"Will you shut up!" shouted Cormac, raising the volume on the television.

Denise sat back, her cheeks burning with anger.

"The rejuvenation of the Harbour District is being seen as the biggest project of its kind ever to happen in the country. A project management company has yet to be appointed by the government to head the Harbour redevelopment. But speculation has been rife within the construction industry, with the two main players tendering for the contract being O'Keefe Architects headed by Simon O'Keefe, and Projectrum, the company that oversaw the development of the inner-city facelift, headed by Edel Garry."

As the newsreader moved on to another story, Cormac turned off the television.

"Fucking fantastic!" he shouted. "But we are going to have to move fast to make sure nobody else gets their hands on Heavey's Mill. I think I'll head out for a few drinks to celebrate." He walked past Denise and, seeing she was looking out the windows, said "What's wrong with you?"

She swallowed her anger and humiliation at how he had shouted at her and turned around smiling unpleasantly. "Nothing. Just glad to be rid of you for a few hours, that's all."

* * *

Edel Garry rolled away from Simon O'Keefe and sighed, pulling a sheet up over her waist.

Simon lay beside her on his back breathing heavily for a while, before turning on his side and looking at her.

"You're amazing," he said, stroking her face with his index finger. "I've never felt this way about anyone before. You make me feel . . . young again."

She looked at his handsome face, and his silver hair that made him look older than his fifty-two years.

"You make me feel young again too," she answered back softly.

"But you *are* still young," he said, leaning over and kissing her lips.

Was thirty-eight still young? Edel wondered as she kissed him passionately. I suppose it is when you look back at it from fifty-two, she reasoned. She wondered if he really knew her actual age or just guessed from how she looked. She did look great for thirty-eight. She had interesting aristocratic features that had matured into an unusual beauty during her thirties. As her company Projectrum had grown in stature over the past few years, she had realised how important image was and had employed several image consultants and beauty consultants to refine her looks and her wardrobe. Now, she was completely confident with her looks. Her soft highlighted hair reached just below her shoulders. Her doe eyes were always made up to the last, her sallow skin soft and supple. The same soft and sallow skin that Simon O'Keefe was now stroking.

"I'm tired of all this hiding around, Edel. I'm tired of meeting you in hotel bedrooms all the time."

She looked around the luxury suite of The Westin and sighed. "I know. It's hard, but what can we do?"

"We can go and live together. I love you so much!"

She looked at him and smiled sadly. "If only it could all be as simple as that. But you have a wife and I have a husband."

"But what is the point of us living in these loveless marriages when we only love each other?" He was becoming upset.

Edel unleashed the belt that was strapping one of her wrists to the bedpost. "You know I couldn't want anything more in the world than to leave Dessie for you. But I can't. I have my children to consider."

"I have children too."

"It's not the same. Yours are all grown up. I have four young children – eight, six, four and two. I couldn't disrupt their lives by taking them away from their father." Tears began to drop from her doe eyes. "Even if it means that I have to stay in a loveless marriage and away from you."

"Oh, my darling!" Reaching forward, he kissed her passionately. "I love you, I love you, I love you and –"

Her mobile started sounding loudly beside them. Ignoring his ravishing kisses, she reached forward and grabbed it.

"Ignore it!" insisted Simon.

"I can't. It's Dessie."

"Fuck him. Don't let him ruin our happiness."

"I have to answer it. There might be something wrong with one of the children!" She pushed him away hard. Jumping out of bed, she ran quickly to the bathroom and closed the door after her.

"What is it?" she snapped down the phone, sitting down on the side of the bath.

"Where the hell are you? Have you seen the time? It's nearly nine."

"I've been tied up with business." Literally, she thought.

"Charles won't go to bed until you read him a night-time story. Cassandra won't eat anything. I can't get Joseph to do his homework –"

"Save me the details, Dessie, and just *deal* with it. You know the pressure I'm under this week. I've been working around the clock to try and secure this contract for the Harbour District."

"I can appreciate that but –"

"But nothing, Des. I need you to be a little supportive here. Put Joseph on the phone to me."

"Joseph, your mother wants to speak to you!" Dessie shouted.

Edel could hear all the kids screaming and shouting.

"Yeah?" Joseph came onto the phone.

"What's this about you not doing your homework?" Edel demanded.

"He's making a fuss about nothing. I did my maths."

"I want all your homework done, Joseph, not just your maths, and I'll be checking it at breakfast. Put Cassandra on."

"Mummy?" said a little girl's voice on the phone. "Joseph pulled my hair!" She started crying.

"Sweetie. I want you to be a good girl and just go to bed for Daddy. Would you do that just because you love me so very much?" Edel's voice was sweet and coaxing.

There was a light knock on the bathroom door and Simon popped his head in.

"Darling?" he whispered.

Edel covered the mouthpiece of the phone. "Sorry, Simon, I'll be in to you in a minute." She blew him a kiss and he exited.

"Put your father back on the phone, sweetie . . . Dessie? Now I've issued them their instructions, so I really hope you can deal with them now."

"I am dealing with them. Aren't I dealing with them every frigging evening on my own?"

"Shhh, now calm down," she said sweetly. "It won't be for much longer. I'll have the contract soon."

"They mentioned it on the main evening news, about the Harbour Project."

"What did they say?" she asked excitedly. She had wanted to turn on the news after today's government announcement but Simon had been more interested in tantric sex.

"They just said that the main tenders for the project would be yours or O'Keefe's."

"Is that all they said?" She was disappointed.

"Wasn't it enough?"

"Listen, I'd better get back to work. I'll see you later." She turned off her mobile.

She looked around the beautiful bathroom. Soon, she would be at a reception officially accepting the contract for the Harbour District Redevelopment.

She got up and went out to the bedroom. Simon was waiting there in bed, holding out his arms for her. She went into his arms.

"Let's stay the night here, Edel. I can't bear to leave you."

"You know I can't do that, Simon. And maybe after next week, we might never be able to see each other again."

"What?" he almost shouted and held her firmly by the shoulders. "What are you talking about?"

"It's just reality, I guess. I suppose we've found love over the past few months because we had so much in common since we were both going after the Harbour Project. And even though we were competitors, we still – I suppose – helped each other out. Bounced ideas off each other, let each other know what the other was going to do." She bit her lip and looked down at the floor. "I know I've let my heart rule my head, and given maybe too much information to you – not a good idea since you were my main competition."

"I've never used any of the information you gave me!" Simon was indignant.

"It's too late anyway. I know you'll get the contract next week. And I'm so happy you'll get it – you are the man I love. But that means that Projectrum will have to start looking for projects in the UK to manage . . . I'll have to spend much more time in London . . . and away from you."

"Edel! Is that what has you so worried? Being apart from me?"

"It's not easy for me to hide my emotions any longer." She wiped away a tear from her cheek.

He stroked her hair. "Since we have started going out together, do you honestly think I could have taken anything from you, especially the Harbour Project?"

"What do you mean?"

"Let's put it this way. Me or my management, on my instructions, haven't put our full force into this campaign. I want you to get the job, I always have. There will be other projects, but there will only be one you."

Ain't that a fact, thought Edel.

"Oh, Simon, what can I ever do to repay you?"

"I can think of a few things."

* * *

Denise pushed through the crowd at Stevie's feeling exhilarated. The club was particularly packed that night and she'd had a great time. She had just been on the podium dancing when, looking at her watch and seeing it was half two, she realised she had better go home. A few people had complimented her watch and she told them it was a fake Rolex. It wasn't. But nobody there would believe it was the real thing. She wanted to stay until the club finished but knew it was better not to. It would take her ages to get back into town and then to collect her car from Baggot Street. And she doubted Cormac would be out that late considering the mood he was in that week.

She came to the front door.

"A good night, Denise?" asked Jason.

"Really good." Her cheeks were flushed from all the dancing.

"Listen, love, I just tried to phone a cab for another girl and they said it would be an hour before it arrived. There's a concert on in town, and it's really busy."

"Shit!"

"Why don't I call you a taxi and while you're waiting you go back down and enjoy the rest of the night?"

She thought about Cormac arriving home and no sign of her.

"No. I'll just walk down to the main street and flag a taxi down there."

"I don't know if that's such a good idea, Denise – you know how rough it is around here," warned Jason.

"I'll be all right. Thanks for everything and I'll see you next week." She walked out onto the street.

"Be careful, Denise!" Jason shouted after her.

"I always am!" she called back.

The street was deserted as her stilettos clicked along

the pavement. She figured that the main street was a ten-minute walk away. She felt really cold in her little sequined cardigan and her skimpy dress, now that she had left the stifling warmth of the club. She hoped she would come across a taxi before she froze.

She heard a car drive slowly behind her and, relieved, she turned and waved it down. The black car slowed near her, and then moved on quickly. Seeing it wasn't a taxi, she thought nothing of it and continued her walk. She saw it turn at the bottom of the street and start driving back quickly. It drove past her. She glanced over to it, but the windows were dark and she could see nothing.

She heard the car stop up the road. She turned and looked around. It was turning at the top of the road and coming back to her. She walked on, trying not to appear panicked as she heard it slow down behind her. It passed her slowly, almost stopping where she was. What was it up to? A thousand thoughts flashed through her head. All she knew was she wanted to be home, a million miles from there. She could feel her heart thumping. And she thought about ringing Cormac, or anyone else. But who the hell could she ring and explain where she was and what she was doing? She turned to see how far she was from Stevie's, but she had come too far. And the whole place was so rundown, there didn't seem anywhere to go. The car was coming towards her again. She didn't even look at it, but kept her head down. She waited till it drove past her up the road and then she moved very quickly and ran into a side alley. She hid behind some empty boxes and prayed that the car would not return.

15

Somewhere in the distance, Ali could hear a police siren wailing. She felt safe and warm under the warm covers with Michael sleeping beside her. What a strange turn of events all this was. Strange but nice. She felt she had turned a corner. She didn't know where all this would end with Michael, but she hoped it wouldn't end soon. He seemed very interested in her. And she knew she was completely drawn to him. What would everyone say if they could see them now? After all she had written about him! It was all very quick and sudden, but it had seemed very natural. She wondered about him. They had spoken mostly about her. But she wanted to know more about him. She wanted to know everything about him. His mobile suddenly starting to ring cut into her thoughts and into the silence.

"What the hell . . .?" slurred Michael.

"It's all right . . . it's just your mobile," Ali reassured him quickly.

"Who the hell is it at this time in the morning? What time is it anyway?" Michael reached over and turned on the light, flooding the room with brightness.

Ali squinted to look at her watch. "It's half two."

Michael reached over and grabbed his mobile as it rang again. "What is it?" he snapped.

He blinked his eyes a few times. "Denise? . . . What is it? . . . Listen, calm down and just tell me where you are . . . okay . . . okay . . . I'm going to my car and I'll be with you as soon as I can."

Michael reached for his pullover and pulled it over his head as he got out of bed.

"Who is that?" Ali questioned, her face creased in concern.

"A friend." He shook his head a few times to try and get awake.

"What do they want?"

"I don't know . . . she's in some trouble and I have to go."

"What?" Ali was incredulous.

He went over to her and gave her a hug. "I'm really sorry about this. Try and go back to sleep and I'll be home as quickly as possible."

"Is this a girlfriend or something?" Ali was alarmed.

"No, of course not. Just a friend . . . I'd better run." He reached over and kissed her forehead. He was dressed in a few seconds and out into the night, slamming the front door behind him.

* * *

Denise crouched without moving a muscle. She had been

hiding along the alleyways off the street for half an hour, all the time the black car driving slowly by, looking for her. It was as if the occupant or occupants had at first been uncertain or trying to make up their minds about her but, soon after she had hidden, it became clear that they were no longer uncertain – they were single-mindedly searching for her. It was terrifying.

Occasionally she could hear the car stop and a car door open and footsteps searching for her. Then the car door would open and shut again and the car would move on. It was a cat and mouse game with her taking the opportunity to move to another alley when the car sounded distant. She didn't know what to do. She was terrified. She contemplated phoning the police, but they would take her name and address and bring her home and Cormac would find out where she had been and so would everyone else. She had tried to ring Stevie's to see if Jason or one of the other doormen would come and get her. But nobody was answering the phone there. When the car had parked very near her, she had her finger on Cormac's number ready to phone him and face the consequences. And what consequences they would be if he found her dressed like this where she was! She could ring Martha or any of her friends, but she would face social ruin. And then she had thought of Michael. Maybe he was the only one she could trust. Realising she could be dealing with a life-and-death situation, she made the call to him.

Her phone vibrated noiselessly as she had put it on silent.

"Michael?" she gasped down the phone. "Where are you?"

"I'm on this street called Fairway Street that you said you were on. But there's nothing here except boarded-up shops and derelict buildings."

"Where are you on the street? It's so fucking long!"

"Maybe it would be better if you just stand on the pavement and wave until I see you."

"No!" She peeped out from behind the rubbish-bin onto the main street and saw an old disused kebab shop across from her.

"Look for an old kebab shop – it's all red on the outside – and park outside it," she urged.

"I don't understand –"

"Just do it!"

She watched attentively until she saw Michael's car pull up and park outside the kebab shop. She jumped up quickly, ran out across the street and opened the passenger door. Hurling herself in, she locked the door behind her.

"Denise? What the hell is going on here?" Michael stared at her in complete confusion. He hardly recognised her. She looked completely different with her big hair and make-up and the get-up she was wearing.

"Just let's get out of here. Please!" She couldn't help shaking.

They drove in silence through the city streets. They left behind the under-privileged areas where Michael had found Denise and slowly approached the city centre.

He glanced down at her bare legs in the mini-dress, and the light cardigan barely covering her exposed arms.

"There's a coat in the back if you're cold," he said.

"No . . . no, thanks, I'm fine." She had stopped shaking

by now. And she just felt relieved that she was away from that street and the car that was stalking her.

"Do you want me drop you back to The Pavilions?" he asked.

She felt shook up.

"Do you want to come back to mine first? You look like you could do with a stiff drink and clean-up before you go home to Cormac."

"That would be nice," she managed.

He turned the car towards Adelaide Road and soon was parking the car in the street.

As she got out and walked up the pathway to his house, Michael hoped none of the neighbours were watching. She looked like a prostitute. He quickly opened his front door and let her in.

They walked up the stairs.

"The bathroom's down there if you want to clean up," he advised.

"Thanks." She walked down the corridor and into the bathroom. Looking at herself in the mirror, she turned on the hot tap and started to wash off the garish make-up.

Michael went into his bedroom. Ali was sitting up in bed, her face full of concern.

"Are you all right?" she asked.

"Yeah. Fine. Just a friend who was in trouble." He bent down and hugged her. "She's here."

"Oh!" Ali didn't know what to make of it all. But maybe Michael was true to his image in the papers after all – never a dull moment and full of surprises.

"I'm just going to go out and see if she's all right. She

probably won't be staying that long."

"I see." Ali didn't know whether to be cross or not.

He kissed her forehead and walked out of the room. Before closing the door, he turned to her and said, "If you wouldn't mind just staying in here until she's gone, I'd be grateful."

Ali just stared at him, bemused.

He found Denise sitting on the couch, her legs crossed. She had cleaned off some of her make-up, but still had a lot on. Michael reckoned it would take a trowel to get all that muck off her face.

"Drink?" He went to the drinks cabinet.

"Whiskey."

"Anything in it?"

"Just ice."

He poured them both a whiskey and handed her one. He then sat opposite her.

"Denise . . . what the hell is going on?"

"You won't tell anybody about tonight, will you? I didn't want to disturb you, honestly I didn't. But I couldn't think of anyone else to trust."

"Of course, I won't. I take it Cormac doesn't know where you were?"

She managed a laugh "What do you think?"

"I think Cormac Cunningham would wonder what his Society Queen wife was doing in Fairway Street dressed like a hooker, cowering from some madman."

"It's not as bad as it looks." She took a swig from her drink.

* * *

If Michael Farrell had thought that she would stay in the bed, while he was out talking to some mystery woman, then he hadn't reckoned on Ali O'Mara being an investigative journalist with a burning curiosity. She stepped out of the bed and pulled Michael's dressing gown around her. She quietly slipped out of the bedroom and over to the circular staircase. She crept halfway up it and crouched there, so she could just glimpse Michael and the woman he was talking to.

"Do you want to start by telling me who was chasing you?" Michael asked.

"I haven't a clue." She ran her hands through her hair. "I was just making my way to the main street to get a cab, and then this car started following me. It was very scary."

"Well, of course, it was! But just being in that area during the day would be scary enough, let alone on your own in the middle of the night dressed like . . . well, dressed like that!"

"I know. I was really stupid. I should have waited for a cab." She started to shiver slightly again at the memory of the car.

"But, Denise," his forehead creased, "what's going on?"

She didn't want to tell him anything. She had gone through twelve years of her life, knowing everything about everyone, but nobody knowing anything about her. It had kept her safe and untouchable.

Sensing her thoughts, Michael said, "I'm sorry, it really is none of my business. You're a friend who was in trouble and I helped you out. You don't owe me any explanation or anything. I won't tell anyone about tonight."

She looked at his warm and sympathetic face. "You've always been a good friend to me and the Cunninghams. We couldn't have had a better friend."

"You've all been always very good to me."

"I remember when you came and worked at the sales office at Cunninghams. You were this young lad . . . and look at you now."

"You were always very supportive of me. Right from the beginning, when maybe everyone else was giving me a hard time."

"I felt you were an outsider, like myself." She knocked back her drink.

Rising, he got the decanter and filled her glass.

"You were never an outsider, Denise. You're the centre of the Cunningham family, the centre of Dublin society."

"Maybe." She looked at him directly "I was at a nightclub tonight, Michael."

"A nightclub?" He was confused. "On your own?"

"'A place called Stevie's, ever heard of it?"

"Eh . . . no."

"Well, you wouldn't have. It's not for people like you. It's not for anybody we know. It's for what people we know would call the dregs of society. It's not too far from where you found me tonight. It's full of criminals, prostitutes, pimps and some very nice but very poor people as well."

"And what were you doing there? Were you doing something in connection with that charity you're involved in?"

"Ha!" Denise roared with laughter. "No. They would all be scandalised if they knew I was there, Michael. I'd be thrown off the board and become a social pariah. My charity might raise money for people like that, but they don't want anything to do with them."

Michael rubbed his forehead. "I might be thick or something, but what brings a society princess, the wife of one of this county's biggest businessmen, to a place like that on her own?"

"Because I love it! I love it there. Tonight wasn't a one-off. I go there once a week and have been going there once a week for the past eight years. I'm a regular." She downed her drink.

"And what do you there?" Michael was incredulous.

"I live! I enjoy myself. I dance. I talk. I can dress like this. I can do whatever I want, say whatever I want without watching everything I say and do all the time."

"Like it's escapism or something?"

"Yes . . . maybe."

"But then you must be really unhappy in your life to need that?"

"But I'm not, that's the whole point. I know how really lucky I am. I just need this release once a week."

He looked at her as if she were mad.

"There's no point trying to explain. You won't understand," she said, looking into her drink.

"Well, tell me then," he said. "I want to understand."

* * *

June Power was a young naïve girl of nineteen born into a poor working-class family. A dreamer was how everyone described her. Dreams of a world a million miles away from her nice but poor family and neighbours. A girl who lived for films and reading romantic books. A girl who dreamed of a nice house to live in with a wonderful husband. She left school early and managed to get a job in a local factory. She was lucky to get the job, as jobs around there were very scarce. Her highlight every week was to go to the local dance with her friends. Entering the dance-hall, June didn't see a drab building, tarted up with cheap lights. She was entering a fantasy world, like one in films or in books. She was a good-looking girl and dated a few local lads, but none of them lit her fire. None of them could match the man she had invented in her head – a mixture of twenty different movie stars and thirty fictional characters.

"Get your head out of the clouds, girl," her mother would say to her. "What's going on in your head will get you into a lot more trouble than any danger in the real world."

Did she care? She would laugh happily and skip out the door to work in the factory. Herself and her family lived in a tiny terraced house. It was an old community where everyone knew each other. It was the early seventies and the same terraced houses were now being knocked and replaced with high-rise flats. Even though there was much talk about it, it hadn't affected her street yet. Politicians would call to their door regularly and tell them that it would only be a matter of time before their little council house would be gone and they would be rehoused into a new luxury flat. It sounded exciting. June couldn't wait for this bright new shiny flat for her family.

One night at the local dance, she spotted a man standing at the bar. He seemed to be looking directly at her as she sat amongst her friends. She pretended to ignore him and laughed along with the others. But when her friends all went up to dance she stayed seated.

Seeing her on her own, he approached her and sat beside her and asked, "Can I buy you a drink?"

She pretended to talk posh and put her head into the air. "No, I've got my own Coca-Cola, thank you."

"Do you live around here?" he asked.

"Just a few streets away." She turned and looked at him "You're not from around here."

"No, just doing a bit of work in the area . . . on the new flats."

She was lost in his eyes which seemed to bore into her.

"You're beautiful," he suddenly said.

She felt her heart beat fast and came over all funny. Those were words she had been waiting to hear all her life.

"Thank you," she whispered back. "So are you."

He roared with laughter "Hardly! You're funny. Do you want to dance?"

She nodded and smiled.

He held her tightly as they danced. She was enveloped in his aftershave. She had never smelt anything like it before and it was making her weak at the knees.

They danced continually for an hour, his eyes boring into hers constantly.

"I think I love you," he whispered into her ear and she

felt faint.

He seemed older than everyone else at the dance. And he was much better dressed in a sharp suit. Her friends looked on at her enviously as he led her over to a private table for just the two of them.

He went to the bar and got her another Coke. Then discreetly he opened his blazer and showed her a bottle. "Let me put a drop of this in your Coke. You'll love it."

"I don't drink," she protested.

"A little will do you no harm." Discreetly, he poured some alcohol into her glass. "Go on, taste it," he urged.

She raised the glass and sipped it. "It's strong!" she gasped.

He laughed loudly, and she enjoyed him laughing and drank some more.

"I want to know your name and everything about you!"

"Why?" she asked.

"Because I told you that I'm in love with you."

She giggled. "There isn't much to tell. My name is June Power, and I've lived all my life here and work in a clothes factory."

He stroked her arm. "Your skin is so soft."

She was glad the lights were dim, because she was blushing so much.

They danced again and she rested her head against his shoulder as they danced to the slow numbers. And when he reached down and kissed her, she was elated.

"I can't live my life without you," he said as they walked down the street after the dance, holding hands.

She felt so happy, she could cry. She knew he would come for her one day and take her away.

"Let me drive you home," he said.

"It's only a short distance," she said.

"Get in, love," he said.

She looked at his shiny new car and stepped into the passenger seat. He sat gazing at her and it was like her life had only just begun.

"I really want to marry you," he said, stroking her face.

"But you hardly know me!" she protested.

"You don't have to know someone long to know everything about them. Do you understand me, June?"

"Oh yes, I do," she agreed.

He started the engine and drove out to one of the deserted building sites where the flats were being constructed.

They started to kiss.

"Will you meet me tomorrow in the dance-hall at the same time?" he asked through breaks of kissing her.

"Of course I will!"

"You wouldn't let me down, would you, June? You would never let me down?"

"Never!"

"We need to plan the rest of our life together, June."

"I know." She was kissing him passionately but as his hand travelled up her leg and under her skirt she got a shock and pulled back.

"What's wrong?" he asked, continuing to kiss her.

"I – I can't!" She pushed his hand away.

"Why? We're going to be married, aren't we?"

"Married?" She stared into his eyes.

"Of course!"

"I – I don't know!"

"You don't want to marry me?" His face was consumed with hurt and she felt terrible.

She couldn't imagine not having this man in her life for ever more.

"Of course, I want to marry you."

He started to kiss her again, and when his hands started to push up her skirt, she didn't want to struggle.

* * *

"You wouldn't let me down, June, would you?" He stared into her face. He was parked at the top of her street.

"Never!" she whispered.

"You'll be there in the dance-hall tomorrow, at nine?"

"Yes."

"You promise me? You solemnly promise me?"

"Don't look so worried. I'd never let you down. Of course, I'll be there and we can plan the rest of our lives together. I love you too." She leaned forward and kissed him passionately.

"You had better go. Your family will be worried."

She got out of the car.

"Wait – your name!" She called as he drove off. "What's your name?"

But the car had turned the corner and gone.

* * *

He didn't turn up at the dance the next night. She waited there expectantly for the whole night. Waiting and hoping. When the dance had ended and there was no sign of him, she was consumed with fright that something had happened to him.

Maybe she had misheard him. Maybe he meant the next night or the next. And she went back night after night, waiting for him, but he never arrived.

She went up to the building sites where they were building the new flats.

"I'm sorry," she asked a group of labourers. "I'm looking for a man."

"Will any of us do?" asked one of the labourers, and they all roared with laughter.

"What's his name?" asked another.

"I don't know . . . but he's working on one of the sites. He's about thirty and good-looking with blond hair . . ." She trailed off as all the labourers looked at her as if she were mad. And as she turned and quickly walked away she realised she must be mad. Or stupid. Or both. She cried and cried for days and nights as she realised she had been a complete fool for this man. But that was only the beginning of her worries as she soon realised she was pregnant.

* * *

The next few months were just a haze of confusion and terror. Her family were horrified when they realised she was pregnant and no sign of a father. And something happened within June. A light went out. Over and over again she went over that night until she was filled with exhaustion thinking about it. She had a baby girl and she called her Denise. The neighbours were scandalised. But they didn't have much time to be scandalised. Because suddenly the bulldozers came in and flattened their community and they were all dispersed to different tower blocks.

"She's a single mother. Get her to go down to the council and apply for her own flat. She'll go to the top of the list being an unmarried mother," advised a family friend to her parents. She couldn't stay around her parents' flat for much longer. They were coping very badly with the shock of her and the baby. That on top of losing their little house and being placed on the ninth floor of a tower block which was a completely alien feeling to them. True for the family friend, June got a flat very quickly. And suddenly she was alone in a flat up a tower block, a long way from her family and friends. The dreamer in her was dead and the only thing she could do to get through the day was drink.

* * *

One of Denise's earliest memories was being in the kitchen in the flat and looking up at the kitchen sink. There was a bottle of lemon washing-up liquid on it. And she could see past the washing-up bottle out the window and across the city. The city lay out in front of her from their high-rise flat, and it held great wonder for her. Denise never remembered her mother being young. She seemed to have been born middle-aged. Her once-beautiful face was lined and hard; her eyes held little expression. It was just the two of them in that flat. Her mother never worked, but she didn't spend much either. So the money they got "on the Social" gave them what they needed. Her mother loved her, she knew that. She just didn't love life any-more. She had started life with such hope and now it had all disintegrated. In a way it was like the new flat complexes they were moved to. The people had moved out there with hope that a new life was starting for them, leaving behind their tenements. But it soon became obvious that an urban nightmare had been created. The flats quickly disintegrated into a soulless ghetto with no sense of community. The people might have taken great pride within their own homes, as did June, but it was a losing battle when the halls and community areas were filled with graffiti and vandalism, when the lifts rarely worked, and you had to climb steps up ten floors to get to your flat. And as time went by, the littering of public areas with syringes was a sure indication that Dublin was taking its place as the heroin capital of Europe.

"You've been blessed with looks," June would tell her daughter, "but more importantly you've been blessed with a brain. Your looks might get you out of here, but your brain will keep you out of here. Don't be stupid like I was. Whatever you do, don't mess up. You'll only get one chance to get out and away from a life here. Don't mess it up, like I did." June never stopped giving her daughter this advice. She had been trapped in the flats, but if her daughter could escape maybe she could make a life for herself elsewhere.

And as Denise grew up and looked around at the deprivation, her mother's words ran very true. She didn't want to be there; she wanted to escape. She was friendly with lots of kids, but she never got too close. She took great pride in herself and her appearance. She wasn't academic – even if she was there wouldn't be much of a chance to develop her education in the school she attended. But she kept her mind alert and open, learning about life as much as she could. By the time she was a teenager, the flats were a dangerous place to live, as the drugs took control and with them crime and AIDS. When her friends started going to the local discos and wanted her to go too, she declined. She attracted a lot of attention by the way she looked and how she held herself. But when anyone said anything derogatory to Denise, her mother would say, "Don't mind any of them – you'll have the last laugh, when you escape from here."

A lot of guys asked her out, but she said no to them all, much to their anger.

"You're a stuck-up bitch!" a couple of guys roared at her one day as she walked through the playground in the communal area to her block of flats. She walked past three of her friends pushing prams and another pregnant, by the time she got to the entrance of her block. As she opened the door and got to the lift, she cursed as she discovered it was broken again and she would have to walk up the stairs. She opened the fire-exit door and began the walk up.

* * *

She was seventeen and thinking hard about what to do with her life. She really didn't have much education and there were no opportunities around there.

She took a teacher aside after school.

"I want to be a receptionist," she told him. "Can you help me get on a course?"

The teacher was only too delighted to help her and, before she knew it, she received a government grant and got on a FÁS scheme.

"I'll try and get you on a course locally, so you won't have far to travel," said the kindly woman organising courses.

"Oh, no!" Denise shook her head. "I don't want to go on a course around here. I want to go on a course in the city somewhere."

"Well, if you go on a course around here, I might be able to place you on a government-assisted job in a local factory."

Denise smiled at her, but her eyes were steely. "I want to go on a course in the city. And I'm going to be such a good receptionist, I won't need a government-assisted job."

Excited, Denise got the bus into the city centre to start her course. She got a shock when she met all the others in her class as they seemed so rich and well spoken compared to her. But she wouldn't allow herself to be intimidated. If she could get this far, she wasn't going to turn back now. The course lasted a few months and over the time Denise worked really hard. She came top of her class and was quickly placed in a job as receptionist in a hotel. It was amazing for her to earn good money, but the job didn't stimulate her. She wanted to be out front meeting people. She waited for a few months there, building up her CV. She knew what she was and where she came from, but she also knew what she had to offer: looks, a quick mind, an easy charm and also a great sense of style. And a receptionist job could bring her into the environment she wanted to be in. She was always scouring the papers for jobs and she sent her CV off to prestigious companies, but always received rejection letters, to her bitter disappointment.

"I wonder why I'm not even getting interviews," she complained to a colleague who had just been offered a job with an airline.

Her colleague looked at her, embarrassed. "It's your address, Denise. They aren't going to want to see you when they see where you're from."

Denise hid her shame, but learned from her advice. She quickly rented a tiny apartment in a better area. She asked her mother to move with her.

"No. It's too late for me. I'll only drag you down. You fly as high as you can. You're out of here. Now keep running."

Over the next three or four years she became a first-class receptionist. Her manner and looks made it easy for her to get any job she wanted, especially as she trained her accent into a soft neutral tone. Companies that would have laughed at her before, she was now turning down. She had matured into an incredible looker and was constantly being asked out on dates by guys she worked with. She went with a few, but she knew what she was waiting for.

She then got a job in an architects' firm on the front reception. The pay was amazing. She became a trophy with all the architects asking her out, but she said no to them all.

Except one for a while . . .

She didn't even socialise that much, but went home, preparing herself for the day she knew would come that would change her life.

That day came when Cormac Cunningham walked into Reception. She smiled graciously at him and asked him to take a seat. She could see from his face that he was completely taken with her. She had turned his head. She made some enquiries and found out who he was and that Cunningham Homes were hiring the firm to do some work. Cormac came in for some meetings and couldn't keep his eyes off her. It wasn't long until he asked her out. They were married in six months.

* * *

Michael listened fascinated as Denise finished speaking and stared down at her drink, which she was gently swirling around in its glass. He didn't know what to say or think. He had only ever known Denise as being the epitome of class and elegance, a style leader. He found it hard to believe her real background. There was never any hint of it. Although she was always warm and friendly, he always knew she was a private person despite being in the public eye, and he just saw that as another element of her breeding.

"Did . . . does Cormac know about your background?" he asked curiously.

"Yes. Of course, I told him everything before we were married. Not at first . . . I didn't know where we were going, but when we became serious I had to tell him. There was no way I could hide it from him."

"Of course." Michael knew the great pride Cormac took in having a society wife as a showpiece and couldn't imagine the man happily marrying a nobody from the flats.

"I know what you're thinking, Michael." She smiled bleakly at him. "How could he have married someone from my background when he had so much to offer?"

"No, I wasn't —"

"Cormac is a perfectionist. He expects it in others and expects it in himself. The funny thing was, because of how I looked and carried myself he thought I was perfect. Does that make sense?"

"Yeah . . . I guess."

"Regardless of my background he was completely intrigued by me . . . and he wanted me.

"I'm no victim, Michael and I never have been. Even when we started dating I never let Cormac get away with any of the shit he gives everyone else. And he needed that.

Someone to stand up to him."

"So you married . . ." Michael carefully searched for the right words but there was no way around the situation, "you married Cormac . . . for his money?"

She ran her fingers through her hair. "It's so easy to say that. I married Cormac because he was everything I wanted. He was everything I was waiting for and when he walked into that reception that day, my life started."

"But your marriage is so volatile," said Michael.

"They don't come more volatile. Let's face it, Cormac is a terrible bully and he would treat me in the same despicable manner he treats everyone else if I let him. In fact, he would treat me worse. A marriage of great unequals like me and Cormac is bound to suffer from jealousies and feelings of inferiority. Did she marry me for my money? Am I replaceable by a younger more beautiful wife? Does she really find me attractive? Does he have all the power because he has all the money? Our marriage quickly became a battleground. There's a part of Cormac that wants to own things, go to war with people, conquer whatever there is to be conquered. My mother told me years ago that looks would get me through the door of success, but they wouldn't keep me there. And she was right. I have a good brain and I use it. And I'll never be going back to the flats."

They sat in silence for a while.

"Do the rest of the Cunninghams know your background?"

"Not everything. Me and Cormac hid a lot from them. Let's put it this way, they knew he wasn't marrying royalty. But he had gone out with such bitches before me that they were relieved when demure little me came on the scene. For the first four years of the marriage, I kept a very low profile. I just stayed at home and cooked and cleaned. Then people got used to seeing me around and started to invite me to things. It's funny, but because they slowly got used to me nobody really asked too many questions about where I was from. It was as if I was always there and slowly I became Denise Cunningham, this society princess, as you call me."

"And now you're risking it all by going to trashy nightclubs? If everyone knew that, you'd be a laughing-stock."

"Michael, I never had a youth. I was the snobby bitch in the flats who was trying to perfect my looks as an escape route when everyone else was out enjoying life. Even when I was working as a receptionist, I rarely went out. I was at home preening myself for when someone like Cormac would come in and give me a life. And then I went straight to being a society wife. I've had no youth. Going to Stevie's once a week makes me feel young again – brings me back to the people I grew up with and being amongst them just a little bit helps me make sense of the huge gulf that I have crossed. And that release once a week can let me be this perfect woman for the rest of the week that Cormac and the Cunninghams and the charity and everyone else expects me to be. Would you deny me that?" Her face was pleading, almost as if she was looking for Michael's approval.

"Of course not. You're a very brave woman. Just be a

little more careful, next time, eh?"

She smiled and nodded. "I took a stupid risk walking down there to get a taxi tonight – I really must be gone from the flats for a long time to have lost my street savvy like that. I've taken up enough of your time. I'd better be going home."

"Come on and I'll give you a lift."

"Not at all. You've work tomorrow. Just call a cab for me, please."

As Michael took out his mobile, Ali crept back down the stairs to the bedroom and closed the bedroom door.

*   *   *

"Thanks, Michael – for everything." Denise hugged him close at his front door.

"Any time." He kissed her cheek. "Are you all right?"

"I'm fine. Don't look so worried, Michael!" She tried to laugh lightly. "Don't worry about anything. I'm fine and Cormac's fine. Okay?"

"Okay." He smiled and nodded.

She turned and walked down the path to the waiting taxi.

He closed the door firmly and leant back against the door thinking about her. Suddenly the world seemed very cold to him and he wanted safety and comfort.

He crept down the corridor and into the darkened bedroom.

"Are you awake?" he whispered as he got into the bed.

"Just about," Ali turned and looked at him. "What's

been going on?"

"I'll explain it tomorrow to you." He got in beside her and put his arm around her. She cuddled him back.

For some reason, he felt terribly bad thinking about Denise's upbringing.

Sensing his unhappiness she held him tightly.

*   *   *

Denise quietly opened the apartment front door and checked for signs of Cormac. Seeing there was silence, she quickly dashed across the living area and down the hall into the bathroom and put on the shower. Throwing off her clothes she stepped in.

"Denise? Is that you?" Cormac shouted from the other side of the bathroom door, banging on it.

She groaned, realising he had been waiting for her.

"Well, who else the fuck do you think it is?" she shouted back.

"Where the fuck have you been? It's five in the morning!"

"I was over at Martha's and didn't notice the time going by."

"Until five in the morning?" he roared.

She turned off the shower and wrapped a bathrobe around herself. She threw her clothes into the laundry basket and checked her appearance to make sure all make-up was gone.

Opening the bathroom door, she walked straight past her husband into the lounge.

"Your fucking mobile was off – I've been trying to phone you for the past two hours."

"I didn't realise you cared," she snapped, going into the kitchen and pouring herself a glass of water.

"I've been shaking with worry about you, thinking you might be injured or something."

"I went around to Martha's, had a couple of drinks and fell asleep. Nothing more dramatic than that."

"How dare you go out for so long and not let me know!"

"Why? You do it all the time."

"That's different."

"Why?"

"Because I can take care of myself".

"I've news for you – so can I."

Putting down the glass of water and going out to the living room she looked at his tired worried face. He seemed to be trembling slightly. And then she realised she was trembling too.

"Cormac," she said.

"What?" he snapped.

She walked over to him and looked at him closely and to his surprise put her arms around him and held him tightly.

"Let's just for once . . . be quiet," she whispered into his ear.

16

Honey and Lisa took a seat at Brown's for lunch. "Well?" asked Honey as she took up the menu and began to peruse it.

"Well, what?" asked Lisa.

"Don't play coy, Lisa. It doesn't become you. What did you do about Michael?"

"I took your advice and pretended the whole sorry saga never took place."

"Good girl. And how did he react?"

"He did the same."

"As I said he would."

"Of course, you're always right." Lisa began to look through the menu.

"Thank God somebody has a brain in this family."

"Have you ladies decided yet?" asked the waiter politely.

"We're both on diets so we're having a light lunch," Honey informed him. "I've been asked to sing at a

166

friend's daughter's wedding so I need to be slim and trim and she –" Honey pointed over at her daughter, "is after a husband, so really needs to keep her weight down."

"Mother!" Lisa snapped, smiling apologetically at the amused waiter.

"Sorry, Lisa, if the truth hurts." Honey squinted at the menu – vanity refused to allow her to wear glasses. "We're both going to have brown-bread sandwiches, I want chicken in mine and she wants pastrami."

"Thanks!" Lisa raised her eyes, and snapped her menu closed with irritation.

The waiter looked anxious and said, "The bread is sliced thick."

Honey looked at Lisa and sneered at her. "A bit like yourself, Lisa." She turned to the waiter. "It will be fine."

The waiter nodded. "And do you want some dressing or mayonnaise? Otherwise it's very dry."

Lisa sat up and sneered in turn at Honey. "A bit like you, Mum. Mayo on mine, please."

The waiter uncorked a bottle of white wine and departed.

"Make sure it's low-fat mayonnaise for her!" Honey shouted after him.

Lisa poured them both a glass of wine.

"So, I know you're dying to tell me. Whose wedding are you singing at?"

"My friend Moya's daughter – you know, Rosanne?"

"Oh yeah." Lisa nodded.

"Beautiful girl, beautiful husband. Sure there's no need for an engagement ring, their child will be a diamond in

167

itself. But speaking of the engagement ring. You should see it. The size of a small country."

"From what I remember of Rosanne that more aptly describes her arse."

Honey looked un-amused and sipped her drink "At least she got herself a husband, fat arse and all. Unlike you . . . we try to sell . . . but nobody buys." She shook her head.

"Are you singing at the church?" Lisa tried to re-direct the conversation.

"No."

"At the reception?"

"Well, not officially."

"So you haven't been asked to sing at all then?"

"You know every event I go to is the same. They'll all be shouting and pleading 'Honey, give us a song!' and they'll shoo the band away and expect me to entertain the masses."

"It's hard for you," Lisa said sarcastically.

"But I always rise to the occasion." Honey raised her glass and sipped. "So what's the plan of action with Michael now since throwing yourself at his feet and professing undying love didn't work?"

Lisa cringed at the memory. "What can I do? Let the dust settle anyway."

"Have you been out drinking with him – since you made a show of yourself?"

"No. It just hasn't seemed appropriate."

"You need to get back into your old routine with him as quickly as possible. Let's face it, whatever chance you have of getting him when he's pissed, you'll never stand a chance when he's sober."

"You're so encouraging." Lisa felt annoyed. "Maybe I should just face the fact the man isn't interested in me and move on to pastures new."

"Eh – what pastures new exactly? Look, if you were ten years younger, you might stand a chance with someone else. You should have hitched a ride on someone else's bandwagon back then. It's too late now. You've invested too much time in Michael to let him go – in fact, we all have . . . Well, look who just walked through the door."

Lisa turned to see Denise talking to the doorman.

"Only fancy-smanzy herself . . . Oy! Denise!" Honey hollered across the restaurant.

Denise felt a shiver as she heard her mother-in-law's roar and turned to see Honey and Lisa. She had a meeting with the charity in an hour and a half and she had hoped for just a quiet lunch on her own reading the paper. No such luck now.

She smiled and walked over to them.

"Who are you meeting?" Honey asked as Denise got to their table.

"Well, nobody actually. I have to be at Forward's office in a bit, so I was just going to grab a bite to eat."

Honey looked at her as if she had two heads. "Eating on your own? I never heard of such a thing. Don't ya have friends or something to eat with?"

Denise controlled her rising irritation. Everything Honey said was meant to undermine her.

"I was supposed to meet Martha here, but she just rang to say she couldn't make it," she lied.

"Well, grab a chair and join us then," Honey ordered.

The waiter quickly brought a chair over and Denise sat down.

"And what would madam like to eat?" asked the waiter.

"Could I have just a medium leaf salad with some caviar on the side, please?"

Honey whispered loudly to Lisa. "It's far from it she was reared."

Lisa nodded and shrugged.

A text came through on Denise's phone and she checked it.

"You're always getting texts coming through. You'd swear you had a secret lover," Honey said, studying Denise's face.

"It's from the charity saying the meeting is delayed." Denise turned off her mobile and sat back.

Honey and Lisa. Honey truly was the mother-in-law from hell. A weaker character would have been destroyed by her years ago. But Denise had encountered far worse than Honey growing up and just about managed to take her in her stride. Honey had such a way with her that she managed to get away with everything she said. She had a knack of lulling people into a false sense of security and giving compliments that were quickly followed up with insults and then compliments again. She was quick-witted and quick-talking and she left those who couldn't keep up with her very quickly behind. No doubt that was a policy which had brought her from a midlands farm to being a minor show-band star and onwards to being very rich indeed, married to Paul. Denise knew you didn't go into battle with Honey. You tried to not get angry with her, armoured yourself against her remarks, and if you could get in the occasional barb you were doing well.

Lisa and Denise had a friendly but distant relationship. Lisa, like Cormac, had been spoiled when growing up but they had also had distilled in them the idea that everything in the world was theirs for the taking if they worked hard and outwitted everybody else. And Honey and Paul expected their children to be winners. Lisa seemed to hide behind her big blonde hair and overly glamorous but un-chic clothes, her cigarettes and her drink. Lisa had had a great life partying and answering to nobody but now, only because she was getting older, were the insecurities of her life hitting home. She had never managed to achieve a long-term happy relationship. She had fallen for Michael a long time ago and refused to accept there was no future there. Working hard and being demanding had got Lisa everything she wanted in work, but she seemed only to be able to adopt the same principles to her love life and they didn't work in that area.

Thinking about Cormac, Denise realised he was the same.

"We've just been talking about Michael and Lisa and where their non-existent relationship is going," Honey informed Denise.

"Oh please!" Lisa raised her eyes to heaven.

"Oh really?" Denise crossed her legs.

"What do you think of it all?" Honey enquired.

"They are great friends and I think that's brilliant."

Denise gave Lisa a supportive smile.

"What's so great about that?" Honey looked confused.

The waiter came and put their food in front of them.

"Thanks, very," said Honey as he left. "What about him, Lisa, the waiter?"

"What about him?" Lisa creased her forehead.

"He's cute. Why don't you ask him out on a date?"

"The waiter!" Lisa was horrified. "I'm not going out with a waiter. And even if I did and I brought a waiter home, you and Dad would have me shot."

"That's what you think! Me and Paul would be delighted with anybody at this stage. Anyway, we're not snobs. We didn't say anything when Cormac brought Denise home and announced he was marrying her, did we?"

Denise twirled her fork around her plate, refusing to give Honey the satisfaction of seeing that she was upsetting her.

"And Denise has been nothing but an asset to this family. I don't care what people say about her behind her back and what faults she might have – she's no slut."

Denise ran her fingers though her hair in an unfazed fashion and tried to ignore Honey.

"Actually, Lisa, you should try and get some tips off Denise to see how to snare a man. She was one smooth operator when she was dating Cormac. Any tips for Lisa, Denise?"

Denise smiled contentedly. "If it's meant to be it's meant to be. You can't dictate love."

"Ain't that a fact?" Honey smiled. "I wish they'd turn

that music down. I don't know why these restaurants always play such loud music you can barely hear yourself think. I remember growing up on the farm and when it was dinner-time my parents always had music playing on the radio and we weren't allowed to talk until dinner was over."

"You often find children who are told to be quiet a lot tend to overcompensate when they are adults," said Denise, looking innocent.

*　*　*

Denise managed to slip away from her luncheon companions early. As she walked back to her car she felt the events of the other night seemed a million years away. It had been terrifying being followed and it had shaken her. It was a stupid mistake setting off on her own like that. She wondered if she had been stupid telling Michael everything. Probably, but if she could trust anyone it would be Michael. And it was a relief to actually talk to someone about her life.

17

Ali rushed into work. She was late as she'd had her carpet fitted in the apartment that morning. She walked through the offices at the newspaper feeling happy but confused.

What a strange turn of events! After they were together, Michael had driven her into work the next day. That night she had been exhausted and had gone to bed early.

She opened her office and took a deep breath as she saw the office was filled with roses. She couldn't help but smile. What a sweet and romantic thing to do! She had never suspected the man she had castigated so many times in print for being an unscrupulous businessman would have such a soft side. As she took off her coat and smelt some of the roses, she supposed it made sense. Michael loved big gestures and fanfare. He was like that in business so it would follow through he would also be like that in his love life.

It made sense to her now why she had got some funny

looks from her colleagues as she had walked through the building. If they knew who the roses were from!

She sat down, picked up the phone and dialled Michael's number.

"You're very sweet," she said when he answered.

"I know! They cost me a bloody fortune, all those flowers!"

"What am I to do with them all? There's so many of them I can hardly work from the overpowering fragrance."

"How do you think I can work? When I am left with your lingering fragrance in my head."

"Oh shut up!" She laughed. She touched the petals on the vase nearest her. "I'll have them sent down to the children's hospital – they'll be nice in the wards."

"The children's hospital?" At the other end of the line, Michael felt his big smile disappear. "Don't you want to bring them home to your new apartment?"

"Well, they'll only wilt in a couple of days. They're so lovely it would be nice for other people to enjoy them too."

Her bloody social conscience! thought Michael. "I'm sure the kids will enjoy them." He tried to keep the irritation out of his voice. "So you're still on for dinner tonight?" he went on, sounding upbeat.

"Wouldn't miss it for the world."

* * *

Lisa steadied herself, then did a quick rap on Michael's door and entered smiling.

"Guess what I just sold?" she crowed.

"Your soul?" He sat back in his chair and put his hands behind his head.

"Nah – I sold that a long time ago. The house on Church Avenue."

"Well done! I was a bit nervous with that one. They were asking far in excess of its true worth and wouldn't listen when I tried to guide them a little more realistically."

"Well, I just sold it to a local family who want to stay in the area but want to move to something bigger." She smiled triumphantly.

He had seen her in action and she would have put every bit of her energy into that house to try and sell it. She was a great auctioneer. And a great girl. She would make somebody a great wife some day. He was glad that their little embarrassing encounter was forgotten. It was probably just down to the drink anyway.

"So I thought to celebrate, we'd finish up a little early and head over to The Pembroke for a few drinks." She sat down on his desk, crossed her legs and swung them in a childlike fashion.

"Eh – I would really love to." His face creased with anxiety. "I've something on, I'm afraid."

"Oh, if it's some bloody stupid pilot's lesson, then just cancel it and let's get pissed."

"Eh . . . no." Why don't you just come out and tell her you're going on a date? You're a free agent who can do what he wants . . . Michael had never told Lisa about any dates or relationships he had. Deep down he knew she had feelings for him and so never wanted to upset her. But maybe it was the wrong policy. Maybe he should be honest with her and then she would know the score and any repeat of that embarrassing episode wouldn't be repeated.

"I'm off out on a date actually."

Lisa's smile dropped for a second and she looked shocked. She had the smile plastered back on almost immediately.

"A date! How exciting. Who with?" she asked brightly.

"Oh, nobody you know." He started to tidy away papers on his desk.

"Well, don't be so coy. What's her name and where did you meet her?"

"Look, it's no big deal. It's just a date, that's all."

"You're always so secretive about your love life. You can tell me, you know. Just because I don't have a love life doesn't mean I resent everyone else having one."

He looked up at her. She seemed genuinely comfortable with the subject.

"Her name's Ali – son." He decided to keep the finer detail that it was Ali O'Mara to himself.

"Alison. That's a nice name. Very respectable name." She looked to be thinking hard. "It's a sensible name, Alison. I went to school with an Alison. She was the most sensible girl you could meet. Never drank, never smoked, a bit square, you know. But the most sensible girl you could meet. I wonder if it's the same girl?"

He raised an eyebrow. "Doubtful."

"Well, don't stop there. Tell me all about her. I have this image of anyone called Alison being like that girl I went to school with, so you need to either verify that she was like this girl or paint her in a whole new light so I'll never think of an Alison in the same way again."

"Oh, I don't know." Standing up, he started to file papers away in a filing cabinet. "She's kind of hard to describe."

"Intriguing, I love it! The last thing I ever thought an Alison could be – intriguing! Is she pretty?"

"Yes . . . I guess."

"You guess? This isn't sounding too promising to me, Michael."

He turned around from the filing cabinet and looked at her. Unusually for Michael, he looked very serious.

Get out, Lisa screamed at herself. Get out before you make a complete fool of yourself and do or say something you'll never recover from.

She jumped off the desk.

"Shit!" she almost shouted.

"What's wrong?" He was startled.

"Shit, I've an appointment for a viewing I completely forgot about. I'd better run." She raced to the door, just stopping before leaving to turn and say brightly "Good luck with the date!"

"Thanks!" he called after her.

She walked through the outside office. There were four estate agents at their desks there busily talking on the phone. She walked past them and down the corridor to her own office. She entered and closed her door firmly behind her and turned the lock. She went and sat at her desk. Only then did she let the tears run and suddenly she was stifling sobs, anxious that none of her co-workers outside would hear her.

* * *

Michael looked at his watch. She was late and he felt himself become slightly anxious.

He was seated in the corner of the restaurant Tribecca.

He saw her come in and, talking to the hostess, take off her coat and hand it to her. She surveyed the restaurant and, spotting Michael, smiled at him and made her way over. He found it hard to take his eyes off her. He was drawn to everything about her.

"Sorry, I'm late. I got tied up at RTÉ."

He stood up and kissed her lightly on the lips. She felt awkward and hoped nobody she knew had seen. He spotted her reaction and as they sat down he looked at her, perplexed.

"Do you want to tell me what that was about?" he asked.

"What?"

"The look of horror when I kissed you?"

She looked confused and then lightly placed her hand on his hand. "I'm sorry. It *was* a look of horror, wasn't it? I'm really not sure what's going on here, are you?"

"I thought it was pretty straightforward. Boy meets girl. Boy likes girl. Girl hopefully likes boy. Happy ever after."

She sat back and stared at him and then laughed. "You come across as very innocent at times. There's nothing wrong with your boy meets girl scenario, except for the fact of who the boy and girl are."

"How do you mean?"

"Oh come on, Michael, you're not that innocent! You stand for everything I fight against. You stand for everything I despise about our society. I've built my career on attacking people like you, and not just people like you, but actually *you*. You know what I did, last night?"

"Took a bubble bath?"

"I went and looked through loads of old articles where I've written about you and the Cunninghams. Do you know what adjectives I used to describe you?"

"Not really."

"Grasping, greedy, nasty, a law unto himself. I'm just finding it very hard to match this public persona you have to this sweet guy in front of me."

"Those were your thoughts on me, not the real me."

"Oh, come on, I've seen all those antics you've got up to over the years. Do you remember that time during a launch of a rival's development when you personally stood outside the estate, having invited the press, and gave out leaflets to all the potential buyers directing them to your estate down the road because it was much better value for money?"

"Yeah – and I'm not going to apologise for that. I got lots of publicity, as well as all your man's customers and we were sold out in a week."

"But do you not think that's wrong?" She sat forward.

"I think it took a lot of balls to do it on my part."

"But it was such an unnecessary thing to do."

"You might think it was unnecessary. But I tell you that builder was in trouble financially and needed sales quickly."

"Everything is just about money these days, and it really pisses me off."

"So are you saying you don't want this to continue any further?" He looked nervous.

"I do want it to go further because I really like you," she said. "But it would also destroy me if it got out that I was seeing you. That fucking Honeymoon Murder fiasco nearly finished me . . . if people found out I was seeing Michael Farrell, after all I've said and written about you, they would say I was the biggest hypocrite of all time and I'd have to leave the country or something."

"You're saying we are seeing each other then?"

She looked at him for a while before putting her hand under the table. He did likewise and they held hands hidden from everyone's view.

"Yes." She smiled at him.

* * *

They were walking back to Michael's through the quiet night streets after leaving Tribecca. His arm was casually around her as she listened intently to him talking.

He was singing the Cunninghams' praises.

"You really admire them, don't you?" she asked.

"How could you not? Look at Paul Cunningham. He's just from a small farm somewhere and he started off fifty years ago working for himself and look what he's built up."

"How did he start up?"

"Just started doing any kind of building work he could

get. Then he started employing another couple of fellas and it just went from there. By the sixties he was building the new housing estates springing up around Dublin. Then he even branched into the entertainment field and bought a pub and a couple of dance-halls. Do you know how clever he was? On a Friday evening he would take over a table in his pub and sit there with his sheet of names of employees and the wage packets. Then his workers would come in and queue in the pub and he would tick off their names and hand them over the wage packet. Then he used to have a special cut-price meal served to his workers in the pub and of course the workers would eat their great feed, and the money Paul had just paid them would go straight back over the bar back into Paul's coffers as they drank the night away. And if they hadn't spent enough then, they would get free passes into Paul's dance-halls and spend the rest of their money there!"

"It's no wonder he ended up so rich." Ali found the whole thing disturbing. She had met Paul Cunningham at a few political events and found him to be humourless and un-engaging but he obviously had a very cunning mind. She was worried that Michael seemed to hold him in such awe. Worried but intrigued.

"Do you know what else he used to do? If any of the workers came looking for a sub, he would give it to them without question. And do you know why? A lot of the workers had a permanent sub going on purpose so that their wages were always short – then when they gave the packet to their wives the wives thought they were on less money."

"And the subs would just go on drink in Paul's pub?"

"You got it in one."

Ali could imagine the wives and families of the workers coping on a lesser wage as the permanent subs were drunk in Paul's bar and dance-halls.

They reached Michael's door and he opened it, letting them in.

"It's immoral earnings." Ali tried to keep her voice from sounding patronising. "The Cunningham family fortune is built on ill-gotten gains, if what you're saying is true."

"No, it isn't," Michael objected. "Nobody forced those men to go drinking in Paul's pubs. They could have fucked off home and stayed in."

"You know what the culture was like back then. All they had to do was go to the pub."

"Exactly. If they hadn't spent their wages in Paul's pub, then they would have gone to another pub. It might as well go back to the hand that fed them in the first place and make their jobs more secure."

Ali walked up the circular stairs and sat down.

Michael came and sat beside her.

"And I guess that's where he met his wife," said Ali. "In one of the dance-halls?"

"Yeah, Honey was very popular on the show-band circuit and she was employed to sing at one of his dance-halls. They got married soon after."

She sighed. "I suppose people meet in the most unlikely of places."

"They sure do. I remember I was showing this

apartment once to this girl, ended up going out with her and she was a total nut."

"And that's supposed to me, I guess?" She arched an eyebrow.

"No, another girl I met last week," he said seriously.

She sat up concerned. Only when he started grinning did she slap him across the shoulders and sit back.

18

Cormac looked at the man at the other side of his desk and felt his temper rise.

The man was a contractor they had employed on site. He had agreed a price with him for work to be carried out. The man had failed to complete the work to specifications but was now in his office demanding payment.

"That bill should have been paid two months ago and I can't wait any longer. I want a cheque today," demanded the man.

"You can want as much as you like, but you're getting nothing outta me until you come back and fix that work and not leave it in the fucking mess you left it." Cormac's voice was loud but even.

"The work is done – you can go out and see it's done."

"It's not done the way you were directed to do it. The engineer will never pass it so you can whistle for your money because I'm going to have to waste my time and my money getting someone to fix your sloppy work."

"I'm going legal on this. You'll be hearing from my solicitors today."

"Good and I hope they're better solicitors than you are a joiner. Now fuck off out of my office!" Cormac looked down at the papers in front of him and started to read them.

The man, consumed with anger, stormed to the door and went to open it. The door had been sticking for a while and Cormac had kept meaning to have it fixed. The result was that the contractor's dramatic exit was ruined as he unsuccessfully attempted to let himself out. Cormac pretended to ignore him for a couple of minutes as the man's frustration grew to boiling point.

Eventually Cormac looked up and said loudly, "Don't bother with the door – use the fucking window!"

* * *

Shysters! The world was full of shysters, thought Cormac as he walked down the steps from his site office and towards No 1 Glenwood. Everybody always out for money. To try and do you out of money if they can. People trying to fiddle invoices. Trying to add in extras they never did. Or in the case of the eejit he had just argued with doing shit work and expecting payment for it. When he handed a Cunningham Home over to the buyer, the buyer expected it to be perfect. With all these programmes on the television obsessed with house-buying and redecoration, everyone considered themselves to be an expert at property these days and when someone bought a property they went through it with a fine-tooth comb to make sure it was perfect. And it was perfect because he made sure it was. But all these shysters didn't care about the end product. They didn't care about Cunningham Homes or their reputation. All they cared about was the money. And Cormac knew just how to deal with them.

It was the day of the photo shoot for *The Times* and from the array of expensive cars parked in the driveway at No 1, he realised everyone was already there.

A couple of workers were just finishing off the cobble-lock driveway as he walked up.

"Would you get a fucking move-on? This was supposed to be finished yesterday! They're taking the fucking photographs today!"

He walked in and saw the photographer and his assistant setting up their equipment in the sitting-room. As he looked around the finished place, he had to admit Denise had been right to direct Susan away from the way she was going. The cool clean contemporary image the house had was perfect. Susan was now working on No 2 Glenwood which was to be the showhouse and he made a mental note to tell her not to copy this style.

He walked through to the kitchen where he found Lisa and Michael chatting away to Niall Williams from *The Times*.

"Where's Denise?" Cormac asked as he joined them.

"Upstairs, beautifying herself," answered Lisa.

"When are you changing yourself, Cormac?" Michael asked.

Cormac glanced down at his immaculate Italian

designer suit. "But I am changed!" he said, and as Michael and Lisa started laughing and he knew Michael had been joking he added, "You're such a smart arse!"

Lisa went over to him and started to smooth down his silvering hair.

"I know Denise is the star of this show, and you're only a prop," she straightened his tie, "but let's put your best foot forward as well." She buttoned the middle button on his blazer and stepped back from him to look. "But you don't scrub up too badly."

Cormac sat down on one of the high stools that were situated around the huge island in the middle of the kitchen.

"Do you need to interview us or anything?" Cormac questioned Niall. He felt a bit agitated. Denise loved this kind of thing, but it made him feel nervous. And there wasn't much that made Cormac nervous. However, he knew the publicity would be invaluable.

"No, it's okay. I've already given your interview for you," said Michael, smirking.

"Yes, quite a detailed interview as well," said Niall, looking through his abundance of notes.

Cormac was glad, knowing that Michael would get every positive point across.

"Yes, in fact you came across as so charming during the interview, I hardly recognised you!" laughed Lisa.

"What about the Harbour District, Niall? Have you heard any developments on that yet?" quizzed Cormac.

"Everyone's waiting for the big announcement as who gets the contract," Neil informed him. "Word on the street is O'Keefe's will get it. They are much longer established and have more experience than Projectrum."

Hopefully, thought Cormac. He knew Simon O'Keefe and that would strengthen his chance of getting Heavey's Mill.

"Having said that, Edel Garry is a woman that it's very hard to say no to," said Niall.

Lisa viewed Michael across the kitchen island, dying to know how his date with the mysterious Alison went. She was obviously a woman Michael couldn't say no to. Whereas she herself was obviously a woman that Michael could very easily say no to.

"I'm sorry for delaying everybody," said Denise, coming into the kitchen. "I'm ready whenever you are."

All eyes turned to look at Denise.

"You look fantastic!" said Michael. Everyone else thought the same. But none of them said it.

"Love's young dream!" whispered Lisa to Michael as they looked at Denise poised on the sofa with Cormac's arm around her for the photographer.

"Come on, Cormac. Give us a smile!" pleaded the photographer.

Cormac tried to smile but it just looked strained.

Denise beside him was relaxed and smiling naturally for the camera.

"Come on, Cormac. You have a beautiful wife, a beautiful home – you've everything in the world to smile about!" urged the photographer.

Cormac forced a wider smile, but it just looked like a ridiculous grin.

"I know what'll make him smile. Think of all the money you'll make when you get the front page of the property section with these photos – they'll be rushing to buy here!" called Michael.

"It's no good," sighed the photographer. "They won't print these photos. They look unnatural."

"Ah, for fuck's sake, just get on with it!" Cormac snapped, losing his temper.

Denise put her hand on his knee and squeezed it. "It's all right, Cormac, relax." She looked reassuringly into his eyes. She rarely saw a look of vulnerability in Cormac's eyes. But it was there then. She put her arm around him. "Just pretend there's nobody else here."

Cormac held her a little tighter and they smiled for the camera.

"Great!" said the photographer.

He took them around the house, taking photos of them in the different rooms.

"It's going to look good," said Neil. "Should start a lot of interest in Glenwood."

"Let's fucking hope so!" said Cormac as the photographer started to pack away his equipment.

"How was your date with – sorry, what was her name again?" Lisa asked Michael, as they left the house and made their way to their cars.

"Alison? It went well actually." Michael tried to sound natural.

"Do I need to buy a hat yet?"

Michael grinned. "Hardly."

* * *

"Niall, I'm heading into the Ice Bar for a few drinks if you want to tag along?" Cormac offered.

"I might pop in for one. Thanks, Cormac." Niall had formed a close friendship with the Cunninghams over the years. They threw a lot of advertising revenue his way, and he threw a lot of free editorial theirs. A harmonious relationship.

Cormac had felt unnerved from all the photo-taking and couldn't wait to get into town for the night. He felt exposed from the whole process.

He went into the kitchen where he found Denise inspecting the cupboard space.

"We won't know ourselves with all this extra room," commented Denise.

"I've ordered the removal lorry for first thing Tuesday morning and so you'd better have everything sorted by then," he threatened.

"It will be." Her voice turned to ice at his tone. Any vulnerability she had seen in him earlier was long gone.

"I'm off over to the Ice Bar with Niall and a few others. So I'll see you whenever." He turned to leave.

"But, I didn't bring my car with me. I got a lift with Lisa."

"Well, then you should have got a lift back with her, shouldn't you?"

"It would be nice if you offered me a lift back," she said.

"Look, I'm late to meet Steve Foyle at the Ice Bar already. If I drop you home, we're going into rush hour. I'll be tied up for hours." He reached into his wallet and threw two hundred euro bills on the table. "Grab yourself a taxi."

He turned to leave.

"You're that anxious for a fucking drink, you're going to leave me out here waiting for a taxi for a couple of hours?" She felt her cheeks burn.

He turned and faced her and smiled. "Does it piss you off that I'm going?"

She saw enjoyment in his eyes. "No. It pisses me off that I'm stuck out here with no transport home."

"This is your new home, so you might as well get acquainted with it while you wait for your taxi."

She walked past him. "You'd better run and get your drink. Give you a bit of confidence again after you realised I completely upstaged you today."

* * *

Cormac got into his car angrily, slammed the door and tore out of the driveway of No 1 Glenwood.

She was one smart bitch. She had seen how much he relied on her to get him through that stupid photo session and didn't mind telling him at the earliest opportunity. She knew he hated being vulnerable and was running away to be distracted by the nearest bar. It was gloves off. But wasn't it always gloves off between the two of them?

He dialled Michael's number on the mobile.

"Michael. You slipped off before I said goodbye. Big

night out tonight in the Ice Bar. Get your ass in there
ASAP."

"Eh, sorry, Cormac. I've got other plans."

"Well, cancel them."

"Sorry, can't get out of them."

"Ah! You've a new woman on the scene." Realisation
dawned.

"Something like that."

"Well, who is she then?"

"You wouldn't know her."

"Right. Well, you know where we are if you want to
join us."

Cormac hung up the phone. He knew it was great
marketing and everything, but he would just let Denise do
any publicity things like that in future. He was a behind-
the-scenes man. *He* liked to call the shots, not some lousy
photographer. He quickly started to dial another number.
He wanted a big crowd out tonight.

19

It was two in the morning and Ali and Michael looked in each other's eyes in the darkened bedroom. Michael had his head resting on his hand, while the other stroked Ali's arm.

She toyed with the diamond necklace that he had sent into her office by courier that afternoon.

"You're doing all the wrong things to romance me, Michael," she said, glancing down at the diamonds.

"That's why you're in my bed then, is it?"

"No, I mean flowers and diamonds and stuff . . . they just don't interest me," she said earnestly.

"Don't tell me you're going to send that necklace to the children's hospital like you did with the flowers?"

"Of course, I won't. I really appreciated the effort too – but really, no more grand gestures, hey?"

"Okay," he conceded.

"It just makes me wonder what kind of vacuous bimbos you've gone out with in the past that you feel you have to do these things."

"I don't feel I have to do it, I just wanted to show you I like you."

She started stroking. "You can show me in much nicer . . . and cheaper ways."

He was curious. "Don't you like jewellery much?"

"Really, what's the point of it? I can't understand women who are like magpies – you know, drawn to glittering and sparkling objects just so they can possess them."

He thought of Lisa and Denise, rarely seen without being adorned with a piece from their impressive jewellery collection.

"You're very unlike everyone else I know," he said.

"Good! Considering the people you know . . . I'll be back in a minute."

Ali got out of the bed and Michael watched her naked form leave the room and walk down the hallway to the bathroom.

* * *

The taxi pulled up outside Michael's house and the back door opened. Out poured Cormac, Steve Foyle and three female companions.

"It looks like Michael's asleep," said Steve looking up at the house.

"Ah, Michael's always in the mood for a party," said Cormac walking up the path.

They had been partying hard all night. They had gone

to a nightclub and consumed copious amounts of champagne.

"I haven't seen Michael in ages," giggled one of the women as Cormac searched his pocket for the key.

"Well, now's your chance to rectify that!" Cormac opened the door and they all trooped unsteadily in.

Ali came out of the bathroom, switched off the light and began to walk back to the bedroom. She screamed as she was greeted by the sight of Cormac and his friends standing staring at her as she stood there naked.

Michael, on hearing the scream, jumped out of the bed and pulling a sheet around him raced to the main hallway.

"Well, well, well. It looks like you started the party already!" laughed Cormac to Michael as Ali raced into the bathroom and slammed the door after her.

"Oh no!" sighed Michael as he looked at the drunken party now making its way up the spiral staircase to the living-room.

Barbara didn't follow them. Instead, she came up to Michael and stroked his chest.

"Hi, Mikey, long time no see," she cooed.

The bathroom door opened and Ali came storming out. dressed in Michael's dressing-gown.

"What the hell is going on?" she demanded.

Barbara continued to stroke Michael's chest and gave Ali a disapproving look. "Who's she, Mikey?"

Michael grabbed Barbara's hand and threw it away from him.

"Suit yourself, grumpy!" grimaced Barbara as she went up the spiral stairs to join the party. Loud music and much laughter could now be heard from the living-room upstairs.

"Ali, I'm sorry. I didn't know they were coming, honest."

"I nearly had heart failure. I came out naked and they were all standing there *staring* at me. Who the fuck *are* they?" Ali's eyes blazed.

"They're just some friends of mine, that's all."

"And who let them in?"

"Cormac has a key to my house."

"Cormac? You mean Cormac Cunningham?" Ali was trying to take it all in.

"Yeah. It's hard to explain."

"Michael, what are they doing here?"

"Having a party by the look of things."

"Michael, you've got one minute to explain, or I promise I'm calling a taxi and I'm outta here and that's the end of that."

"Look, Cormac's often out late with friends and looking to have another few drinks or whatever after closing time. So he has a key to my house and lets himself in."

"So, this is a regular thing?"

Michael nodded.

"And you don't mind them invading your home at all hours and creating all that noise?"

"Live and let live." He shrugged his shoulders.

"You don't mind because you usually join the party. Now it's making sense. And who are all those slappers?"

"Just friends of Cormac's."

"So basically you let Cormac Cunningham use your home as a whorehouse, is what you're telling me?"

"Mikey!" came a male shout from upstairs.

"Hey, Mikey, get rid of the bore and come and join the party!" called Barbara.

Ali raised her eyes to heaven and walked past Michael into the bedroom.

Careful not to trip on the trailing sheet around him, Michael ran after her.

She threw off the bathrobe and quickly began to put on her clothes.

"Don't go, Ali! Listen, I know it sound a bit strange, but it's not really. Cormac just likes a pad to entertain his friends and he's a good mate, so what's the problem? Besides he does own fifty per cent of the house – I couldn't stop him even if I wanted to."

"He owns half your house!" Ali was incredulous.

"Well, yeah. Do you know how much houses are going for on this street? When this came up for sale I really wanted it but couldn't manage it on my own so Cormac came up trumps. It's a great investment for him as well."

Ali finished dressing and put on her high-heeled shoes.

"Please don't go, Ali," Michael pleaded.

"Go? I never said I was going anywhere." There was a determined look on Ali's face. "If you or them up there think that I'm going to go scurrying into the night you've another think coming."

She walked past him and out into the hallway.

"For fuck's sake!" snapped Michael as he heard her go up the spiral staircase. He threw off the sheet and started to dress quickly.

Ali looked around the sitting-room. Cormac Cunningham was sitting on an armchair, a huge tumbler of whiskey in his hand. He was laughing with one of the girls who sat on the arm of the chair. The other man was stretched out on the couch and she immediately recognised him as the politician Steve Foyle. She looked at the other two women. She recognised Barbara, who was busy mixing drinks in the kitchen, and the other girl as being two of the women who were with Cormac the night she saw him in the Ice Bar.

"Well, look who it is!" said Cormac looking at Ali. "I didn't recognise you with your clothes on, love."

Barbara looked up from mixing her drinks. "Let's call her 'Knickers-off-knickers-on'!" She erupted in laughter.

Ali knew they were all very drunk and were in no mood to go home.

"What's your name, love?" Cormac asked.

She hated the condescending manner in which he was treating her. As if she was just another one of these girls.

She walked across the room and poured herself a vodka. She took a sip and then turned to face everyone.

"My name is Ali O'Mara."

Steve Foyle sat up quickly from his drunken stupor and focused in on Ali.

"Yes, Steve, and how are you? Last time we met was about a month ago when I interviewed you about environmental waste, remember?"

Steve looked nervous. "Yes . . . hi, Ali."

Cormac sat back a little in his chair and studied her.

"We've never had the pleasure of meeting before. But I've always read your articles with great interest. But, you know, every time I read anything of yours again I'll just be reminded of the image of you coming out of Mike Farrell's bathroom in the nip."

Michael came up the stairs at a run.

"Michael, I knew Ali had bought in The Pavilions but I never realised you had brought your professional relationship to a new level."

Michael was completely embarrassed and uncomfortable. "Eh, yes, we've been seeing each other for a little bit."

"Yes, I'm a neighbour of yours now," Ali said happily. "I've passed your wife a couple of times in the lobby." The atmosphere in the room went cold as the three women looked at each other with uncertainty.

Cormac remained relaxed. "We're moving next week. Despite our best efforts, the development has just gone downmarket recently."

"Mikey, can I get you a drink?" Barbara cooed.

"Yes, get Mikey a drink – I think he could do with one," said Ali.

The girl who was sitting on Cormac's armchair suddenly got up and walked over to Barbara. On the counter Barbara had an open envelope of coke. The girl gave Barbara a warning look and closed the envelope over. Barbara nodded and folded it away into a pocket.

Ali saw the whole action as did Cormac.

Cormac stood up. "I think we'll head off – I can feel some agitation in the air."

Property

"I think that's for the best." Steve stood up quickly.

"I don't know why we have to go just because of her." Barbara gave Ali a filthy look.

"I'm not asking anyone to leave – please don't leave on account of me!" Ali threw hands into the air. "I'd love to party just as much as the rest of you – I'm sure."

Cormac went over to Ali and put out his hand.

"The pleasure was all ours." He winked at her.

Her eyes were as cold as ice as she took his hand and shook it. "I'm delighted to see you're everything I imagined over the years."

Their eyes bored into each other for a while before Cormac smiled and turned.

With relief Michael escorted the group down to the front door.

"Mikey, you should have warned us Ali O'Mara was here," hissed Steve.

"Very interesting choice of partner," Cormac said, studying Michael intently. "It's obviously serious?"

Michael paused and then nodded.

"She was never a friend of ours," said Cormac.

"I know," Michael nodded.

Cormac clasped his hand on Michael's shoulder. "I wonder what the press will make of you two lovebirds." He slapped Michael on the back and started laughing as they all walked out onto the street. "Come on, girls, let's find another venue," he said as Michael closed the door firmly and locked it.

Michael climbed the stairs and found Ali sitting on the chair vacated by Cormac with her legs crossed.

"This really seems to be my year for humiliation. I don't know which was worse – being shown up on national television or being seen nude by Cormac Cunningham."

"You didn't have to go up and join them. Cormac would have been none the wiser as to who you were," Michael pointed out.

"No, I didn't have to go up. I could have let them all have a good laugh at the naked bird caught coming out of Mikey's bathroom. They would have joked about that one for a long time. Do you remember 'Knickers-off-knickers-on' – it was *such* a laugh! Let them think of me as just another slapper. And then I could go scurrying off into the night like a frightened fool. No, Michael, I will *not ever* be intimidated by anyone."

"The sensible thing would have been to go back to bed," he offered.

"And listen to their screams of laughter for the night? No, thanks. Now, if you wanted me to go, then you should have said it and I would have gone like that!" She clicked her fingers.

"I didn't want you to go." He stared at her and couldn't help but admire her and her strength and no-bullshit approach. She was so different from the likes of Barbara.

He went over to her and put his arm around her. "I'm really sorry about all that – intrusion."

"Invasion more like. Michael, I knew your life and your circle were very different from mine, but I didn't realise you lived in this chaos."

"There's really no harm in it. They just like to have a

good time. This house is big and I live on my own so Cormac brings people over from time to time. And, yes, I join in the fun. There's nothing bad or sinister about it."

"Michael, that girl Barbara had coke on her. I saw it."

"A couple of the girls do the odd line of coke, so what?"

"Do you take it?"

"No, of course, I don't."

"But you don't mind it being consumed in your home?"

"As I said, live and let live is my motto."

Ali ran her fingers through her hair. "Look, I know you must think I'm the biggest square in the world, but this whole lifestyle is very alien to me. You're very alien to me . . . I mean, to me that set-up looked like there was a scene between Cormac Cunningham and that girl. I might have no time for him or his wife and what they stand for but I don't like to see people messing around when they're married. And you're supposed to be Denise's friend but just turn a blind eye to it."

"I don't know what Cormac does, and that's the truth. He likes the company of pretty girls; he likes the company of a lot of people. That's all I know. I'm not his keeper after that."

"But you wouldn't mind him being unfaithful to his wife under your roof? Live and let live?"

"It's none of my business. I don't know what he does. I've no evidence of him being with another woman."

"See no evil, hear no evil, and speak no evil. Oh Michael! That attitude is everything I'm against, everything I fight against!"

"Does your whole life have to be a crusade?" Michael felt himself becoming annoyed. "Who appointed you judge and jury for this world? You know something? You're so sanctimonious all the time. You're exactly like you are in your writing – judging the whole world from a moral high ground."

"I'm not going to apologise for having high standards."

He looked at her. "No, I'm sorry and you shouldn't have to. But I'm not going to apologise for my friends either. Cormac and Denise – what can I say? They have a very interesting marriage. I honestly don't know what goes on in that marriage or what they do outside it. It's certainly not conventional – and certainly not something I would want. Looking on, they seem to hate each other sometimes. People say she's with him for the money. They say he screws around on her. They say lots. But they're still with each other after a lot of years."

Ali felt guilty that he didn't know she had seen Denise at his house, especially when she was lecturing about truths.

"Michael. That night when you rushed off in the middle of the night. I saw you talking to Denise back here at your house."

"Oh!" He looked alarmed. "Did you hear what we were talking about?"

"I heard what you were talking about – yes. I'm sorry. I suppose I was spying on you. It's the journalist in me."

He rubbed his hands over his face. "You wonder what you're getting involved in? So am I. As you just said . . . you're a journalist. A journalist who likes to expose wealthy and powerful people. A journalist with a track record for damaging the Cunninghams and me for that matter."

"Commenting on – not damaging."

"When you comment it amounts to the same thing. You've certainly gathered a lot of information about us all for your portfolio."

She looked at him straight in the eye. "Do you honestly think I would use my personal life to get info?" He shrugged.

"I think I'd better go." She stood up, removed the diamond necklace and placed it on the kitchen counter.

"You can give that to Barbara next time she calls around with the gang," she said softly.

She walked past him and down the stairs. She put on her coat and left.

20

The front page of *The Times Property Supplement* was an array of richly coloured photos of Denise and Cormac in the different rooms of their new house in Glenwood, under the heading *'Glenwood – A Haven For The Rich & Famous'*.

The article read:

"What better endorsement can any development have than for the developer to take up residency there? Glenwood – the new must-have address for any millionaire entrepreneur, member of the pop aristocracy, celebrity or just the plain moneyed – has just welcomed its first residents who are none other than Cormac Cunningham of Cunningham Homes and his beautiful and highly respected wife Denise. There are thirty-five houses in Glenwood and all have been architecturally designed with the emphasis on individuality.

Situated in the lush countryside of Kinsealy, Glenwood is a gated community with an extensive security system and security service in place. With starting prices at euros 2,000,000, the selling agent Michael Farrell of Farrell's Auctioneers says, 'Glenwood offers complete privacy and protection for people who because of their position and status want to feel completely safe and away from prying eyes. All houses were designed with numerous panic buttons and other detailed security devices and the estate employs a full-time security service." At these prices, attention to detail would be expected and Cunningham Homes have spared no detail in ensuring Glenwood is the very height of luxury. As she shows us around her new extensive kitchen, Denise Cunningham tells us: 'You really have all the peace and quiet of being in the country, but so near the city.'"

Denise quickly read through the rest of the article over her breakfast and decided it was excellent exposure. Not that Cormac or anyone else had rung her to say so.

* * *

Ali felt miserable as she hit the button for the lift. It had been a couple of days since her falling out with Michael and they hadn't communicated. Damn, why did she have to get involved with him? It was obviously going to end up a disaster and now she really missed him.

She was hosting a dinner party the next night and really didn't feel like hosting it any more. But it would be rude to cancel it and maybe she genuinely wanted to show off the new apartment. She decided to go ahead as it might distract her from feeling miserable.

The lift doors opened and Denise was standing inside.
Ali was taken aback at seeing her so close after hearing her
life story. She was also surprised to see how different she
looked from then, as she seemed now a picture of
elegance, hidden behind big sunglasses and a fur coat.

"Are you going down?" Denise questioned politely
with a smile.

"Eh, yes – sorry!" Ali quickly stepped in and pressed
the ground floor.

Ali stood beside Denise and studied her intently from
the corner of her eye.

"The weather is very changeable at the moment, isn't
it?" Denise smiled.

"Isn't it," said Ali.

"I haven't seen you around before – are you new to the
building?"

"Yes." Ali forced a smile.

"There's a great roof garden. Not sure if you've been
up there yet, but it's a great place to top up the tan."

"Thanks."

Denise pulled the fur coat a little tighter around her.

"All we need now is a little sunshine so we can use it!"

Ali was sure Denise had never ventured onto the
communal roof garden when she had her own roof terrace
at her penthouse. Ali felt very uncomfortable, thinking of
the women in Cormac's company at Michael's house and
wondering what on earth he could see in them when he
had someone like Denise at home. You know far too much
about this poor unsuspecting woman, Ali thought, for
once in her life wishing she had ignored her journalistic

nosiness at Michael's house.

The lift doors chimed as they opened.

"Anyway, see you around," said Denise as she strolled out and walked through the lobby.

* * *

Denise immediately regretted turning down the street off Grafton Street. There was a huge anti-fur protest outside a furrier's and she knew her fake fur looked too real not to cause trouble.

The protestors were screaming abuse over their microphones and Denise straightened her sunglasses as she walked past them.

Suddenly a woman jumped in front of her and screamed at the top of her voice: "Murderer! Murderer!"

"Would you ever fucking cop on?" Denise shouted back at her. "Can't you recognise a fake when you it?" She pushed the woman aside and continued to walk.

The woman grabbed a microphone and shouted after her: "Yeah, baby, I sure can spot one big fake when I see one!"

Denise reached the end of the street and sat quickly into her car. She put on a CD and Barry White's deep voice filled the car with "The Trouble With Me".

Denise never really let things get to her, but she felt upset as she pulled out of her parking space. Her life was very protected and the incident with the protestor in the street had unnerved her. She was angry that a stranger felt she had the right to shout at her like that. She had handled the woman with her usual coolness, but in her head she was transported back to the estate she grew up on and the abuse that was shouted at her growing up. "I sure can spot one big fake when I see one!" The protestor's words were ringing in Denise's ears. She reasoned she was still unnerved from the incident with the car that had followed her that night after Stevie's which had shaken her a lot. Then talking to Michael that night had stirred up a lot of buried memories and demons.

She wouldn't allow it all to ruin her day. She was all over the country on the front of the property supplement in her beautiful new home. What more could she want? Not that Cormac or any of the Cunninghams had rung to compliment her. Not even Michael. All her friends had phoned or texted her saying how great it was and how they couldn't wait to see the house for themselves. Oh, what did she care? It was a Friday night and she needed to let her hair down. She never went to Stevie's on a Friday, but she decided that night she would. As she turned a corner for home, she was oblivious to the black car following her.

* * *

Lisa sailed into Michael's office, with a huge smile across her face.

"Do you know the phones have been hopping with enquiries about Glenwood?" she said, sitting on his desk.

"Really?"

Michael looked tired and even uninterested. He had

been in terrible form for a couple of days. Lisa was delighted with this as she saw it was a sign that his relationship with the mysterious Alison had come to an end.

"It was a great idea of yours to have only private appointments to view the showhouse as opposed to open house. It's adding a feeling of exclusivity to Glenwood, and stopping every dog and its mother from trailing in for a look."

"When are we doing the first showings?"

"I've made some appointments for Monday. But some of the people ringing have been very high calibre. You know Jeff Knowles of Knowles Technology? He's viewing on Tuesday. You know his company was recently floated on the London Stock Exchange and he's worth millions. And I've had an enquiry from the agent of someone he would only describe as a Hollywood star. I'm dying to know who that is. And, of course, a couple of record agencies have been on enquiring on behalf of their pop totty. I tell you, if some of these big names buy, Glenwood will be the address to have."

"Good, we'll be able to put up the prices and that should keep Cormac happy."

"Yeah." She placed a hand on his shoulder. "Unlike you. Michael. What's the matter?"

"Ah . . . nothing."

"Is it . . ." she smiled sympathetically, "Alison?"

"Yeah . . . I think it's over."

"Ahh," she sighed sympathetically. "Well, what's meant to be is meant to be. You know what I always say?

If it don't come easy then let it go."

Yeah, a spoilt brat like you who has had everything handed to you on a silver plate would say that, Michael thought.

"You know what you need? A night on the piss with good old little me."

That was the last thing he wanted. "Thanks, Lisa. But I'm not good company at the moment."

"You're always good company."

"No, I'm just going to go home to watch some TV. Thanks, anyway."

21

In all her years going to Stevie's, Denise had never been there on a Friday night before. If it was possible it seemed even more packed than usual. She was delighted to be there and having a great time. Cormac had come home after work to change before he headed out for his usual Friday-night pub crawl. He had seemed in excellent spirits, which she took to mean he was delighted with the press coverage for Glenwood. Which she took to mean lots of people had paid him gushing compliments about it all day.

She downed her vodka and headed out to the floor. On a Friday night they seemed to play some eighties tracks. Blondie's "Atomic" was blaring and she lost herself in the music.

Green eyes stared across the crowd, fixed on her and watched her every move.

Denise could feel the bodies move in rhythm as she closed her eyes and let the soundtrack gush over her.

The man moved over to the bar and caught the barman Sam's attention with his green eyes.

"A bottle of Carlsberg," he said.

Sam opened a bottle and put it in front of the man.

The man handed him twenty. "You can keep the change."

Sam looked at him suspiciously before nodding and smiling.

"Hey," the man called Sam back.

"Yeah?" Sam spoke loudly to be heard over the music.

"Is she a regular?" asked the man. Sam followed the man's gaze and instinctively knew he was speaking about Denise.

"Oh, that's Denise," said Sam. "We don't usually see her at the weekend. She usually comes midweek."

"Is she easy?"

Sam looked uneasy and stepped back. "No, not Denise. She doesn't come here for that, just to enjoy herself." Sam gave him a warning look and went off to serve somebody else.

Denise pushed back her hair and headed off the dance floor.

She got to her bar stool and sat up on it.

"Sam, another one of these!" She shook her empty glass and Sam had her glass filled in a second.

She took a swig and turned around so she could look at the dancers.

"Where have you been all my life?" asked a man's voice beside her.

She raised her eyes to heaven at the corniness of it all,

and began to turn around to tell the speaker to get lost, when she heard him say, "And why didn't you stay there?"

She stopped for a second, surprise jolting through her, then she slowly continued to turn, knowing who the speaker was.

She looked him straight in the face and then she slowly smiled.

"Ryan," she whispered.

"The very same." His face broke out in a grin.

A hand gripped his shoulder and Jason's booming voice said, "Move on, mate. She doesn't want you annoying her."

"Get off!" snapped Ryan and shook Jason's hand away.

Jason went to grip Ryan again.

"No, Jason, it's all right . . . I know him," intervened Denise.

"Right, sorry, Denise. Sorry, mate." Jason slipped off into the crowd.

They looked at each other for a while.

"How long has it been?" Denise asked.

"About twelve years."

"That long?"

* * *

Denise had been working on reception at the architects' firm for two months and all the single guys, and some of the not-so-single ones, had all asked her out. She had politely declined all offers.

When Ryan Cantwell came to work at the firm in his

first position as an engineer, he wasn't aware of this. On his first day, he had gone up to Reception and did a double- take on seeing Denise before boldly going up to her and asking with a great big smile: "Where have you been all my life?"

Denise looked up from her magazine, completely unimpressed, and gave him a withering look.

Feeling a complete fool and annoyed with her aloofness he snapped, "And why didn't you stay there?" before walking with what dignity he could muster down the corridor towards the offices.

As she watched him march off, she couldn't help but admire his quick wits.

She was used to all the other guys continually flirting with her even after she had refused their advances many times. She was always polite and coolly flirtatious back to them as they continued to try their luck with her. But she noticed after their initial encounter, Ryan kept a distance from her and kept their contact purely professional. "Could you fax this for me?" or "Any messages?" was as deep as it got in his conversations with her. She wasn't used to his cool manner. She was the one who was usually cool with people. It vaguely intrigued her, especially as he seemed to be a very popular guy within the company. After work, there was a big drinking culture in the firm and everyone would head over to the pub for drinks. Whenever Denise went over, she never really drank and never stayed that late, but there would always be a few of the directors all about her when she was there – all looking for her attention. She wondered how quickly they would move away from her if they knew where she was from. She wondered how quickly she would be viewed as a slapper in the company and lose all respect if she was stupid enough to sleep with one of them. She might just be a receptionist, but she had crossed a huge gulf from the flats to being here and she knew she could keep going now she was on the ladder. She knew it would only be a matter of time until she met the right person who would give her the life she wanted and she would be safe. The guys she had met could offer her a very good life, but she hadn't met the man yet who could offer her it all. And she wouldn't mess up her life like her mother by falling for any false promises, dreams or chancers. Although she never showed it, she was deeply flattered that the directors would give her so much attention in the pub, but she found her own attention being directed over to Ryan – Ryan who seemed to be in the pub every evening after work, and always had a big gang of friends around him – and continued to look at her in the same cool manner in which she had viewed him on his first day at work.

One evening, she decided to try and break the ice when they were standing side by side at the bar waiting to give orders.

"Yeah?" asked the barman, looking at the two of them to see who was first in line.

"Three pints of Heineken, two Carlsberg and a Guinness please," Ryan ordered.

"Isn't it a case of ladies first?" Denise asked, looking at Ryan and raising an eyebrow.

Ryan looked at her, seemingly embarrassed, before

saying, "Oh, yeah, you go ahead first."

Denise was about to laugh and say "Only joking" when one of his crowd shouted his name, and he quickly turned and went to join them in some dispute they were having over football. Denise was left standing at the bar, feeling irritated because now he must think she was a real bitch after her attempt to be friendly backfired.

A couple of days later, Denise went into the newsagent's around the corner during her lunch break. Ryan was standing at the magazine shelves, leafing through a magazine.

"Are you going to steal that?" she asked as she walked past him, with a smile.

Ryan looked up at her and his face looked serious and perplexed. "Don't you like me or something, Denise?"

Denise stopped in her tracks and felt guilty. "Yes, I do . . . I do like you."

She quickly turned and walked off. She couldn't help thinking about Ryan all that afternoon. And that evening when she went back to the small apartment she was renting she started feeling upset.

Ryan had only been friendly on his first day – she didn't have to be the Ice Queen back. She was so used to getting attention that she was stopping being considerate of other people's feelings. She wanted to escape the flats more than anything in the world, and she was getting there, but she didn't want to become a bitch on the way. Her looks might have been a passport out of the flats, but weren't a passport to treat people in a rude or condescending manner.

The next morning Ryan came in very late and looked stressed. He had probably been drinking till all hours the night before. The Managing Director, George, had been screaming looking for Ryan and Denise, realising he would be in big trouble, adjusted his diary to show he had an appointment with a client.

"Ryan!" Denise called him over. "George has been going mad looking for you," she whispered, "so I said you were at a meeting . . . look here . . . I inserted it in your diary and everything, okay?"

Ryan was amazed at her intervention. But his overwhelming relief at being spared the wrath of George was bigger than his amazement at her action.

At lunch, he came up to her and was embarrassed as he said, "Thanks for doing that this morning – you saved my neck."

She smiled up at him and shook her head. "It was no problem."

"It would have been a big problem for me if George knew I was late. You know what he's like." He nodded at her and made his way to the lift. As the lift door opened he turned around "Do you want to come out to lunch, my treat? I owe you one."

"It really isn't necessary." She looked down at her packed sandwiches – her impoverished upbringing made her do her accounts very meticulously.

"Seriously, I'd like to." He became agitated. "But if you've something else on –"

"No, I don't actually . . . I'd love to go to lunch." She stood up and grabbed her handbag.

They went to a pub around the corner where they ordered lasagne and chips and had Pepsi with it.

"Nice and healthy," Ryan joked as he tucked in.

"Where were you last night anyway to cause you to sleep it out?"

"Me and some of the guys went to a nightclub – didn't get home till after five."

"On a school night? You're mad."

"You're only young once, aren't you?"

"I guess."

He spoke a bit about himself. He was from the west coast. Son of two teachers. His father was a woodwork teacher and he had encouraged an early interest in engineering. Ryan had come up to Dublin to study engineering, and the firm was his first permanent job. He lived with three friends from college. His life seemed very uncomplicated and normal to Denise. He warmed up as they continued to eat and she enjoyed his company as he started being the same way with her as she had observed he was with their other colleagues.

As they walked back to work, they were chatting like old friends.

They passed a hotel and there was a wedding party arriving. The bride and groom looked overwhelmingly happy as they gazed into each other's eyes.

"At what part do we throw up?" whispered Ryan, making Denise laugh.

They hit it off like a house on fire after that. Ryan would always stop at Reception to chat away to Denise and a secret bond developed between them where they would have codes for different people in the company and moods they were in.

"There's a chill in the air in Bruce Willis's department today," Ryan would say as he faxed at reception.

"Thanks, I'll avoid going there. Barbra Streisand's voice went up to a new octave at a meeting in the boardroom this morning . . . I think Naomi Campbell's days are numbered."

Denise really enjoyed his company and they began to have lunch together regularly and go out for a drink after work.

They even made a joke out of their initial encounter. When one would see the other, the first thing they would say was "Where have you been all my life?" and then the other would respond with "And why didn't you stay there?"

One night, Ryan was back at her apartment and she cooked them a meal. They had a few to drink and laughed a lot and before either of them knew what was happening they were kissing passionately.

Ryan woke in the middle of the night and reached out for Denise, but the bed was empty.

He sat up, feeling completely happy with life. Even though he had lots of friends, there was a part of Ryan that was a loner. A part of him that felt he never could get really close to someone, no matter how much he wanted to. He wondered if he would ever find love. And then suddenly he had met Denise and everything made sense. He jumped out of bed and put on some clothes. The weather was cold outside, and a light snow was falling against the windowpane. He looked out at the snow falling silently on the ground. He opened the bedroom door and peeped out. He was shocked to see Denise sitting on the couch, wrapped in a dressing gown-crying softly.

"Denise?" He rushed to her and sat beside her, putting his arm around her. "What's wrong, love?"

She was suddenly sobbing into his jumper and he rubbed her back silently.

"I'm so stupid. Why did I let this happen?" she said between sobs.

"I don't understand."

"It'll ruin our friendship. I'll lose a good friend." He looked at her and tried to smile. "You might lose a friend, but gain a boyfriend."

"I don't want a boyfriend, Ryan. There's no future for us as a couple. I'm so sorry."

He was confused and upset but continued to rub her back as she sobbed, until they both fell asleep.

* * *

All the memories came flooding back as Denise gazed into Ryan's green eyes at Stevie's.

What amazed her most was that he seemed not to have changed a bit apart from his eyes. His eyes were very different from how they used to be and gave him a whole different look. They had lost their youthfulness.

"What are you doing here in Stevie's? You're not living around here, are you?" she asked.

"No, I've been living in London for years. I'm just back

for a few days and was visiting friends nearby and we ended up coming in here. I haven't been to a nightclub in years." He laughed. "What about you? Are you living locally?"

Denise blinked a few times and she quickly came back down to earth. What would she say she was doing in a place like this? Ryan might know people locally, so she would have to be careful not to expose herself. Part of her was disappointed to see Ryan there and hanging out with people who went to Stevie's. He had potential and she had hoped he would find a better place for himself in life.

"I don't live close by, but not too far away."

"How mad is this? After all these years! Are you married?"

Oh, how she wished she had bumped into him in Grafton Street or somewhere where she could be honest.

"Yes, married for a few years."

"Is he here?"

"Eh, no. At home watching television." She gave a little laugh. "What about you? Are you married?" She looked down at his ringless fingers.

"Divorced."

"I'm sorry to hear that."

He shrugged. "Shit happens. Last I heard, you had gone off with some rich big shot."

"It's so long ago I can't remember."

"I remember."

"How long are you back for?" she asked, quickly changing the subject.

"Just a couple of days."

"You're still in engineering?"

"Still in construction, yeah. You working?"

"No, not any more."

They stared at each other for a long while. Denise suddenly remembered how late it was and glanced down at her watch.

"I'd better run. It's getting late."

"The husband will be wondering where you are."

"Something like that. Ryan . . . back then . . . there was a lot of things going on in my life and in my head at the time . . . I'm sorry if I ever hurt you." Denise couldn't help it, but her eyes filled up with tears.

Ryan looked at her and nodded. "Please don't worry about anything that passed between us in the past. It's forgotten."

She reached forward, enveloped him in a hug and kissed his cheek. Then she silently got up and walked away.

* * *

When she got back to the penthouse she felt very sad. Meeting Ryan again had stirred up so many memories and the realisation of time passing was very moving. She peeped into the bedroom and saw Cormac was sleeping. They would be moving to Glenwood the following week and she was suddenly really looking forward to it. She wanted to start a new chapter in her life. In the bathroom she looked in the mirror and felt embarrassed that she had met Ryan dressed in this tarty way. She had been so taken aback at meeting him that she hadn't given any thought to the way she was dressed. Strangely, Ryan hadn't appeared to be surprised by her appearance either.

22

"It's just amazing," complimented Ali's sister-in-law Úna as she looked around the apartment.

"Look at the attention to detail," remarked her brother James.

"You must be delighted you've finally got your own place," Úna followed up.

Ali wished she had cancelled the dinner party as her spirits really hadn't lifted and she wasn't in the mood for the chattering classes that night.

There had been no contact between her and Michael and, instead of getting over him, she was feeling worse as each day went by. As much as she loved all the people gathered around her dinner table, she found them all boring after Michael's company.

"The place is trumps," said Tim. "The furniture is just really cool too."

Ali slapped her fork on the table. "Okay, we've established the fact that the damned apartment is great –

can we now move on and talk about something else?"
There was an uneasy feeling around the table as they all
exchanged looks.

"I'm sorry," said Ali, running a hand through her hair.
"I've just been under a bit of pressure recently with that
honeymoon fiasco and moving house and everything.
Seriously, I do appreciate all your compliments and I know
I'm lucky to have got it. It's just I am now an official
member of the rat race, aren't I?"

"What do you mean?" Úna quizzed.

"Well, they got me, didn't they? I am now a home
owner. I bought into this whole big fantasy about
acquiring goods that we are all reared on."

"Considering the amount of people who can't afford
their own place, you should feel lucky," said James.

"Well, that's just it, isn't it? Forget the fact that I'll be
chained to exorbitant repayments for the next thirty years
– I'm brainwashed to think I feel lucky. You know, when I
was shopping for all this furniture and TVs and DVDs etc,
I was struck going around the shops about how we are all
brainwashed into thinking we are lesser people if we don't
have anything. There was everyone, so many young
couples, convinced they had to buy and buy more. As far
as I can see it it's all a big sham so a few families at the top
can just get richer and richer by convincing everyone else
to buy more and more of what they build, make, sell."

Úna threw her napkin on the table. "Oh, for fuck's
sake, Ali! Why don't you just enjoy the experience of your
first home instead of overanalysing everything? I
sometime wonder why you didn't just go and live on a

kibbutz or something years ago!"

"Maybe I should have. I might have been happier there."

Ali stood up, put the plates on top of each other and walked to the kitchen.

"Look, everybody," she said, turning and doing a little twirl. "Dressed in a beautiful Karen Milan cocktail dress, about to stack my NEF dishwasher and will be serving my home-made tiramisu in exactly five minutes. Aren't I a marvel? How wonderful is my life?"

She continued into the kitchen and closed the door behind her. She flung the dishes in the sink, poured herself a large glass of white wine and took a gulp of it. She was being a bitch and she knew it. She had invited people over for dinner and now she didn't have the good manners to be hospitable. She was taking out her disappointment about Michael on those closest to her, and that wasn't fair. Maybe she had been too judgmental with him? Why couldn't she have just enjoyed his company without commenting on everything? She felt terrible about eavesdropping on Denise Cunningham. She really didn't want to know all that stuff about her.

The door opened. In walked Tim and closed the door behind him.

"OK, what's the matter?"

"I'm very sorry. Just give me a few minutes in here and I'll go out and plaster a smile on my face."

"What happened and who is he?"

"That obvious?"

"I'm afraid so."

"What the hell is wrong with me, Tim? I just can't keep from being Ali O'Mara, esteemed journalist. It's no wonder all my relationships end when I deal with them in the same way I deal with an investigative story. I don't blame Richard for running away from me as soon as he got his Bafta."

"Let me remind you it was you who kicked Richard out, and for good reason as he was screwing around on you. That never had a future in it anyway."

"Maybe." She took a gulp from her wine. "Maybe I should have done what everyone else seems to do and not make a stir and just suffer in silence."

"Ali, one thing you will never do is suffer in silence. Come on, I'll help you dish out dessert."

She nodded and spread out the dessert plates.

"Tim?" she asked, slicing up the tiramisu.

"Uh huh?"

"You're a man-about-town. Do you know of a girl called Barbara?"

"Barbara who?"

"Don't know. You remember when we were in the Ice Bar a while back? There were three girls with Cormac Cunningham. She was the dark-haired one. Early thirties, good-looking girl."

He started to laugh lightly. "You mean Barbara Whelan."

"Why are you laughing?"

"She's a coke ho'!"

"A what?"

"A coke ho'. She would sleep with anyone for a line of

coke. She's been on the scene for years. Came from a good family. Did a bit of modelling in her youth and got to know a few important people which gained her access to some privileged circles. She developed an addiction to nose candy along the way and lost all self-respect."

"I don't think I'm getting the full picture here."

"I don't know all the specific details about Barbara Whelan. But I know a coke ho' would do anything for her fix of coke. They're known to go into toilets in exclusive nightclubs and have sex while enjoying coke. Not exactly prostitution but not exactly Mary Poppins either."

*   *   *

Ali had handed around the plates of tiramisu, apologising for her earlier bad form. She was now pretending to smile and to be in good form, but her thoughts were pre-occupied with what Tim had told her in the kitchen.

There was a knock on the door.

"That's funny. Nobody rang the buzzer from downstairs," said Ali, making her way to the door.

"Probably one of the neighbors complaining about the noise," joked Úna.

Ali opened the door.

Michael was standing there looking sheepish.

"I was going to bring the biggest bunch of flowers and chocolates with me, but I remembered what you said about not being impressed by grand gestures. So, I just brought me instead."

She bit her lower lip. "Hi." She smiled.

Hearing the chatter of her guests, he frowned. "I'm sorry. You're entertaining. It's a bad time for you."

"No . . . you're fine. Come on in." She reached forward and drew him in by the arm.

"Everybody, this is Michael," said Ali, leading him over to the table.

"I hope you like tiramisu, Michael, because you've missed everything else," said Úna.

"I only like tiramisu if it's dripping in alcohol." He smiled at Ali as he took a spare seat and pulled it up beside her.

Tim stared at Ali and mouthed the word "No!" at her.

She nodded, shrugged, and took a spoon of desert.

* * *

Much later when all the guests had gone home, Michael and Ali curled up on the couch.

"I thought I wouldn't see you again," she said.

"Wouldn't you have contacted me?" he stroked her back.

"No . . . I'm horribly stubborn . . . horrible in many ways . . . I really do regret listening in to that private conversation with Denise."

"I'm sorry I accused you of using our relationship to get a scoop."

"Well, I don't blame you the way I went marching up to all those people and scared them off in a few minutes."

"They were quite intimidated, I think," he chuckled.

"Did you miss me?" She looked into his face seriously.

"I really tried not to, but I did."

"Good. Thanks for coming back." She squeezed him tightly. "We're the most mismatched couple you could meet, but I'm willing to give it a go. Are you?"

"I've a feeling life won't be easy with you, but – I'll give it a go too. What a romantic way of putting it!"

"That's me – last of the great romantics . . . I'll try not to be so judgmental, but I can't change myself either. I am what I am. I am nosy and criticising and when I see something wrong I holler about it."

"You really piss me off with your ways, but I don't want you any other way."

"I do find your life completely alien to me – I really was shocked with the invasion of those awful people."

"Well, life might not be easy with you, but it won't be straightforward either with me." He raised his glass. "Do you want to drink to that?"

She raised her glass and clinked his.

"Apart from an alcohol-drenched tiramisu," he said, "that's the best offer I've had all day."

23

"Please be careful with that!" Denise pleaded at the removal men as they banged an antique table against the door.

She looked around the chaos that their living-room had descended into and sighed loudly.

She wondered where on earth Cormac had found these cowboys who were posing as removal men. They were obviously got through a friend of a friend and at a knockdown price, because they hadn't a clue what they were doing.

"Good to see everything is going well," said Cormac as he entered the apartment and walked past her towards the study.

"It's not going well at all." She walked quickly after him. "They're damaging everything."

"We're after paying a lot of money to Susan Haughey for a load of new furniture. We shouldn't be bringing much stuff with us from here," Cormac pointed out. He had already put the penthouse on the market and advertised it as fully furnished so he was alarmed to think that Denise might be plundering it.

"We are bringing some stuff with us, Cormac. And I'm talking about all our personal things as well. They dropped a box of delph earlier and everything was smashed."

Cormac looked through files for documents. "I'm busy trying to get things sorted for a meeting this afternoon, so you deal with it. Soft furnishings are your department," he snapped.

"And bullshit is yours," she said, before turning and leaving.

Four hours later and Denise was still in the penthouse, even though everything they were taking with them had been moved. She sat looking at what had been her home for four years, now stripped of any personal elements. Stripped of any indication that they had ever lived there. She had been happy there and now she felt the wrench of leaving affecting her more than she thought it would. Cormac had packed his files that morning and headed off to his meeting, instructing her to lock up after her. No sentimentality there.

As she gazed across the city views for the last time, she realised she had never lived in a house before. In a strange kind of way the views from the penthouse had reminded her of the views from the flats when she was growing up. She went to the door of the penthouse and took one final look around before exiting. As she turned the key, a tear fell down her face.

* * *

Ali pressed the button of the elevator and waited for it to arrive, feeling elated over Michael being back in her life. As the door swung open she got a surprise to see Denise there, looking as if she had been crying. Denise quickly put on her dark glasses and smiled.

"Hi again," said Denise.

"Hi," Ali forced herself to smile back, wondering what had upset her. "I found that roof garden you were recommending. It's gorgeous."

"Isn't it? I'm moving, so I won't get a chance to use it again."

"Oh!" Ali remembered the feature in the property supplement. "Well, the best of luck with it." Ali studied Denise intently.

"Thanks. See you around." The lift doors opened and Denise walked out.

24

Denise took her seat beside Martha at the boardroom at Forward.

"So, how did the move go?" asked Martha.

"A nightmare to be honest."

"I drove past there on Sunday. They look gorgeous. You're very lucky."

Denise smiled. "I know I am."

Tony came in and sat at the top of the table.

"Hi, everybody. Great work on the fundraising for the new play centre for Jobstown. There's some great ideas there and I think we can really make it happen. Denise, I particularly liked your idea of selling tickets for a luncheon cooked by celebrities where each table gets to eat lunch with the celebrity who cooked the meal."

"Thanks, Tony. I've made a few calls on that one and I've already got a few names of people who are interested."

"Excellent. Now, I've a bit of a surprise for you. A very pleasant one I have to add. I'm sure you've all heard of

Aston, the British construction firm?"

There was a general grumble of acknowledgement and nods around the committee table.

"Well, Aston are moving into the Irish market. They contacted me some time ago about making a donation to Forward. They asked me to keep it strictly confidential until it was finalised. But I'm happy to inform you that Aston are making a donation of 100,000 euros to Forward!"

"Wow!" exclaimed Martha as everybody erupted in excited chatter.

"A brilliant and very generous donation, I'm sure you agree. And what's more, this isn't a blank cheque from Aston. They are going to take an active interest in how the money is spent and want to adopt us as their charity in Ireland permanently. And this is coming from the highest level at Aston, with the Chairman of the company wanting to join the committee here at Forward. If there are no objections from anyone here on the board, I would be delighted to accept him onto the board." Tony looked around at the committee who all shook their heads and smiled.

"Excellent. If you can be patient for just a minute," said Tony, rising from his seat and leaving the boardroom.

"That's all very unexpected," said Martha. "Tony is a dark horse."

"Tony will be anything you want him to be as long as there is a pay-off for the charity at the end of it." Denise smiled wryly.

The door opened, and Tony re-entered followed by a

tall, impeccably dressed man.

Denise looked up, smiling. Her smile faltered as she took the man in.

"Ladies and gentlemen, this is the Chairman of Aston, Ryan Cantwell."

Ryan smiled and nodded at the crowd.

Denise stared at Ryan in disbelief.

"Please, Ryan, take a seat beside me," urged Tony as he sat down.

Still smiling, Ryan sat down and looked at everyone individually and nodded. Everyone smiled back, with the exception of Denise who had confusion written across her face.

Ryan spent no longer nodding at Denise than he did in the case of everyone else.

"Thank you, everybody, for allowing me to join Forward," said Ryan. "You know, Aston is one of the biggest construction firms in the UK, but I think a lot of our success is down to the fact that we care about the communities we build in. We don't just build, take the profits and run, but rather make sure that we are contributing to the community. And we like to give to the community. That's why when we decided to enter the Irish property market, at the same time as looking for suitable sites we started to look at the charity work being done here and decide who we could best do some work with so we can help improve Dublin. As I looked around, there really was no option for me but Forward."

"He's a dish, isn't he?" Martha whispered to Denise.

Denise stopped staring at Ryan in shock and quickly

looked down at her notes on the table.

She spent the rest of the meeting with emotions racing from confusion to fear to curious to furious. Ryan being the chairman of Aston was revelation enough. How and when did he become the head of such a major corporation? Whenever she'd thought of him, she knew he would do well, but she'd imagined him as being a middle-management engineer in a middle-sized company. Not running one of the biggest firms in the Britain! She tried not to look over at him, but when she could catch a glimpse she was shocked to see his suave, tailored and affluent appearance. Even more shocked to observe the cool confidence of his manner. Which brought her to realise you would never find a man like that in Stevie's, so what the hell was he doing there? Which led her to be terrified about the fact that he had seen her dressed like a tart there! And even worse that her wonderful sheltered world had just been invaded by an ex-lover. She felt exceptionally exposed.

"Right, so, we'll call it a day, until next week." Tony wrapped up the meeting.

Everyone started moving and they all headed in the direction of Ryan to shake his hand and welcome him.

"Are you coming to get a closer look?" said Martha, heading in Ryan's direction.

"I'll be over in a minute," said Denise who headed out down the corridor after Tony.

"Tony, can I have a quick word?" asked Denise.

"Of course, Denise." Tony stopped and smiled at her.

"It's just . . . well, it's just, we don't usually accept

somebody onto the committee without going through the normal procedures of nomination, then seconding etc."

"I know, but then we don't normally get donations of 100,000 euros free gratis, do we?"

"It's just I hope our need for money doesn't also mean greed. I mean we don't know anything about this man's reputation, do we? Is he the type of person we want on the committee at Forward?"

Tony was very tempted to turn around and say that Cunningham Homes weren't exactly angels and had sometimes a very nasty reputation but it didn't stop her from being on the committee. But no, he had too much respect for Denise to insult her.

"I think everyone knows of Aston; their reputation speaks for itself. I've met Ryan numerous times and found him to be nothing but commendable. And I like to pride myself on being an excellent judge of character." Tony smiled at her and walked off, indicating he wanted to hear no more of her negativity.

Slowly she turned and watched the committee walk down the stairs, all chattering among themselves. Realising she had left her handbag in the boardroom, she waited until they were all gone before going in. She hurried across to where she had been sitting and reached down to get the bag.

"Oh, hi! I'm sorry . . . I just forgot my folder." She looked up and saw that Ryan was in the doorway. He moved across to where he had been sitting and picked up his paperwork.

Denise stared at him, not knowing what to say.

"This is mad, isn't it? Meeting again like this?" He beamed a smile at her.

"Isn't it?"

"We haven't seen each other in years. And then we bump into each other twice in a matter of days. What's the chance of that?"

"Very slim. Of all the charities in all the world, you had to walk into mine . . . or something like that."

He laughed. "Something like that. Anyway, I have an appointment at three, so I'll see you at the next meeting, I guess."

And then he was gone.

* * *

Cormac was on the phone to Honey while Denise sat up in bed flicking through a magazine, trying to keep her mind off the day's activities.

"What do you mean you won't attend your cousin Jenny's wedding?" Honey was saying. "You were very close growing up."

"We weren't close growing up! You used to force us to hang out together, but we hated each other, and I'm not taking a day off from work to attend the wedding of somebody I can't stand."

"You know what your problem is, Cormac? You've got no sense of family. If you ask me that's why you haven't been blessed with children. Life is funny with things like that. It senses you aren't family-orientated and so won't give you any children."

"I don't know what you're banging on about, Mum."

"You, that's what! You take all the perks and give nothing back. I wonder where you would be if you hadn't been handed a thriving company. I wonder where you would be if you had to make your own way in the world. And you won't even attend a family wedding in return."

"Cunningham Homes has never done better since I took over, and you know it."

"Success is easy to build on success. Me and your father worked every hour God sent to establish that company."

"Listen, I'm not getting into all that. I'm not going. I can't anyway because Denise has something on that day."

"Oh great!" whispered Denise as she threw her eyes to heaven. "Put the blame on me."

"Denise? And what pressing hairdresser's appointment can't she get out of that day?"

"It's with her charity."

"Charity begins at home, tell her."

"All right, all right, I'll go," snapped Cormac.

"Good. Talk to you tomorrow."

Cormac muttered something to himself and started to read the paperwork on his lap again.

Denise shook her head as she flicked the pages of her magazine. "The reason why she always gets her own way is because nobody has the balls to stand up to her."

"And you do?" Cormac shot back.

"I don't let her get away with as much as everyone else does."

"Anyway, we're going to Jenny's wedding."

Denise laughed "Oh, no, my dear. *You* said you would go. I didn't. I like Jenny less than you and going to her first wedding was bad enough."

"She made comments about us not having children again."

"She really isn't a shining example to encourage motherhood," Denise said.

"And yours was?" Cormac said.

Denise looked up for a second and looked at her husband, the pain showing in her eyes for a split second, before she smiled brightly.

"No. Which just proves my point we should never have children, since neither of us has any good role models."

"Excuse me, I had a very good upbringing –"

"No, Cormac, you had a very rich upbringing. There's a difference." Denise flung the magazine on the floor, turned off her bedside lamp and turned her back on her husband.

She couldn't stop thinking of Ryan.

"Do you know Aston Construction, Cormac?" she asked after a while.

"I know of them, yes. Why?"

"Seemingly they are moving into the Irish market."

"And how would you know that?"

"I met the chairman of the company today, an Irish guy. He joined Forward."

"That's just what I fucking need! Another competitor for land."

* * *

All those years ago, Ryan couldn't help himself from falling in love with Denise. Even though she tried everything to stop him from doing it. He was young, at the beginning of his career and now he felt he had met the woman of his dreams. Life was good for him.

"So I turned around to Jacob and I shouted at him 'If you want it done you can do it your bloody self!'"

Denise laughed as Ryan concluded a story about an incident at work. They were in the pub having a few drinks. They had been seeing each other for three months, even though they kept it a secret from their work colleagues.

They sat in silence for a couple of minutes as Denise looked down into her glass of wine, and Ryan gazed happily at her.

"Oh, Ryan, why don't you go and find yourself a nice girl?" urged Denise.

"I have found myself a nice girl!" he retorted.

"No, you haven't. Emily in Accounts is mad for you to ask her out. I heard her discussing you in the canteen."

"Emily in Accounts! How could I go near her once I've been with you? Nice as Emily from Accounts is."

"Ryan, I'm being serious. You're wasting your time with me. We don't have a future together."

"But why? I like you. you like me. We're a happy family."

She couldn't help smiling at him. "You're quite mad, do you know that?"

"I'm mad about you."

"Don't, Ryan, please. I really like you, but I know what

I'm looking for in life and I'll know it when I see it. And I know you're not for me."

"Come on. We're going to be late for the cinema." He grabbed her hand and pulled her up.

They went back to Ryan's house first so he could change into casual clothes. They often did that on their way out. She would sit there and be sociable with the three guys that were Ryan's friends from college. They would offer her a can of beer which she would gratefully accept and sip while making polite conversation while they all stared at her as if she came from another planet.

"Are we ready?" Ryan came bounding into the room.

"Yeah," Denise stood up and put on her coat. "See you guys."

Ryan put his arm around her and they went out the front door.

"Wonder what they're saying about us now?" she said.

He laughed. He could guess. And, as it happened, he was dead right.

"Phew! She's some looker," one of them was saying. "Ryan's done well for himself."

"They kind of look mismatched though, don't they?" remarked another. "She looks like she should be with some fella driving a Porsche, not our Ryan."

Deep down Ryan felt the same thing. In his head he had them living in a nice house in a suburb with him doing well at work. But he knew that was the life Denise never wanted.

* * *

They were lying in each other's arms in her bed in her flat.

"I . . . I care for you, Ryan," Denise said. "I really do. But that's not enough for me, do you understand?"

"Uh huh," Ryan whispered, glad the darkness hid the tear rolling down his face as he realised this girl had the ability to break his heart and yet he couldn't move away from her.

* * *

"Fred offered me a promotion at work," Ryan informed Denise excitedly over lunch.

"Brilliant! I'm delighted for you," she said genuinely.

"For us, babe, delighted for us," he urged. "I'm heading home at the weekend to see my family. They would love to meet you, if you want to come with me?"

"No, thanks . . . I wish you didn't speak of me to them."

"Why? It's normal to speak about the love in your life to your family. Don't you ever speak about me to your family?"

Denise sighed. "Come on. We'd better get back to work or we'll be late."

As they walked back to the office, he thought as he had countless times before that she never spoke about her family and when he pushed her on it she closed up completely.

He was determined to get to the bottom of it. After work, he borrowed a friend's car and waited outside her home on a Thursday. She was never available on a Thursday and he wondered where she got to. The chances were she went to see her family. She came out of her flat and walked down the road to the bus. He waited until she got on to the bus and then he followed it.

She swapped buses in town and, as he continued to follow her, he became concerned as she seemed to be heading towards a very deprived area.

It was getting dark and as the bus came to its last stop, he saw her getting off. He parked and set off on foot at a safe distance. He watched her walk through the empty playground and into a rundown tower block. She was in there a couple of hours and then she re-emerged and headed towards the bus stop to wait for her bus.

Not knowing what to do, he went back to his car and sat in and drove up to her.

"Hi there!" he said cheerily as he opened the window. "Fancy meeting you here!" He grinned at her.

Denise was shocked to see him "What the hell are you doing here?" she demanded. "Did you follow me? How dare you!"

The bus arrived at that moment. She got on and it took off immediately.

He called around to her flat that night and spent a couple of hours ringing the bell which she ignored. The next day at work she was as cold as ice to him. This went on for a couple of days. Then after work one night he went up to Reception.

"Denise, please don't do this to me. Whatever you do, don't ignore me in this fashion. I'm sorry I followed you, I wasn't thinking straight. You never tell me about your background or family. I just wondered what you did on a

Thursday because you're never around. I'm really really sorry."

"You had no right to follow me." She looked very upset.

"I know."

They walked back to her flat and she poured them both a strong drink and suddenly she was telling him everything. About her mother and her upbringing and where she was from. Afterwards he just stared at her.

"So you see, I'm not some princess on a pedestal for you to adore. I'm a girl from the flats. So why don't you just leave me alone now and go find someone else?"

He put his arms around her. "Oh, Denise!"

And suddenly she put her arms around him and she wanted to be close to him.

"I never talk about it to anyone. But I'm tired of pretending. I'm glad you know."

"I'm glad I know as well. As if it could ever make me love you less. It makes me love you more."

The next morning, for the first time Ryan felt they had finally concreted their relationship and found each other as equals. She stood in the small kitchenette cooking them a fry and laughed and joked away with him. They both called in sick and spent the day together.

"Denise, you know this promotion I've been offered?"

"Yes." She nodded.

"Well, it's subject to me spending three months in Africa working on some dam being built. How do you feel about that?"

"You going to Africa? That promotion is a great

opportunity. Of course, you should go."

"You wouldn't mind me being away for so long?"

She shook her head.

"You know this promotion means a lot. And Fred was saying that if I apply myself I might be offered a senior position in the next couple of years."

"You'll go far."

He bent over and kissed her forehead. *"We'll* go far, love. I'm going to do everything I can to make sure you have the life you deserve. And when I get back from Africa, I want to make this permanent. You know – engagement, and marriage and stuff."

She smiled weakly. "When are you going to Africa?"

"They're just waiting for me to give the go-ahead, and I was waiting to speak to you first. Now you say you don't mind, I'll be off in two weeks."

* * *

She saw him to the airport.

"I really wish I wasn't going," he said as they stood together hugging.

"You'll be fine."

He rubbed his eyes. "I meant what I said. When I get back I'm going to make life perfect for us."

She took out a handkerchief and dabbed at her eyes as well. "Don't you dare cry or you'll set me off as well."

"I'm going to spend the rest of my life making you happy."

"Just enjoy yourself over there. It's the opportunity of a

lifetime. You'd better go – they're boarding your plane." She pushed him away.

She waved to him as he walked down through security. He turned and smiled and waved at her one last time. She smiled and waved back, knowing she wouldn't see him again.

Two weeks later, Denise was sitting in Reception when Cormac Cunningham walked in.

Cunningham Homes was employing their company to design a new estate.

Cormac immediately did a double-take as she literally turned his head.

"I've an appointment with Fred Kelly," he informed her, trying not to stare.

"And who will I say is here for him?"

"Cormac Cunningham."

"I'll let him know," Denise said, picking up the phone. "Cormac Cunningham here to see you, Fred . . . uh huh." Hanging up the phone she said, "If you can take a seat he'll be with you shortly."

Cormac sat down and glanced over at her as she busily did some paperwork.

"What do you have to do around here to get some coffee?" he asked.

She looked up at him, bemused. "Not much. Just go down the corridor to the kitchen and pour yourself a cup."

He laughed lightly. "I see."

Cormac had a meeting in there every day that week. Each day he enjoyed a little more banter with Denise. On the fourth day he asked her for a date. She declined. On the fifth day he asked her again. She accepted. And suddenly Denise knew she had met the person she had been waiting for all her life. The man who made sense of everything in her life. It was a whirlwind romance and they were engaged very quickly.

When Ryan returned he went straight to her flat only to get a severe shock. Denise didn't live there any-more. And there was no forwarding address. The next day he rushed into her workplace only to find a new girl sitting in Reception. He went rushing around the building, trying to find out where she had got to.

"Denise? Nobody knows," explained a colleague. "There's a rumour she started seeing Cormac Cunningham. You know we were doing work for them. Anyway, she gave in her notice and she's been gone at least a month by now."

Ryan couldn't understand it.

* * *

All the memories came flooding back as Denise lay on her side staring into the darkness.

Cormac had put away his paperwork and she could feel his warm body close to hers.

"Are you awake?" he whispered.

"How could I be, with all that rattling of papers you made?"

She felt his hand stroke her arm.

"I wish you wouldn't," she said.

"Why?"

"Because I like it." She turned to face him and they kissed. "I shouldn't let you near me after all those slappers you're with."

He nuzzled her neck. "What slappers? I've never been unfaithful to you."

"Oh sure!" She kissed his lips "Stupid I am not. I hear the whispered rumours."

"You shouldn't listen to rumours."

"Hard not to when I've got a close coterie of friends who feel it their duty to tell me what my husband gets up to . . . for my own good, of course." She stroked his back.

"And what do you say to them?" His removed the straps of her slip.

"I refute all their claims, thank them for their concern and ask them not to repeat it."

"That's my girl! You don't believe them, do you?" She moved on top of him. "Cormac, I don't know and I don't really care."

25

The couple, Declan and Louise, who were in their late thirties, had a look of joy and fear written across their faces. They had obviously fallen in love with the period red-bricked terrace house in Ranelagh, hence the look of joy. The look of fear was caused by the knowledge that their budget wouldn't allow them to go much further. Lisa had shown the property to them before and they had made an offer of 900,000. Subsequently Lisa had received a further offer of 950,000 from another family. The couple, who were clearly nervous, had requested a second viewing before they made another offer.

"Well, what do you think?" asked Lisa as they finished the tour and re-entered the lounge.

"It's exactly what we are looking for," said Louise. "I love it the second time round even more." She looked to her husband for confirmation.

"It's our dream home," Declan announced simply.

"It's a fine house. And as I'm sure you are aware period

properties in this area are much sought after."

"We know," Louise sighed. "We've viewed everything that has come on the market for the past year and we just keep being out-priced."

"It's frustrating, isn't it?" Lisa nodded sympathetically. Always a good touch to let the buyers think you're identifying with them, she knew. Then she cut to the chase. "Will you be making a further offer?"

Declan and Louise looked at each other nervously and nodded.

"We'll offer the million," Declan said cautiously.

"Excellent," said Lisa, knowing the other interested party would offer another fifty before close of business.

"But that's our final offer," Louise spoke quickly. "There's no point in saying anything else. Our budget can't go any further. We'll be eating beans on toast for the next ten years as it is with that."

Her honesty was unusual, thought Lisa. And she knew they weren't bluffing.

"Do you think there will be any further offer?" Declan asked, looking nervous.

Lisa thought for a few seconds. She decided to match their honesty to avoid raising their hopes. "Well, to be honest, yes. The other party are as interested in this house as you are and they do seem to have more money to play around with."

Both of them looked close to tears on hearing this news.

"We would be happy here for the rest of our lives." Louise sounded desperate. "I'd do anything to get this house."

"I'm sorry," Lisa shrugged.

"Well, thank you for being frank with us," Declan said as he put his arm around his wife and headed towards the front door.

"Wait a second!"

They both turned around and looked at her.

"Could your budget run to an extra ten thousand?"

They looked at each other, confused.

"I suppose another ten thousand could just be manageable." said Louise.

"I like you two – I have from the moment I met you – and I can see how much you want this place – just call me an old romantic, but I would really like to see you two make a home for yourselves here."

They looked at each other nervously.

"What I'm suggesting isn't exactly ethical . . . and would amount to a good deal of trust . . . and discretion . . . on both our parts."

"Go on," urged Declan.

"I can fix it for you to get this house, but I would be compromising my principles, and I would expect a small amount of compensation for that."

"Like ten thousand?" Declan face creased in cynicism.

"Exactly . . . If you bring ten thousand into my office tomorrow, in cash, no cheques, I'll inform the vendor that your offer was the top one received and I'll tell the other bidder that we have a received a substantial bid that I'm confident they won't be able to match and put them out of the picture."

"That really stinks badly." Declan looked very nervous

and very angry.

"I'm only trying to help you. If you don't want to . . ."

"Declan, are you thinking straight?" snapped Louise. "How long have we been looking for a house? I can't take much more of this. And this is the house of our dreams, as you said yourself. Who cares how we get it?"

Declan thought hard for a while. "All right, I'll bring the money into your office in the morning," he confirmed.

"That's fine . . . I hope you'll be very happy in your new home." Lisa closed over her briefcase and smiled.

* * *

Lisa took the last swig from her wineglass and then grabbed the bottle and refilled it. She was out having dinner with a few girlfriends in Bang. Dinner had been devoured as had dessert and even though it was now half eleven they were making no effort to leave as they ordered more wine. She looked around the group. They'd been great fun when she was in her twenties as they partied around town, but now she found most of them a bit of a duty call. Most of them were now married, some separated and some even moved on to their second husbands. And there she sat, without even a boyfriend to interest them with.

Susan, a red-haired beauty who had always fancied herself and had ended up married to and recently separated from a banker, was divulging the intricacies of her break-up to her captive audience.

"Do you know what the bastard did last week?" she

said, flicking back her luscious hair. "He told our ten-year-old, you know, Benjamin, that he had a big surprise for him at the weekend. So Benjamin goes over to his house all excited for his big surprise. And do you know what the big surprise was? His new girlfriend!"

There was a general gasp of "No!" around the table.

"Benjamin came home to me in tears. He said he thought his surprise was going to be a new bike."

"Instead, it was an introduction to his dad's new bike!" Lisa said loudly and burst out laughing. There was a general look of disapproval towards Lisa who was unable to contain her giggles.

"Lisa, I could hardly expect you to understand. You don't have children, so you can't understand the heartbreaking effect a break-up can have on a child." Susan said icily.

"Oh, just buy him another computer game or trainers or something."

"You know, if I didn't know you, I would think you were just trying to be funny. But the truth is you actually believe that."

Lisa threw her head back and closed her eyes. "Please, spare me the disapproval. I disapprove of myself far too much. There's no room for you do it as well."

"One day, Lisa, when you've sold every house in Dublin and made all the money in Ireland, you're going to look at the bottom of that wine bottle and it's going to be empty and you're going to find that a very lonely place."

"How could I ever be lonely? When I have friends like yourselves to rivet me with your interesting lives! It really intrigues me why parents think other people are as interested in their children as they are."

* * *

The elevator doors opened and Lisa swayed down the corridor to her apartment. Her head was swimming from the alcohol. It's no wonder she had drunk so much when she had to put up with such boring company all night. She would give that gang a wide berth for a while. She had plenty of other gangs she could socialise with. She reached her door, and searched through her handbag, looking for the keys unsuccessfully. Irritated, she emptied the contents of her bag on the floor. She looked through the mess, found her keys and opened the door. She then got on her hands and knees, scooped everything back into the bag and crawled inside. She got up, slammed the door shut and put on the lights.

Lisa's apartment was in the Docklands. One whole wall at the bottom of the living area was glass which looked out onto the rejuvenated docks. Lisa had exactly three pieces of furniture in her apartment. A white couch, a television, and a double bed in the bedroom. The cream carpet apart from the odd wine spillage looked as new as the day it went down. She had lived there for three years and kept meaning to get more furniture, but never bothered. It wasn't as if she spent much time there anyway. She was always out at work or socialising or over at her parents. So she just never got around to furnishing the place properly. Anyway, she liked it like that. She hated clutter. And it wasn't as if it would be her home forever. She would move on, get a house, get married or something, so what was the point in making the place all homely? She stumbled into the kitchen and dragged out a bottle of wine from the fridge and, opening it, brought it and a balloon glass into the living-room and sat down on the couch.

Her thoughts immediately turned to Michael, Michael who had been in foul form last week, and hadn't come into work that week. He had his mobile off. It was all very obvious that his relationship with Alison was over and he was very upset about it. He was probably sitting at home looking into a glass of wine, feeling terrible – just like her.

There was no reason why he should be on his own when he had her. This was a golden opportunity. She should go over there now. It was a small window of opportunity. In another week, he might have found a new Alison and then he would be out of her reach again. Maybe forever. She downed her wine.

* * *

"I heard you on the radio today," Michael said to Ali.

They lay in each other's arms in bed at his house.

"What did you think?" she asked.

"You're were all right."

"Just all right?" She looked at him, surprised.

"Yeah, you weren't bad."

"You're killing me with your enthusiasm here."

"You were excellent and you know you were," he

conceded.

"Well, I wouldn't say excellent." She faked modesty. "I'd say I was all right."

"You!" He shook her mockingly and kissed her.

Their doorbell screeched into the night silence.

"Who the fuck is that?" said Michael, concerned.

"Well, we know it's not Cormac Cunningham. He wouldn't bother with the niceties of ringing a doorbell."

Michael got out of bed and threw some clothes on as the doorbell continued to ring.

He hurried out of the room.

* * *

Lisa stood at Michael's door with her finger pressed on the doorbell.

The door swung open and there stood Michael, looking very surprised to see her.

"Michael!" She fell into his arms and kissed his lips before pushing him aside and going into the hall.

"Lisa, you've been drinking."

"Ten out of ten for observation." She climbed up the spiral staircase into the living room.

"Lisa, no! You can't stay! I'll get you a cab on the street." Michael tried to keep his voice to a whisper, as he followed her up.

Lisa made straight for the drink and poured two glasses of wine.

"Here, a drink for you, a drink for me." She forced a glass into his hand and clinked the glasses together.

"Lisa. Really you can't stay. Please!"

"Can't was a word I was brought up not to use." She took a drink. "Michael, I've been very concerned about you. In terrible form last week – and not turning up this week – well, I know what the problem is. You've been dumped by what's-her-name and you're feeling low about yourself and your life. I know – I've been there. But I'm here for you as always." She placed her hand on his cheek.

He took her hand and pushed it away. "I'm absolutely fine. I just wanted some time off. I'm going to get you a cab."

"We are so alike, Michael. Two peas in the same pod. And we've been so busy building the business together that we haven't seen what's under our noses."

"And what's that?"

"Us."

* * *

Ali could hear voices and threw her eyes to heaven, wondering what on earth was happening this time. For once mind your own business and stay out of it, she told herself.

Just turn over and go to sleep. She thought for a minute, then jumped out of bed and put some clothes on. She walked down the corridor and climbed up the staircase, listening.

She observed the glamorous blonde talking closely to Michael.

"I've been thinking a lot about us, Michael."

"Lisa, there isn't any us. I've told you before, I love you as a friend . . ."

"Aren't you going to introduce us?" asked Ali as she came into the room.

Lisa turned abruptly and looked at Ali in surprise.

"What's the maid doing here at this time of night?" Lisa asked, looking at Ali from head to toe.

"Lisa, this is Ali." Michael sighed loudly.

"Ali? Ali-son." The penny dropped with Lisa. "Ali O'Mara. You've been seeing Ali O'Mara?" A strange expression of bemusement mixed with anger was written across her face.

She threw her hair back and approached Ali quickly with her hand outstretched.

"I'm very pleased to meet you. I'm Lisa Cunningham."

"What is this place?" snapped Ali. "Grand Central Station for the Cunningham family?"

Seeing her offered hand was being ignored, Lisa retracted it and lit herself a cigarette instead.

"Do you smoke, Ali?" Lisa asked, offering her packet.

"No, I don't," Ali snapped. "Michael, what is going on here?"

"Well, nothing, my dear," said Lisa. "I'm just dropping by to see a work colleague and a dear friend."

"At three in the morning?"

"Is that the time? I didn't realise it was so late. So, Michael . . . I didn't realise we were throwing in a free auctioneer with every apartment built by Cunningham Homes?"

"We just clicked and we've been seeing each other,"

explained Michael. For some strange reason, he felt as if he had been found cheating on Lisa, which made no sense at all.

"Do you often have office meetings at three in the morning at each other's houses?" enquired Ali.

"Well, when you're as close as me and Michael you can meet at any time any place. Our lives are completely open to each other. We're just like an old married couple really." Lisa looked over at Michael and smiled happily.

"Really?" Ali was not amused.

"You'll have to forgive me." Lisa gave a little laugh. "This is just all so unexpected . . . it will just take me a little time to get used to it. You two a couple? After all the things you wrote about Michael over the years!"

"It was unexpected for us as well." Ali felt she had to explain herself.

"And after all the things *you* said about *her* over the years, Michael!" Lisa laughed loudly. "You used to describe her as a little communist feminist bitch! You used to say she had a problem with the whole world. You used to say she was so stuck up her own ego that no man in his right mind would have anything to do with her. You used to say –"

"Thank you! I think I get the general idea," interrupted Ali.

"It's just the whole irony of the situation of you two being together is too much! When's the wedding? Can I be bridesmaid? That's me! Always the ride and never the bride!"

"Lisa, it's late. I'm going to call you a taxi." Michael

went to the phone and dialled a number.

"Thank you, Michael. That's so considerate of you. You're always so considerate. One of the things I love most about Michael is his consideration. Yes, I really must go and leave you two lovebirds to continue with whatever you were doing."

Despite the wide constant smile, Ali noticed that Lisa's eyes had filled with tears.

"Sorry for this interruption. I'll be sure to phone next time. It's just Michael's home has always been open house."

"I had gathered that."

Michael hung up the phone. "It will be another hour until they can get a taxi."

"Don't worry about me. I'll just flag down a cab out on the street."

"I'll go out to make sure you get one," said Michael.

"Anyway, it's been so nice to meet you," Lisa went over and put out her hand.

Ali nodded and shook her hand tentatively. She watched the two of them go down the staircase. She sat down and ran her fingers through her hair, then rubbed her temples.

A few minutes later, she heard the front door slam and Michael came up.

"I'm really sorry about that," said Michael.

Ali looked up at him. "Okay, Michael, do you want to try and explain to me what that was all about?"

"She had been drinking and came by."

"I'm not blind and I'm not stupid. What's the story

between you two?"

"There is no story."

"Well, she seems to think otherwise."

Lisa has always been a really good mate of mine. She's a business partner. She's a drinking buddy. She's –"

"In love with you."

Michael stared at her angrily and then sat down and sighed. "I know."

"And are you in love with her?"

"No! Of course not! Look, once, many years ago, we both had too much to drink and ended up together."

"Great!" Ali threw her hands in the air.

"It was a stupid mistake on my part and I've never repeated it."

"It's all so bizarre! Why don't you just go off with her? Get married to her. You're practically a Cunningham anyway so just make it official and marry them!" Ali was angry.

"Lisa is not my type. I never thought of her in that way."

"Well, you did for one night at least."

"I was drunk! I'm very fond of her but I've no interest in her that way."

"Michael, the Cunninghams own eighty per cent of your company. Fifty per cent of your home. And by the look of it, one hundred per cent of your ass! You are Cunningham property and I don't think they'll allow you to have your own life. I don't think you can have a relationship with me and be part of them."

"I'm my own man."

"It doesn't look like that from where I'm standing."

"Do you want to finish it?"

"I'm having a déja vu."

Michael got up and, going to sit beside Ali, put his arm around her.

"Why don't you just give me a chance and see how my life really is. Yes, the Cunninghams are a part of my life, but they aren't that bad. Why don't you give them a chance? Give me a chance?"

Ali leaned over and kissed Michael. "All right."

26

Lisa pushed open the door of her parents' house and slammed it behind her. She walked across the marble hall and into the lounge, avoiding looking at herself in one of the numerous mirrors she passed.

Honey was sitting on the couch, talking on the phone. Paul was seated on an armchair reading the newspaper.

"That's just fine, sweetie. I'll see you at seven." Honey concluded her phone conversation and replaced the receiver. "Ahhh!" she then shouted, after taking one look at her daughter. "What has you looking like shit?"

"Copious amounts of alcohol and no sleep," answered Lisa pouring herself a drink from the decanter.

"Yep, that should do it every time," said Honey. "It's barely twelve, Lisa. A bit early for a drink, isn't it?"

"Hair of the dog."

"And why aren't you at work anyway?"

"I'm taking the day off."

Paul peered up from behind his newspapers "Aren't

you supposed to be busy selling Glenwood?"

"Let Michael do it today." Lisa was looking at herself in the huge mirror over the fireplace and thinking of Ali's brown hair. "Do you think I should stop dyeing my hair and go back to my natural colour?"

"Darling, a girl that looks like you needs all the help she can get. Stay blonde," Honey said. "Besides, you started dyeing your hair at thirteen. Can you even remember what your natural colour is? I think you might find your natural colour is grey at this stage."

"Cheers. Here I am feeling like shit, and you're making me feel worse."

"You look like you feel . . . what the hell is wrong with you? Why aren't you out selling houses instead of looking in the mirror feeling sorry for yourself?"

Lisa turned quickly and sat down on an armchair. "Whatever is wrong with me? Michael!"

Paul raised his eyes to heaven and continued to read the newspaper.

"What's the latest instalment of the sorry saga?" questioned Honey.

"Do you know who he's seeing now? Ali O"Mara!"

"The journalist?" Honey shot Paul a concerned look, which he matched.

"The very bitch."

"And how long has this been going on?" Honey was incredulous.

"Since she bought an apartment in the Pavilions. Do you know what the stupid thing is? I was scheduled to show her around that afternoon but Michael said he wanted to because of all the horrible things she had written about him. If I'd gone they would never have met. I wish I had."

"Oh, if wishes were fishes we'd eat well tonight," Honey's face was creased in worry. "If you had any kind of ability you'd have that fella wrapped up in a marriage years ago and out of harm's way."

"Ali O'Mara?" said Paul. "She's dangerous. What the fuck is he doing seeing that wagon?"

"I always suspected he had a weak heart," said Honey. "That girl hates us and is so full of shit, she'll try and turn Michael against us"

"The question is what do we do? Michael has put us on the map, he's a brilliant auctioneer and a lot of our runaway success over the past ten years has been down to him giving us the edge in marketing . . . I don't know if we can do without him."

"And why should we lose him?" said Honey. "I think we might have to become best friends with Miss O'Mara."

"Oh, no, you're not!" Lisa half laughed.

"Why should we lose our star player because of your lack of sex appeal? We're going to box clever on this one. We're going to forget about all those horrible things she has written about and embrace her with open arms." Honey nodded to herself. "If we go against her we'll only lose Michael, and as you said we depend too much on him. She won't last long anyway. I've always suspected Michael suffers from that attention deficit disorder the way he can never sit still for a second, and the way his mind jumps from idea to idea. She's just a big novelty and a challenge at the moment. He'll soon tire of her . . . I mean how serious can it be?"

"She's achieved an awful lot in her life," said Lisa, picking up the paper and looking at Ali's column.

"Yeah, big tits and ambition work every time," said Honey.

* * *

"I'd better get going into the office," Ali said.

It was eleven in the morning and she and Michael were in the kitchen having breakfast.

"Ah, take the day off. Let's hang out together."

"I can't. I've too much to do."

"C'mon. The two of us seem to always put work first. Let's put ourselves first for a change." Michael picked up his mobile and dialled his office. "Mandy? Just letting you know I won't be in today."

"There's been a lot of enquiries about Glenwood, Michael."

"Just give them to Lisa. She can look after them." Michael hung up the phone and handed it to Ali. "Your turn."

* * *

"For fuck's sake!"

Cormac roared so loud workers could hear him down the road and quickly dived for cover. Cormac was standing in one of the kitchens in one of the completed houses at Glenwood after his foreman had informed him there had been a break-in during the night and the kitchen

269

appliances had been stolen.

"How many houses have been raided?" demanded Cormac.

"About ten. I checked all the other houses and they still have all the fridge freezers and cookers and everything else."

"This is a fucking inside job. There's no way anyone broke in through security. Fucking bastards!" Cormac thought hard for a minute. "Who else knows the extent of the theft?"

"Only me," said the foreman.

"Okay. Keep it that way." Cormac marched out of the house and towards his office. He knew exactly what he would do. He would turn the situation around to his advantage. He wouldn't report the theft until tomorrow. That night he would organise a contact of his to come in and remove the appliances from the rest of the houses that hadn't been robbed. He would then file an insurance claim for all the houses, and make a tidy profit from the goods he would sell on. Unethical? Yes. Did he care? No.

It would be risky if anyone had moved into the site. But since he and Denise were the only residents, there would be no witnesses.

Walking into his office, he was unnerved to find Paul sitting at his desk looking through his paperwork.

"How many sales have we had since launching Glenwood?" Paul asked, not looking up from the papers in front of him.

"I'm not sure. Shouldn't Lisa be the one you ask that?" "I've just left Lisa at home blubbering into her wine.

There's going to be no sense from her for a while. Michael is seeing that bitch Ali O'Mara, according to Lisa."

Cormac laughed. "Oh, she found out, did she?"

Paul looked up, concerned. "You knew?"

"Yeah, I found them together a little while back."

Paul's voice was angered. "And you didn't think it important?"

"No, I didn't think anyone cared who Michael was screwing."

"When it happens to be somebody who's our enemy, I think it's very important."

Cormac felt himself go red with frustration and anger.

Paul stood up. "If you'd let me know earlier we could have done something about it."

"Like what exactly?" Cormac asked angrily.

"Just get on to Michael and find out exactly how the sales are going here. There's a lot at stake here and I don't want to risk anything because of all your incompetence."

Cormac marched to his desk and picking up his phone dialled Farrell's.

"Mandy, is Michael there?"

"Sorry, Cormac, Michael's been out for a couple of days."

"Lisa?"

"She won't be in either."

"And who the fuck is doing showings at Glenwood in that case?"

"Er . . ." Mandy decided to play dumb.

Cormac abruptly put down the phone and dialled Michael's number.

"Yes, Cormac?" Michael had the roof down in his car and they were heading down the country for a day out.

"Michael? You sick or something?"

"No. Just taking a brief holiday."

"A brief holiday? In the middle of our launch at Glenwood?"

"Lisa is taking care of it all."

"She's nowhere to be seen. I've got millions out here, we got the front page of the fucking newspaper and you're telling me there's nobody doing showings?"

"I'm sorry, Cormac. I thought it was being taken care of." Michael pulled over.

"If somebody could get this fucking show on the road, I'd be very grateful!" shouted Cormac as he slammed down the phone.

* * *

"That was –"

"I know who it was," said Ali.

"I have to go back." He looked apologetic.

"What was I saying about you being Cunningham property?" she sighed.

Michael turned the car and speeded back to Dublin.

27

Denise walked down the grand staircase at Glenwood and strolled across the hallway into the lounge. It was dark outside and all the construction workers had long left the site. She felt odd as this was the first house that she had ever lived in. She had gone from the flat she grew up in to living in a small apartment in town to living in a series of penthouses with Cormac. She was used to having people nearby and found it strange and isolating being in the big house behind security gates. She looked forward to when other people would move into the estate. A text came through on her mobile and she opened it. It was from Cormac, telling her he would be home very late. She went into the study, turned on the computer and typed in the web page address for Google. Then she punched in *Ryan Cantwell* and *Aston Construction*. She waited as the search engine did its job. A few seconds later numerous entries were displayed on the screen to her amazement. She glanced through them. They were everything from interviews in the British press to publications of speeches he had made over the years. She tapped on one heading that read *'Ryan Cantwell – An Insight into the Future of British Construction'*. With growing amazement she scanned down the article, realising just what a heavyweight Ryan had become. He had filled her thoughts since turning up and she didn't know what to make of it all. He seemed to have changed a lot. But then judging by what he had achieved in his life he must have changed a lot. But then the gestures, the expressions, the infectious smile were all the same. She clicked on to another report about him and realised she would be sitting at the computer well into the night.

* * *

Denise glanced at herself in the car-window mirror. For a woman whose appearance attracted a great deal of attention, she didn't really spend much time looking into mirrors. But as she prepared herself to go into the meeting at Forward, she felt unusually insecure. She got out of the car, walked down the street and up the steps into the grand Georgian building. She stopped for a quick chat with the receptionist and then realising she was late, made her way hurriedly up the stairs to the boardroom. She opened the door and walked in. A few heads turned and nodded at her, but the rest were too busy being enraptured by Ryan who was speaking loudly and boldly. The sight of him sitting at the top of the table, speaking as if he was conducting a meeting irritated her. She quietly walked to her normal seat and sat down.

"From what I'm seeing and what I'm hearing, Forward is not keeping pace with what is happening in the charity world and is in danger of falling behind. We live in an age where there is overkill in the charity market. And make no mistake, charity is a market like any others. The public is being inundated with charity appeals and to a certain extent charity fatigue has set in. What we need to do is think how we can make Forward stand out from the others. How can Forward reach out to the public like no other charity can?"

The committee members started nodding and mumbling agreement.

"He's great, isn't he?" Martha whispered to Denise.

"Smashing." Denise didn't bother trying to hide her sarcasm.

"I took the liberty of getting my marketing department at Aston to do some surveys just to find out what people's attitudes to Forward are, and I think you'll find the results very interesting." Ryan stood up and picked up a pile of papers in front of him. He walked around the board table handing a copy to each person.

With growing annoyance, Denise took the paper from him as he passed by and flung it on the table in front of her.

"You're more that welcome to take home these surveys and study them at your leisure," Ryan said.

How kind, Denise thought.

"But to save you time now I'll sum it up quickly. Forward is seen as a charity of the elite. It's seen as a ladies-who-lunch-and-bored-businessman charity. A charity that revolves around expensive balls and lunches."

Denise couldn't restrain herself from speaking up. "Those expensive balls and charities are what fund our projects through the year."

Ryan looked at Denise directly and smiled at her. His smile was disarming and threw her.

"Yes, Denise, of course they do. But we're in danger of being pigeon-holed and if Joe Public doesn't see us as anything other than a club for the rich to feel good about themselves, then they won't bother with us. And no matter how much we earn from these top-notch events, it's the support of the public that will make us a mainstream charity and that's what we can't do without." He continued to smile at her after finishing speaking and held her gaze.

And being the centre of his attention for a minute made her realise that the way he had been treating her as just another committee member up till then had been angering her.

She sat back in her chair and picked up the survey, pretending to read it as Ryan continued to speak to the board.

* * *

"Excellent points," gushed Martha as the meeting ended and people were leaving the boardroom.

"Thanks. Sometimes, it's just good to get a fresh perspective on everything." Ryan held the door open for her and followed her out.

Denise thought hard for a few seconds and then

quickly went after them.

She found Ryan on his mobile out in the corridor.

"Jodhi, just finishing up here, so I'll head straight over to the Berkley Court. Can you keep them occupied till I get there? Good." He closed over his mobile.

"Ryan, could I have a word with you?" Denise asked, stepping forward.

"Eh, sure. It'll have to be quick though. I'm late for a meeting."

"I'll try and not take up too much of your time." She indicated the boardroom.

He went back inside and she closed the door after them. She stood against the back of the door for a minute looking at him.

"Yeah?" he asked eventually, and smiled with a confused look.

"I've just been wondering over the past few days what you're doing back in my life?" she said.

"Back in *your* life?" He laughed for a few seconds. "Denise, I'm back in Dublin, that's all."

She walked away from the door towards the centre of the room.

"If you had just joined Forward, I might just think it all a coincidence. Bizarre, yes, but it could be a coincidence. But the fact you were out at Stevie's as well. That is too much of a coincidence."

"No, it isn't. Actually my company has been looking at some land up near there that I had been inspecting that day and I wanted to get a feel of the area."

"Up near Stevie's?" Denise sounded unbelieving.

"Sure. Building land is very hard to come by in Dublin, you know."

"You know, I was thinking about it. It wouldn't be the first time you followed me. You followed me back to my mother's home one night when we were seeing each other."

"Back to the flats? Yeah, I did. I was worried about you, and wanted to know where you were disappearing to . . . is *that* what this is all about? You're worried about exposure. That I'll tell everyone about your background, or that I saw you swinging around a podium in Stevie's a couple of weeks ago? Don't worry, that's not my style. Your sordid little secrets are safe with me."

Denise became enraged. "Sordid? There's nothing sordid about my life. How dare you! I'm just wondering why and how you've been around every corner I've turned recently. And to be honest, I'm finding that very disturbing."

"Denise, you still think every guy you meet wants to fuck you, don't you?" He opened his briefcase, riffled through the paperwork, pulled out a sheet of paper and handed it to her. It was a letter from Forward to Ryan dated back a few months, inviting him to become involved with them. "Tony approached me about joining Forward on hearing Aston were opening offices in Dublin. As you can read from the letter, I had been recommended to him by some contacts in London who I had done charity work with."

His mobile rang and he answered it.

"Jodhi, sorry. Got held up."

Ryan made his way to the door. He left the room talking on his mobile without another look at Denise. Denise was left looking at the letter from Tony. It listed all the board members at the bottom of the page and her name was the first one.

* * *

Michael flew through the doors of Farrell's, stopping at reception.

"Any calls?" he asked Mandy, hassled.

She handed him a list.

"Where's Lisa?"

Mandy shrugged.

"And enquiries for Glenwood?"

Mandy handed him a second sheet. He took it and walked on through his team of staff, busily making deals on the phones. He should have appointed one of them to deal with Glenwood. But owing to the importance of the development he had wanted Lisa and himself to handle the site directly. He went into his office, and closing the door sat down and looked through the long list of enquiries. He immediately spotted a few millionaire entrepreneurs, some members of the Irish music aristocracy, a Hollywood-based Irish actor. A very promising list indeed. Looking at the dates they had phoned, he realised how unprofessional Farrell's must have come across as, by not dealing with the enquiries quickly. He picked up the phone and rang Lisa's number, but it rang out.

28

Jodhi Barbeaux was a stunning girl of twenty-eight who had worked as Ryan's PA for five years. Her mother had been French and white, her father British and black. She had been brought up mainly in British boarding schools and her accent mirrored the education she had been given.

"I can't say exactly when Mr Cantwell will be able to return your call. Also, I can't say when I expect him back. I'm sorry, I will pass on your messages as soon as I see him." She hung up the phone and got up from her desk. Ryan had been staying in a suite of rooms at The Westbury. She now walked from the room she was using as an office and into the lounge where Ryan sat with an engineer, maps and plans spread out over the huge glass coffee table.

"Fred Golden from BP has been on again for you. That's his fifth message this week," Jodhi informed the men as she took a seat opposite them. She put on her reading glasses so she could see the plans more clearly.

"Could we have access from the site at both angles as well as from the front?" Ryan asked the engineer as he peered at the plans.

"In theory, yes, and you would be then allowing yourself much more access and in return a higher density of units."

"Hmmm . . ." Ryan sat back thinking. "And if we were allowed more density, then I could justify spending more for the site."

"But it's a very big 'if' that you would be allowed so much access. One of those roads is very near the sea, and I don't think they'll give you planning for access out there. It really all depends on what the Harbour Project management team envisage for the area and we won't know that until after they appoint that management team next week. Is that all?"

"Yep, thanks for that – you can go," Ryan acknowledged and the engineer exited the suite.

Jodhi looked at Ryan who was deep in thought, looking down at the map. She had seen that look on her employer's face many times before. It was a look that he had something he wanted. Something worth fighting for and he would fight all the way to get it. He was like that with everything. Even with staff. She had been working for a rival firm when he had spotted her. He made a financial offer she couldn't refuse and she had been with him ever since.

"Is this Heavey's Mill worth all this effort you're putting into it?" asked Jodhi.

"It's going to be the centrepiece of this new Harbour

District which is going to be the biggest redevelopment Dublin has ever seen."

"So why look so worried?"

"Because everyone else knows that too. Which means it's going to go for a hell of a lot of money."

"More than Aston can afford?"

"More than I'm comfortable asking Aston to spend."

"So, move on to a less risky project," Jodhi urged.

"The higher the risk, the higher the pay-off. Make me a coffee, would you?"

Jodhi stood up and walked into the kitchen.

"Oh, I forgot to tell you. Kate rang for you as well," she called from the kitchen.

Ryan looked up from studying the plans.

"Kate? Did she say what was it about?"

"No. She didn't say it was urgent."

When she returned and handed Ryan his cup, she said, "You should call her, Ryan." She took her seat again and sipped from her own mug.

"I know. I will." He was occupied with the plans again.

"Ryan. She rang last week and you didn't return her call then either."

"I know. I said I'd call her when I get a chance," he snapped. "I want this fucking mill!" He spoke with conviction. "I've been gone from Ireland for years and nobody knows who I am over here. They don't give a shit that I've become an industry chief in the UK. To get their attention I need to play their game their way. And that means building the biggest apartment block they can imagine on this site."

"People only care what's happening in their own backyard," Jodhi agreed. She smiled. "What will Denise think went she sees you at the press launch of the Harbour development next week?"

"What will she think when I buy Heavey's Mill from under her precious husband's nose?"

* * *

"Did you hear what I said?" Cormac asked.

Denise had been riveted to the laptop, reading a speech that Ryan had made at a conference the previous year.

"What?" she asked, irritated at the interruption.

"The press conference for the announcement of the project company for the Harbour Project is Wednesday evening. Don't forget. And wear something sexy. It looks like Simon O'Keefe will get that contract and he's always had an eye for a pretty face."

"I'm not sure if that's a compliment," said Denise, who was well aware that her glamour was an invaluable asset to her husband and had no qualms about using it to help them get ahead.

She scrolled down Ryan's speech on the internet and started reading again.

"We're nearly finished up here at Glenwood, so I won't be at the site office as much," Cormac informed her. "Going to be in town concentrating on getting the final phase of The Pavilions finished."

"When will you be finished there?"

"In a few months."

"Where to then?"

"I'm hoping we'll have Heavey's Mill by then and we'll be heading there."

"And if we haven't Heavey's Mill?"

"Then we've just run out of work."

Denise looked up, alarmed. She was fully aware that their industry relied on having building land and that they were coming to the end of their land bank. Building land was so hard to get, she realised how important the Heavey's Mill site was to their future.

"Don't worry, I'll pull out all the stops for Simon O'Keefe on Wednesday," she said.

"That's my girl," said Cormac.

29

Michael heard a disturbance outside in the main office and got up from his desk. Opening his door he saw Lisa having a go at an employee.

"I fucking told you enough times not to close the sale until you've received the deposit cheque!"

"They seemed so genuine. I never thought they would pull out."

"You're not paid to think. You're paid to do what I say. You don't have a genuine buyer till you get the deposit, so *never* take the house off the market until you have that cheque in your greedy little fist!"

"Lisa, could I speak to you a minute please," interrupted Michael, taking Lisa's arm and gently bringing her to his office. "What's all that about?" he asked, closing his door.

"You know what it's about. A sale has fallen through."

"A bit of an overreaction on your part."

"Since when did you become employer of the year?

285

Your motto with staff has always been burn and turn!"

"I know, but the best of us can't stop a sale from falling through. Why do you have to be like this? So hard on yourself and everyone else?"

"You're right, of course. I need to get more in touch with my feminine side. I'm going to make them all sandwiches tomorrow for lunch, and cut the crusts off and everything."

"You're being ridiculous."

"Of course, I am. I love being ridiculous. I'm better at being ridiculous than anything else."

Michael went over to her and grabbed her shoulders.

"Can't you be serious for once? I'm sorry about what happened the other night. About me and Ali."

"I don't think I understand you. You're sorry about being with her or just that I found out?"

He let her go and walked to his desk.

"I'm a free agent, Lisa. You make me feel guilty for seeing somebody. There's nothing between us."

"But, of course, I know there's nothing between us. It's glaringly obvious over the past few weeks. Since the lovely Ali arrived on the scene and took your heart."

"I don't know what I can do to make things right between us."

Dump the bitch! Lisa screamed inside.

Michael sat down at his desk and sank his face into his hands.

"I care a lot about you, Lisa. But not in that way. And after all this time, can't you just be happy that I've found somebody who makes me happy? That I've finally found something just for me?"

She stared at him. She was so used to Michael being full of jokes and full of fun that seeing him like this was unsettling.

"Oh, Michael! You don't want to take me too seriously." She sat on his desk and ran her fingers through his hair. "I'm glad you've found happiness, really I am. You deserve it. Now, come on, let's get back to work. Glenwood. What enquiries have we had?"

He looked up at her. "This sheet of names."

She tore the sheet in half and handed him one half. "I'll take the top half and you take the bottom, how's that?" He nodded and smiled. "Thanks, Lisa."

She got up and quickly walked to the door.

"Are you okay with everything?" he asked cautiously.

"Of course, I am."

"You know you're my best friend, and I'd really like you and Ali to become friends as well."

Cold day – hell, thought Lisa.

"I'd like nothing more," Lisa said quickly before exiting.

30

Lisa waved to the security guard as she drove her car into Glenwood and pulled into the showhouse drive. Glancing over at No 1, she saw that Denise wasn't at home. She got out of her car and entered the house, turning off the alarm. She went immediately into the kitchen and turned on the heating. Then she went around the house, checking everything was in order and leaving the doors opened in the correct positions to show off the house to its best advantage. She then lit a couple of scented candles and put soft soothing music playing. She looked through her appointments for the day. She had spaced them out, leaving an hour for each viewing. For houses of this calibre and this price, people needed an unrushed feeling while they were viewing. Her first client was due any minute and she saw his name was Thomas Grange. The doorbell rang. She went and opened it, wearing a big smile plastered across her face.

"Ms Cunningham?" asked Thomas, a slightly nervous-looking man in his forties.

"That's me. Thomas? Come on in and make yourself at home."

"T-t-thank you," the man said, edging in beside her. "Nice weather we're having."

"Isn't it? Now if you want to take a copy of the brochure?" She handed him the booklet. "And I'll show you around."

She wasn't sure about this one. Over the years she had picked up a sixth sense and something wasn't quite right about Thomas Grange.

She walked confidently into the lounge. "As you can see the room is dual aspect, and so you get the sun in the mornings and the afternoons."

"What kind of heating is there?"

"Underground heating. Also, to encourage energy efficiency because the houses are very large, they are fitted with solar panels."

"I like this house a lot, don't you?" he said quietly.

"Well, yes, I do –" Lisa began.

"Yes, it's very nice," Thomas said, looking out the window.

"These double doors lead through to the dining-room, where in turn another set of double doors lead through to the kitchen." Lisa walked through, followed by Thomas. "Again, light is a main feature throughout the houses."

"I love the light," said Thomas. "I don't. It gets on my nerves after a while," he then said.

Feeling a little perplexed, Lisa decided to speed up this viewing.

"This door then leads back into the hall, and the stairs as you can see." Lisa began to climb the stairs, followed by the man.

"I hate these stairs," said Thomas. "They're too big. I love the space they give," he then said.

As she walked down the corridor Lisa was fully aware she was dealing with somebody with mental problems. She would act as calmly as possible, not wanting to aggravate the situation. "Through here is the master bedroom. Walk-in wardrobe, a dressing-room and an en suite with a sunken bath." She quickly opened the doors, offering a view of the different compartments.

"Whoever designed this house had disgusting taste," said Thomas nastily.

"Well, it's a matter of taste –" began Lisa.

"Shut up! They had excellent taste," Thomas contradicted himself. "Only *you* would dislike a house as beautiful as this." "I'm entitled to my opinion the same as everybody else," he snapped.

Feeling completely unnerved, Lisa quickly walked out into the corridor and into another bedroom.

"The second bedroom is also light and airy," she said.

"She's a stupid bitch," said Thomas quietly. "No, she's not. Why are you being so horrible about her? She's just doing her job," he again contradicted himself. "Look at her there, with her blonde hair all tarted up. I can't stand her." Just shut up and concentrate on the house!"

"Lovely view of the rolling countryside," Lisa said, standing at the window.

"Yes, it's very nice," said Thomas. "Yes, it's very nice!"

he mimicked his own voice. "It's a horrible house and I refuse to live here." Well, too bad. I want to," he insisted to himself.

Lisa looked on alarmed as Thomas had a full-scale argument with himself out loud about the house.

She knew she should feel threatened, but with everything going on with Michael all she felt was annoyance.

"Look!" Lisa interrupted Thomas loudly. "Will the two of you shut the fuck up and argue about it later. Let me know when you've both come to a decision!"

* * *

Jodhi who was driving Ryan's black Mercedes was stopped at the security gate going into Glenwood.

"I've an appointment at the showhouse for three," she told the security guard.

"Second house down. She's already there."

"Thanks." Jodhi drove on through the huge electronic gates. She scrutinised No 1 as she drove past slowly and then pulled up outside the showhouse.

Lisa opened the front door of the house.

"Thanks for dropping by," Lisa said to Thomas with a false smile.

He nodded, quickly went to his car and drove off. She threw her eyes to heaven.

Jodhi got out of the car and walked up the cobble-lock driveway.

"Lisa?"

"Yeah." Lisa glanced down at her appointment sheet. "Jodhi Barbeaux?"

"Yes." They shook hands and Lisa drew a line through her name on the sheet. "It's extremely well positioned. The space between the houses is great."

"The whole development had been built to offer the resident as much privacy and space as possible."

As Lisa showed her through the house she observed that the girl was relatively young and wondered how she could afford the price tag at Glenwood. She hoped she wasn't another time-waster. That was the trouble with the spread that they had got on the front page – it could attract a lot of people who were just curious.

"It's a big house for just one person. Are you married?" asked Lisa as they came back downstairs and into the kitchen.

"No." Jodhi took out the brochure and looked through the site map. "We want a property near the front of the site. Would No 3 be available?"

"Yes, it is available. The asking price is 2.4 million for that house," Lisa looked at Jodhi sceptically.

"I realise that. The property is for my employer."

Lisa felt herself becoming angry. "Well, don't you think he should come and look at the house himself then?"

"That won't be necessary. We'll take No 3."

Lisa looked at Jodhi incredulously. "Listen I'm not taking any booking on the whim of a secretary. If your employer is a serious buyer then get him to make an appointment and we'll take it from there."

"Excuse me, do you have a problem with me?"

"Not you personally, darling, but I've quite a lot of viewings and I'm not going to turn a serious buyer away on your say-so."

"I am a serious buyer. If you're not interested in selling the property, that's fine. I'll take our custom elsewhere."

"But who is your employer?"

"That is none of your business." She took out a cheque. "I have a deposit cheque here for fifty thousand for No 3."

Lisa was bewildered as she took the cheque, scanning it for some clue to the identity of the mystery buyer. It was a company cheque from a solicitor's in London.

"Whose name will I put on the sales invoice?"

"The property is being bought in trust by Felladales solicitors in London. Good-day to you." Jodhi nodded and left the house.

31

The foyer at The Westbury was buzzing with people on the Wednesday evening as they made their way to the function room where the Harbour District Press Reception was being held. Ali mingled with the crowd. She felt nervous, as Michael had told her all the Cunninghams would be present. She searched the crowd looking for Michael, but he didn't seem to have arrived yet. She spotted Edel Garry, holding court with a crowd around her. She studied her from a distance. Although not conventionally pretty, she definitely had allure and stood out in a crowd. Word on the street was that the contract had already gone to Simon O'Keefe; his firm's experience left Edel's in the shade. But still Ali decided she would like to organise an interview with Edel anyway. A woman fighting in a man's world was always a cause close to her heart.

"Ms Garry?" Ali stood beside her. "Ali O'Mara." She put out her hand and smiled.

Edel viewed the hand with suspicion for a second, although smiling throughout, and then reached forward and shook it.

"The best of luck tonight," said Ali.

"Thank you," Edel nodded.

"I was wondering if I could do an interview with you? Over the next week or so?"

"Oh!" Edel thought for a second. "Yes, I'd love to. But it's going to be hectic getting things sorted . . ." Edel trailed off.

Ali felt the woman was speaking as if she would be getting the contract.

"Yes, I'd like to do the interview," Edel then said firmly. "Contact my office and we'll arrange something. This is my husband, Dessie."

A man standing beside Edel turned around when he heard his name being mentioned. He looked hassled but affable.

"Hello," he said pleasantly and shook Ali's hand. Edel used the opportunity to delicately edge away and start talking to another group.

* * *

Honey and Paul stood in the middle of the crowd, Honey's loud voice booming over everybody else's.

"So, go on. Tell me, Steve. Who's getting the contract?" she demanded.

"I haven't a clue, Honey," Steve said coyly.

"Of course, you know. You're making the announcement,

aren't you?."

"I'm sworn to secrecy. More than my job's worth."

"You're dirt, Steve, pure dirt. You won't be getting any extra shepherd's pie when you're at our house in future."

"Ah, Honey!" Steve laughed.

Paul observed Denise working the room expertly, talking to all the right people.

"She knows how to do it, doesn't she?" Paul said to Honey.

Honey looked over at her daughter-in-law. "That's why she's still here. That fecking eejit of a daughter of ours isn't coming. Says she can't face seeing Michael and his new bint."

"She would want to cop on to herself," Paul said gruffly. "Michael is more important to our company that she is, so she needs to just get on with it."

*   *   *

"Simon, you remember my wife Denise, don't you?" asked Cormac.

Simon O'Keefe had been gazing across the room at Edel, and tore himself away to focus on Denise.

"How could I forget? Very good to see you again," he said, taking Denise's hand.

She leant forward and gave him a kiss on the cheek.

"Is it a little premature to offer congratulations?" asked Denise.

Simon looked uncomfortable. "Eh . . . just a tad, I'd say."

"I've been telling everybody that with Simon O'Keefe in charge down at the Harbour it will be the biggest success this city has ever seen," said Cormac.

Simon's gaze again drifted over to Edel, whose husband had just put his arm around her waist. "Ah, well, I don't know about that. We've a lot on at the moment, and something like the Harbour deserves a company's full attention."

"Which I'm sure you'll give. I'd love to come by your office next week to have a chat about a couple of ideas I have about the old Heavey's Mill site there."

"Eh . . . sure."

"Better still," said Denise, "why don't you come up to the house some evening next week and we'll have dinner?"

* * *

Ali had been subtly studying the Cunninghams from across the room. Honey and Paul seemed over-confident and larger than life. She wasn't sure if she was glad or not when she saw Michael arrive. She smiled over to him and he winked at her. She edged around the room to where he was talking to a group of auctioneers.

"Running a little late," she whispered to him.

"Got held up with some viewings at Glenwood."

"How long do you think this will go on for?"

"Probably another couple of hours. Why?"

"Because I can't wait to get out of here and be alone with you!"

Unseen by anyone he put his hand behind her and rubbed the base of her back.

"I see your second family are all here," she said.

"Come on over and meet them."

"No, Michael. I don't want to."

"Look, you're going to have to meet them sometime, so it might as well be now."

"I just can't, Michael. Not after all the stuff I wrote about them."

"Are you frightened of meeting them?" he smirked at her.

"I'm too clever for you to try to use reverse physcology on me. Of course I'm not frightened of meeting them."

"Well, come on then."

"I was only saying the other day; you can't get a better investment than property. And when it come to property you can't get better than a Cuningham Home," Honey was saying out loud to a few people around her.

"Hi, Honey," Michael said, moving in beside her.

"Ah, Michael!" Honey threw her arms around him and kissed both cheeks, before looking at Ali with curiosity.

"Paul, Honey, this is Ali O'Mara," said Michael.

"Ah, this is the little girl we've been hearing about." Honey looked her up and down with a smile.

"It's nice to meet you. Michael has spoken very highly of you," said Ali.

"Which is more than you've ever done," Honey said but continued to smile.

"But that's in the past now," said Paul. "Any girlfriend of Michael's is a friend of ours."

298

Ali felt herself going red.

"We're having a few people over for dinner on Sunday – why don't you two come and join us?"

"Oh, I'm not too sure –" began Ali.

"I'm cooking your favourite, Michael – pork," Honey tempted.

"I think we'd love to come over, wouldn't we, Ali?" Michael smiled down at her.

Ali sighed. "Sure. What else would I be doing but sitting at home and filing my nails?"

Honey burst out laughing. "Ah, you're dirt, Ali, pure *dirt!*" Honey seemed to put extra emphasis in her catchphrase.

"Anyway, I'd better circulate. Nice meeting you." Ali smiled and turned to walk away.

"We'll see you at two. You're a great girl," Honey said and slapped Ali across the ass.

Ali paused in disbelief, and then quickly walked on.

"She's not so hot," Honey said to Paul, watching Ali and Michael walk off. "I don't know what all the fuss about her is. I think we'll manage her just fine."

* * *

"They're great, aren't they?" said Michael, later on to Ali.

"Hmmm." Ali tried to smile.

"They liked you. I could tell,"

Ali wanted to say that firstly it was glaringly obvious they couldn't stand her, and secondly she didn't want them to like her. She didn't want anything to do with them. They were everything she imagined only worse.

"Listen, I'm not so sure about this lunch on Sunday, Michael."

"Why not?"

"I just think we might be forcing something here that isn't going to work."

"They're going way out of their way for you and so I think you should meet them halfway, don't you? You heard what Paul said – the past is in the past."

"Have you two gone public with your relationship? Because you're looking very much like a couple here tonight," said Cormac's voice behind them.

They looked around to see Cormac and Denise standing there.

Suddenly conscious they might indeed be looking like a couple, Ali stepped away from Michael.

"No, we're treating our private life as private," said Ali.

"Denise, this is Ali," said Michael.

Denise studied Ali. "You live in The Pavilions." She bit her lower lip as she recognised it was the journalist Ali O'Mara and digested the information that Michael was seeing her.

"Yes . . . if you'll excuse me, there's somebody over there I want to interview." Ali walked away.

"Cormac, get your poor old mother a drink!" Honey shouted across the room and, sighing, Cormac headed over to the bar.

"How long has this been going on?" asked Denise.

"For a while."

"And it's serious?"

Michael nodded.

"They won't let you keep her, Michael. She's their biggest critic."

"Denise, you might have to do what they say, but I'm a free man. I can see who I want when I want. And they'll just have to get used to Ali, because she's around for the long haul."

"Michael, go look at your finances and see how much of a free agent you are. They own you lock-stock and barrel."

Michael sighed loudly "That's business. This is my personal life."

"I don't think it matters."

"I thought you were on my side."

"I am. I'm just pointing out the facts to you. They won't want her around. And maybe if I'm honest, I don't want her around either. She's written some vicious stuff about us all."

"Well, you'll all have to get used to it, because she isn't going anywhere."

* * *

Cormac handed his mother a drink.

"Thanks, pet."

Paul was staring at Ali circulating the room.

"What are we going to do about her?" he asked. "We can't risk losing Michael over her."

"I think you should stop worrying about it," said

Cormac. "What can she do?"

"You know the reason why I've got what I have? Because I sense out threats at the start and weed them out before they can do any damage. And that's what we need to do with her."

Denise joined them.

"We need Michael, and that's the bottom line," said Paul. "You're all very good at managing, Cormac. You manage the company very well. But you're not a showman. Not like Michael's a show man. You can't keep our name up there like Michael has been doing. You can't bring in the sales and the marketing that Michael does. You can't close deals like Michael can. You can't source land like Michael can. If we get Heavey's Mill it will because of Michael's prowess."

Cormac felt himself burn with anger.

There was a noise from the microphone at the top of the room.

"Ladies and gentlemen, if I can have your attention please," said Steve Foyle.

Denise stood close to her husband, sensing his hurt over Paul's words.

"Are you all right?" she asked.

"Yes," Cormac snapped. "Just fuck off!"

"Ladies and gentlemen, it has been a long wait to begin the Harbour Project but finally the mechanisms are in place to begin what will be Dublin's biggest-ever rejuvenation project. The final piece is to appoint the company that will oversee this rejuvenation. We are here tonight to learn who has been appointed. There has been some tough competition and the proposals we received were fascinating, uplifting, inspiring. But the decision has been made that the company that will oversee the Harbour Project is Edel Garry at Projectrum."

Applause came from around the room amidst much chatter and many gasps.

Edel smiled and turned and kissed her husband. Then she walked through the crowd and up to the podium. She shook Steve Foyle's hand and stood in front of the microphone. On the giant screen behind her the film featuring Projectrum's proposal for the Harbour area began to play, showing computerised visions of what the district should look like after redevelopment.

"One thing I've noticed since qualifying as an architect is that the more things change the more things stay the same," said Edel into the microphone. "This was never more true than with the Harbour district. In yesteryear the Harbour area was the lifeline of the city as it was the connection with the outside world as the constant flow of shipments came in and out. But as the decades passed the area went into a decline and finally became the wasteland it is today. But now it is poised to again become an epicentre as we build a city within a city. An area, close to the city centre, close to the sea, but self-contained where a community of people can live, work and play and never leave the confines of the district if they so please . . ."

"I can't believe it," said Cormac to Denise. "She doesn't have the experience to oversee something of this scale."

"Well, somebody thinks she does."

Denise heard somebody enter the room. She glanced

over and did a double-take as she saw Ryan walk in accompanied by a beautiful dark girl. She watched in disbelief as he walked through the crowd and seemed to be greeted by a lot of people with smiles and handshakes.

* * *

The speeches were over. Denise had been unable to take her eyes off Ryan the whole time. She picked her moment and went up to him and tapped him on the shoulder.

"You seem to be everywhere I turn these days," she says.

"Well, it's big city but a small town." Ryan smiled at her.

"What are you doing here?"

"I do run a major construction company, Denise, and this is the announcement of a major construction project. What are you doing here? Drumming up some charity funds?"

"Hardly, I'm here with my husband."

"Oh, is he interested in doing some work in the Harbour area?"

"You'd have to ask him yourself," Denise wasn't about to give anything away.

"Because if he is I'm not sure if his company is big enough to take on some of the projects that will be going on down there. I'd say Projectrum will be looking for the biggest and the best, like Aston."

Denise looked at him in disbelief. Before she could think of a retort, Jodhi interrupted.

"Ryan, I've been speaking to Edel Garry and she would like to meet you if you've a minute."

"Of course. If you'll excuse me." Ryan nodded at Denise and moved on. Then he turned and said, "Incidentally, are you going to the Forward charity lunch this week?"

She looked at him in amazement. "Of course, I am. I'm giving a speech there. I have been on the committee for six years, Ryan. You're the newcomer."

He shrugged and smiled.

Open-mouthed, Denise watched on Jodhi cut through the crowd surrounding Edel and got her attention. Suddenly Ryan was shaking hands with Edel and they were chatting closely.

"Who was that?" asked Cormac, sidling up beside Denise.

"Just a guy who's on the committee at the charity. Come on, let's go home."

* * *

"Edel!" Simon O'Keefe almost breathed the word as he came face to face with Edel as she mingled through the crowd accepting congratulations.

"Simon." She took his hand and squeezed it.

"I have to see you," he whispered.

"It's a little awkward. Dessie is here."

"I have to see you soon, I'll go mad otherwise. When?"

Edel looked around feeling uncomfortable. "Tomorrow at two?"

"Where?"

"The Burlington."

*   *   *

Denise sat at her dressing-table removing her make-up. Cormac turned off the shower in the en-suite, and came out wrapped in a bathrobe.

"I can't fucking belief it! Edel Garry won over Simon O'Keefe!" he said.

"I guess a pretty face isn't going to work with Edel," commented Denise.

"It would have been so easy if Simon was in charge. He would have been behind us all the way. I don't know what this Garry woman is like."

"Well, there's only one way of finding out, Cormac. Arrange to meet her as soon as possible. I saw her talking to a number of developers there tonight. You'd better get in quick or else risk losing the Mill." She couldn't help thinking of Ryan's words. "How much do you think it will go for?"

"I'm thinking of a figure around eighty million. But I'm going to have to get Michael to do a more accurate estimate."

"Can we afford that much?"

"We can afford it if we shift Glenwood quickly. The banks will have to help though."

"Speaking of which, what do you think of Michael seeing Ali O'Mara?"

"Just what we need."

"You don't seem shocked?

"I knew already."

"How?"

"I saw them together?"

"When?"

Cormac became uncomfortable as he remembered the circumstances. "I called over one night to Michael's and she was there."

"Oh," Denise raised her eyes and turned to concentrate on her face, "no doubt pissed in the middle of the night with one of your whores."

32

Simon O'Keefe rolled over and looked at the hotel bedroom ceiling.

Edel stepped out of the bed and tied a bathrobe around her. Scattered on the ground were the day's newspapers, most of them carrying the announcement of her appointment somewhere on the front page.

"How does it feel to have the world at your feet?" asked Simon, picking up one of the papers and seeing the face of Edel smile from the front page.

"Exciting, frightening. It means a lot of hard work ahead." She came and sat beside him on the bed.

"Well, I'm here every step of the way for you. Like I was when you were submitting your proposal."

She reached out and held his hand "I'll always be grateful to you, Simon. You've done a lot for me." She squeezed his hand tight. "Which is why what I'm going to say is all the harder for me."

He sat up, concerned. "What is it, Edel?"

"I can't go on seeing you, Simon." She wiped a tear from her eye.

"What?" he almost shouted. "What do you mean?"

"Just what I said. I have to stop seeing you."

"But why?" he asked in anguish. "I don't understand. Things are going so great between us. And now you've got the contract, there's all the more reason to stay together."

"Oh, Simon, don't make this any more difficult than it is! I want you so much, but I can't put myself first, Simon. I've four young children and they need me."

"But I'm not stopping you being with them."

"Don't you understand? I have to give my marriage the best shot for the sake of my children, and that means not seeing you any more. Do you understand?"

"No, I don't!"

"Thank you, I knew you'd see it from my point of view." She got up and gathered her clothes and went into the bathroom. She dressed quickly and then combed her hair and fixed her face in the mirror. It wouldn't do being caught coming out of a hotel bedroom looking like she had just been fucked when her photo was all over the front pages. She'd had to meet Simon one more time, she owed him that. But he'd served his purpose, moving out of the way so she could get the contract. The secret was how to leave without him feeling negative or bitter towards her.

She glanced at herself in the mirror and came out of the bathroom. Simon was sitting up in bed, looking confused and upset.

She went over and sat on the bed again.

"If you ever see me out somewhere or my photo in the

paper and I am smiling, do not think I smile because I am happy. I smile because it stops me from crying."

"Oh Edel! This sacrifice is too much! You have to think of yourself or your own happiness with me."

She wiped away a tear. "That's me, Simon, always putting everyone else before myself. I'll never forget you." She leaned forward and kissed him and then quickly walked out of the room. Walking down the corridor she opened her bag and switched on her mobile.

Stepping into the lift, she phoned her husband.

"Dessie, you'll have to collect the kids from school. I'm stuck in a meeting."

"Edel, I'm in the middle of something. I have a job too."

"Yes, a job that will have to take second place to mine now I have this contract."

"Didn't it always?"

"Don't be smart. Just collect the kids."

"Will you be home for dinner tonight? You missed dinner all week and the kids are screaming to see you."

"Of course I'll be home, Dessie. I always put my family first."

* * *

Denise looked around the restaurant as she spoke. She normally could do these charity speeches in her sleep. But the fact that Ryan was there was completely unnerving her. He had taken a whole table and filled it with prominent figures from the property-development world.

There was extra champagne being ordered constantly to Ryan's table and much joviality, causing the other more sedate tables to look on with slight amusement and envy.

"And that's why all your continued hard work and fundraising activities are not only appreciated by us all at Forward but more importantly by the children your support continues to help. Thank you."

The audience applauded as she stepped down and walked back to her table. A jazz band started playing as she took her seat beside Martha.

"Well done." Martha chinked her champagne glass against Denise's. "Are you okay? You seemed a little on edge?"

"I'm just a bit tired. Had a late night last night," answered Denise as she looked over at Ryan who had just finished telling a joke and causing his captive table to erupt in much laughter.

"They seem to be having a lot of fun," remarked Martha.

"They are a bit loud and crude, I think."

"He's certainly bringing a lot of life to the charity, isn't he?"

"I think he's using us to create a profile for himself," Denise didn't try to hide the irritation in her voice.

"But don't all the businessmen on the committee do the same thing? In fact, you could be accused of furthering your husband's profile with your involvement."

Denise looked at Martha with a warning shot. "And is that what you think?"

"I didn't say that. What's wrong with you? You're so

tetchy lately."

"I'd better be going. I'll talk to you later." Denise stood up, got her handbag and started moving through the restaurant. A lot of people were beginning to leave and Ryan was saying goodbye to everyone at his table as they thanked him and drifted off.

He turned and came face to face with Denise.

"Ah, Denise, great speech," he complimented.

"Thanks." She went to walk past him.

"Can I tempt you to join me in a glass of champagne? Otherwise this half a bottle will get thrown out."

"I don't think so."

"Oh, come on. Half a glass won't kill you."

Looking around the restaurant she saw it was emptying quickly. Not knowing why, she pulled out a chair and sat down.

He sat down beside her and filled two glasses for them.

"You still like to be the heart and soul of a party, don't you?" she said. "It was the same years ago when we worked together. Always in the pub straight after work enjoying the craic with everyone."

"Strangely enough, I don't socialise that much any more. Only with business colleagues or clients."

And who were all these people at your table then?"

"Just business contacts. I hope we didn't make too much noise during your speech."

"Well, you didn't exactly stay silent."

"Sorry . . . I hope we didn't distract you."

"Hardly."

"That was an interesting night – the press launch of the

Harbour area."

"I suppose."

"So that was your husband you were with."

"Cormac, yes."

"He wasn't what I imagined at all . . . he's a lot older than I thought he would be."

"He's only a few years older than me."

"I'd have never put the two of you together."

"Opposites attract."

"Money and beauty attract."

She looked at him wearily.

"I'm disappointed in you, Denise. You sold out, didn't you?"

"What are you talking about?"

"Sitting there on Reception and running away with the first rich guy who came on to you."

"It wasn't like that at all." She was becoming angry.

"You know what the worst thing is? If you hadn't sold out and married Cunningham, you would have made it through life yourself. All you needed was a bit of confidence in yourself and you would have gone far instead of being trapped in this loveless marriage."

"You don't know anything about my marriage. We love each other very much."

"Well, then you obviously haven't heard the rumours that he's shagging everything around town and out nearly every night of the week doing it."

"How dare you!" Her cheeks blazed.

"But I suppose you have your own life. Swinging around a podium in a sleazy club in slutty outfits. Seems like a beautiful and wonderful marriage to me."

"And what about you, Ryan? What's your story? Who's in your life?" She went on the defensive.

"I've been married, lovely girl called Kate. But it didn't work out. And at least I had the courage to know when it was over and get on with my life instead of staying in a sham like you."

She was completely taken aback to find out he had been married and wanted to know more, but her anger at his intrusion was her overwhelming emotion.

"You don't know anything about my life, Ryan, or my marriage. Just because you've climbed up in the world doesn't mean you're an expert on everybody else's life."

Standing up, she grabbed her handbag and stormed off.

33

Honey fussed around the set dining-table checking it looked fine for when her Sunday afternoon lunch guests arrived. Lisa was sitting on a couch looking on.

"I can't believe you're inviting that bitch to lunch," said Lisa.

"Your father insisted, and you know I agree with him. What's the saying? Better to have your enemies inside the tent pissing out than outside pissing in. Besides, I don't know what all the fuss is about. She didn't seem any great shakes to me. We'll have a collar put on her pretty quickly."

Lisa went to look in the mirror and started studying her face close-up. "I read this article that said you should get satin pillowcases. It stops wrinkles developing during the night."

"Too late for satin for you. It's straight to the Botox at this stage," said Honey, taking a final look at her dinner table. "I don't know who to put her sitting beside. She's written something nasty about everyone who's coming at some stage or other."

"Maybe they'll all fall for her charm like Michael did." Denise and Cormac walked into the room.

"Something smells good," said Cormac.

"It's beef, your favourite," Honey informed him. She looked Denise up and down. "Have you put on weight?"

"No, I haven't –"

Honey reached forward and touched Denise's stomach, smiling gleefully. "You're not –"

"No." Denise removed Honey's hand disdainfully. "I'm certainly not."

*   *   *

Ali looked at herself in the mirror after changing outfits ten times. She hadn't known what to wear to the Cunninghams'. Was it dress up or dress down? She imagined everything they did would be over the top so had finally opted to dress up.

Her mobile rang and she saw it was Timothy's number.

"Hi, Ali, just checking if you were heading into town and wanted to meet up for some lunch?"

"I'd love to but I can't. I'm going over to the Cunninghams' for lunch with Michael."

Timothy roared with laughter. "I'd love to be a fly on that wall."

"Oh, don't, Timothy. I'm dreading it."

"Why go then?"

"Because it's important to Michael."

"I don't believe it, Ali. Next thing you'll be going to their political fundraising, and joining charity committees, and writing articles about how poor estate agents are misunderstood."

"No, I won't. Stop being ridiculous."

"They'll pull you in and you'll be one of them."

"I'm seeing Michael. The rest of them don't matter."

"We'll see."

* * *

Michael pulled into the Cunninghams' front drive and Ali looked up at their house in amazement.

"Nice small gaff," she remarked as she got out of the car.

"Looks like we're running a little late," said Michael, going past the array of cars parked.

"Now there's a surprise." Ali had realised that good timekeeping was not one of Michael's strong points.

They climbed the steps and he rang the doorbell.

Honey opened the door. "Michael!" she said, kissing him on both cheeks. She looked Ali up and down. "Oh, glamour, glamour!" She waved them in. "Follow me through!"

They all went into the drawing-room. There was a group of twelve people sitting and standing.

As Ali entered the room she felt the atmosphere go icy as everyone looked at her. She recognised most of the guests were people she had either exposed or written unflattering criticisms about.

"Everyone, this is Michael's new squeeze, Ali O'Mara. I'm sure you all know of her," said Honey, heading over to the punch-bowl on the drinks cabinet. "We're all drinking punch, so you can have the same." She filled two glasses and handed them to Michael and Ali.

"Thank you," said Ali.

"I just love your dress," said Honey, reaching down and pulling up the hem of Ali's skirt and rubbing it.

"Thank you," said Ali again, feeling very awkward, as Honey's action was exposing a good swathe of her legs.

"I love that colour and material – it's the exact same as the curtains I have hanging in the upstairs bathroom."

Ali found herself sitting between Cormac and Michael and opposite Lisa who just looked on, uncommunicative, not eating, just drinking her wine.

"So, Ali, tell us all about your exciting life in the media," said Honey, who was sitting at the top of the table.

Everyone stared at her, most having been her victim at some stage, needing no explanation about what she did.

"Oh, it's not that exciting really. Just a job, you know."

"I heard you on the radio the other day giving out shite about tax breaks for the wealthy," said Honey.

Everyone's icy stares turned into glares.

"Yes, well, you know, I'm paid to give an opinion on different things in society and I have to give a balanced view. I have to speak for the poor sections of society who can't speak for themselves." Why do you sound like you're apologising? Ali scolded herself.

"Myself and Honey made it up from nowhere and nobody helped us along the way," said Paul.

"But you two were obviously strong and talented people who achieved what you did." Did I just say that? Ali thought.

"Bullshit! We worked every hour God sends – and there's nothing stopping anyone else doing the same," said Paul.

"Some people are born into such disadvantaged areas that there is no way out for them," said Ali.

"I don't agree," said Denise smoothly. "I think if you want to really get somewhere nothing will stop you."

Ali looked at Denise, remembered where she came from and felt guilty over her comment.

"I'm not saying there's no exception, but as a rule it's not that easy," said Ali.

"Nothing's easy in life, except to poke fun at other people who are trying to achieve something," said Cormac.

Ali became irritated. "If you are suggesting I poke fun at people in my articles then that's not fair. I give a balanced view –"

"In your opinion," interrupted Cormac.

"Yes, in my opinion," Ali's voice rose.

"And you're always right?" said Cormac.

"In my opinion, yes, I am right. That might not be the same as your opinion, but in a democracy we're entitled to express our opinions and believe we are right."

"Well, you weren't right about that Honeymoon Murder, were you?" There was a glint in Cormac's eyes. "You fucked up good and well there, and in front of the whole nation as well."

"I was going on information I believed was correct."

"Well, you were wrong, and maybe you should keep that in mind next time you decide to put your poisonous pen to work and write something from some imagined high moral ground."

"I think," Michael said loudly, "we should try and steer the conversation to neutral ground."

Everyone went silent. Ali felt her cheeks blaze red as she took a sip of wine.

"Yes, I agree," said Lisa. "How many children would you like to have?"

* * *

It was early evening and Honey was singing "Crazy" at the top of her voice to her assembled guests. Ali stood in the shadows at the back of the room. She was furious with the way she had been attacked by all and sundry. Once the Cunninghams had all got their digs in, all the guests decided to start settling old scores with her as well. A retired judge sitting beside Honey had lambasted her knowledge of the legal system and savagely attacked her over her covering of a case he had presided over a couple of years back.

She actually felt like crying after the whole event. Michael had defended her at every opportunity, but it hadn't stopped the venom from being delivered to her. She looked over across the room at Michael who had been hijacked by Lisa for the past hour and watched them laughing and joking together.

She wiped away a tear.

"You're going to have to develop a thicker skin if you're going to survive around here," said a voice beside her.

She turned to see Denise was the speaker. She quickly wiped away another tear that was threatening to spill over and cleared her throat.

"There's nothing wrong with me," said Ali quickly.

"Well, that's not what you look like. You can't blame anybody really. You've been attacking the people in this room in print for years. What did you expect? That they would welcome you with open arms?"

"I didn't expect anything. I'm only here for Michael because I know how much you all mean to him. But for that I'd be with my own friends."

"The chattering classes discussing what's wrong with society and blaming the people in this room for causing it? A word of advice, Ali – I wasn't one of these people when I started seeing Cormac either."

Don't I know! Ali thought.

"But you adapt. You don't rock the boat that much. You fit in."

"You're asking me to change my very soul. To become somebody else. To give up my career in that case."

"It depends how much you want Michael. Because he's one of them and he'll never be able to change. Of course, you could just make life easy on the two of you and finish it with him now. Lisa will always be there to pick up the pieces."

Ali looked over as Lisa put her arm around Michael

while laughing loudly.

* * *

Michael opened the front door of his house and let them in. They walked wearily up the stairs and he took her in his arms.

"Wasn't so bad, was it?"

She was shocked. "Could it have been any worse?" she said sharply.

He looked at her, alarmed. "There were bound to be some teething problems, but it worked out okay in the end, didn't it?"

"Michael! It . . ." She trailed off as she remembered Denise's words.

"What?" He looked at her, full of concern.

"It went fine," she said and put her head against his shoulder.

"Do you know what would be really cool? How about all your family come over here for dinner during the week and I'll cook up something special? Wouldn't that be great?"

"Yeah," said Ali, smiling and looking up at him. "I'd like that."

34

Denise snapped the laptop shut, angry with herself. Not only had she read every scrap of information she could find about Ryan, but now she was beginning the process of re-reading articles. It was unhealthy, she told herself, and she wouldn't allow herself to do it any more. It was getting dark outside and looking at her watch she saw it was nearly nine.

No word from Cormac, and as she walked through the grandeur of their new house she felt terribly restless. She sat down on the sofa. She wasn't sure if this move to Glenwood had been the wisest. She had loved the feeling of lots of people nearby that the penthouse had afforded her. She had loved the nearness to town. She could pop out anywhere quickly. Now she had to get into the car and make the journey into the city, and find parking etc etc. It was hassle. And now that construction work had practically finished at Glenwood, even the security guard at the gate wasn't there any more. So here she was, in a ghost town of unoccupied mansions, behind a huge security system, isolated from the outside world. A real gilded cage, she thought to herself. Though she had seen some activity in a couple of the houses and she presumed residents would be moving in shortly. Maybe that would make her feel better. Who are you kidding? she asked herself. Okay, maybe Glenwood wasn't quite her cup of tea, but what was really the problem with her was the fact that Ryan Cantwell had invaded her life.

Ryan who had turned out to be so charming and witty and powerful. Ryan who knew everything about her. Nobody knew everything about her. That's how she liked it. But Ryan knew her back before she was anybody, knew where she originally came from, knew what made her tick, and even had discovered her secret excursions to Stevie's. One minute she was safe and secure and happy, and then he had showed up and she felt very exposed and vulnerable. She was furious about how he had passed comment on her marriage. Like he had a right to. And he was wrong in what he had said. Okay their marriage might look unconventional on the surface . . . but . . .

She'd taken the measure of Cormac very quickly when she'd met him. He was a spoilt man, used to barking orders and getting his own way. Not particularly charming. Denise had discovered that charm was something people developed because they needed things from other people. But Cormac didn't need anything – he had been handed everything as his birthright. But he was witty and funny, even though it was a black and sometimes cruel humour. He was used to getting what he wanted and when he saw Denise, he wanted her. But Denise was used to people wanting her, and she certainly wasn't just going to jump when Cormac clicked his fingers. When she finally agreed to go out on a date with him, the rules of their relationship had already been set by their various interactions at work. She wouldn't let him get away with anything. Any order that was barked at her, she would bark back. Cormac wasn't used to people standing up to him, but Denise was more than able for him. Their dating got off to a fiery but exciting start.

About a month after dating they were out eating in a restaurant.

"Keep Saturday free. I've got tickets for the theatre," Cormac said to her as he looked through the menu.

"Sorry, I've something on Saturday," said Denise truthfully, as she scanned the menu.

"Well, cancel it then," said Cormac.

"You must be joking! It's Thursday night. If you want to make plans with me for Saturday, you need to let me know before now."

"It took me ages to get these tickets, so I'm not missing out just because you're getting fake tan put on or whatever you're doing."

"I'm not asking you to miss out. Take someone else."

"I might just do that. You know there are a lot of girls who would be delighted to be out with me."

She shrugged. "Go with them. I wouldn't be on my own for long, I can assure you."

Jealousy erupted inside Cormac and they sat in silence for a while looking at the menus.

"I'll take my mother on Saturday. She wants to see that play," Cormac said eventually.

Denise looked up and couldn't help smiling. "I've tickets to the theatre for the following Saturday if you want to go?"

"I might be busy," he said sulkily.

"Well, as long as you let me know by Wednesday, or I might have to bring my mother."

He looked up at her and, seeing her grinning, couldn't help from smiling.

"Are you ready to order?" asked the waiter.

"Yes, I'm going to have the beef and she is going to have the duck," said Cormac closing his menu.

Denise bit her lip as she decided now was the time to try out the French she had learned from the classes she was going to every Tuesday evening.

She turned to the waiter and in French she explained she didn't want the duck and that sir didn't want the beef, but they would opt for monkfish instead.

Cormac looked on in amazement, not understanding a word being said. Denise hoped the waiter wouldn't ask for too much detail to expose her scant knowledge.

"What did you just say?" asked Cormac, once the waiter had gone.

"I ordered monkfish for both of us," she said.

"But I never have fish when dining out."

"Well, you need to broaden your horizons and not be so narrow-minded."

"And you're the one who's going to help me do that, are you?" he asked smirking.

She chinked her glass against his and said, "With your looks and my brains, we should go a long way."

Cormac looked at her in astonishment.

As their relationship became very serious, Denise couldn't help thinking about Ryan and his imminent return. She realised Cormac was the man she had been waiting for even though their relationship was very challenging. Maybe because it was so challenging. She thought about writing to Ryan and saying it was over. Or waiting until he arrived back and explaining what had happened. She had never promised Ryan anything. In fact she had more than emphasised along the way it wasn't for ever and that it would end. But he was so insistent and that's why their relationship had continued. Because Ryan could be so dogmatic, she decided that the best thing to do was make a clean break of it. As she and Cormac started to discuss wedding plans, she gave in her notice at the firm and moved flat. She didn't leave any forwarding details. She knew she was taking the coward's way out. But knowing Ryan, this was the only way to do it, to convince him there was no future for them. She needed to allow him to move on with his own life as well. He was a talented engineer and should do well in life. He would meet someone nice and they would live happily in the suburbs somewhere. The last thing he needed in his life was someone like her. Someone with a thirst to be someone and a hunger to get somewhere. In a way she and Cormac were very similar in that way. Neither was particularly straightforward about life and they would never be Mr and Mrs Average.

One thing Denise felt she had to be honest about was her background. She didn't want this huge secrecy in her relationship to her husband. She didn't want the fear he might find out she was from the flats one day. She didn't go into too much detail, but she told him where she came from. She wasn't sure how he would take it because he came from such wealth. He didn't care in the least. He was used to people coming from nowhere and making good in their lives, including his own parents. Cormac was many things but he wasn't a snob. And she loved him for that. And once she had told her husband, she filed her past away, never to be talked about again.

After they got married in a low-key ceremony and the years passed by, their relationship became even more entrenched in the original challenges. Their initial power games became more like a struggle as they refused to give in to one another. People can become immune to their own behaviour and, because they had never been polite to each other, their rudeness grew and grew. What had initially attracted them to each other became what they disliked in each other. As Cormac became more established as a businessman, Denise saw him become more demanding and used to getting his own way which in turn made her more obstinate. And as Denise grew in confidence and became an important social figure, Cormac became more insecure about her. Even though they always shared moments of closeness and humour, their marriage often resembled a battlefield between two strong characters, neither of which would yield to the other. Petty thoughts and fears entered their marriage and were blown up out of proportion. Misunderstandings and jealousies became prominent. Although Denise's background was never an issue for him, he wondered had Denise ever really loved him and he could at times feel bitter towards her. She in turn realised that if she was a weaker person he would more than happily break her spirit.

Finally their marriage began to function on a new level that seemed to work. They began to lead separate lives and yet were also together. Denise was well aware that there were other women in Cormac's life. How did she feel about it? Life was tough, she knew, and you had to accept certain situations. She knew what true misery was like and so she knew when she was happy now. Safely ensconced in her new life, she began to think about her background and realise how lucky she was to get away from it. Lucky and clever. But she had been so single-minded about leaving that life behind, she felt she had never had a youth. She had never enjoyed herself freely. And as the pressure mounted with her new social status and within her marriage, she began to escape to Stevie's. Those nights out alleviated all the pressure.

Feeling restless now, she decided she didn't want to spend the night on her own in the house.

Lately she had been finding her friends a bit boring. There were any number of people she could phone up and arrange to meet. But she didn't want to listen to their petty problems or talk the usual small talk. She decided she would go to Stevie's and let her hair down.

35

Ali opened the bottle of wine and poured two hefty glasses in the kitchen of her apartment. Walking into the living area she handed a glass to Timothy and sat down opposite him.

"When are they releasing the next phase?" he asked, looking out at the crane towering over The Pavilions.

"Michael said in a few months."

"What will they be going for?"

"According to Michael about forty grand more than I paid for this one."

"Phew! That's a nice quick profit."

"I know I'm lucky I bought when I did."

Timothy laughed. "Listen to you! Going out with an auctioneer, discussing how much you've gained on your property. I'd never have believed it."

"Neither would I!" She took a sip from her glass.

"How's it going with Michael?"

"Just great. My whole family was over at his house on

Tuesday. He cooked a fantastic meal and was the utterly charming host. They all loved him. He had my mother dancing at two o'clock in the morning!"

"You're joking!"

"Sure you saw what he was like the night he came over here."

He studied her. "So why the long face?"

"Michael has effortlessly fitted into my world, but I'm having real difficulty with his. Last Sunday at the Cunninghams' was a nightmare. I hated them; they hated me. The only one I got on slightly with was Denise, and I think that's because I only feel sorry for her."

"Why?

She thought about Denise's background. "Er . . . because she's married to Cormac. That's plenty of reason to feel sorry for her."

"And what did Michael make of it?"

"Oh, Michael is just like a big kid. Unless something hits him in the face he's oblivious to it. He thought it went okay."

"And have you tried to talk to him about it?"

"We've had so many disagreements about it all that I don't want to bring it up again. I mean, they are really important to him. His father remarried when his mother passed away and he's not really that close to his real family. He's much closer to the Cunninghams. And, as I said, he's made such an effort with my life that I think I just need to swallow my pride and not rock the boat . . . just put up with them."

"He means that much to you?"

"I was miserable without him when we broke up."

"I never thought I'd see the day when Ali O'Mara would compromise her principles."

"Well, where the hell has not compromising got me? All my relationships have ended because I was so headstrong. And I always put my career first and where has that got me? A career won't love you back. Besides, look at my career, the glory days are over."

* * *

Denise came out of the house, locked the door behind her and got into her car. She drove down the driveway and out onto the main road of the estate. She looked down the road and saw just a handful of construction workers tidying up things and finishing off jobs. In front of the house three doors down from her, she saw a big removal lorry and she felt delighted to see someone was moving in. Deciding to be sociable, she turned the car and drove down and parked behind the lorry. She got out of her car. All the houses at Glenwood were behind high walls, and she walked through the gateway and up the driveway where a black Mercedes was parked. She rang the doorbell and waited for an answer. She wondered who had moved in. Cormac had mentioned that a member of a prominent boy band and his fiancée had bought one of the houses and she was thinking about getting them involved with something to do with Forward if she became friendly with them.

The huge glass doors opened and Denise looked at the dark woman standing there coolly.

She recognised her from somewhere and was searching her mind.

"Can I help you?" said the woman in clipped tones.

The distinctive accent jogged Denise's memory and her confusion. She remembered the woman was Ryan's PA at the launch.

"Who is it, Jodhi?" asked the very recognisable voice of Ryan from somewhere in the house.

"I'm not sure," said Jodhi. "Again, can I help you?"

"Who has bought this house?" Denise demanded, her face filled with confusion.

"That is none of your business – I must warn you that this site is serviced by an excellent security system. All I have to do is activate it and this place will be swarming with a private security firm within seconds."

"What the hell are you talking about? You don't need to inform me of anything about Glenwood. My husband *built* this estate!" Getting angry, Denise pushed Jodhi out of the way and marched into the hallway.

"I'm contacting security right now," warned Jodhi, heading to a panel inside the door.

"Ryan!" Denise shouted.

"What's all the fuss?" Ryan said, emerging from the lounge in a dressing-gown and drinking a cup of coffee.

"This madwoman has just stormed in and I'm calling the police," said Jodhi.

"That's not a madwoman. That's Denise," said Ryan and as he observed the furious expression on her face added, "Well, maybe she is a madwoman on second thoughts."

"What the hell is going on here, Ryan? Have you

bought this house?" demanded Denise.

"Jodhi, it's okay. You don't have to call in the army. Denise, do you want to come into the lounge?"

Denise stormed into the lounge. He closed the door after them.

"What do you think of the interior? All my own choice," he said as he waved his hand.

The house was done out in walnut floors with strong masculine leather furniture.

"I don't give a shit about your interiors! Why have you bought this house?"

"Well, according to *The Irish Times'* front page because it's the best exclusive development to be launched in Dublin for years."

"Don't be smart with me," Denise's voice was almost a roar. "I'm sick of your stupid games. It's bad enough that you're on my committee but now you're living two fucking doors away from me!"

"Language, Denise! You're not acting like the society lady now, but then I suppose you never really left your roots behind, did you? Always only one step away from the flats. You can take the girl out of the flats but you can't take the flat out of the girl."

Out of frustration and without thinking her hand went to slap across his face. The sound of the smack shocked both of them. She quickly pulled her hand back and covered her mouth in shock. Ryan gently rubbed the red mark on his cheek.

She walked quickly past him and out the front door.

Sitting into her car, she tore off down the road.

Reaching the front of the site, she pressed the button that had been installed on her dashboard. The high security gates gently opened and then she tore off down the country roads. Her mind was spinning. What was he doing in her life? What was he trying to do? And why had she reacted the way she had? She had never hit anybody in her life. She was usually so cool and in control, never letting anything affect her. She pressed down on the accelerator.

* * *

Ali entered the glass office block and walked up to the concierge desk.

"What floor is Projectrum on, please?"

"Eighth floor, the top floor."

"Thanks."

She got into the lift and pressed '8'. She was looking forward to interviewing Edel Garry. After she had won the Harbour contract, it had almost been impossible to get through to her. She had left a dozen messages at her reception, none of which was returned. Finally she managed to get her mobile number from a contact and got to speak directly to her, reminding her she had promised an interview. It was a common phenomenon that Ali had witnessed over the years. Somebody who was just regular and easily accessible suddenly hit the big time and as they went into supernova they became almost impossible to reach.

The lift doors opened and Ali stepped into the wide open-plan office. There seemed to be a staff of about fourteen at different desks working on different projects.

"Here to see Mrs Garry," Ali informed the receptionist.

"Hello, good to see you again," said Edel who seemed to appear from nowhere, taking Ali by surprise.

Ali shook her hand.

"Do you want to follow me through?" suggested Edel and Ali did as she was bid.

"So this is the nerve centre of everything?" commented Ali as she saw the different architects working at their desks. The whole office had a hushed feeling. A feeling of calm and concentration that was in direct contrast to the newspaper offices Ali was used to.

"Yes, this is where it all happens." Edel opened the door of her office and held it for Ali to enter. The office was large and spacious with floor-to-ceiling windows offering a breathtaking view of Dublin. Or, more importantly for the career that Edel was in, the many cranes towering over the Dublin skyline.

"Take a seat, please," said Edel as she sat down behind her desk in her swivel-chair.

Edel Garry seemed to exude a regal air. Her brown shoulder-length hair was pulled back in an Alice band that day. She was dressed in a red business suit. Only her doe-like eyes betrayed the cool exterior.

Ali had done some research on Edel before the interview and strangely the same comment was passed about her by many: "She's a woman very hard to say no to."

"You've shocked a lot of people in the construction industry with your appointment as project manager of the Harbour area," began Ali.

"Have I? It's something I'm very excited about. As you

336

probably saw from my proposal I have a lot of exciting ideas for the area."

"I just want to check a couple of background details if you don't mind? You studied architecture in UCD. Then you worked for some leading architecture firms, before you went out on your own ten years ago and formed your own project-management company."

"Yes, I guess I was at the right time and the right place. The construction industry was just beginning to explode and so it was the right time for me to start my own company."

"In the first year of starting Projectrum you were appointed to oversee the city centre rejuvenation. It was what launched you. That was a big project to be awarded to a small and new company. What made you stand out from the competition to get that project, do you think?"

Sleeping with the minister who was awarding the contract, thought Edel. "I've always felt you should be original in everything you do. Although imitation is the best form of flattery, I avoid it. I try to avoid looking at other people's work, so that all my ideas are innovative and come from in here." She put a hand to her heart.

"After the successful overseeing of the city centre rejuvenation, your name was made and you continued to get lucrative government contracts. But the Harbour Project is so big, there's many who don't think you can handle it."

"People have been saying that I can't handle things since I started my career. I've proven all of them wrong to date."

"Do you think people have been saying that because you're a woman?"

"This is still a male-dominated industry, so there is probably an element of that."

"Do you think being a woman project manager has been a disadvantage to you?"

She thought about the number of times she had used being a woman to her advantage over the years. "I think it's irrelevant really to me. If it colours other people's perceptions that's for them to deal with."

"You've been married for twelve years and have four children."

"Yes, I met Dessie at college. He's an architect as well. He's my anchor and I adore him."

"Do you find it hard in this hard business to be there for the children?"

"No, I always make time for my kids. If it's a case of a meeting or time with my kids, the kids win every time."

"So what's your plan for the Harbour area?"

"I want to oversee a community that offers the very best quality of life to people. I think property development has been all about big profits too long. I want to work with the developers to put something back into society."

As Edel continued speak about her dreams, Ali couldn't help but be impressed by her vision. She wasn't sure if Edel Garry was someone she would like, but she certainly was drawn to her. And she knew that here was someone who was going to be a big name and a powerful player.

36

"I'd say the Cunninghams are a little upset they don't have free range of your home any more," said Ali.

They were curled up on the couch in his house.

He looked at her with a cautious smile. "I suppose".

"I wonder where Cormac is going now for his little late-night parties and trysts?"

"I wonder."

"At least now you can go to bed with the knowledge that you're going to have good night's sleep without a circus arriving in on top of you."

"The bags are already disappearing from under my eyes."

She hit him playfully across the chest. "I wish you could be serious for once."

"I am being serious. I owe you so much. You reclaimed my home and made it my own . . . well, half my own since you're here nearly every night."

"You might joke, but one of those sluts had a load of

cocaine on her – and that is a class A drug. If it was ever caught in your home you'd be in serious trouble."

"I didn't see anyone with cocaine."

"Then you must be blind . . . of course, why doesn't that surprise me? Anything you don't want to see you simply decide not to see. You're the most classic example of head in the sand I've ever seen. You let that ridiculous situation with Lisa continue for years instead of simply making it clear there was no future for the two of you years ago. Yes, there would have been a little hurt pride, but then you and she would have moved on. But no, you had to let her build it up into this fairytale in her head." She smiled up at him. "There will be no more dodging reality now I'm around. I'm one gal who likes dealing in the here and now and likes everyone to know where they are."

"Indeed. Speaking of bags under my eyes, I'm feeling exhausted. Think I need an early night."

"And you work too hard, another thing – what has you so tired?"

"Just doing so many viewings at Glenwood. Eighty per cent of them have just come to nose around – see how the other half live – and we've had a bit of a setback over the Harbour re-development."

"How so?"

"We were banking on Simon O'Keefe, who is one of ours, being the boss down there, but they gave it to that woman instead."

"Edel Garry? I interviewed her yesterday."

"What?" Michael raised his voice and sat up. "You

interviewed Edel Garry? How did you manage that? She's impossible to get through to since she was awarded the contract. I've left loads of messages at Projectrum and she hasn't returned my calls. They never give out her mobile seemingly."

"I guess I just have the right contacts to arrange these things."

"What's she like?" He sat forward, interested.

"A bit cool. Obviously intelligent . . . impressive . . . I don't know. Read what I've written about her in the paper tomorrow."

"If I'd known you were meeting her I could have got you to talk about me and arrange a meeting."

Ali sat back affronted. "Excuse me, I'm not Denise Cunningham. I'm not some little woman whose purpose in life is to glorify her partner and promote his business."

"More's the pity. You could have smoothed a very rocky road for me there. Make sure you write a glowing complimentary interview, none of your assassination stuff, in case she ever finds out we're seeing each other and she holds it against me."

"I can't believe I'm hearing this!" Ali's face was a mixture of horror and amusement. "If you think for one minute I would compromise my journalistic reputation to smooth some business deal for you, you can stop kidding yourself!"

"Oh, don't worry; I know you could never do something like that." He sat back and folded his arms in a sulking fashion.

She went to cuddle him, but he pulled away and scowled.

"Don't be like that!" she cajoled.

"I'd compromise myself for you," he said.

"Would you now?" She looked at him in amusement.

He nodded.

She sighed and, reaching over to her handbag, took out her mobile. Looking through her numbers, she sent a text.

A few seconds later, his mobile bleeped.

"What was that?" he asked.

"I just texted you her private mobile number." He jumped up happily and kissed her.

"Now, I really had to call in a favour to get it. So don't you dare ever let on where you got it from."

* * *

The interview of Edel Garry was accompanied by a very flattering photo of her sitting at her desk with the view of the cranes in the background. The heading read:

'Edel Garry – Starchitect.'

The article read:

"When you enter the hushed offices of Projectrum it exudes a feeling that nothing could ever go wrong there. Maybe it was this aura of confidence and capableness that led to the government entrusting the Harbour re-development to Projectrum over fierce and stiff competition. Edel Garry has a regal air about her as she leads you into her office. She's a woman who has achieved much in her career in this traditionally male-dominated sector. A woman who has got there on her own merit. A woman whose ideas are original, socially inclusive and yet at the cutting edge. What's more, this starchitect coolly oversees her thriving business while at the same time being a dedicated wife and mother of four young children."

"For fuck's sake – what are you doing to O'Mara? There's not a note of disapproval in the whole damned interview!" said Cormac, tossing the paper onto Michael's desk.

He was in Farrell's discussing the sales figures at Glenwood.

"Give Ali her due, when she meets people she keeps an open mind. Let's face it, she hadn't met any of us when she wrote those articles about us. If we had met her and given her interviews, maybe she would have written really good things about us."

Cormac looked at Michael. He was always aware Michael could be a little naïve, but surely not that naïve.

"I'd say more like Garry pushed all the right buttons." Cormac scanned through the article. "Yep, she's saying all the right things – responsibility of architects and developers, designing eco-friendly environments, affordable housing. O'Mara fell for her crap."

Michael became irritated with the way Cormac spoke of Ali in such a derogatory way.

"Well, maybe we should be more aware of stuff like that."

"Oh, fucking save me from all that crap! Don't you fucking start spewing out O'Mara's philosophy on life. It's bad enough we have to listen to her, but I don't want to hear it second-hand from you as well. Go get a job as a social worker if you're going to go soft on me."

"I'm just saying we could learn from the way Edel handles the press."

"The only press being handled around here is you screwing O'Mara. Anyway, I'm out with Barbara and a few of the others tonight. Why don't you come along and have a bit of fun before you forget how to."

"You're so fucking cynical, Cormac. No, I'm staying in and watching a DVD with Ali. Why don't you give Barbara and the others a miss and try doing the same with your lovely wife?"

Cormac raised his eyes. "Ah, give me a break . . . Come on. Let's get down to business. We're no nearer meeting Garry."

Michael sat back and smiled. "Well, we might be a little nearer. I managed to get my hands on her evasive mobile number."

Cormac was impressed. "How did you do that?"

"Ali gave it to me." Michael savoured the look on Cormac's face.

"Maybe she's good for something."

"Shall I ring Garry or will you?" Michael enquired.

"You're the one with the gift of the gab. I'll leave it to you."

Michael dialled Edel's number. "It's ringing," he whispered.

"Hello?" said Edel's smooth voice.

"Ah, Edel? Michael Farrell here from Farrell's Auctioneers."

"How did you get this number?" she quizzed coolly.

"Your Reception gave it to me. I've been trying to get hold of you for while."

"It has been hectic since our appointment. I haven't even looked at my messages at Reception."

"Completely understand. You must be under huge pressure."

"Nothing I can't handle."

"Of course. Anyway, I'm not going to waste any of your time. I'm going to get to the point. I would love to meet up with you at your earliest convenience to discuss a couple of ideas."

"I'm sure I'd love to hear your ideas, but I am very busy –"

"Completely understand. But I really think you'd be interested in what we have to say and it won't take that long."

"Friday morning at twelve, my office," Edel said quickly and she hung up the phone.

37

Denise looked at Ryan sitting down the board table at Forward. As had become customary, he was dominating the meeting, putting forward his ideas and plans, which irritatingly were always innovative and good. Not that she cared about that. He was very businesslike that day, his easy good humour replaced by seriousness. He barely acknowledged her and purposely looked past her very quickly when he was addressing the committee. It compounded her guilt at hitting him. She despised physical violence. Growing up where she had, she had seen enough of it around and hated it. She was angry and very surprised with herself that she had resorted to that, whatever the circumstances. Herself and Cormac had been married for years in the most conflicted of marriages and never once raised their hand to one another, or would ever dream of doing it. She would have to address the situation as soon as the meeting was over.

"Okay," said Tony, wrapping things up. "Thanks to

everyone and to you, Ryan, especially for that great input.
See you all on Thursday."

"Fancy an afternoon cocktail?" Martha asked Denise, as
everyone got up to go.

"Eh, thanks but no. I just need to sort something out so
I'll give you a call later, okay?"

"Okay," Martha shrugged and headed off.

Denise waited for Tony to stop talking to Ryan and
then approached him.

"Can I have a word?" she asked.

Ryan looked at her suspiciously and, surprisingly,
blushed.

"Why not?" he said.

They waited a few seconds for Tony to leave them
alone and close the door.

She just came out and said it. "About the other day . . .
I'm sorry I slapped you."

"It was the first time a customer who'd just bought a
two point four million house off you got hit, I'd imagine."

"There is no excuse for what I did. I didn't mean it. I
don't know where it came from."

Ryan nodded and looked down at the floor.

"It's just been quite a shock with you turning up like
this after all these years . . ." she trailed off.

He nodded.

"I'm giving you the opportunity to say something here.
Maybe explain what you're doing here," she pushed.

There was a rap on the door. They turned around and
saw Jodhi walking in.

"Ryan, you'll miss your meeting at three if we don't

leave now," she said.

"Coming right now . . . I'll see you Thursday, Denise."
He walked past her and out of the room.

"Well?" asked Jodhi quietly as they descended the
grand stairs.

"We're getting there . . . slowly but surely," answered
Ryan.

* * *

Edel pulled her car up in front of the giant derelict
Heavey's Mill. Looking at her watch she realised she was
slightly early. She stepped out of the car and looked
around the dilapidated landscape. There was a wind
blowing in from the nearby sea. It was hard to imagine the
transformation that would be taking place here over the
next few years, to turn this industrial wasteland into a
thriving community. It would take someone with excellent
leadership skills and vision. In short – it would take her.
Life was hard and it was easy to be passed over and be
stepped on. You had to be exceptionally shrewd to get on.
She could easily have just been sidelined along the way.
But she knew just how to handle people to get what she
wanted. Simon O'Keefe had left messages for her which
she hadn't returned. She had explained the situation and
he would come to understand in time.

She saw the black Mercedes approach down the dusty
road. All the developers had been angling for a meeting
with her since Projectrum had been awarded the contract.
It was great to be in the position to pick and choose. She
deserved it after everything she had done to get there. She

had started with the biggest. Aston was a company she had long admired. And she had thought it innovative of Ryan Cantwell to suggest meeting actually at the Harbour as opposed to some plush office or hotel.

"I hope you haven't been waiting for long," said Ryan, stepping out of his car and walking towards her. Jodhi got out on the other side and joined him.

"Not at all." She shook both their hands.

"Congratulations again," said Ryan.

"Thank you." She cast a discreet eye up and down him. She liked the look of Ryan Cantwell.

Ryan turned away from Edel and, folding his arms, stood staring up at the Mill, entranced.

"It's magnificent, isn't it?" he said.

Edel smiled. "Hardly magnificent in its present state. And a typical example of a Victorian industrial building is what it was in its prime."

Ryan walked towards it and held his hands up in the air. "I love it! I've loved it from the first day I saw it."

With a bemused smile Edel walked towards the building. "I've always admired passion in a person."

Ryan turned to look at her. "I think you have to be passionate in this game. If you aren't, what else is there?"

"Money . . . some would say," said Edel.

"But did the great architects of the Georgian and Victorian era think about money, or were they dedicating themselves to leaving something to posterity?"

"I would imagine a bit of both." Edel leaned against her car and folded her arms.

"Aston Construction has an excellent track record at

developing period property sensitively," explained Jodhi, handing Edel a large book. "As you can see from this book, we have carried out much work in the London Docklands – in Yorkshire and in the Manchester area."

Edel took it and, without looking at it, opened her car boot and put it in.

"I'll look at it later – I'm already aware of the work you've carried out – I take it you are interested in Heavey's Mill?"

Ryan looked at her and closed his eyes for a few seconds. "Every so often I see a building that I believe I have to develop. That's the feeling I get about Heavey's Mill."

Edel nodded and looked lost in thought for a couple of minutes.

"This site is the epicentre of the Harbour development. It's going to be the showpiece for the whole district and as such there has been much demand for it. Why should I give it to you rather than anyone else?"

"Because I can make this work exactly as you see it. I can make this the most exciting development Dublin has ever seen."

"And how exactly do you propose to do that?"

Ryan laughed. "What? You want to know right here and right now?"

"No – but soon. I will be inviting the developers that I think have the financial might, the vision and the experience to develop Heavey's Mill to submit to me a full proposal, including drawings, plans etc of what they plan to do at this site. Expensive I know – but it is the only way

I can be sure that whoever is allowed to buy this site has the right development." She walked to her car and opened the driver's door.

"And are you asking me to submit such a proposal?" Ryan asked.

"Yes, I am," said Edel getting into the car and driving off.

* * *

Edel sat in her swivel-chair, her back to her desk, looking out at the cranes reaching over the Dublin skyline. It had been an interesting meeting with Ryan Cantwell. The success of the Harbour rejuvenation depended on big names being involved. And Aston was surely a big name. She was now waiting for the representatives of Cunningham Homes to arrive. Cunningham Homes was not a name that inspired admiration in her, but again they were too big a name to ignore. But their reputation for ruthlessness and flashiness, not to mention their being a firm part of the old boy network that had controlled this country for years didn't impress her.

A knock on the door and she spun her chair around.

"Cormac Cunningham and Michael Farrell," introduced the receptionist.

Edel stood up and, smiling, shook their hands.

"Gentlemen, please take a seat," she offered.

"You're a hard woman to track down," said Michael.

"Not hard enough obviously. I checked with Reception and as is policy they never gave my mobile number out to you."

"I can have a way of getting what I want." Michael leaned closer and, smiling, winked at her.

"So I've heard," Edel sat back coolly. "Anyway, let's cut to the chase. What can I do for you?"

"We are interested in buying Heavey's Mill," Cormac said with a smile.

"Isn't everybody?" returned Edel.

Cormac glanced at Michael before looking at Edel. "Ah, yes, but does everybody have the money to buy it?" Edel shrugged her shoulders. "In today's market – yes."

Michael coughed. "Look, there are a lot of developers out there, but I'm sure a company of Projectrum's stature will only want to deal with the crème de la crème. And that's what Cunningham Homes is."

"I'm not saying you aren't. But I am saying: what can you offer that nobody else can?"

"It's simple. We can pay more money for the Mill than everyone else can."

Edel closed her eyes for a few seconds and joined her fingers together like a temple.

"The development of the Harbour area is not just about the money." She opened her eyes. "I could put that site up for auction in the morning and just let it go to the highest bidder. But I want to learn from the mistakes made before. I want the Harbour area to be a shining example of urban renewal, not just in Ireland but internationally. And this is government land and so, of course, we want to raise the necessary funds but I want to know what you plan for Heavey's Mill. I want a full planning programme submitted by you as to what you are planning to do with the site."

"But that would mean employing architects and engineers. It would end up costing tens of thousands with no guarantee we'll get the land." Cormac looked concerned.

"That's what I want. Take it or leave it. I will have the land valued over the next couple of weeks and put the sale price as that evaluation. All reputable companies who wish to then be considered and have the funds to buy the Mill will be judged on their proposal."

"That's not how we do business. We make an offer on the land, buy it and build," said Cormac.

"This isn't normal building land. The success of the Harbour area is at stake here."

"Can we ask who else is involved?" asked Michael.

Edel thought for a moment. "I can't see why not. I believe in business being open. So far Aston will be submitting a proposal. I have meetings with several other developers over the next few days." Edel glanced down at her watch. "You'll have to excuse me, boys. I'm on the school run this week and I'm running late."

38

Cormac came into the house and flung his briefcase at the couch.

Denise was standing at the large front window, discreetly hidden behind the curtains watching the procession of cars turn into Ryan's driveway.

"What's wrong with you?" questioned Denise, observing a Ferrari pull in through Ryan's gateway and disappear behind the high walls.

"Had a meeting with that stupid bitch, Edel Garry, today."

"I take it that it didn't go well?" She could hear loud laughter and much merriment from open patio doors at Ryan's house.

"We've got our work cut out for us with her."

"What's she like?"

"Don't know. Can't get a handle on her. Cool customer. She's putting Heavey's Mill out to tender and the best proposal will get the site."

"Is that so bad? Cunningham Homes are known at the top end of the market which is a huge plus. Just propose a luxury development."

A car pulled up outside Ryan's and because the driveway was full, it parked out on the road. Denise observed the four guests getting out of the car and that the two men were dressed in tuxedos and the two women in cocktail dresses.

"This Edel Garry is unknown territory. It's a whole different ball-game with her. She told us today that the British firm, Aston, will be tendering. I mean what the fuck are they coming here for? Isn't there enough building in London?"

Denise quickly turned around and looked at Cormac. "Aston? That's the firm Ryan Cantwell is the head of." She looked alarmed.

"Who?"

"Ryan, the fella I told you had joined the committee at Forward. If you listened to a word I ever said, you'd remember."

Cormac thought for a second and remembered Denise saying something about it. "And what's he joined Forward for?"

Denise decided to be very careful. The last thing she wanted was for Cormac to know about herself and Ryan. "I don't know. From what I can see, he's out to make a big splash in Dublin . . . eh, he's also one of our new neighbours."

"What?" Cormac was perplexed.

"He's bought No 3, and from what I can see he's

having quite a party there tonight."

Cormac walked quickly over to the window, and pushed Denise out of the way to get a good look at the arriving cars.

* * *

"Ali, can I have a word with you?" asked her editor Barry.

"Sure," Ali looked up from her computer screen as Barry closed her office door and sat on her desk.

He looked at her for a minute suspiciously.

"Barry?" she prompted.

"Not sure how to approach this, so better just come out and say it."

"You usually do."

"Are you seeing Michael Farrell?"

She felt herself go red. "What makes you ask that?"

"Because you've been seen together a lot."

"You can do nothing in this town." Ali sat back annoyed.

"No, you can't. You of all people should know that. Well?"

"Well, what if I am?" She looked at him defiantly.

"So it's fucking true." Barry nodded to himself cynically.

"Have you a problem with that?"

"Where do I start? You're Ali O'Mara, the social conscience of this country – you can't go out with Michael Farrell. He's a shyster, publicity mad, egocentric and . . . need I go on? Or will I just get out a few of the articles you've written about him to remind you what he's like?"

"I know what Michael comes across as in public. But he's also funny, and kind and exciting and terribly naïve at times –"

"Would you ever shut up? I can't listen to it. That fella and that Cunningham lot are just one step from a tribunal."

"Nothing has ever been proved, Barry, or else they would be up before a tribunal. And if anything was proved about them, I would be the first to write a lambasting feature about them."

"Well, that's just my point, Ali. You can't speak with authority any more if you continue to see Farrell. People are very clever now, and for better or worse your fancy fella is the face of today's greedy property market, and you will be guilty by association."

Ali threw her hands into the air. "What are you expecting me to do then?"

"Well, I thought it was obvious . . . dump him."

Ali's eyes glinted with danger. "You can't tell me who I can or cannot see, Barry."

"I know I can't." He softened his voice. "I'm speaking to you as a friend. Ali, this will have serious consequences for your career. Sure you've had a hard time recently – when the scoops stop coming – it is hard. But it happens to all of us. We all go through lean periods. But it will come together for you again. Don't throw it all away."

She looked at his middle-aged features, his hard hooded eyes, his lined face. He was an old hack. Over the years, she had been over the pub with Barry countless of times, sitting beside him at the bar, listening to his old war stories. He was an alcoholic. Didn't even know it himself. Despite this, she had always felt privileged in his company, sharing ideological debate with this super intelligent man. Being inspired by him. She admired him. But she didn't want to be him.

"How's your wife, Barry?" she asked, sitting back.

"Janet? What the fuck's she got to do with anything? She's at home baking cookies, or watching soaps or whatever she does in the afternoon."

She sighed. She could say so much. Point out to him how empty his life was. She could say how he had always been a role model for her, but now her biggest fear was to end up like him. But it wasn't her place to say it. He had his own demons to deal with and she didn't want to say anything to hurt him.

"Thanks for your honesty, Barry. I appreciate what you've said. I'll keep it in mind. If you don't mind, I'd better rush – I've an interview at four."

* * *

"We got this call from MIM Management today saying one of their clients wanted to be shown around Glenwood," said Michael.

They had been having dinner out at The Apple Shaker and were now walking back to his house. Ali had been a bit anxious over dinner, conscious of people spotting them together. And even now as they walked through the darkened warm streets, she was slightly uncomfortable with his arm around her waist in case they were seen.

"They represent all the actors, don't they?" asked Ali.

"They sure do. They wouldn't reveal which one of their clients it was though. Everyone was playing guessing games all day in the office seeing who it might be. It must be a major-league star for them to be able to afford Glenwood."

"Must be," agreed Ali.

"We tossed a coin for who would show them around. Lisa won."

"Lucky Lisa."

"Are you all right . . . you seem very quiet tonight?"

"Yeah," she forced a smile. "I'm fine I guess. Just had a hard day. Can I ask you something?"

He looked at her anxiously. "I guess."

She stopped walking and looked at him. "Have you ever done anything illegal?"

"Oh, here we go again." Michael threw his hands in the air in exasperation."

"Look, I'm sorry . . . I'm not having a go at you or anything like I did before. I just want to know. I need to know."

"You've heard something?"

"I'm a journalist. I hear a lot of things."

"Do you really think I'm so bad? That I'd break the law?"

"Just answer me truthfully, please. Have all your business dealings been legal? Because, if not and it got out that we were seeing each other, it would destroy me."

"No. No, I haven't done anything illegal."

"I'm sorry for asking, but I needed to know."

"But you should know me by now. You should know I wouldn't do anything wrong."

"I know you wouldn't. It's just the Cunninghams. I'm sure Cormac has done lots of things."

"You know, you should give Cormac a break. Okay, he comes across as aggressive and hard, but if you knew Cormac like I know him, you'd know he has a very good heart."

"Please tell me where he keeps it."

"I'm serious. I know him well. You know, he sponsors loads of kids out in Third World countries."

Ali looked at him cynically. "I'm sorry, I find that very hard to believe."

"I'm completely serious. Nobody knows that, not even Denise. But I know because he makes the payments through Farrell's and I see them go out every month."

"Well, it must be some tax-dodging scam."

"If you're not going to have an open mind, there's no point in telling you any more." Michael went to walk off.

She grabbed his arm. "No, I'm sorry. Go on."

"That's not all he does. He donates to charity all over the place and nobody ever knows. He even makes anonymous donations to Denise's charity and she doesn't know."

"I'm intrigued. Go on."

"You know how he roars at his staff and everything? Okay, he does give them a hard time, but he just expects the same commitment from them as he gives. And I tell you he gives the best money and the best bonuses to his staff. And if ever any of them are in some kind of trouble, he's straight in there helping them out, and he insists nobody ever finds out. Last year one of his foremen started developing a gambling problem and his home was about to be repossessed. Cormac got in here, staved off the bank, and got the guy into some help programme. The man got back on his feet within six months and is now working away solidly. Even with Denise, he doesn't deny her anything."

"Maybe financially. But he's still out with the likes of that Barbara every night."

"As I said to you before, Cormac and Denise's relationship works on a different level. I think I know what the problem is. At the beginning of their relationship, he was very much the more powerful of the two. But as time went on I think he got frightened that she had outgrown him . . . and, you know, maybe he's right."

She stood there, taking it all in. Then she put her arm around his waist and they continued walking back to his house.

"Remember it's a cocktail party over at Honey and Paul's" said Michael. "And don't forget to keep Sunday week free. We said we'd go for dinner there as well."

* * *

Lisa went around the showhouse at Glenwood, checking everything looked fine for MIM's client to arrive. Sales had been great at Glenwood and there weren't many properties left. She hoped that MIM's client would be a big name. They could release it to the press and make it an even more sought-after address.

She had been working hard with Michael, selling. It was as if everything was normal. And maybe as far as Michael was concerned it was. But it hurt her so much to feel he was gone from her . . . and to realise she never really had had him in the first place. But she wasn't out of the game yet.

She had left the heavy security gates at the front of the estate open so they could drive straight in. And as she looked out the window she saw a silver Audi pull in through the gates of the showhouse. She went to the front door to open it and watched as the back door of the car opened and out stepped a tall dark handsome man, hidden behind huge sunglasses. She immediately recognised him as Hugh Fitzroy. Hugh Fitzroy was a major-league actor who had managed to conquer Europe and America. A working-class hero who had lost none of his earthiness and yet managed to have star appeal.

Coming from her background, Lisa had grown up with so many important people around that she never got starstruck. However, as the sun shone down and sparkled off Hugh's huge shades, she did feel herself go slightly woozy.

She pulled herself together and went into professional mode.

"How's it going? You the auctioneer? Marge at MIM said there would be a bird here to meet me all right."

Lisa looked at him in amazement. "Yes – Mr. Fitzroy, isn't it?" She held out her hand for him to shake.

"The one and only . . . impressive gaffs, I have to say."

"Aren't they? All individually architecturally designed."

"A bit like meself." He moved his glasses up, and his bleary and bloodshot eyes looked her up and down, squinting in the sun, before he put the shades back on. "So when does this magical mystery tour start?"

"Right now if you want. As you can see all the houses are protected by high walls, protecting your privacy from your neighbours." She walked into the hall and he followed her. Lisa decided privacy and security would be the chief selling points to Hugh Fitzroy. "The whole site has a ten-foot wall surrounding it, which has a laser running over it. Basically this means nobody can get over the wall without the place being swamped by the private security firm employed to protect Glenwood. The front entrance is served by electronic wrought-iron gates. Each house will be given an individual code to press into the pad on the way in and even on the way out. Glenwood has been designed with security as one of the main features."

"It sounds like it's fucking Fort Knox."

"Well, Mr Fitzroy, for the people who are moving here their protection is most important."

"That's why MIM sent me out here. Said it would keep all the fame-hungry shits out and that nobody would see in. No straying paparazzi."

"That is something you will be guaranteed at Glenwood." She led him through the living-room through to the kitchen. "Look at that high wall at the end of the garden, completely protected – and I'm pleased to say that we do have houses left with the swimming pool as per the showhouse."

She turned around. Hugh had picked up an ornamental decanter filled with whiskey and was pouring himself a large drink. He downed it in one.

"Nothing like it. When you've had a hard night on the razz, the best thing is to start on the sauce first thing."

Lisa couldn't hide her bemusement. "I've found the same thing myself."

"Get out of it! I bet you're a one-Martini-a month bird."

"Why? Do I look all prim and proper or something?" She flicked her hair back.

"Maybe a bit."

"Well, compared to those LA whores you hang around with, I guess I do," Lisa said.

He looked her over and smiled. He walked back into the sitting-room and went over to the drinks cabinet. "I hope none of this shit is coloured water?"

"No, it's all real alcohol. But it's for ornamental purposes not for just anyone to come in and help themselves."

Hugh grabbed a bottle and poured two drinks out. "Ah, but I'm not just anybody. I'm a movie star!"

"As my mother would say, you can't make a dainty meal out of a cabbage."

"Huh?"

"Forget it."

"Drink?" He held out a glass to her.

She thought for a second "Why not?"

Four hours later and the lounge in the showhouse was littered with empty decanters. Lisa was stretched out on one sofa, while Hugh was stretched out on the other.

"You just don't know how hard my life is," Hugh informed her with a slur. "It's just non-stop work. In front of those fucking cameras. And then when you're finished with that, you have to smile for the fucking cameras and the fans . . . often you have to smile even though you don't feel like it . . . poor me . . ."

"Any photo I've ever seen of you in the paper, you are either scowling or look totally pissed. You should try being in my high-heeled shoes. Meeting all these stupid people all day long selling them houses. Having to put up with their crap. Meeting sales targets . . . poor me."

"I thought you said your family built these gaffs."

"They did."

"Well, what's your problem then? Just set your own targets."

"It's not as easy as that. It's even more important to get those targets when they are for yourself. Is your driver still out there?"

"Yeah. Don't worry about him. MIM pay him to keep me out of trouble." He sat up and looked at her, laughing. "But I pay him twice as much to stay out of my way."

"I like your style." Lisa joined his laughter.

He looked at her oversized handbag on the floor and the top of the book in it.

"What you reading?" he asked.

She struggled forward and took out the book. "It's called *Women Who Love Too Much*."

He leaned forward and emptied the decanter into their glasses. "Isn't the word 'themselves' missing from that title?"

"I need it. I need to educate myself to stop me from

loving too much."

"And who are you loving too much?"

"This fucker called Michael. Well, actually I kind of hate him now . . . love, hate, what's the difference? I've loved him for years . . . but he doesn't love me . . . chosen some fool with her arse on the ground . . . it's hard being me."

"You think that's hard? You should try my life . . . all these bints who just want you cos you're frigging rich and famous . . . they wouldn't have looked at me five years ago."

She raised her glass and drank. "At least they want to be with you! My man doesn't want to be anywhere near me . . . he doesn't give a shit I'm rich!"

"Any more booze in this joint?" Hugh looked at the empty decanter.

"Looks like we've drunk the place dry . . . I'd better be going home." Lisa staggered up and took a look around the mess they had created all day. "Well, I'm not clearing all this up," she stated.

"Well, I sure as hell am not." Hugh struggled to his feet.

"Oh, fuck it, who cares?" said Lisa, as she staggered to the door. "Your driver can drop me off as I'm too pissed to drive."

Hugh followed her out.

Lisa turned and looked at him, suddenly remembering.

"Are you taking the house, incidentally?"

"Oh, yeah, the house . . . ah, sure, why not? It would be rude not to."

39

Michael looked at Ali seated beside him at the Cunninghams' dinner table and smiled at her. All his earlier worries were evaporating. She was fitting in just fine. Sure there was the occasional barb, but that was the Cunninghams' way. Nobody was safe from their humour and you had to learn to slag back and get on with it. He knew somebody as tough as Ali, a woman who'd brought down two ministers, a union and a hospital board, could more than handle the Cunninghams once she got used to their ways. And it was important that she did get on with them. They were like a surrogate family to him. His own stepmother had damaged his relationship with his own family and the Cunninghams had stepped in and given him everything he needed. He reached under the table and gave Ali's leg a little reassuring squeeze.

Feeling Michael's hand on her leg, she discreetly turned and smiled at him. How could she get through the rest of the day? Listening to their ranting self-importance.

And listening to their fawning guests. And if that wasn't bad enough, Honey's caterwauling would finish proceedings. She reached forward for her glass of wine and knocked it back.

"So Hugh Fitzroy is definitely going ahead with buying number 6," Lisa informed them, who had been recounting her tale of meeting the actor.

"What's he like? Anything like his image?" questioned Denise.

"The exact same. Drinking, and smoking and cursing. A real scream."

Honey gave her daughter a knowing look. "It's amazing – drunks always manage to seek each other out. Just like sluts, they always find each other as well."

"Actually, Hugh Fitzroy was one of the most difficult sales this auctioneer has had to encounter. His ego is immense. All he wanted to do was talk about himself," said Lisa.

"Well, fuck it, who cares what he's like? He's a coup for Glenwood and should push the prices up," said Cormac. "A bona fide movie star at Glenwood. What more could we ask for?"

"I wonder if he's into doing charity work?" asked Denise. "He's from a pretty deprived background, isn't he? Forward might interest him."

Honey looked at her daughter-in-law. "If the poor fucker is from a shite background, the last thing he wants is to be reminded of it. Some of us can leave the past behind."

Ali cleared his throat. "Actually, from what I know, that

is all a contrived image by his management."

"And, of course, you'd know," snapped Honey.

"Well, yes, actually I do." Ali looked at her defiantly. "We know the inside track on everybody."

"Well, bully for you! Well, you keep that bit of news about him buying at Glenwood to yourself. That's not to be aired in one of your columns. Or anything else you hear around our table is strictly confidential."

Ali controlled her temper. "I'm not a showbiz columnist; I write about serious issues. The state of the health service is much more important to my readers than where Hugh Fitzroy is buying."

Cormac sat back in his chair and looked at Ali. "If she wants to write about it, let her away. Extra publicity for Glenwood. You can write something that benefits us for a change."

"I refuse to be your mouthpiece either," Ali said firmly.

Lisa looked at Michael. "I have to say, Hugh is a very handsome man. I was very taken with him."

"Well, now, Lisa, how about you and him together?" pushed Honey.

"Oh, Mother, stop!" said Lisa, but she was laughing, and she was still looking at Michael.

"Why not?" asked Honey. "Every shit finds its shovel."

"I think there's only room for one star in this family, Honey," commented Denise.

"Honey, that was a fantastic meal," said the elderly gentleman guest to Honey's right. "And when are we going to hear you sing to finish off a perfect meal?"

"Well, if you're very good, I might start now,"

promised Honey, touching the man's chin. "Right, everyone, into the drawing-room."

Everyone started to make a move as instructed.

"You okay?" Michael asked, stroking Ali's arm as they got up.

"Of course I am." Ali smiled at him.

As everyone sat around the drawing-room listening to Honey blasting out "You're Just Too Good To Be True", Lisa stared at Michael sitting beside Ali, stroking her arm, and she knew what she had to do.

*   *   *

Since the construction at Glenwood was completed, Cormac had ordered the moving of the site offices from there and had them moved to the last phase at The Pavilions. For his own office, he took one of the apartments that was completed and used that as an office. He was used to using prefabs that weren't particularly glamorous. But the first-floor apartment he was using as an office was extremely comfortable. He brought in Susan Haughey who did it up nice. She had the main living area as a reception area. The main bedroom was turned into Cormac's office. The smaller bedroom was left as a bedroom in case he was staying over. It suited his needs perfectly, since Michael's house was now off limits. He now had a new city-centre base to continue the party after all the pubs were shut.

That afternoon, Michael, Paul and Lisa were in his office and the topic of conversation was Heavey's Mill.

"If it ain't broken then don't fix it, that's what I say," said Lisa. "Cunningham Homes has a formula and it works a treat. High-class homes with excellent finishes. Turn the whole of Heavey's Mill into the most exclusive apartment block this city has ever seen."

"You haven't met Edel Garry," said Cormac. "I don't think that will be enough for her. All this tender business – she's looking for something else."

"I agree," said Michael. "She's not looking for just a run-of-the-mill development. She's looking for that bit extra and I haven't a fucking clue what that could be."

"Well, get your thinking caps on. You all get paid enough to come up with something," snapped Paul.

"Extra high ceilings? Appliances all included? Beautifully landscaped by award-winning gardeners?" suggested Lisa.

"That's all run-of-the-mill these days," said Cormac.

"Concierge? Swimming pool for residents?"

"Okay, it's high spec, but it still isn't going to impress Edel Garry," dismissed Cormac.

"I don't hear you coming up with any idea," Paul accused his son.

Cormac looked at his father, annoyed.

"But we're on to something here," mused Michael. "Residents' swimming pool, I like it. And the concierge. Five-star treatment . . .".

Lisa nodded her head at her brother triumphantly.

They sat in silence for a couple of minutes.

"In fact, that's it," stated Michael excitedly. "Five-star treatment. We'll put a fucking five-star hotel in there!"

"In Heavey's Mill?" Cormac looked excited.

"Exactly." Michael jumped up, and started to walk around the office excitedly. "Let's face it, what's out in the Harbour Area now? Fuck all! There isn't even a Spar shop out there. What is there to attract people out to live there? Sweet fuck all."

"But that will come in time," said Cormac.

"It will come in time, yes, but Edel Garry is trying to create a vibrant community now. If we put a five-star hotel in there and make Heavey's Mill a mixed development, the place will take off like a rocket. It will attract people to live there because they will be living beside a fabulous hotel. Edel Garry will love it because it will be bringing permanent jobs and tourism into the Harbour. She doesn't want to create a ghost town out there. I'm telling you it would work a treat."

Everyone sat in silence for a while thinking.

"He's right," said Paul. "That's exactly what we need in our tender."

"But we're losing valuable building land doing that," Cormac pointed out.

"We can get a major hotel operator in and they can pay for it. And what we're losing in space, we can make up by adding on to the price of the apartments as an extra cost for the privilege of living beside a top-class hotel."

* * *

Denise walked through the patio doors and out into the afternoon sunshine. Going over to the side of the swimming pool, she took off her bathrobe and stretched out on a sun lounger, dressed in a black swimsuit. She smoothed on some sun cream to protect her from the strong sun and settled back for an afternoon of relaxation. Perhaps there were some advantages to living out at Glenwood. Although she regularly sunbathed on the patio back at the penthouse, there was no comparison to the joy of having a swimming pool. As she lay there allowing her body to soak up the sun's heat, she felt a shadow cast over her. She opened her eyes and shaded them from the sun. She sat up abruptly, seeing that Ryan was standing over her.

"Sorry, I was ringing the doorbell, but you obviously couldn't hear back here."

Denise got up quickly and went to the table, getting her bathrobe and quickly putting it on.

"What do you want?" she asked angrily.

"I just wanted to apologise really."

"Apologise?" She was taken aback.

"Yeah . . . I had no reason to pass judgment on your marriage or your life."

"No, you hadn't," she agreed.

"I'm sorry if what I said hurt you. With the position I have with Aston, I've just got used to speaking my mind, and maybe I should think before I speak sometimes."

"Maybe you should."

"Look, maybe I am invading your territory here unintentionally. I probably haven't given enough thought to how you might feel. I think I'll resign from the committee at Forward and just find another charity to join."

"I see." She was very surprised. "I have to say I wasn't happy with you joining Forward. But you're there now."

"I know, but if it's making you feel uncomfortable I'd rather leave."

She thought for a while. "You've been an excellent contributor to Forward, and actually have breathed new life in the place. The charity is a very important part of my life, and I don't want it to suffer because of me."

"You want me to stay then?"

"It's not what I want but it's what's beneficial for the charity."

"Well, if you're sure." He turned to walk away.

"I wish I could understand what's happening in your head," she said after him.

"The hardest thing is always finding out what's happening in somebody's head," he said and walked around the corner.

40

Ali was sitting at the table in her apartment at her laptop, finishing off an article, when she heard a knock on her door. The knock broke into her concentration and she felt irritated as she went to answer it, confident it wasn't for her. These apartment blocks were so big, there was always some visitor lost.

She looked through the peephole and saw Lisa standing there. Completely thrown, she contemplated not answering it. But her curiosity got the better of her and she undid the bolt.

"Hi," said Lisa. "Are you busy?"

"Not overly so. Michael's not here, if you're looking for him."

"I wasn't . . . I was looking for you."

"I see. Well, you'd better come in then."

Lisa walked past Ali into the living-room.

"Do you want anything to drink?" asked Ali.

"No, I'm fine." Lisa turned and faced Ali.

"What's all this about, Lisa?" Ali folded her arms.

"It's about you and Michael."

Ali smiled in confusion. "What about us?"

"I want you to leave Michael, Ali," Lisa said evenly.

"What?" Ali gasped and squinted her eyes, looking both amused and confused.

"It's as simple as that . . . leave Michael."

"Well, I admire your straightforwardness, if nothing else."

"I'm not here to be a bitch, Ali. I'm not here to demand you leave him. I'm not here to threaten you –"

"Well, I guess I'm glad to hear that."

"I'm here to beg you to leave him."

Ali walked to the other side of the room.

"I'm in love with Michael, Ali."

"I'm aware of that and I'm sorry you are, because it's not reciprocated."

"I understand him, Ali. I understand him more than you ever could. I've invested years into him. You've barely been going out with him two or three months."

"Lisa, you've been friends with him for years. Michael and I have been in a relationship."

"We weren't always just friends, or didn't he tell you?"

"He's told me everything. I know you had a drunken one-night stand a long time ago."

"It meant a lot to me." Lisa looked sadly down at the ground.

"I'm sure it did, but you have to move on in life. We all do!"

"He's the only man for me. It's either him or nobody."

Ali felt very disturbed. "Lisa, you can't put limitations on yourself like that."

"Ali, look at you. You're bright, you're beautiful, you're strong, you're confident – you can get anybody you want."

"As flattering as that is, it's crap."

"You could leave Michael tomorrow and you'd have him replaced in a week – you can move on to someone new. I can't. Please leave him to me." Tears were forming in Lisa's eyes.

"I don't know what to say to you," said Ali.

"All I want is for you to go. Me and Michael were meant to be together. Does he really mean that much to you . . . honestly? Is he not just an entertainment to you? Who could be easily replaced?"

"No, he's not –"

"I need you to think very hard about it, Ali, because you're ruining my life if you continue seeing Michael. Thanks for hearing me out."

Lisa turned and left the apartment.

* * *

Denise looked over at Ryan's empty seat at the boardroom in Forward. They were halfway through their meeting and there was no sign of him. Remembering their conversation, she felt a straight desperation that he wasn't going to show up. Maybe he had thought it best after all to leave Forward.

"Excuse me, Tony," Denise interrupted. "I just wanted to follow up something on one of Ryan's suggestions he made last week – do you know if he's coming today?"

Don't tell me he's left the organisation, she pleaded quietly.

"I'm not sure where he is, Denise. He's a busy man, maybe he got held up. Anyway, as I was saying, Adidas have agreed to sponsor a charity run . . ."

Denise tuned out as Tony's voice droned on, as she concentrated on Ryan's empty chair.

* * *

Things had been falling behind in London while Ryan had turned all his attention and energy to Dublin. He took a 6 a.m. flight to Heathrow and by eight stormed into the head office at Aston, which was situated in the Docklands. He loved taking the place completely unawares, and caught a few off them off guard. He quickly went through a series of meetings with departmental heads, and had the whole place shipshape by three.

He glanced at his watch. He was due to meet Kate shortly, as Jodhi had reminded him and he was now running late. He swept out of Reception and into an awaiting taxi.

"Where to, guv?" asked the driver.

"The city. A little place called Jimmy's. You know it?"

"I'll find it." The taxi took off.

He wished Kate had picked a meeting place other than Jimmy's. When they had begun dating, they had gone into the little deli all the time. That was ten years ago, when he had been an engineer working for a large construction firm based in the city. His career was advancing at breakneck speed and everyone knew he was heading to the top. He met Kate at a Christmas party. She was the daughter of one of the directors of his firm. His wife was on a shopping trip to New York, so he had brought Kate instead. She was lovely. Porcelain skin, big innocent blue eyes, brown slightly curled hair. They had got talking and she was taken by him. She started coming up with excuses to visit his workplace, pretending she was seeing her father, and started bumping into him and they would chat. They started dating. She had worked in personnel for a bank, not far from his offices, and they met at Jimmy's after work for something to eat every evening. They were engaged within six months and married within a year. She was perfect wife material for a rising executive. She had her own connections with her father, which helped accelerate his career. They bought a lovely house in Surrey. Everything was picture-book perfect.

The taxi pulled up outside Jimmy's and Ryan paid the driver and jumped out.

He walked into the place and scanned the restaurant, spotting Kate seated at what had been their regular table. She looked up at him and waved. The big blue eyes were still there, but they had knowingness now. She still looked lovely, he thought.

He sat down opposite her.

"Two cappuccinos," he instructed the waiter.

"How are things?" he asked her.

"Good."

"How's the bank?"

"Always busy. You?" she asked in her soft English accent.

"Trying to get a big project going in Dublin."

"That's nice. It will give you an opportunity to spend some time at home."

"Yeah. It's changed a lot, hardly recognise the place sometimes."

"You'll adapt to it, Ryan. You always do."

He heard a note of weariness in her voice. Weary from him.

"Thanks for meeting me," she said.

"I'll always make time for you, Kate. Just because we aren't married any more, doesn't mean we aren't still friends."

"Don't, Ryan." She looked down at the red-and-white squares on the tablecloth.

The waiter placed two cups in front of them.

Kate looked up and smiled at Ryan. "The reason I wanted to meet you for a chat is about the house in Surrey."

"Yeah?"

"I was just thinking. It's really stupid for us to keep it still. I know you said at the time of the divorce to hold on to it for another while as it was a good investment. I just feel funny still having it, and it's not serving any purpose. I think we should just sell it and take the profits."

"Oh, I see. Is it a case of the money?" he said anxiously. "Are you short? Because if you are, I can sort you out straight away."

"No, it's not the money," she said firmly. "You know

it's not the money. It's the house. I feel I can't properly move on until we have it sold."

"I see. We had a lot of good times in that house."

"I know. And that's why I want to sell it. I don't want it as a reminder any more."

"And where will you move to?"

"Do what you did. Get an apartment in the city."

"Well, whatever you want. I just want you to be happy."

"Well, selling the house will make me happy."

They sat in silence for a while.

"You always make it sound like I'm the one to blame for the break-up. It's you who wanted the divorce," Ryan said eventually.

She looked up at him. "Yes, I wanted the divorce . . . and you still don't realise why, do you?"

He shrugged. "No."

Her porcelain skin creased in stress. "I had to separate from you just simply because of how you are acting today . . . this indifference. Okay, we'll sell the house – no big deal. When I told you I wanted a divorce, it was the very same thing – okay, whatever makes you happy, Kate."

"I did want just whatever makes you happy," he confirmed.

"But I wanted you to need me." Her face went sad. "And you never needed me. From the moment I met you, I was infatuated with you, but that was never returned. You were so consumed with rising in the world. Getting to the top, being someone. Whenever we were together, your mind was on something else – work, I don't know. I gave up trying to figure it out in the end."

He sat back. "Don't hate me, Kate." There was a pleading in his voice.

She forced a smile and willed the threatening tears away, and reaching forward touched his hand softly. "I don't hate you, Ryan. I could never hate you. Listen, let's stick to the point. Are we in agreement to sell the house in Surrey?"

"As I said, if that's what you want."

"Good, I'll contact Foxtons in the morning then. I'd better get back to work." She glanced at her watch. "I'll miss an appointment if I don't. You were half an hour late," she accused him.

He sat forward and looked anxious. "Oh, I'm sorry. I got delayed and –"

She smiled broadly. "That's all right, Ryan. I'm used to it." She stood up, bent over and kissed his forehead.

He watched her step out of the restaurant into the bustling street.

* * *

Ryan was sitting at his desk in his London office which offered a great view of the City Docklands under the reddening evening sky. He looked out at the view pensively.

Jodhi knocked on his door and entered.

"I just need your signature on these documents. I'll leave them on your desk for you."

"Thanks," he said.

"Everything went okay today . . . with Kate?" she asked.

"I guess so. She wants to sell the house."

"Right. How was she?"

"Seemed all right. She's lovely, isn't she?"

Jodhi smiled. "Yes, she is."

"Why couldn't I make it work then?"

"She wasn't for you . . . and she knew it."

"I wish she had been. Life would have been so much simpler if she had been. I met her two years after Denise. In that two years I had changed so much. I was so destroyed when I returned and found that Denise had gone off without as much as an explanation. You know if I had never met Denise and just met Kate, we'd probably be happily living in Surrey. Have a kid or two by now."

"But you did meet Denise first," said Jodhi.

"I know."

41

Ali walked into her work building, deep in thought. Lisa's visit had completely thrown and upset her. She could take Lisa the bully, Lisa the spoilt brat, Lisa the drunk, Lisa the self-obsessed; she wasn't sure she could take Lisa the victim. It was a fairly convincing show she had put on in her apartment. As a journalist, Ali had always taken the side of the victim, and it was hard now not to feel sorry for Lisa when the full extent of her pain over Michael was laid bare to her.

As she walked towards her office, she wasn't sure if she was becoming paranoid, but people seemed to be giving her funny looks.

She went into her office and sat down. Someone had left a copy of *The Independent* on her desk. She picked up the scrawled note left on it, which read: *'I told you so – Barry.'*

She picked up the paper and was greeted with a photo of herself and Michael having dinner in a restaurant. They looked very intimate. The heading read: *'Farrell & O'Mara – They Meet Their Match.'* She quickly read the column which read: *"Auctioneer Extraordinaire Michael Farrell has been secretly dating journalist Ali O'Mara, The Independent can reveal today. The relationship has been an open secret in property and media circles for some time. Farrell, who is notorious for his colourful marketing campaigns in selling new developments, has raised many eyebrows with his new liaison, as O'Mara has been a leading critic of the manipulation of the property boom by ruthless developers and their estate agents. The pair met when O'Mara was buying her apartment from Farrell's main client, Cunningham Homes. O'Mara has openly and viciously criticised Farrell in numerous articles over the years, which makes their relationship all the more surprising.'*

* * *

Denise looked at Ryan's empty seat in the boardroom during the next meeting and was filled with anxiety. She had been watching his house and there had been no sign of him coming or going over the past days. She burned with curiosity about where he was. And nobody on the committee seemed to know either. She had this terrible feeling he wasn't going to come back to the charity. And that gave her a panicked feeling, when she knew she should be relieved. As she headed out the M50 back to Glenwood, she wondered had Ryan been saying goodbye to her when he came into their back garden. He had been talking about leaving Forward and staying out of her way. Maybe he had decided to do it after all. Maybe he would just disappear without another word. She wondered what it would be like if she didn't see him again. It made her feel very lost. He had come storming into her life and confused her completely and turned everything upside down. Then just to leave without an explanation, without giving her a reason, as she had done to him all those years ago! What goes around comes around, as they say. Maybe that had been his plan all along, to somehow pay her back. She was caught in the thick of rush hour and there seemed to be major road works, which basically meant her car was crawling along and the journey home was taking forever in the heat. She cursed herself for not leaving town earlier to avoid all this traffic mayhem. She knew Cormac had a meeting that evening with an architect about Heavey's Mill, and he had said he would be leaving home at eight, so she had wanted to cook them an early meal. Too late for that now. Eventually she reached Glenwood and pressed her code into the pad at the gates.

She drove into the estate and into their driveway. She was tired and exhausted from the traffic as she let herself in the front door.

"Cormac?' she called.

"In the kitchen," he answered.

"The traffic was atrocious, got caught up for a couple of hours." She walked into the kitchen and saw Cormac seated at the table, eating a steak dinner.

"I cooked dinner myself," he explained.

"Well, there's a surprise! You cook so rarely, I thought you had forgotten how."

"When you weren't home by six, I thought there wasn't

much point in waiting for you much longer." She looked at his plate. "That actually looks lovely. Maybe I should be late home more often and let you do more cooking." She walked over to the pan and cooking pots on the cooker. "I'm actually starving. I missed lunch." She took a plate and opened the pots. Then stared down at them seeing they were empty.

She turned around and looked at him.

"Where's mine?"

"You're what?"

"My food, of course."

He shrugged. "I didn't cook you any."

She stared at him in disbelief. "You mean to tell me that the first time you've cooked anything in two years you didn't bother making anything for me, even though you knew I was coming home?"

He shrugged again. "I didn't know you were coming home. I didn't know you'd be hungry." He finished off his dinner.

"Every night you come home, I never know what time to expect you. Often you've eaten out anyway, but I always cook for you and have it ready for you, even if it's burned black in the oven. I still have the good manners and the decency to cook for you when I'm cooking for myself."

"If you wanted me to cook for you, you should have rung me and asked me to."

"You are so selfish, it's unbelievable." She shook her head slowly.

"I don't know what the big deal is. Order a fucking

Chinese or something. I have a little more important things going on in my life than arguing about who cooked what for who. For fuck's sake, you're not back in the flats now with all those people screaming and fighting about petty little things to make their lives more interesting. You'll be fighting over who's doing the washing-up next!"

Denise blinked back tears. Her background was off limits. No matter how vicious their arguments got, that was never mentioned. It was something she had always admired Cormac for.

"This isn't about the dinner." She raised her voice. "This is about you never thinking about anyone else but yourself."

"And you're so respectful to me, are you? Did you ever listen to the way you speak to me?" He rose up from the table. "Who the hell would you be if I hadn't married you? You were sitting on Reception, and that was a major step up from where you started off."

"Oh huh!" Denise laughed cynically "It's all coming out in the wash tonight, isn't it? You must have been dying to say that for years."

Cormac took up his plate. "You might have the rest of Dublin fooled with your airs and graces, but not me. Just because you're all over the social pages." Walking over to the sink, he flung the plate into it.

"I can't believe this! You don't object to my profile when it's used to help you sell your developments!"

"Big fucking deal. So you smile for a couple of cameras when we open a showhouse? Cunningham Homes was here long before you arrived, and it will be here long after you're gone."

"I'm going to keep that in mind next time you ask me to do a photo shoot. Next time you want me to smooch some contact or client – because you're completely unable to charm anyone yourself."

He turned and looked at her angrily. "Careful what you say."

"Well, if it's all coming out in the wash tonight, I've a few things I want to air as well. You talk about my background. I wonder where you'd be if you hadn't been born a Cunningham. Would you have been able to make it in the world yourself without it all being set up for you already?"

"You know how much Cunningham Homes profits have gone up since I took over."

"I also know this country has witnessed the biggest building boom ever since you took over! You'd want to be a buffoon not to have got profits up. You think just because you can roar and shout at people that makes you a good businessman. But your social skills are fairly limited to shouting and being demanding. That's what you hate: you need me, more than I'll ever need you."

"Darling, I'd have you replaced in the morning, and I wouldn't think twice about it. Girls like you are two a penny."

"Why don't you head off to the Ice Bar and drink the night away with your buddies and your whores? That's about as good as your social skills can go."

They stared at each other, both consumed with rage. Their faces red, their eyes brimming with tears of anger.

"What will it cost me to get you out of my fucking life?" he demanded.

"I will bring you down."

They continued their staring match until Cormac turned and stormed into the lounge. She heard the front door slam, and his car tear out of the driveway and screech off.

*   *   *

It was only when she knew he was safely gone that she allowed herself a good cry. She rarely cried. It wasn't in her nature to do so. She didn't believe in letting life get you down. You had what you were given and you could either wallow in self-pity, or try your very best to have the best life for yourself. But that night she let the tears flow freely and loudly as she lay out on their bed. Once she started crying she found it hard to stop. The argument had been so vicious, so horrible. It was the worst they had ever had, each dragging out the very things they knew would hurt the other the most. She sat up, and wiped away the tears with her hands. She was sick of it. Tired and sick of this battleground of a marriage they lived in. His words were ringing in her ears: "How much will it cost to get you out of my fucking life?" She quickly got up and went into her dressing-room. She parted the rails of clothes and reaching into the back, she pulled out a black sequined dress.

*   *   *

Two hours later, Denise was on a podium at Stevie's

twirling around to the loud music. She wasn't going to stay in all night crying and feeling sorry for herself. It had never been her style and, as she lost herself in the atmosphere at Stevie's, her argument with Cormac drifted to the back of her mind. As the song came to an end, she walked down the steps from the podium and waded through the crowd on the dance floor, feeling energised. She went to the bar and pushed to the front of the queue. She gave in her order and as she waited for her drink, she glanced around the bar.

And saw Ryan sitting at the end of the bar.

She was shocked to see him and excited at the same time. She took her drink and walked down to him.

"Where have you been all my life?" she asked.

Ryan looked up from his drink and smiled. "And why didn't you stay there?"

"We were wondering if you would ever show up at the charity again," she said.

"I was wondering that myself."

"I didn't see you at Glenwood either. Where have you been?"

"I had to go over to London to sort some things out."

"And what are you doing here tonight."

"It's a place you can lose yourself in, isn't it?"

"Yes, it is."

"Is everything all right? You look different."

"Ryan, I'm standing here in a Lycra mini-dress that cost ten euros from Top Shop, seven-inch stilettos and more fake diamonds than a gypsy's curtain – of course I look different!"

Ryan laughed. "True. But besides all that . . . you've been crying."

"I'm here to have a good time and forget about life, not to drag out problems. What are you here for?"

"The same thing."

"Then shut up and let's enjoy ourselves. What are you drinking?"

"A Bacardi and Coke."

It was just what Denise needed. She completely forgot about the argument with Cormac. She wanted to dance and forced a reluctant Ryan up on the dance floor. After a while, he seemed to enjoy it as much as she as they danced to Gnarls Barclay's "Crazy". After every few drinks, they escaped to the bar, where they would knock back a drink before returning to the dance floor.

"How can you keep going? I'm exhausted!" shouted Ryan.

"You're getting old, Ryan. Just shut up and enjoy the music."

"It's okay for you. You can sleep on in the morning. Some of us have to work."

"You aren't getting any sympathy from me."

"As if I ever expected any from you!"

"Oh, shut up and keep dancing!"

* * *

"We can share a taxi," said Ryan as the night drew to a close.

"No, it's okay, I'll get my own."

"Denise, that's ridiculous. We live two doors down from each other."

"I'm not risking being seen arriving home with you, Ryan. Besides, my car is parked in town."

"So?"

"So I have to go and collect it."

"Leave it there till tomorrow. It's stupid to go all the way into town only to go out again. And you've been drinking besides. You'll get yourself arrested. Just get a taxi straight from here. It will take half the time."

"No," Denise snapped. "I have my routine so just leave me with it, okay?"

"I can't understand your life at all."

"Well, some of your behaviour isn't exactly normal either."

"What exactly?"

"You still haven't explained what you're doing here. In Dublin. At Forward, at Glenwood, at Stevie's and now from what I hear at Heavey's Mill as well."

"Heavey's Mill is a prime piece of real estate."

"Which my husband desperately wants and that is common knowledge."

He looked at her for a while. "Can I meet you tomorrow evening?"

"I don't know if it's appropriate for me to be seen out with you."

"You're here with me tonight."

"I'm hardly going to meet anyone I know here, am I?"

"You're frightened of what people will think?"

"Someone in my position, with my husband's family

reputation, has to be careful how she conducts herself in public."

"You sure weren't being careful swinging around that pole on the dance floor."

"As I said, I'd never bump into anyone I know here."

"You bumped into me."

"Which is no coincidence?"

"Meet me tomorrow for a chat. Look, we're both on the same charity committee – of course, we have to meet up to talk about projects."

Denise thought for a moment. "Okay. Ocean Bar at eight."

42

Denise had spent the day thinking and relaxing. By the time she got home the previous night, she was exhausted and had fallen into a troubled sleep. Cormac hadn't arrived home, and by the time she woke at eleven the next morning, she realised he hadn't bothered coming home. A further indication of how serious this argument was compared to the others. As she sat in her dressing-gown in the afternoon, looking out at the sun twinkling on the water, she felt a strange sense of unreality. They should be used to shouting at each other at this stage. And maybe that was the problem. They were so used to shouting at each other they didn't know when to stop. She looked at her watch. She had arranged to meet Ryan at eight, and she was looking forward to it.

* * *

She arrived into The Westin early, went down to the bar

and ordered herself a glass of wine. She still hadn't heard from Cormac and hell would freeze over before she picked up the phone first.

Ryan arrived in on the dot and waved over to her. He approached her smiling.

"How do you feel today?" she enquired.

"I had a meeting at eight this morning and so I've been feeling pretty tired. A glass of red, Chilean," he ordered from the passing waitress.

Denise sat back and smiled at him.

"Something funny?"

"I remember a time you only drank Harp. Hardly knew what wine was, let alone what country it originated from."

"I've moved on."

She nodded. "Yes, you have. Sometimes, when I look at you at the meetings, I wonder if you're the same person at all."

"Ah, I haven't changed that much."

"True . . . sometimes you say or do something, and I go right back fourteen years."

"Working at the architects' office – you on reception, me tied to an office desk."

"Me in my tiny little flat . . . you in your house-share with your college crew."

"Having lunch nearly every day."

"In a bar on your insistence."

"Going out at night."

"To a bar at your insistence."

"I suppose I seemed pretty uncouth to you at the time."

"No . . . you were fun . . . great fun." She nodded. "You were a really good friend. I felt I could trust you with everything."

"You could have trusted me with anything. I'd have done anything for you."

Nancy Sinatra's 'Bang, Bang, You Shot Me Down,' was playing in the background.

"I know that. I have apologised for hurting you."

He looked at her and smiled. "A quick apology in a nightclub?"

"It was a long time ago. It was the best I could do. I never promised you anything. In fact, I warned you over and over again not to get involved with me. I warned you we weren't suited."

He raised his glass "Yes, your honesty was never in question. I just didn't believe you when you said it. But you meant every word."

"I meant every word. Where I come from, you don't fuck up chances. I knew what I wanted and I wasn't going to settle for anything less."

He raised an eyebrow. "And I was less, was I?"

"Of course not. That came out all wrong. You were a great guy, just not for me."

"Well, at least you got everything you wanted in the end."

"Yes, I did." She sipped her wine. "And well done to you. You've done really well. I'm really impressed."

They sat in silence for a few minutes.

"What's happened?" he asked.

"Happened?"

"I could always read you like a book. Something's happened."

"Everything's fine."

"I'm a friend, you know. You can tell me anything. You just said so."

She thought for a minute. She had loads of friends, but nobody she ever trusted to tell things about herself to. It had been a trait all her life. The one exception had been Ryan years ago.

"It's nothing really – just an argument with Cormac."

"That's pretty normal for a marriage."

"This was pretty bad. Cormac is everything I ever wanted in a husband. All my married life, I had to nearly pinch myself to make sure that I realised how lucky I was. It's just lately . . ."

"What was it about?" Ryan probed.

"He didn't cook me dinner." She looked angry.

"I . . . see," Ryan said slowly, as if trying to understand.

"I know it sounds ridiculous. Look, nobody understands what goes on in a relationship apart from the two people in it, so it's impossible to explain to you."

"I want to try to understand."

She sighed and sat back. "Myself and Cormac have always fought like cat and dog, and I can handle it. I'm nobody's victim. It's just lately, I want more. My marriage doesn't feel right to me. And it used to."

"Are you unhappy?"

"I'm not unhappy, because I realise how fortunate I am. I'm just not satisfied any more . . . I hate him." She shocked herself with her own words. She wasn't sure where the words came from, or how long she had been thinking them. Or why she said them.

"Oh!" Ryan looked shocked as well.

"I'm sorry. I shouldn't have said that," Denise said quickly. "I don't want you to have to hear something like that."

"Look, I don't care what you say about him. He means nothing to me. But I do care a lot that I'm hearing you say that, because your happiness is important to me."

She looked at him, perplexed. "Why would you care how I feel? Especially considering how I treated you years ago?"

They sat in silence for a long while. Ryan felt overwhelmed with anxiety. He had rehearsed the lines in his mind hundreds of times. But now that he had the opportunity to say them, it was almost impossible to get them out. The bar was nearly empty apart from them, in the dimmed lighting. Sting's version of "The Windmills Of Your Mind" was playing. Say it – he shouted at himself. It's now or never – say it!

Ryan placed his hands on the table and, looking down at them, spoke slowly. "I want you to come and live with me . . . I want you to leave Cormac . . . and come and make a new life with me."

He looked up from his hands on the table at her.

Her eyes widened. She let his words sink in as she searched his face for something – she wasn't even sure what.

"Well . . . eh . . . you're very brave to say that."

"I know. But I mean every word. I've been wanting to

say that for years. I feel there is a connection between us. Nobody makes sense for me, but you."

"I'm expecting you to turn around and say this is a practical joke or something."

"I've never been more serious about anything in my life . . . I never got over you; I never could. I wondered about you for years. One day I was home visiting the family and I picked up some magazine in the airport and there you were photographed at some function with your husband, Cormac Cunningham. I couldn't believe it. And when I saw you, I knew I had never got over you and I couldn't stop thinking about you. Of course, I knew who Cormac was, him being in the same industry. I did some research and found out all about you – I found out about your work at Forward."

"And what about Stevie's? How did you find out about Stevie's?"

"I followed you around for a couple of days . . . I'm sorry. It was despicable of me, and I know that. But when you walked out on me all those years ago, what did you think happened to me? Did you ever think how that affected me?"

"Of course, I did. But I thought it was the best way to do it. The least messy and complicated."

"I had my whole life mapped out with you."

"Those weren't my plans."

"I know, but when I was in Africa, all I thought about was you. And then when I got back and found out you'd gone off with some rich fella, unable to contact you I fell apart . . . I literally didn't know what to say or do. I stopped functioning almost. And then I went to London and slowly started rebuilding my life . . . a bit wiser, harder. And all the time, I wanted you. So, I'm sorry that I followed you around, but I couldn't believe I had found you and I wanted to know everything about you." He reached over and touched her arm and pulled a face. "I guess I love you."

"Well . . . I don't know what to say . . . but I wanted you to say it . . . but, Ryan, you really don't know me any more. You're thinking of that girl back then. And I've changed so much, much more than yourself. I've become spoilt and used to my luxuries and I'm sarcastic and uncompromising. You only have to see my marriage with Cormac to realise that. We're at each other's throats all the time. I've become complicated. Twelve years of marriage to Cormac and the Cunninghams will do that to you. I mean, you know about my life – one minute in the social pages, the next swinging around a pole. Is that normal?"

"What's normal? I had the perfect marriage to the perfect girl and I didn't want it. Can you explain that to me?"

"But what makes you sure you want me?"

"I just am."

"But what if it didn't work out?"

"There are no certainties in this life . . . but I would do everything in my power to make sure it does work." Denise looked down at her watch and saw it was nearly eleven.

"There're a lot of things in my life that have come back to hit me recently. Where I come from, how I even came about, my upbringing. I didn't care or think about them before; I was just too happy to be away from it all and enjoying my new life. But maybe you can't escape things forever, maybe they do come back to you . . . it's making me wonder a lot about my life. I'm not the self-assured girl you think I am."

"But there's that connection, isn't there?"

"Yes, there is."

"I know you, Denise. I always have. As I look at you now, I know you. Does Cormac?"

"Sometimes I feel he doesn't know me at all . . . I don't know what to say, Ryan. There's an awful lot here for me to think about." She looked at her watch again. "I need to get home." She reached behind her, and put on her coat. He finished his glass and went to stand up. They walked in silence through the lobby and out onto the night street.

They headed down towards the taxi rank.

"I'm not the girl I was, Ryan."

"I know what I want and I want you."

They reached the first taxi in the queue.

"As I said, I need to think about this a lot. So where do we leave this?" she asked.

"What about if I phone you during the week?"

"Okay." She scribbled down her number and gave it to him. Then, "Aren't you going to open the taxi door for me?" she asked, grinning.

"Is that part of you being spoilt and demanding?" he laughed.

"It sure is."

"Oh, sounds like my life is going to be a drag." He

reached forward, opened the door, and she sat in. "I'll phone you," he said as he closed the door.

He watched the taxi driving away.

*   *   *

Ryan closed the door of his house after him and leaned against the door-frame.

"How did it go?" Jodhi asked from the living-room.

He rubbed his eyes and walked through the double door to her.

She looked up from the company accounts she was reading, and removed her reading glasses. He looks exhausted, she thought, as he staggered over and sat down.

"Well . . . I told her."

She closed over her reading and sat forward. "And?"

"I said it all. Said it as I had planned it over the years."

"And what did she say? How did she react?"

"She . . . I don't know . . . well, she didn't laugh out loud, slap me across the face or storm out . . . she reacted calmly . . ."

"Which is a good sign?"

"Which is how I imagined she'd act. She said she needs to think about it. Well, I never expected her to fall into my arms and declare undying love."

43

Ali felt incredibly exposed after the photo of her and Michael having dinner was published in the paper. That kind of thing didn't happen to people like her. It happened to celebrities and models and rock stars, but not to journalists. Why would people even be interested in who she was dating? She knew they wouldn't give a damn usually, but it was just because it was a flamboyant and well-known figure like Michael. It was the irony of the whole situation that people were interested in. She hated it all. She hardly came out of her office all day, and when she did she felt she was been stared at. Michael had been away at a conference that night and when she spoke to him on the phone, he just said they'd talk about it when he was home. That night she had gone home to her apartment, locked the door and drawn the curtains as if she could shut out the world.

Her life had been invaded by that article. She felt incredibly strange. She had built her career on exposing people and commenting on them, and now she was realising what that had felt like for them.

The next day she was out doing interviews for most of the day, and she went to Michael's in the evening, waiting for him to return from Galway.

Hearing the key in the lock, she felt relieved he was back and when she saw him come up the stairs and into the lounge, his cheery smiling face was a relief for her and she went to him and held him tight.

"Hey? What's all this?" he asked, rubbing her back.

"I just feel terribly vulnerable after that photo of us appeared in the paper."

"You vulnerable? Nah . . . What's the problem? We were photographed having dinner, big deal? It's not quite the same as some sex video on the internet of us, is it?"

She managed to laugh. "You're always so upbeat. But doesn't it bother you?"

"The press has been writing things about me since I launched my first, and if I can say excellent, marketing campaign. Bugger them, I don't care."

"I suppose if you look at it like that . . ."

"Come on. Are you trying to tell me that the great Ali O'Mara is going to let this get her down? I don't think so."

* * *

Michael had spent the whole night giving her a pep talk, and she got swept away with his cavalier attitude. What business was it of people?

A work colleague was leaving work the next day, and

was having leaving drinks at O'Neill's in Suffolk Street. She was contemplating not going, but then she realised that would be stupid.

She was late finishing an article and walked through the still sunny evening streets to the pub. She pushed open the doors, and made her way through the packed bar. The newspaper staff had taken over a large section of the pub, and by the look of them they were already well oiled. As she walked through them, she felt their stares and their whispers. She went over to Barry and a few other friends and ordered a round of drinks.

Nobody in the circle was bringing up the photo and Ali was relieved at that. But as the night progressed, she felt it was hanging over them all awkwardly and she wished somebody would mention the damned thing.

She made her way to the ladies', went into a cubicle, took out her mobile and rang Michael.

"Everything all right?" he asked.

"Yeah, it's fine – and thanks for all your support last night."

"Don't mention it. See you later."

She closed over her phone and was about to come out of the cubicle when she heard two women's voices. She recognised them as two work colleagues, Penny and Kitty.

"What do you make of her?" asked Penny.

"She has a nerve, I'll say that for her. Only she could make a career out of slagging someone and then end up riding them!"

"To be honest, I never really fell for that 'woman of the people' routine she does. Well, it's just as well he has money, because it's only a matter of time before her career is over."

"Well, somebody who becomes the news can never be taken seriously enough to report the news any more, can they?"

"No way. Well, I wouldn't feel sorry for her. She's sold out, plain and simple. Sold out on everything she pretended to believe in for an easy and cushy life with your man."

"I hear she's over at the Cunninghams' every Sunday."

"I heard she's about to start writing articles about how poor developers and auctioneers are misunderstood."

"Well, I heard she's about to join the Forward committee with Denise Cunningham."

"I heard she's leaving journalism and going to work for the Cunninghams full-time as their Public Relations Manager."

There was a pause, then the two women said in unison: "Sold Out!"

* * *

Ali had developed a pattern of being unable to sleep, tossing and turning, everything spinning through her mind: what her colleagues and people thought of her; Lisa coming by her apartment and pleading for her to leave Michael. This relationship was causing so much trouble, Part of her wished she had never met Michael. But then when she saw him soundly sleeping through her insomnia, she felt like she couldn't be without him now.

*   *   *

As Michael's car pulled into the Cunninghams' driveway, she felt her stomach tightening.

"Michael?"

"Ah, ha!" He concentrated on parking beside a Bentley.

"We're not going to come here every single Sunday, are we?"

"No . . . once you're part of the gang, and you're all comfortable with each other, we'll skip every second Sunday. How about that?"

"That would be nice to spend time together – just the two of us."

She hadn't bothered discussing her worries with Michael. She had given him such a hard time when they started seeing each other that she was amazed he had stuck around. If somebody had been as abusive to her, she would have told them to sling their hook. But he had put up with all her criticism and probing, so the least she could do was sit through dinner with his friends.

They climbed the steps up to the front door and rang the doorbell. Honey swung the door open.

"Hi there," she said and looking up at the bright sun said, "Well, at least you brought the weather with you, if nothing else. Come on in. Got your favourite for lunch today, Michael – duck."

"That's nice – who's over for dinner?"

"I've got Father Don O'Sullivan, back from Boston. I've got the Kellehers," she lowered her voice, "who just sold their company and got millions. We've got Senator Keane and, of course, Tommy Fagan, who my heart goes out to – he's having such a hard time of it at the moment."

Because he's up on charges at one of the tribunals, thought Ali.

"I just had to throw his name into the pot today and invite him over," said Honey.

Ali's heart sank with each name being mentioned, all of them were people she had crossed paths unpleasantly with in the past.

* * *

Denise saw Michael and Ali enter the lounge with Honey and smiled at them, before she drifted back into her thoughts. Ryan's announcement had taken her so much by surprise that she wondered sometimes had it happened at all. Maybe she had dreamed the whole thing up. All kinds of emotion were raging through her from terror to excitement, and every other emotion in between. She didn't know what to do. Cormac had come home the next evening, and they ignored each other. The next day, he went into work, even though it was Saturday and hadn't come home till four in the morning. Then on Sunday, they had got ready without saying a word to each other and come over to the Cunninghams which was the normal ritual. She had to meet Ryan again. Was he joking her? Was he trying to get one back at her after what she had done to him all those years ago? She had so many questions she needed answering before she could think about this further.

* * *

"I didn't realise you were in a relationship, Michael. How long have you two being seeing each other?" asked Father Don, when they were all seated at the table.

"About three months,' said Michael, smiling at Lisa

"Every shit finds its shovel," said Honey who was going around the table giving everyone more helpings. "More spuds?" she asked Ali.

"Oh, no thanks, I've more than enough –" Ali objected, as Honey scooped out a huge potato from the central dish with a ladle and plonked it in the centre of Ali's plate, causing the gravy to splash out over Ali's white top.

"Oh, sorry, darling!" said Honey, grabbing a napkin and starting to mop away the splashes.

Ali managed to hide her annoyance. "It's all right. It doesn't matter –"

"Oh no!" said Honey, stopping wiping and looking at the top. "I think I've ground it in now!"

Ali looked down at her ruined top and felt herself go red.

"Not to worry," said Honey, walking back to her chair at the head of the table. "It doesn't look like it cost much."

"Do you want me to run home and get you clean clothes?" offered Michael, concerned.

"No, it really doesn't matter," Ali insisted.

"This dinner is delicious, Honey," complimented Tommy Fagan.

"Isn't it? I got the recipe from Bridie Hogan – you

know, that friend of mine that had all that bulimia nonsense going on." Honey paused and thought for a second. "There's an irony in there somewhere, getting a recipe from someone with an eating disorder." Honey started to laugh.

Ali looked down at her in disgust, struggling to keep her anger under control.

"Any more word of Hugh Fitzroy?" Paul asked Lisa.

"Yeah, he's due to sign contracts next week. I met him during the week, and drove him around showing him new places that are opened. He's been in California for a while, so he's a bit out of touch at home."

Ali had been nervous of Lisa all day because of their encounter. Lisa had been unusually quiet and had a look of sorrow about her, accentuating Ali's guilt.

"He was saying that his management insists he keeps his weight down and goes to the gym all the time so he doesn't become fat and unemployable. He said all he wanted to do was go to pubs and drink beer and eat burger and chips."

"Of course, Michael and Ali will be joining Hugh Fitzroy now, with them having to escape the paparazzi and the publicity glare," Cormac said, looking amused.

Ali had wondered how long it would take for one of them to mention the photo.

"Yeah, how's about that?" asked Honey. "What does it feel like to be a celebrity couple?"

"A bit embarrassing!" said Michael.

"And what do all your media friends think about you dating Michael?" asked Honey.

"They actually had the good manners not to mention it. I wish I could say the same for everyone else," Ali said.

"I tell you what, it's been a great week for Cunningham Homes," said Cormac, smiling wickedly. "So many people were phoning me and congratulating me, saying what a coup to have Ali O'Mara behind us. After all the criticism we had from you, it really turned everything on its head that you're now seeing one of us. What better endorsement could we have for a Cunningham Home?"

"Enquiries were up ten per cent at the agency," said Lisa dryly.

"You know we've been approaching the press all wrongly. In future if someone writes something about us, we won't sue them. We'll just shag them!" Cormac roared with the laughter.

"Very funny!" commented Michael, with a cynical smile on his face. But he was unaware of the increasing anger creeping across Ali's face.

"You know, now that the photographers will be following you around and snapping at you, you're going to have to tidy up your image, Ali," said Honey. "You'll have to watch the old weight – you're at the age now where everything can go pear-shaped – literally. And you need to sex up the old wardrobe a bit, throw away those dowdy clothes you wear and invest in something a bit glamorous. Let Denise take you around to a few shops and take a leaf out of her book. She'll show you how to put on a bit of lippy."

Ali threw her fork down on her plate, causing everyone to look at her in surprise.

"You really think you're all so clever and funny, don't you?" Ali's voice was harsh and loud.

"Don't think it, darling. Know it," said Cormac.

Ali got to her feet. "I've had enough of all of you and your misplaced superiority. Why don't you all take a good look at yourselves, before you start commenting on others!"

"She can dish it, but she can't take it," said Lisa.

"You know, I have really made an effort with you people. I've really tried my best for Michael's sake. But I just can't take you anymore. Just because you have money you think it gives you the right to be rude and offensive, and your money just does not impress me enough for me to want to be around you lot. I've been compromising myself being in your company, and I'm ashamed I've done that. I don't want to turn into Denise, willing to put up with all this crap."

"How dare you come to our dinner table and insult us!" said Honey.

"I can because I'm speaking the truth."

"You're filth, O'Mara, pure filth!" spat Honey.

Ali turned and looked at Michael's face, full of concern, "I'm sorry, Michael. I really tried, but I can't do this any more." She looked at Lisa's face that had changed from sad to smug. "You got what you wanted. I'm outta here." She stormed away from the table and slammed the front door after her.

She walked quickly past the designer cars in the Cunninghams' driveway and out the gateway and quickly down the tree-lined avenue. She wanted to cry, but was too angry to allow herself to.

"Ali!" shouted Michael, as he raced after her. "Ali, will you stop and talk to me!"

He caught up with her and grabbed her arm, swinging her around.

"Michael, just leave me alone, and go back to your friends."

"I don't want to. I want to talk to you."

"There's nothing to talk about, Michael. We're from two different worlds, and neither of our worlds will accept the other. I'm not willing to compromise myself any more. We were mad to ever think this would work."

"But it is working. We get on great, don't we?"

"We do, yes, but that's not enough. I can't stand those people."

"I'm sorry, I shouldn't have tried to force it. It's a very volatile environment, where everyone slags each other off. It's a bit tough at the beginning, but then you get used to it and just slag them back."

"That's not slagging, Michael. That's pure rudeness and insults, and I'm not taking it any more."

"And you shouldn't have to. They did go way over the top today, and I'm sorry . . . I'm sorry you had to listen to them. I won't force you to be in their company again. Come on home and just talk to me about it."

She looked at him and looked down at the pavement.

"Your life would be so much simpler if I just walked away. My life would be so much simpler."

"And when did Ali O'Mara ever choose the simple option?" He smiled crookedly at her.

She sighed and turned and started walking slowly. He started walking beside her and put his arm around her.

* * *

"She did what?" shouted Michael.

"Lisa begged me not to continue seeing you," confirmed Ali.

"And what did you say to her?"

"I didn't have the opportunity to say anything. She just stood in my apartment, practically crying, saying that she and you were meant to be together and I should just leave you alone and get on with my life."

"And why didn't you tell me this before?"

"Because I wasn't sure what to do. She put forward a very convincing case. I don't like to ruin people's lives. She made me feel very guilty about seeing you. I don't know. I felt all my previous relationships ended because I was dogmatic. I've been looking at my life and here I was, more awards than I knew what to do with, highly respected, but suddenly not sure where I was going any more. And then I met you, so bright and breezy and carefree . . . and I thought maybe I'm taking everything too seriously, maybe I need to lighten up. I tried to be subdued, tried not to be so in control and less serious. But I can't, Michael. I can only be myself."

Michael sat down beside her and hugged her. "I don't want you to be any one else but you. I'm sorry if I ever gave you the impression otherwise. I just wanted you to accept me for who I was as well . . . so I wanted you to be a part of my whole life. The Cunninghams mean a lot to me, but not nearly as much as you. And I don't want to put you into any situation where you're not comfortable. The way I look at it, our relationship is nobody's business but ours, and that includes the Cunninghams, your work colleagues, and the whole country."

*   *   *

Cormac and Denise had been sitting in silence as he drove them back to Glenwood.

"Well, it looks like we've seen the last of O'Mara," he eventually said.

It was the first time they had spoken since their row.

Denise continued to look out the passenger window as she spoke. "You didn't all have to be so rude to her."

"Fuck her. We don't want her around."

"Michael is a good friend of ours – we should respect what makes him happy."

Ali's outburst had been on Denise's mind. Her passion as she defended herself.

But most of all her remark "I don't want to turn into Denise". It wasn't something Denise had needed to hear.

44

Michael drove to the office, feeling increasingly annoyed. The Cunninghams had gone way over the top yesterday, and he felt they showed him a lack of respect by being rude to Ali.

Parking the car, he walked the short distance to work. Ali meant a lot to him. Sure he had had a lot of different relationships, but when he met Ali he knew she was the one for him. With his other relationships, he had always felt the need to almost hide them from the Cunninghams, because of Lisa's feelings for him. But for her to go over to Ali's and interfere like that was unbelievable.

"Will you ask Lisa to come into my office when she gets in," he instructed Reception.

At his desk, he looked through his diary. He was due to meet with Cormac at their architects' at twelve to start the ball rolling on their proposal for Heavey's Mill. The Cunninghams would have to realise that he wasn't their property; he wasn't a second act in their lives. He was his own man and he could do whatever he wanted.

* * *

Lisa came into Reception smiling. She was feeling good. It hadn't been that hard to get rid of O'Mara after all. Just press the right buttons and off she went. In a few weeks' time, Michael would be thanking her for getting rid of her.

"Any messages?" Lisa asked breezily.

The receptionist handed Lisa her message sheet. "And Michael asked for you to pop into his office."

"Okay." She nodded and she headed to Michael's office. Get rid of that smile, she told herself. You don't want to look triumphant.

"Hi, Michael!"

Michael looked up. "Hi."

"Michael, I just want to say that I'm really sorry about what happened yesterday. I think you have to agree that we all went out of our way to include Ali as best we could, inviting her around to the house all the time and just treating her like one of our own. Speaking to her like an old friend. But, you know, I guess she just had her mind set not to fit in."

"Don't bullshit me, Lisa. You all have been working overtime to get rid of Ali. Treating someone with the familiarity of an old friend is one thing, being downright insulting is another. I'm really pissed off with everybody after yesterday. You had no right to talk to my partner like that."

Lisa was upset. "Well, that's the thanks we get for

opening up the hospitality of our home to that stupid cow!"

"Hospitality like that we can do without."

"You'll be thanking us in a few weeks that she's gone."

"She's not gone anywhere. We're still very much together. In fact more so."

Lisa looked angry.

"And also she told me about your little stunt, calling around to her house and playing the victim. Lisa, I've tried to let you down softly over the years and be considerate to your feelings. But the message isn't getting through to you. Nothing is ever going to happen between us. We're friends, that's all, and with your antics you're now putting that friendship very much at risk."

Each word was like a slap across the face to Lisa. She quickly got up and left the office. Michael felt bad saying what he had said. But he had no option. Sure, the Cunninghams had been like family to him over the years, but it was always on their terms. He wasn't their property and it was time he asserted that.

Michael arrived deliberately late to the meeting with the architects. He didn't want to have to talk to Cormac beforehand.

"So what we're looking for is the very highest spec of apartments for Heavey's Mill," Cormac explained. "We really want to push the boat out with this development. The very best of everything has to go in, under-floor heating, state-of-the-art kitchens, plasma televisions built into the walls, Jacuzzi baths. We want each apartment to resemble the presidential suite of a top hotel. As if the apartments are part of the five-star hotel we aim to put in the middle of this development."

"We want this proposal to scream out to Edel Garry so we get the Mill," said Michael.

The meeting completed, Cormac and Michael walked out of the building to their cars.

"Sorry about you and O'Mara breaking up, old chap," said Cormac, slapping Michael on the back.

"Despite all your best efforts, we're still together," Michael informed him seriously.

Cormac looked surprised.

"Did you honestly think a few insults from you lot would have her running to the hills? I think after the career she's had, you should have realised she's more than a match for you and isn't going to be intimidated. She's here to stay, and since you all can't accept that, we'll be staying out of your way."

Michael got into his car and speeded off.

* * *

By Tuesday, Denise's nerves were strained waiting for Ryan's call. Wondering if he would call at all. So much had been going through her mind and she had so much to say and ask.

Her mobile rang on the Tuesday afternoon.

"Hi," she answered.

"Hello, Denise, it's Ryan. How are things?"

She felt awkward. "Fine, fine."

"Are you around to meet up?"

"Eh, yeah . . . but I have to be careful in case we are seen. I want to avoid town, if possible."

"Wherever you say is fine by me."

Denise thought for a few seconds. "How about the Ocean Bar? It's a bit out of the way."

"Sure, when?"

"This evening at seven?"

* * *

Ryan waited nervously and expectantly, looking out at the water from the Ocean Bar.

Denise hadn't sounded over-enthusiastic when he had phoned her. She had sounded cautious. But then why wouldn't she be? Maybe she would meet him and just say politely that she had considered his offer, but it wasn't for her. He knew he would have to prepare himself for that.

She came through the door, and he waved over at her. She walked over and sat down opposite him.

They sat in awkward silence until Ryan said, "How was your weekend?"

"It was fine."

"Did you give what I was saying last week any thought?"

She sighed and smiled. "You don't hang around, do you? When did you become so forthright? I haven't been able to think of anything else."

"And," he cleared his throat, "any decisions?"

"It's not something you can just decide on like that," she clicked her fingers. "I mean I don't know how serious you are."

"I've never been more serious about anything in my life."

"But it's been so long since we were together . . . what if it didn't work out?"

"There are no certainties in life, Denise. That's one thing I realise – but I will do everything in my power to try and make this work between us."

"But what would we do? What would our lives be like together?"

"We'd . . . just live."

"That sounds very nice and simple. But it's too simple."

"You only have one life, Denise. Do you really want to spend it with the wrong person?"

"I have a very good life with Cormac – I don't want for anything."

"Is that enough for you? When I'm offering you complete happiness?"

"What I keep hearing in my head is you saying 'There are no certainties in life'. You know, Ryan, I've made a very good life for myself, and I've seen with my mother's life how a wrong move can destroy you. This is such a huge step for me to take when, as you said, there are no certainties."

"Isn't the risk worth it, though? To leave a wrong situation and come to me? I know you, Denise, I know what can make you happy." He reached over and grabbed her hand. "I'll make you happy."

She felt a shock at the touch of his hand.

"I'm not saying there aren't feelings there." She was

nervous saying the words. She pulled her hand back. "I have to be careful, Ryan. I'm well known around this town. If I was seen with you . . . I've never been unfaithful to Cormac. In all these years, I've never even looked at another man. He's always made it clear, if there was even a slight rumour of an affair, I'd be out. But the funny thing is, he never had to make that clear. It would never cross my mind to have an affair."

"But I don't want to have an affair with you. I want us to be together permanently, for the rest of our lives."

"I know. But where would we live?"

"Anywhere you want."

"I can hardly move two doors down to you in Glenwood."

"I'll sell the house in Glenwood, buy whatever you want."

"You know how insecure my childhood was, Ryan. I need to know what I'm doing. I need firm plans and arrangements. I'm not going down in life, I've come too far." She got to her feet. "That's all I can say right now. I'd better be going."

"Wait, Denise! I feel we're no nearer to knowing what we're doing."

"This is all a big shock for me, Ryan. You can't rush me. There's an awful lot at stake here."

"I know – and I'm not going to rush you. If you come to me, I want you to be completely sure that it's what you want."

"Goodbye, Ryan."

45

Ali had taken a couple of days off work to renew her energies. And as she walked through the Reception of the newspaper, she felt more in control and confident than she had been for a long time. It was true what Michael had said, this was their relationship and nobody else's business. She felt empowered after standing up to the Cunninghams.

She stopped at the coffee machine and noticed a couple of the receptionists staring at her.

"You got a problem?" she asked sharply, and they scurried off trying to look busy.

She switched on her computer at her desk and Barry walked in.

"You busy this afternoon?" he asked.

"Not overly so."

"Got an interview for you to do. The public relations department of Aston Construction have been on about their MD, an Irish guy called Ryan Cantwell. Seemingly he's making a play for Heavey's Mill and about to become a serious player in the Dublin property market. Due to your new connections with the property world, I thought you might want to do it."

She sat back and looked at Barry squarely. "I'll do it because it sounds like an interesting story. Barry, I need to have a chat with you about what's been going on here recently."

"Fire ahead."

"I appreciate how you spoke to me about my relationship with Michael as a friend. I don't appreciate how you spoke to me as my editor. My job should not be affected in any way by who I see. My position here should not be affected by my personal life. And I'm not prepared to put up with comments from you or anybody else. There are laws to protect me and I wouldn't hesitate to use them, if I felt threatened."

"What? You might sue us for harassment or something?"

"If I had to, then yes," she said with determination.

"And I don't doubt you would." He left down a sheet of paper in front of her. "There're the contact details for Cantwell." Before he left, he smiled at her slightly in the way she had become accustomed to call his smile of admiration.

*　*　*

Ali drove out to Glenwood. She pulled into the huge entrance to the estate and looked up at the very high walls and electronic gate. She picked up her mobile and dialled the number of Cantwell's assistant, Jodhi, who she had been speaking to that morning.

"Hi, it's Ali O'Mara. I'm just outside the front of Glenwood."

A few seconds later, the electronic gates opened and Ali drove through. As she drove past No 1, she saw Denise's car parked in the driveway. Ali wondered how these people could live in this enclosed environment. She found gated communities stifling. She drove through the gateway of Ryan's house and parked on the cobble-locked drive. Getting out of the car, she went to the front door and rang the doorbell.

Jodhi answered the door.

"You found the place all right?" asked Jodhi, beckoning her in, removing her reading glasses and placing them in her pocket.

"Yeah. They are impressive houses, aren't they?"

Jodhi looked bemused and shrugged. "Can I get you anything to drink or eat?"

"No, I'm fine, thanks."

"I'll show you through to Ryan then."

They walked down the wide hallway to Ryan's study.

Ryan was sitting behind his huge desk, talking on the phone.

"I'll probably be in London for a couple of days next week, so come up to my office, say Tuesday, and we'll go through it then . . . fine . . . okay."

He put down the phone and stood up, smiling at Ali.

"Ali, nice to meet you and thanks for driving out here

to see me." He stretched out his hand for her to shake.

She took in the tall handsome man, with the slightly curled brown hair, and his accent which was a mix of Irish and London.

"No bother at all." She sat down. "Have we met before?"

"I think very briefly at the launch of the Harbour Project."

She nodded her head and smiled. Yes, she remembered him. She hadn't had a clue who he was at the time, but had observed him mixing very easily with people and he had quite a crowd gathered around him at the end of the evening, hanging on his every word. She was impressed he remembered her, as they must have only said the quickest of hellos. Judging from the intensity of his green eyes, she guessed he was a man who let nothing slip past him and who remembered every little detail, no matter how trivial.

"Do you mind if I tape-record this interview? It just makes it a little easier for me when I'm writing it later." she asked.

"Fire ahead."

She placed the miniature tape recorder on his desk and pressed a button on it.

"I took a read through the piece that your PR department faxed through – so this is a case of local boy made good, is it?" she asked with a cynical smile.

"Local boy who worked his ass off and managed to accomplish a couple of things on the way, maybe." He matched her cynical smile with one of his own. When he was told the name of the journalist the paper was sending over, he had done some quick research on her to update what he knew about her, and was amazed to find that she was the Cunningham frontman's recently acquired girlfriend.

"Rising to the top of a major international firm, no mean feat, seriously," she acknowledged.

"I got lucky with my opportunities; right time, right place; right time, right face," he said in a blasé way.

Looking at his eyes that seemed to get more intense by the second, she figured this man left nothing to chance, and she would hazard a guess his rise was carefully calculated and manipulated, despite his relaxed and easy-going manner.

"I got a list sent through to me of some of the developments you've been doing in the UK over the past five years . . . pretty impressive, especially in the London docklands. So what has you coming over to Dublin?"

"I think the Dublin property market is one of the most exciting markets in the world at the moment, and it was something I very much wanted to bring Aston to."

"Nothing to do with the fact that the Dublin property market is outshining the London one at the moment then?"

"Well, of course, I have to start new projects in locations that will yield the biggest profits for our shareholders."

She couldn't contain herself. "That's just what we need, another greedy developer in this country."

He was taken aback. "I would have thought it was

showing great faith in the Irish economy that we're willing to invest here."

She allowed herself a little laugh. "Do me a favour. You're not here for the good of our health, but the good of your wealth." She knew she was overstepping the mark, but she didn't care.

"You know, ten years ago the Irish economy would be screaming for a company like Aston to set up here."

"Well, why didn't you come here ten years ago then?"

"I wish we had and we wouldn't be in the position now that we have to pay huge sums of money to get a foothold with land here."

"Well, that's your own fault for not having had the vision."

"Ten years ago, I was stuck at the drawing board as an engineer with no power to direct anything but the pen in my hand," he said truthfully.

They looked at each other suspiciously.

"Am I missing something here?" Ryan asked then. "Because this doesn't feel like your normal straightforward interview to me." He waved his hand back and forth gesturing the space between them.

"I'm sorry," she conceded. "You know, I don't think I'm the person who should be conducting this interview. I'll ring my editor and have him send somebody else over. This is being organised by your people to be a flattering feature about you, and I'm in no mood to write anything flattering about any developer at the moment." She ran her hands through her hair.

"Can I ask why?"

"Because I got a little too close for comfort to some and I'm just really off them at the moment."

"Judging by some of the articles you've written in the past, it sounds like you were never on them," he said. "I get your paper delivered to my office in London every week – I quite admire what you write, as a rule."

"Should I be flattered?"

"When I left Ireland, there was a lot wrong with the place. Certain people thought they could do what they wanted, answerable to nobody. People like you changed all that. It needed to happen."

"Why am I feeling lately that nothing has changed?"

"Maybe you've been hanging out with the wrong people. Look, Ali, big business isn't always bad – it can be good. It doesn't just gobble up everything in its path and spit it out. Apart from that press release you got from our PR, what did you learn about Aston?"

"I have to admit – nothing."

"Then you don't know that we have consistently been named in the top five companies in the UK to work for. That our developments have consistently won awards for social planning. We've built our success on catering to people's needs – and I mean real needs, not gold taps in the bathroom."

She sat back, interested. "Well, in your opinion what are the real needs?"

"Actual living space. I'm sick of these apartments like rabbit hutches and dressed up to the nines to disguise the fact that you can't swing a cat in them. We always deliver good realistic living spaces. Then I'm talking about open spaces. We always give at least twice the amount of communal space that is required by law."

Ali found herself being slightly impressed as she thought about the tiny courtyards The Pavilions were built around.

"Then I'm talking about child-care facilities. All our developments have crèches and nurseries. Childcare is such an important thing in today's society and I just think it's neglected, don't you."

"Well, yes, I do actually."

"And I'm talking employment. When you're developing something large scale, it should be mixed use so that firms can locate there and people can live beside their work. I mean I grew up in a rural setting in Galway, and I could never understand why people should have to spend vast amounts of time to get to their fucking work place. If there is better planning and firms were encouraged to be beside developments, there's no reason why most people shouldn't live a ten-minute walk – or drive at least – from their workplace. Don't you agree?"

"In an ideal world, but how many people actually do?"

"Exactly, and all that, Miss O'Mara, is why I'm bringing Aston into the Dublin property market. I'm talking social aims here, not just profits."

At last, thought, Ali, somebody talking a bit of sense.

"You put a convincing argument to get your hands on Heavey's Mill. That is your aim, isn't it?"

"Of course, I want Heavey's Mill. I'd love to turn that place into a world-class development, a showpiece for the new Ireland and the envy of the world."

She put her head to one side and shrugged. "In that case, I wish you the best of luck with it." She reached forward and turned off her tape recorder. "Thanks for your time. I take it your PR people can email me some photos over."

"Anything you want." He rose from his desk and followed her out to the hall and the front door.

"So, you going to tell me what has you so dispirited about developers?" he asked as he opened the front door for her.

"Nah, I better not."

"Why do journalists ask all the questions and never give any answers?" he laughed.

"Just a habit of the trade, I imagine."

* * *

"How have they been with you since?" Ali asked Michael. They were seated in Bang having an early evening dinner.

"I haven't seen sight nor sound of Lisa. She hasn't shown up for work. Probably on the piss with her new drinking buddy, Hugh Fitzroy."

"Ah, and you thought you were irreplaceable! The first movie star that came along, and you're quickly forgotten," Ali teased.

"My broken heart! What will I do to survive?"

She reached under the table and touched him. "I'll help you in any way I can to get over this."

"Ali! Not in public, you never know when a passing paparazzo might photo us," he said, loving it.

She took her hand quickly away. "That isn't as bizarre as it sounds."

"You can save your 'help' for later," his eyes twinkled at her.

"As tempting as that sounds, I can't. I'm going straight home to write up this interview I did today. I'm under a tight schedule for it."

"That's the guy from Aston?"

"Yeah."

"That's the fella after Heavey's Mill. What's he like? No harm in finding out about the competition."

"Pretty impressive actually. I was expecting some asshole like Cormac, but he's pretty clued in. I'd say you have quite a fight on your hands to get Heavey's Mill."

"We'll get it. We always do." He winked at her. He loved winding her up with his cockiness.

46

Denise had waited until Cormac had left the house before getting up. She had lain in bed deep in thought. She and Cormac were still barely on speaking terms since their argument. As she drove down to the shop to get a Danish for breakfast and the paper, she was completely distracted and racked with indecision. The whole situation felt unreal to her and she kept thinking she would wake up from a dream and find Ryan had never shown up again. She fixed herself a coffee and sat down at the kitchen table with the Danish and the paper and started flicking through it. She stopped suddenly as she was confronted by a huge, and very good, photo of Ryan under the heading *'The Boy Done Good'*.

Amazed, she creased the paper over and began to read.

"We're well used to success stories coming out of this country. We've had our rock stars, our film stars, our writers, our entrepreneurs. It's something we take for granted. The latest name to join this golden circle is Ryan Cantwell. As they used to

say – remember the name – he's going to be big. The fact is Ryan Cantwell already is big; it's just that we're only beginning to hear about him now. The reason why is because he's been London-based for the last number of years, very quickly but very discreetly becoming one of the most important men in business over there. But now he's back in Dublin and flexing his muscles as the head of Aston Construction. And he has his eye firmly on Heavey's Mill which is to be the centrepiece of the new Harbour Project. I approached him cynically, sarcastically and angrily, but he completely disarmed me with straightforward talk and common sense and actually made me believe that here is a man who cares. Cares what he builds, cares what he's selling and cares about the people who he sells to – unusual or what? The fact that he has joined the committee of the charity Forward and has made a considerable financial contribution is impressive. The fact that he never mentioned this once during the interview is more impressive . . ."

Denise grabbed her coffee and took a slug, before quickly continuing to read.

* * *

Ali sat at her desk reading through the Cantwell interview with pride. She had, as always, written the interview as truthfully as she could. But this interview was more than a straightforward job. All her critics who said she would end up as just a mouthpiece for the Cunninghams were proven wrong. She had written a very flattering piece about their competition and in doing so asserted her independence and credibility. She was very proud of the feature.

* * *

Michael was speaking on the phone to a potential customer. "Sure, I have a spot in my diary at three if you want me to come over and evaluate your house . . . yeah, we've actually sold two houses on your road already this year and all properties in that area are very much in demand . . ."

He looked up, startled, as Cormac came storming into the office.

Marching up to Michael's desk, he grabbed the phone out of his hand and slammed it down.

"What the fuck do you think you're doing?" demanded Michael.

Cormac flung the paper with Ali's interview in it into Michael's face.

"Take a good look at the handiwork of that bitch you call your girlfriend!" Cormac shouted.

"What are you talking about?" Michael took the paper, and quickly looked at it as Cormac ranted on.

"An interview with Ryan Cantwell of Aston Construction. She's so far up his hole, it's unbelievable." He adopted a silly girlish voice. "Ryan says he likes a good mix of social housing. Ryan won best development of the year last year in the UK for his energy-efficient Docklands development. Ryan won an award for most innovative living designs. And the piece de resistance when she says – there's nobody in this city better positioned to turn Heavey's Mill into a first-class development!"

Michael was scanning the article, dismay written all over his face.

"She's completely undermined us getting Heavey's Mill. Everybody will be reading that and seeing it as an excellent reference for Aston and putting us into the shade. How fucking dare she?"

"Okay . . . okay . . . this is a bit of a blow for us –"

"A bit of a blow? That's the biggest fucking understatement of the year. She has tried to put us out of the running for Heavey's Mill!"

"She didn't do it on purpose. She's a journalist who was sent to do a job and did it."

"When are you going to wake up and smell the coffee and stop being a moron? She's always written negative pieces about us and this is just part of her campaign. You need to keep that bitch on a leash."

Michael stood up, enraged. "Don't you dare speak about her like that! You've insulted her enough and I'm not taking any more of your crap."

"She really has you pussy-whipped, hasn't she? What happened to the old Michael Farrell? The guy who was always game for a laugh. Liked the good life, enjoyed a laugh with the gang. Loved a party. Loved being a winner and getting one over on the next guy."

"I grew up, Cormac . . . and I got sick to death of being the second act in your life – of being the supporting actor to you – you and your family."

Cormac picked up the newspaper from Michael's desk, crumpled it up and threw it into Michael's face before walking out.

* * *

Barry popped his head around Ali's office door.

"Well done, girl, good article!"

She raised an eyebrow. "High praise indeed. Usually you just give me a grunt."

Laughing, he walked off.

Her mobile rang and seeing it was Michael's number she answered it quickly.

"Hiya!" she said cheerily.

"Are you busy?"

"Not particularly."

"I'm just outside your building. Can you come down?"

"Give me two secs."

She walked quickly to the lift that brought her down to Reception, and out into the busy street where Michael stood dragging on a cigarette.

"And to what do I owe this nice surprise?" she asked, kissing him.

"This!" He held up the paper with the article she wrote.

"What's wrong?" she asked, trying to work out his mood. He wasn't his usual happy-go-lucky self. But he wasn't angry either . . . more agitated, upset.

"What did you go and have to write that for?" His voice was calm but upset.

"It's just an interview, Michael. Nothing to get worked up about."

"Ah, come on, Ali. You weren't born yesterday and neither was I. You're after singing this guy's praises and you know he's our main competition for Heavey's Mill."

"I can't or won't let anything stand in my way of doing my job," she said assertively. "I've compromised myself enough over this relationship. I'm not going to give somebody bad press just because he's your business rival."

"Well, why did you have to do the interview at all? Why didn't you just walk away and let somebody else do it?"

"Why should I?" Anger crept into her voice. "I've never walked away from anything in my life."

"Are you trying to tell me you were that naïve you didn't know the impact this article would have on the Cunninghams' bid for the Mill?"

"I'm saying I'm not allowing the Cunninghams to affect my integrity as a journalist, and that means if I'm impressed by their rival, I'll say I am."

He stared into her eyes. "So, you did know the impact it would have then?"

"I didn't consider them at all in the equation. Doing a good, honest interview was my priority – my only concern. But, so what if it damages their chances, Michael? If you want me to be honest, I'll be honest. I don't want them to get the damned Mill. They need to be taken down a peg or two. And besides they would only turn the Mill into a playground for the rich."

"You still don't get it, do you? How can you be so blind? When you attack them, you attack me. I'm in business with them. Them not getting the Mill means me not getting it." He threw his cigarette on the ground and stamped on it. He began to walk down the street.

"Michael, where are you going?"

"I just need to be on my own for a bit."

"Michael!" she called after him, but he kept on walking.

47

The Garry home was a Victorian three-storey redbrick in Ranelagh. They had bought it four years ago when Projectrum's star began to rise. They were very heavily mortgaged.

Edel drove her car off the main road and into the gravel driveway. She saw Des's Rover was already parked there. As she approached the house, she could hear the kids screaming inside. She put the key in the front door and opened it. Her two eldest were on the hall floor aggressively fighting each other as they called each other every name they could think of. Her third child was sliding down the banister. She could see Des, red-faced and stressed out, in the drawing-room changing the youngest one's nappy on the ironing board. She put her briefcase on the sideboard and, as she walked past the fighting duo, she swooped down lifting the child on top, effortlessly dangled him in the air as she walked on, and caught the third eldest as she spun off the end of the banister. She carried the two into the dining-room and deposited them at the table in front of their homework.

"I don't want to hear another word from either of you this side of eight," she commanded.

"But, Mum, Cassandra kicked me in the shin and –" began her son Joseph.

"Save it! I don't want to hear. Not a word till eight."

Her daughter Cassandra who had been fighting on the floor had now begun to cry loudly.

Edel bent over quickly, producing a handkerchief and quickly wiped away the tears.

"Nobody likes a cry baby." Her voice was soothing yet firm. "Have you finished your homework?"

"Yes." Cassandra forced her sobs to stop.

"Then why don't you go and play with Jenny next door."

As she entered the drawing-room, Des said accusingly, "You're late – again."

He looked almost comical, his shirt-sleeves pulled up, the shirt marked from where the baby had vomited, his face frustrated as he finished putting the nappy on the baby.

"I had a meeting on site down at the Harbour. The traffic was terrible getting back."

She took up the baby from the ironing board and, holding him close, walked into the kitchen.

"You're dinner is in the microwave," said Des, following her in.

Still holding the baby, Edel started the microwave to heat up her dinner.

"Is there any luck getting that new au pair?" he asked. "I can't keep leaving work early to pick up the kids."

"If I thought an au pair was the solution I'd get one in the morning. But after that German girl I couldn't bear another one in the house. We're lucky we have a house standing with her habit of smoking pot and falling asleep without putting the damned things out. Those young girls just aren't responsible enough."

"Well, what are we going to do then?"

"We'll manage . . . we always do."

Des rubbed his face. "All we've ever had is a succession of au pairs that don't last long. It's no wonder the kids are becoming maladjusted."

"There's nothing maladjusted about my children, Des. They are just spirited, something they will need as they go through this life."

A scream from the dining room indicated that the two children left in there to do their homework had just begun a fight. This was followed by a huge crash that signalled the breakage of a number of plates.

"For fuck's sake!" shouted Des, racing off into the dining-room to inspect the damage.

"Des, I've told you before, don't swear in front of the children!" yelled Edel. As she cradled her youngest to her chest while Des started screaming at the two children in the dining-room and they started screaming at each other, Edel reached over to the paper on the table and opened Ryan's interview. She had been very impressed by it. Very impressed by him. As she looked at his smiling photo, she wondered what he'd be like in bed.

* * *

Until the legalities of his house at Glenwood finalised, Hugh Fitzroy was staying at a suite at the Morrison Hotel. The Morrison suited him just fine. Not just because he loved its chic sophistication, but also it was in stumbling distance of all his favourite pubs and clubs in the city. Lisa walked over to the large drinks fridge in the sitting-room and inspected its contents. She took out the two miniature vodkas that were left and walking over to the couch handed him one and emptied the other into her glass of Coke.

"Looks like you've run dry," she said, as if it was a natural occurrence that she had played no part in when in fact they had spent the afternoon knocking back every drop in the bar.

"Fuck!" He reached over to the phone and dialled reception "Man, Hugh Fitzroy here. What is this – the prohibition or something? The bar is empty up here." He hung up the phone.

It rang immediately. He let it ring until it went through to the answering machine.

"Hugh, it's Gordon here at MIM. Hugh, we've been searching for you all day and no sign of you. You can't just disappear like this. This can't go on. Call me as soon as you get this." The bleep indicated the call was over.

Hugh swigged back from the vodka bottle. "See what I have to put up with? On a fucking daily basis. I wish they'd all just fuck off and leave me alone. Do you know what that fucking asshole suggested to me the other day? A spell in some drying-out clinic. I said to him, 'Man, you would do anything to get a headline'. But I'm not going to be a part of something just because he needs publicity." He knocked back the vodka.

"Everyone is furious with Michael over that article that O'Mara wrote," said Lisa. "They are seriously angry. You should have heard my father this afternoon. Phew! I'm delighted. The golden boy is losing his shine all right." She drank her vodka and Coke. "Sure is losing his shine. You should have heard the way he spoke to me in his office. He treated me like I was a nobody. You should have heard the tone he used to me. He owes everything to me and my family. Whoever heard of him before we picked him up?"

"You know, I've got one more year left with the contract with MIM, and I'm seriously thinking of not signing up again. Like I'm hot, man. I can sign up with anybody I want. Somebody who can understand my needs and not just see me as a money-making machine."

There was a knock on the door.

"Come in!" roared Hugh.

The waiter opened the door and pushed the drinks trolley in. He was trained not to ever show any emotion when he entered rooms except courtesy. But he nearly laughed as he saw the vision in this room. Hugh Fitzroy was sprawled all over the couch looking wasted. While his dyed-blonde companion was seated in an armchair, obviously also wasted, but trying to sit up and look composed for his benefit. Around them were scattered lots of empty miniature bottles.

"At last!" said Hugh. "I was giving up on you guys. There's thirsty people around here, you know."

"Yes, sir."

"And cut out all that 'sir' bullshit. Makes me feel old."

"Of course."

As the waiter wheeled the trolley past them, Hugh shouted, "Stop! You can leave it just there."

"You don't want me to stock the fridge?"

"No. Just there looks fine." Hugh reached over and took a whiskey. "Just perfect, hardly have to move a muscle." He reached into his pocket, took out a hundred-euro note and tipped him.

"Thank you very much, Mr Fitzroy." The waiter nodded, smiling, and left the room hastily.

"Call me Hugh!" Hugh shouted after him. "They all love me, you know. I see it all the time. That's because I'm so down-to-earth and one of them."

"I tell you, Michael Farrell might just think he's been very clever now he's on top of the world. But he'll regret being abusive to me. I don't believe in this revenge-is-a-dish-best-served-cold shit. I say serve it piping hot and throw it right into their face."

48

Ali tried and tried to phone Michael but he wouldn't answer.

"Michael, I know you're angry with me, but we need to talk. Please give me a call," she said, leaving yet another message on his mobile. If only he would phone her back, she was sure they could sort this out. The look of hurt on his face had really got to her. She had never seen him not smiling and carefree before. And she felt bad because she had caused it. The trouble was she actually hadn't really thought about the consequences for Michael when she had written the article. Sure, she knew it would probably annoy the Cunninghams, but hadn't factored Michael into the equation. Maybe because she just couldn't afford to. She desperately wanted to talk to him and dialled his number again.

* * *

"I remember when I was in the show bands . . . I was once the lead in a band called the Horizons. We had a drummer called Benji Hartman. Now Benji was a lovable kind of rogue and had real star quality. Very popular with the crowds, girl in every dance-hall, if you get my meaning. Anyway, one day, Benji started getting ahead of himself and wanted a bigger profile and wanted the band's name to be changed to Benji Hartman and The Horizons. Well, there was just no talking to him that it wouldn't work. So I remember we were due to perform in Limerick and he was insisting he do a duet with me, even though he couldn't sing to save his life. So we fired him there and then. And left him in Limerick, while we headed on for Galway. He was a very popular guy, so we did suffer without him for a few months. But a year later we were still on the road while he was working behind a bar in Limerick. Married a farmer's daughter in the end, we heard." Honey finished off her story to Paul and Cormac as they sat in the drawing-room of the house on Shrewsbury Road.

"Your point, Mum?" Cormac had lost her halfway through.

"My point is that nobody is irreplaceable, no matter what you or they think."

* * *

Denise tried not to look at Ryan as they sat around the board table at Forward. As he came up with excellent ideas and she thought about the feature interview, she marvelled at the transformation in him over the years. She wondered when it happened. Was it gradual? All of a sudden? Was he always like that, but she had been just too blind to see it?

The meeting came to an end and, as everybody began to leave, she held back and glanced over at Ryan. He was doing the same, and when everyone had left he closed the door.

"Hi." He smiled at her, suddenly changing from the serious man he had been during the meeting.

"Hi." She smiled back. "I read your interview."

"Yeah? What did you think?"

"What can I say? It's very good. You came across very well."

He had received many compliments since the interview had appeared, but the one that had mattered most to him was Denise's.

"You are certainly raising your stakes going after Heavey's Mill."

"I want it."

"And you get everything you want, right?"

"Not always."

"It's interesting you're going after the same land that my husband is."

"Is he angry?"

"You'd have to ask him yourself. We're not on speaking terms at the moment."

"Can we meet up soon?"

"I have to attend a dinner tonight."

He put his hand up. "Whenever you want. I'm not

pressurising you."

She thought for a minute. "Tomorrow maybe. But I don't know where. I can't risk being seen around town with you."

"You live two doors up, just come down to me," he said as if it was the easiest thing in the world.

"I'm not risking being seen going into your house. We might be cut off in that gated cage, but some of the neighbours have moved in, and what if Cormac is passing and sees me?"

"Come in the back way. At the very back of the gardens, there's a gap between the walls – just walk through the show-house garden and you'll be at mine."

"This is so stupid."

He reached out and took her hand. "I'll be there all evening."

49

Michael was sitting in his office looking through sales invoices when there was a knock on his door.

"Come in," he called. Looking up he was surprised to see Cormac, Lisa and Paul come in and close the door behind them.

He was surprised to see the serious looks on all their faces.

"What's this? My birthday or something?" His grin disguised his worrying mind.

"Not so much your B-day as your D-day," said Lisa as the three of them gathered around his desk.

"Something on your mind?" Sitting back, he folded his arms.

"There's no point beating around the bush. Let's come out and say it," authorised Paul.

"It's like this," began Cormac. "We've gone out of our way to put up with that trash you're going out with –"

"Hey!" warned Michael.

"We've given her every chance to become a part of us."

"You took every chance to insult her," corrected Michael.

"We could put up with her when she was just a nuisance, but she's gone too far this time," said Lisa.

"She has completely undermined our bid for Heavey's Mill," said Paul sternly, "by endorsing the opposition with that interview she did."

"I agree the article was damaging," conceded Michael. Then he leant forward, his face suddenly animated, "but I've come up with some great ideas to limit the damage, some brilliant ideas which will catapult our bid."

"I'm sure you have," said Lisa, "but that's not the point of this meeting. She is going to continue to undermine us and she's too much of a loose cannon to have around."

"So what do you suggest I do?"

"Very simple – just get rid of her," said Cormac.

"You want me to end my relationship, just like that?" Michael was incredulous.

"It's the only solution," confirmed Lisa. "She's too much of a threat to us, to all of us, including you."

"I can't believe I'm hearing this. I'm not ending my relationship because you want me to. And that's an end to that."

"We're not asking you. We're telling you," said Paul.

"The answer is no," Michael said angrily. "And I'm fierce pissed off with all of you over this!"

"Make life easy on yourself, Michael." Cormac's voice almost softened. "Just get rid of her."

"I'm not letting this conversation go any further."

"Well, in that case," said Cormac, "I don't know how you can fit into our business any further."

"Let me just remind you that it was my name over this business when you came in. I know I owe you an awful lot, but I draw the line when it comes to you dictating to me like this."

"Okay, Michael, if that's the way you want it," said Paul, and the three of them left.

* * *

Michael sat in his living room looking out through the glass wall at the canal in the evening light, listening to classical music. Why had his life become so complicated? Maybe Ali had been right all along. Their relationship was too complicated. They did come from two different worlds – maybe too different to let it work. He had had a great life before he started seeing Ali. He could do what he wanted when he wanted. He didn't feel he had to explain himself or defend himself to anybody. He was out with Cormac and the gang partying whenever he pleased.

Lisa would do anything for him. Everyone had loved him. And he had needed that with a stepmother with whom he had clashed so badly when growing up, and a father who never took his side no matter what. As soon as he was eighteen, he had gone out into the big bad world, craving power and position and fun. In a household where as a teenager he had been arguing every single day, he just wanted no hassle. He wanted no ties, no arguments. He wanted to be carefree. The Cunninghams had amazed him when he had entered their privileged and spectacular world. They showed him everything was there for the taking – you just had to be brave and clever enough. And as time had gone by, he had become cleverer and braver than them all. Then Ali had arrived in, with her intelligence and her conscience and her questioning mind and now everyone disliked him. Maybe he should have just let her go when she tried to end their relationship? Shouldn't life just be as easy as possible? Why cause problems for yourself? But when Ali had stormed into his life, she was like a breath of fresh air. By just being herself, she had made him realise that he was actually bored with Cormac and the gang and their hard partying. He was sick of casual unimportant relationships. That going to the pub with Lisa had actually become a duty call. It was true what he had said to Cormac; he didn't want to be their support act any more. He craved what he missed as a teenager, a close family environment. His own family. Not somebody else's. Being with Ali made him feel he was the centre of his own life. But that didn't stop them from being incompatible.

The doorbell ringing incessantly invaded his thoughts. He sat still, ignoring it.

"Michael, I know you're in there and I'm not going away till you answer this fucking door!" Ali roared through the letterbox, before she resumed ringing the doorbell.

Michael raised his eyes to heaven and, getting up, walked down the spiral staircase and opened the front door.

She was almost surprised to see him and hovered in the

doorway for a while. Seeing him turn his back and walk up the stairs, she entered and followed him.

"You've been ignoring my calls," she accused.

"I told you I needed some time to think."

"Oh, Michael, why are you so upset?" she appealed to him. "I've never seen you like this before. I keep expecting you to break out into a smile and tell a joke."

"You want a joke? Did you hear about the eejit who fell for a journo who tried to destroy him?"

"I didn't try to destroy you. I admit what I wrote was damaging to you but, Michael, believe me I didn't give you a passing thought when I was writing it. I knew it might get on the Cunninghams' nerves, but I didn't think through the consequences."

"Get on their nerves? This is serious fucking business here with millions at stake!"

"I'm sorry . . . I guess I don't understand business at all."

"That's very obvious."

"I still stand by what I said. It's my job to write the truth as I see it –"

"Oh, don't worry, Ali. Your integrity was never in doubt here – never in doubt – the great Ali O'Mara's reputation is as safe as houses, if you'll pardon the pun. The only thing that is in doubt is your feelings for me, because otherwise you wouldn't have caused so much hassle for me. Why do you always have to have the last say? Why is everything a battle for you? Why can't you just relax and take it easy and enjoy life?"

He walked away from her and looked out on the canal.

She looked at him in silence for a long while.

Then she sat down on the couch and began to speak in a low voice.

"I am sorry if I caused hassle for you. And I'm sorry that you think my feelings for you were in doubt, because they were never in doubt to me. I guess I am a battler, aren't I? Never one to walk away from a fight.

When I was a kid, I used to be fascinated how life dealt people different sets of cards. Some people seemed to have so much power, while others seemed to have nothing. I remember watching the trials of war criminals on television, hearing about the terrible things they did . . . but hear they were finally brought to justice. But what intrigued me were the judges and the lawyers prosecuting and the strength with which they did their job. Speaking for those who didn't have a voice. And I thought, was it just luck that those judges were not themselves in circumstances where they could have been victims of those they were now bringing to justice? And I so wanted to be somebody to make a difference in life. I wanted to be in a strong position, defending people, and not one of the victims. When I was sixteen, I was flying, head of this society and every society and on my way to university, already knowing I was going to be a journalist. Then one day, this group in my class decided they didn't like me. They turned on me viciously and made my life hell for a year."

Michael turned around and looked at her.

"Funny, in the face of aggression, how your friends go quiet. I took it for a year, and it really knocked my self-confidence. Then I decided I didn't want to be a victim any longer. And I fought back. And you know sometimes, it was harder to fight back then just to take it. And after a while, they kept away from me. I've never spoken about that to anybody. And I carry it, Michael. I carry it every day. Because I know how easy it is for anybody to be a victim of circumstance. And I will continue to fight anyone who I think is a bully. I have the strength and the position, but I never take it for granted. Like I'm sure those judges at those trials never took their position for granted."

He walked over, sat down beside her, and hugged her.

50

Michael was having lunch in The Berkley Court with a couple of potential clients. They were a small building firm who were building eight townhouses. As the houses were in the heart of Donnybrook, Michael saw them as prime real estate.

"What I would advise for your townhouses is to fit them out with everything. Porcelain tiles throughout kitchens, integrated kitchens with NEF appliances, Jacuzzi baths, plasma TVs. Okay, it's extra costs, but the market you're aiming for is the very top and so they would appreciate these extras, and it would push up the prices." Michael finished his coffee and winked over at the waitress, indicating he wanted the bill.

"And what about press coverage?" asked one of the builders.

The waitress took Michael's company credit card and disappeared off to the register.

"We at Farrell's pride ourselves on having great

contacts with the property supplements. For an exclusive development like yours, I would be aiming to get you the front page of one of the supplements, the same as we achieved with the launch of Glenwood."

The two builders looked at each other, impressed.

The waitress came back. "Eh, Mr Farrell, I'm sorry but your credit card won't go through."

"Well, try it again." Michael smiled up at her.

"Sorry but it's seems to have been rejected." She went red with embarrassment.

"Rejected?" he said it a little too loud.

"Allow us," said one of the builders, reaching for his wallet and also feeling embarrassed.

"No, no!" Michael laughed. "Must be some cock-up with the administration." He reached into his wallet and gave the waitress cash.

* * *

Michael stormed back to the office, feeling humiliated. Damn the bank and its cock-ups.

He dialled customer service.

"Can I give you my account number, please?"

"Yes, sir," answered the customer service representative.

Michael read the number from his card. "I've just had a very embarrassing experience with a couple of clients with this card being rejected. I know it hasn't gone over its limit, because we always make sure it's paid every week."

"I'm sorry, Mr Farrell, but your card has been cancelled."

"Cancelled?" Michael almost shouted.

"Yes, I'm afraid so."

"I'm going to ring our accountants to get to the bottom of this!"

He hung up and dialled the accountants.

"Olivia, Michael Farrell here, can you put me through to Tom there."

"Eh, sorry Michael . . . but Tom's . . ." she paused before speaking quickly, "Tom's in meetings all day."

"Well, will you get him to call me as soon as possible. There's a problem with the company credit cards."

* * *

Denise looked down at her watch. It was nearly nine. She had heard Cormac come in a couple of hours ago and rummage around the kitchen. He had stayed for about an hour and then she heard the front door slam. The two of them were still avoiding each other.

She felt strangely excited about going down to meet Ryan. She wondered what time she should go. She decided she'd better go soon or otherwise it would be too late. She walked to the patio door of the house and through the back garden to the end. True for Ryan, there was a gap and she easily fitted through. Her stomach was full of butterflies as she walked through the gardens and past the swimming-pool of the showhouse. She slipped through the gap at the back and found herself in Ryan's property.

She steadied herself and walked up to the back door.

Should she knock, just walk in? Oh, this is all ridiculous, she thought. She felt stupid and nervous.

Quickly she turned and started to walk back down the garden to the gap.

"Come in this way," said Ryan's voice.

She got a start. Turning, she saw him standing at the opened patio door.

She walked slowly to the patio doors.

"Have you eaten?" he asked as she walked past him into the house.

She looked confused. She hadn't thought about food all day.

"Em, no."

"Good, just come on through here." He gently put his hand on her back and led her into the dining-room. The table was immaculately laid, and there were delicious aromas from a variety of pots and casseroles on the table.

He pulled out a chair and held it for her.

"Ryan! I wasn't expecting all this!" She shook her head in surprise. "I don't know what I was expecting . . ." she added as she sat down while he pushed her chair in.

He began to serve from the different bowls. "I hope you still like Italian food."

"Who cooked all this?" she said, staring down at her filled plate.

"I did, of course." He poured them two glasses of red wine and sat opposite her.

"You! Is there anything you can't do? You couldn't boil an egg years ago."

He laughed. "It's nothing special."

461

"It actually is. It looks amazing," She looked up at him. "I can't believe you've gone to all this trouble."

She picked up her fork and started to eat slowly. It was delicious.

"I was on the phone to Martha today, and I got a sponsor for that wine bash she suggested having."

"That's great. She was delighted, I suppose."

"Thrilled. Should be a good fundraiser for Forward."

He continued to talk about Forward for most of the dinner, occasionally switching the topic of conversation to his work.

After she finished off cheesecake for dessert, she sat back with a satisfied sigh.

"Another slice?" He reached for her dessert plate.

"No! I 'm stuffed. I couldn't manage another morsel."

"Well, shall we finish our wine in the lounge?" She nodded and, standing up, followed him in and sat down on the couch.

"I have a hectic day tomorrow," he said. "I'm meeting with town planners –"

"Ryan," interrupted Denise, "I'm sorry, but I'm really not interested. I think we've more important things to be talking about here than town planning and Martha's fundraisers, don't you?"

The look of surprise was quickly followed by a nod.

She tilted her head and glanced around the room. "You really have done it out beautifully? Who was your interior designer?"

"I didn't use one. I put it all together myself."

"Why doesn't that surprise me? Why wouldn't it

surprise me if you turned around and told me that you painted that oil painting over the fireplace?" She gestured up to the exquisite piece.

"I might be able to do many things, but I'm not up to that standard of painting. That's a Lucian Freud."

She quickly looked up at the painting again, impressed.

"You're just so successful. It's amazing how accomplished you are. Nothing would surprise me if you told me you had done it . . . I feel so . . . unaccomplished beside you."

"I don't want you to feel that."

"You never seem to put a foot wrong. But you seem rehearsed or something to me."

"Not true. I just do or say whatever comes naturally to me." He shrugged.

She stared at him as if trying to read him. "I'm sitting in a house that you bought for two point four million, two doors down from me. Is that a natural thing to do? The lengths that you went to in order to infiltrate my life, following me . . . I don't know whether to be immensely flattered or frightened."

"You've nothing to be frightened of from me. It's like I said – I just wanted to know everything about you. I'd been thinking about you for years, wondering all the time what you were doing. And when I finally caught up with you, I hadn't a clue how to approach you. I was looking for ways to get to know you."

"Ryan, if we ended up together, and that is just an if, where would we live? What are your plans? I really need to know."

"I've been giving this a lot of thought. I mean, I don't want to pull you away from everything in your life. We can stay here in Dublin."

"What, in this house? Living down the road from my ex-husband?" She raised an eyebrow.

"No, I already told you I'll sell this place and we'll go looking for a new house. Anything you want."

"And what about your work in London?"

"When I get Heavey's Mill I'll need to spend a lot of time in Dublin, anyway. Obviously I'll need to go back and forth to London. But it's so near, I won't be away for long. You can come to London with me any time you want."

"You make it all sound so simple, Ryan. But there would be major repercussions here. The fact is, whatever about my relationship with Cormac, I love my life."

"And that's why I don't want to take you away from it."

"Then there's the scandal. I'm well known around Dublin as are the Cunninghams. People will be shocked if I leave Cormac . . . I don't know if I could face everybody."

"I'll be there supporting you all the way. Besides, I'm sure it's in everyone's interest to keep this all as low-key as possible."

She didn't respond to this and he allowed her to fall silent, while he sipped from his wine and watched her think.

At length, she sighed and looked at him.

"I'd better get back to the house. Me and Cormac are still not speaking, so I don't know what his plans are tonight. He might be back early and wonder where I am."

She stood up and he followed her out to the patio doors.

She turned and faced him.

"Thank you for dinner. You've really surprised me doing that." She smiled softly at him. "It was not what I expected . . . but it was lovely."

"I wish you could stay longer. We could have a few glasses of wine in front of the fire, listen to some music."

"I'd better go." She walked a few steps down the garden, then turned around and said, "It sounds nice though."

* * *

Michael turned over on his back and looked at the morning sun stream through the linen curtains of his bedroom. He glanced at his watch and saw it was eight. It was Saturday, so he turned back on his side and began to drift back to sleep. Ali had been at a conference the previous night and had stayed in her own apartment. Somewhere he could hear voices and assumed it was someone in the street.

Then his eyes shot open as he realised the talking was in the house. He jumped out of bed and threw a dressing-gown on. Racing out of his bedroom, he rushed up the spiral staircase to where the talking was coming from.

Lisa stood there with a middle-aged couple, holding a clipboard.

"As you can see it's quite remarkable what they did with the back wall of the house. They literally tore it out and replaced it with this glass wall. A truly unique and amazing effect. The fact that the living-room is on the first floor is very avant garde, and offers a lovely view of the canal."

"What the hell is going on?" Michael all but shouted.

The middle-aged couple, startled, looked at Lisa.

Lisa walked into the kitchen area, ignoring Michael. "The house has oil-fired central heating. If you are interested, I advise you to make an offer quickly, as I have a lot of viewings set up and I know the owners are looking for a quick sale."

"Sale? What the fuck are you talking about?" Michael was shouting. "This house isn't for sale!"

"I think you'll find it actually is." Lisa pulled back the curtains on the front window.

Michael rushed over and, looking down, saw a huge *'For Sale'* sign in his small front garden.

"Who put that there? What the fuck is going on?" Michael demanded.

The couple were becoming agitated.

"Why don't you take a look around the house at your leisure," said Lisa, "and I'll catch up with you in a couple of minutes."

The couple quickly disappeared down the stairs.

"Would you mind keeping your voice down? You're going to scare off my buyers."

"They are not buying this house!"

"Why?" Lisa faked concern "Don't you think they have the look of the serious buyer about them? Maybe not. Not to worry – I have another appointment at nine anyway."

"Well, cancel the fucking thing! My house is not for sale!"

"I think you'll find that my family own fifty per cent of this house and as such they are more than entitled to put it up for sale. You only have the house because my family bankrolled it. They've bankrolled everything in your life. And then you repay us back by going off with that slapper who's out to destroy us."

"She's not trying to destroy you."

"Well, it looks like it from where we're sitting. We're not taking it any more, Michael. You can't have your cake and eat it. So we're taking away your privileges."

"I can't believe you would do this to me."

"Believe it. You're quite dispensable to us. Now, if you will excuse me, I need to get back to my clients."

51

Michael was sitting in Ali's apartment, his head in his hands.

"This is a fucking nightmare. She's showing people around my house all day."

"But how can they do that, Michael? You own fifty per cent, you still have your say."

"No, I've checked it out. When we were buying the place, they wrote it into the contract that they have the right to sell the house, without even giving me notice. I was so delighted to be getting the house at the time that I'd have agreed to anything. I love that house, Ali. It's everything I've ever wanted. I remember when it came on our books and I went around to do an evaluation, I knew from the moment I stepped into it that I had to have it."

"Can you buy out their share?"

"They won't agree to that. This isn't about money. This is about making life as difficult for me as possible. They cut off my credit cards and even my mobile."

Ali was stunned. "They're ruthless. I feel so guilty about that article and everything."

"Well, you know something? I'm glad you wrote that article, because it's shown me what they're like. They never gave a toss for me. You know what Lisa said? She said they were withdrawing privileges, as if I was some naughty kid or something. They've been subtly controlling me for years. Even over things that are trivial. They would be having a cocktail party, and I'd have something on and say I couldn't make it. Then they'd ring up saying they'd delayed the party for two hours so that I could go. And me, feeling guilty, would cancel my plans and show up."

"They had you earmarked for Lisa." Ali shrugged her shoulders.

"That's not proper friendship, like I thought we had. That's just being of use to someone. But it hurts, Ali . . . it still hurts."

She leaned forward and hugged him. "I know."

"It's all right for you. You've got a strong family unit. I never had that."

"Well, you've got me now." She kissed him. "Why don't you move in here? There's no point in your staying at your house. They'll just be invading your space with viewers all the time."

"Thanks, Ali," he smiled at her, "but this is just a one-roomed apartment. We'd be living on top of each other."

"I don't mind if you don't!" She winked at him.

"I think I'd like that . . . But, is this just a stop gap? Or are we kind of officially moving in together?"

She bit her lip. "I think we could call it official."

It was good to see him smile as he said, "I could live with that."

They spent the rest of the weekend clearing all Michael's stuff from the house. He contacted a friend and had all the furniture put into storage.

* * *

It was late Sunday evening and Michael and Ali were looking around the bare house.

"It looks really different empty, doesn't it?" said Michael.

"Yes, it does," Ali agreed.

"I'm just thinking of all the parties that went on in here, with Cormac and the gang."

"Don't think too much about it. We'll get another house once things settle down a bit."

"I don't think I'll ever feel the same about a house again."

"It's only bricks and mortar, Michael. Our next place will be our home, and you'll feel just the same about it in time."

"Yeah, you're right." He took one final look around the place and then they left.

* * *

Michael walked into Reception at Farrell's early on Monday morning.

"Any messages?" he asked the receptionist.

"Just *The Times* was on looking for you."

"Thanks." He went to walk away.

"Oh, and Michael . . . Lisa asked me to give you this box."

He looked down at the box suspiciously and, picking it up, brought it into his office.

He opened it and saw that it was stacked with business cards. Confused, he took one up and read it.

'Farrell's Auctioneers – Michael Farrell – Senior Negotiator.'

Senior Negotiator? But he was Managing Director. He thought for a moment, as he realised what had happened. Grabbing a handful of the cards, he walked quickly out of his office, down the corridor and into Lisa's office.

She was sitting at her desk, reading a magazine.

He threw the fistful of cards into the air, and they floated down gently,

"Senior Negotiator?" he demanded.

"Yes. We had a board meeting and decided, considering what was happening, it was best you step down as MD."

"A board meeting? You mean you and your family cooked it up over a cocktail?"

"We do own eighty per cent of Farrell's. You are very much a junior partner."

"I considered you to be my best friends!" said Michael, outraged. "How wrong was I?"

"As my father would say – business is business."

"And who did you appoint as the new MD?"

"You're looking at her."

"You!" He laughed loudly. "You wouldn't know how to run this place. You're a good estate agent, a very good one, but that's where it stops. You don't have the ability or the concentration to be the MD here. When you're not out having three-hour liquid lunches, you're cancelling appointments due to hangovers. Not to mention trips to the hairdresser's, the beautician and shopping trips with Mother."

Lisa became annoyed. "I can run this place perfectly well. This business is in my blood."

"Pure vodka is in your blood! And all this because you're jealous of me and Ali."

"Jealous! I'm the daughter of a multi-millionaire. Why would I be jealous of you two?"

"Well, it won't work. The funny thing is all these stupid antics are just speeding up our commitment to each other. I've moved in with Ali, so you can do as many viewings in the house in Adelaide Road as you want. And I'm not sticking around here to be a Senior Negotiator. I resign as of now."

Lisa looked stunned.

"We'll see just how long you can keep this place running!" said Michael.

She tried to rally. "You're such a stupid man," she gasped. "You've thrown away everything over nothing."

"I feel free for the first time in ages. I don't have to be at your beck and call any more. I don't know where my future will be going, but I'll be in charge of it for a change."

"You're such a selfish bastard. To just walk out on us and leave us in the lurch like this!"

"You're incredible. You've forced me into this corner and now you're playing the victim? Of course, I shouldn't be surprised. You go through your whole life playing the victim, Lisa. You were handed everything in life and yet you constantly feel sorry for yourself. No matter how mean you are to people it's always their fault. I'm going to clear out my office."

He strode out and down the corridor.

She got up and stormed after him, shrieking. "I'll give you six months! Six months and you'll back here crawling, begging us for a second chance!"

* * *

Honey was on the phone to a customer services rep complaining about a bill that she had received.

"Now I'm either not explaining myself properly or you're particularly thick," Honey told the rep. "It's quite simple. I've been overcharged."

The front door slammed and Lisa came storming into the drawing-room in tears.

"What the fuck is wrong with you?" Honey demanded. "I'll have to call you back," she said to the rep and hung up the phone.

"It's Michael. He resigned this morning."

"He did *what?*" Honey was gobsmacked.

"Everything's backfired. He's moved out of Adelaide Road and in with Ali. And when he found out he had been removed as MD he quit on the spot!"

"And you let him go?" Honey demanded.

"What was I supposed to do? Lock him into his office?"

"If you had to, yes! But he'll be back. When he's given it a bit of thought, he'll be back."

"You didn't see him. He never gets mad or lets anything get to him. But he was really furious!"

"You must have handled it all wrong, as usual."

"Don't try and blame me for all this. It was you lot that came up with this strategy."

"I thought it would work. I thought Michael was too impressed with position and money to risk his future."

"Well, you were wrong."

"I'm never wrong, Lisa." Honey said sternly. "He's changed, that's all. The Michael of old wouldn't have risked it. But there's been a change in him of late. Maybe even before O'Mara arrived on the scene. Maybe he was looking for more . . . Ah well, we'll just have to write him off in that case." Honey sighed.

"Write him off?" Lisa nearly shouted. "You make him sound like a bad investment on the stock market."

"Well, in a way, it is a bit similar."

"He was the love of my life!"

"But you weren't the love of his. So stop acting like a pathetic bitch and get over it."

"I'll never get over him!" She turned and stormed out.

* * *

Ali and Michael were in a little coffee shop around the corner from the newspaper.

"I had no option but to quit."

"Of course you didn't. How dare they try to humiliate you like that! I'm really proud of you for standing up to them."

"Are you?" He looked at her with his crooked smile.

"Of course!" She squeezed his hand.

"This is pure mad. My life has been turned upside down. I've gone from knowing exactly where I am to not having a clue."

Her forehead creased in worry. "And do you regret anything?"

"Nothing at all."

"Well, you don't have to worry about anything financially. You're living with me, and I can take care of the all the bills and everything . . ."

She trailed off as his crooked smile switched into a full one.

"What?" she asked.

"I think I'm all right financially for now. I'm not the multi-millionaire businessman people think I am. But I'm not short for a bob or two. And the sale of the house will be coming through as well. But thanks anyway. It's really nice to have somebody to rely on."

"Maybe you should play golf for a while or something then," she suggested.

"No. I'd go mad. I need to get working very quickly or I'd go mad."

Ali had to admit this was true, with a mind as active as Michael's.

"I'm just wondering what estate agency will touch me. The ones that hate the Cunninghams won't want me

475

because they associate me too closely with them. And the ones who like the Cunninghams won't touch me for fear of offending them."

52

Michael arranged to meet some contacts at different auctioneers to see what the situation was concerning him getting a new job. Although he was told they would certainly find a position for him, he could sense they were nervous. As he had thought, nervous of his position with the Cunninghams. And then they were concerned that here was a man used to running his own show – how would he feel about following someone else's direction? His flamboyant approach to business wouldn't fit into a lot of companies' profiles. In a way, he was too well known. Michael then realised that he wouldn't feel comfortable working for people he had been friends with.

As he walked down Grafton Street after a lunch with another business friend, he was pondering this when he came face to face with Denise coming out of Brown Thomas.

"Hi there." She leaned forward and kissed his cheek. "How's everything?"

He studied her happy face, and came to the conclusion she knew nothing about what had happened.

"Fine, I guess."

"You seem a little out of sorts. Come on, and I'll treat you to a coffee." She linked her arm through his and started walking down the street.

Michael stopped and looked at her. "I should have guessed they wouldn't tell you anything."

"Tell me what?"

"Denise, there's been a lot going on, and I don't want to get you involved. So maybe we should skip the coffee, okay?"

"No, not okay. What's been going on exactly? Michael? We're friends, aren't we?"

He studied her exquisite features.

"Okay, let's grab that coffee."

* * *

Denise stared down at her half-drunk cappuccino and then looked up at Michael.

"How dare they! How dare they treat you like that!"

"Cormac didn't say anything?"

"We're going through one of our real bad patches at the moment. We're barely saying good morning. Not that he would have told me anyway. He knows I wouldn't allow it. I'm going straight over to him and fixing this right now, Michael. I'll have you right back as MD at Farrell's by the end of the day and back in your house tomorrow!"

"Thanks, Denise. I appreciate that. But it's not just

Cormac. It's all of them. It's a united front, I'm afraid."

"Fuck them anyway!" Denise spat, acknowledging there was little she could do in that case. "But you can't just let them get away with all this. You can't let them take your company away."

"They're by far the majority shareholders. I'll still get an income out of it. But by the time their accountants have cooked the figures, it won't be much I imagine. And by the time Lisa has run the company into the ground, it will be nothing at all."

"But what will you do now?"

"I'm just checking out what's out there. I'll be fine." He grinned. "You know me. Nothing will get me down."

"You're a brilliant estate agent and businessman. I've no doubt you'll be back on your feet in no time. But I'll really miss you, Michael. You've been there nearly as long as I have. I always felt we were the two outsiders amongst them."

"In a way we were. But, you know, even though it's all a big shock, I'm glad it's happened. I'm delighted living in Ali's little apartment, doing whatever I want to do. It feels good."

"I imagine it does."

"So – that's the story. I'd better head off."

He stood up and so did Denise.

She hugged him tightly.

"You've been a great friend to me over the years," she whispered into his ear.

* * *

Denise drove straight down to The Pavilions. She walked briskly towards the construction part and approached the security guard.

"Where's my husband's office?" she asked.

"Apartment 45, fifth floor of that building," he informed her.

As she walked through the construction site, the workers gave her second looks. She entered the lobby of the building, where painters and carpenters were busy, and getting into the elevator pressed '5'.

On the fifth floor, she walked down the corridor and opened the door of No 45.

Cormac had turned the three-bedroom apartment into beautiful offices for himself, she observed.

Walking in, Denise saw Cormac's secretary at work in what had been the first bedroom.

"Hi," she said, "have you gone on your lunch break yet?"

"Eh, yes."

"Would you mind going on another?"

"I'll just check it with Cormac –"

"Don't bother. I'll have a word with him."

The secretary nodded and, grabbing her handbag, promptly left.

As Denise walked past the second bedroom, she noticed that Cormac had maintained that as a bedroom. And looking into the living area, she saw it was amply stocked with drink. Obviously, the apartment doubled as Cormac's office and playroom.

She went to the door of the master bedroom and

opened it. Cormac was seated at his desk in front of the wall-to-ceiling windows that looked over the building site.

"I just bumped into Michael," she said, entering the office.

He started and sat back.

"You and your rotten family pulling those stunts on him!"

"Nobody asked him to leave Farrell's – he quit himself."

"You bullied him out. He was a good friend to you and all of us and to treat him so shoddily is a disgrace."

"He had it coming. We gave him ample warnings about O'Mara."

"He's entitled to see who he wants!" she suddenly exploded.

"Shut up. The secretary –"

"I sent her on a break. He's not interested in Lisa, he was never interested in Lisa, and he never will be interested in Lisa. Why don't you all get it through your thick heads?"

"I couldn't give a fuck about him and Lisa. The rest of my family might be obsessed by it, but I don't give a shit. O'Mara's dangerous and Michael's too stupid to see it. Did you read that feature she wrote about Ryan Cantwell from Aston?"

Denise was taken aback at hearing Cormac say Ryan's name. "Yes. I did."

"She said that he was the best man for Heavey's Mill."

"She's entitled to her opinion."

"Take a good look out that window, Denise, because that's the last land that Cunningham Homes owns. There's about another few months' work finishing off this phase of The Pavilions and then we have nothing left to build. A construction firm needs land to continue, and there's nothing out there in the market to buy. We're not like other construction firms who built up land banks over the years. We're desperate here. If we don't get Heavey's Mill, we'll be out of business."

"So why don't you use the brains you were born with and all work together? Instead of turning against Michael, your greatest asset and your oldest friend."

"You don't know anything about business. Why don't you stick to shopping and fundraising?"

"Do you know, the problem here is not just about that article. It's not even about Heavey's Mill. It's about you losing control over Michael. Michael, who you used to click your fingers at and he'd jump into action.. Michael, who you could use in business. You felt you were losing him, so pulled out all the stops to get him back under control. And by doing so you lost him altogether."

"You haven't a fucking clue what you're talking about."

"Well, you won't have him now at those meetings to do all the talking. And Lisa won't have him to run Farrell's. And all you've done is show yourselves to be vindictive and spoilt. As your father always said, you're not a frontman, Cormac, so you better start shopping around for someone new."

"You know, I'm so sick of you. Why don't you just piss off back to where you came from?"

"Well, Cormac, you are really making things much clearer for me."

* * *

It was evening time, and Ryan was with Jodhi at Glenwood.

"The reaction back from the interview is wonderful," said Jodhi. "It's really made people in this country aware of who you are and what you've achieved, and in doing so has smoothed the path for Aston to acquire the Mill. What did Denise think of it?"

"She seemed impressed." Ryan put his hands together. "She almost seemed a little too impressed. I don't want to frighten her away, Jodhi."

"From what you tell me about Denise, success doesn't frighten her away. She seems to be drawn to it."

"I don't know . . . I feel we're no closer to being together than when I started out on all this."

"It'll take time."

"That's what she says. It's as if she looking for flaws in me all the time, almost as if she's looking for reasons not to leave Cunningham and come to me. I can offer her everything she wants. I'd go out of my way to make sure she's happy."

"I put together a programme for when you two get together. She is right in so far as it will cause a scandal. But we also want to maximise it to get the best publicity for Heavey's Mill. Handled correctly, when you and Denise are together, we can really make it work to make Heavey's Mill the talking point in Dublin. People are genuinely interested in her – look at the publicity she acquired for the Cuninghams for the launch of Glenwood. Imagine what we can achieve for the Mill."

"If we get Heavey's Mill, if me and her end up together. She's made no commitment whatsoever so far."

*   *   *

Denise wished she had taken Ryan's mobile number. She was so enraged after her argument with Cormac and finding out what they had done to Michael that she really needed to talk to him. She thought quickly and then set off down the garden to the gap in the wall. A couple of minutes later she found herself at the patio window of Ryan's house. She knocked loudly. She rapped her knuckles on the glass again, realising he might be out. To her relief, she saw him walking to the door, looking perplexed as he unlocked it.

"Denise?" he said as the door opened and she stepped into his arms. "What's the matter?"

"I'm sorry. I didn't have your number and I really needed to speak to you –" She stopped short as she spotted Jodhi in the doorway.

"It's all right. Don't mind Jodhi, she's completely trustworthy," assured Ryan.

"I was just heading back to the hotel anyway," said Jodhi. "I'll see you in the morning."

Ryan put his arm around Denise and led her into the sitting-room.

Denise was concerned. "She won't say anything to anyone, will she?"

"Not at all. She's been with me for years."

"Does she know about us?"

"She knows my feelings for you. That's all there is to know, isn't there?"

"I suppose," she nodded.

"Now tell me what's wrong."

They sat down, and he held both her hands in his.

"I just had such a bad argument with Cormac today."

"Over what?"

"It's a long story. Michael Farrell – you know of him?"

"Of course."

"They've pushed him out over his relationship with Ali O'Mara, the journalist who interviewed you. They've treated him so badly, and he's been such a good friend to us all. I'm so pissed off with them. So angry with Cormac. He has no feelings for anybody but himself. I don't think I can go on in this marriage. I can't even bear being near him any more."

"I've told you that you don't have to. I'm here for you."

"But, Ryan . . . I don't want to get hurt."

"I would never hurt you."

"I'm safe where I am. I'm in control. I'm so frightened to leave it behind."

"And what are you going to do? Put up with this unhappy marriage?"

"I don't know. I'm so confused. One thing I've realised after how they've treated Michael is that I don't think I can stay in Dublin if I leave Cormac."

Her words were a shock to him. "I see."

"They would be too angry and vindictive. I couldn't stay here to put up with all the shit that would come my way."

"And where would you want us to go?" Ryan felt uneasy. He had always imagined them settling in Dublin and enjoying the city together after a while. He also felt uneasy as she was saying she wanted to run. As she had run from him all those years ago. That element was still in her personality.

"London, I suppose. I don't know." She saw his worried expression. "Maybe you don't want me over in London?"

"Of course, I do. I just pictured us here."

"Well, if you don't want me there, you need to tell me. You need to be completely honest with me, because I'm risking everything here for you. If this didn't work out between us, you can just get back with your life. I'd have no life to go back to."

"I understand. I know . . . of course I want you in London. I just thought you wouldn't want to leave the charity and your friends and everything here."

"I don't think I have any choice."

Ryan thought for a while. "Why don't you come over to London with me for a few days? Come over and see where I live and see a bit about my life over there."

"I don't know. What excuse would I give Cormac? We mightn't be speaking, but I couldn't just disappear like that."

"Tell him it's something to do with Forward. I want you to come over."

She thought hard. "Okay. I might be able to get away for a couple of days."

53

Renards was packed and the music was blaring, but still Hugh Fitzroy was attracting much attention. His management had phoned, reserving a table in the members' lounge. A doorman from the club stood beside the table, ensuring that Hugh wasn't bothered by anybody. Lisa sat beside Hugh, matching him drink for drink. She looked around the rest of the people at his table. A couple of models, another actor and a director. She had needed a good night out, and Hugh was always game for that. She enjoyed all the looks they were getting from people. But she would still prefer to be in The Pembroke with Michael. The whole thing had backfired and there was nothing she could do. She'd had a headwreck of a day, meeting accountants and solicitors for Farrell's. Most of what they'd said had gone over her head – she had left all that side of the business to Michael. It bored her.

She looked at Hugh, chatting up the model to his right. Despite his looks, she didn't fancy him. He wasn't her type. But she did enjoy his company. And besides, since Michael had met O'Mara, she needed a new drinking buddy. Hugh didn't need anything from her; he had enough himself. And he was aware that neither did Lisa need anything from him, because of her background. Someone was always looking for something from Hugh. Either the groupies who wanted to boast they had been with him, or the people around him whose livelihoods depended on him. There had been one night, when they had both got very drunk and things had become a bit blurred. She vaguely remembered snogging him and getting undressed. But there was no mention of it after.

* * *

Cormac had also reserved a table at Renards at the opposite end of the members' lounge. He was chatting to Steve Foyle and a few other guests and looking around for Barbara, who had been missing for a while. He spotted her coming out of the toilets, rubbing her nose. He raised his eyes to heaven. She could be a little more discreet.

She flounced over and sat beside Cormac. He reached over to the ice bucket for the champagne and filled everyone's glasses, then topped up his own and Barbara's glasses with Red Bull.

"So when am I going to get to visit your new house at Glenwood?" enquired Barbara.

"Sometime soon," promised Cormac.

"You're always saying that but I still haven't been. Doesn't that wife of yours ever leave the house?"

"I can't risk her coming back and finding you lot having a party there."

"We had a couple of great parties in your last house, remember?" She rubbed his back.

"Yeah, when she was on her trip to New York."

"I don't know why you stick with her. She's such a fucking bore."

"Hey!" He put his finger to her lips. "We don't discuss her – ever – remember?"

She pouted. "I miss Mikey. I miss the great craic we had around at his house. It was open season there."

"Yeah, well, Michael just decided to become one boring git."

"Are we going back to your offices to continue the party after?"

"No, not tonight, Josephine."

"You know, I don't think it's just Mikey who's getting boring and old around here. I think I need to get myself some new friends."

"I think you have plenty of friends and you see them all the time." He looked at her knowingly.

She giggled. "Ah, come on, Cormac. Let me come by your new house – I wanna see it."

"Okay. I'll organise something soon. Promise."

"Hey, guess who's over there," said one of the other girls returning from the toilet. "Hugh Fitzroy!"

"Where?" demanded Barbara.

"Down at the back. And he's with your sister, Cormac."

"He's buying a house up at Glenwood. They've become friends," explained Cormac.

"Come on," said Barbra standing up. "Come on over and introduce me."

"No way. I haven't even met the guy myself," objected Cormac.

"Well, now's a great time to meet him. He's going to be your new neighbour, isn't he?"

She pulled Cormac up and dragged him across the members' lounge.

Cormac felt uneasy as he approached the Fitzroy table. Although Lisa and he worked closely together and were together at many of their parents' social gatherings, they would never confide in each other and avoided socialising together directly.

Lisa spotted Cormac and waved at him. The security guard knew who Cormac was but still gave a quick glance at Hugh who nodded, indicating it was all right to let them join the table.

"I didn't realise you were going to be here tonight," said Lisa, as Cormac and Barbara sat down at their table.

"Hugh, this is my brother, Cormac."

Cormac reached over and shook Hugh's hand.

"Great gaffs you built up there in Glenwood, man," said Hugh.

"Glad to have you as a neighbour. This is Barbara. Lisa, have you met Barbara before?"

Lisa looked at Barbara disdainfully. She was fully aware of Barbara's reputation around town. Barbara seemed to have twenty different boyfriends, most of them married. And she was rumoured to have a coke addiction. Pleasant company her brother kept. She didn't know if

Cormac was one of Barbara's twenty boyfriends, and she really didn't want to know. Reputed to be a great beauty in her day, the constant partying had given Barbara, still in her mid-thirties, a tired look. And Barbara couldn't take her eyes off Hugh.

"Yes, I think we met before," Barbara answered for Lisa, and it was obvious her main focus of attention was Hugh as she stretched her hand out across the table.

"Hugh, I'm Barbara."

Hugh looked up at her through bleary eyes and then looked down at her well-exposed breasts.

"Have I met both of you before?" he asked.

Barbara screamed with laughter. "You're hilarious!" and moved a little closer to him.

Lisa shook her head in boredom and leaned over to Cormac.

"What do you think of Michael's departure?"

"He'll be back quick enough. I've already put out the word that anyone who does business with him is no friend of ours."

"Good. I've done the same with all my contacts." Lisa looked over at Barbara who had moved in beside Hugh and was whispering into his ear.

* * *

A couple of hours later and Hugh and Lisa were falling in the door of his suite at The Morrison.

"I'm fed up with fucking hotels. When am I getting the keys to that fucking house?" slurred Hugh, collapsing on the sofa.

"Whenever you return the contracts and pay the money," said Lisa, taking two miniatures from the fridge.

"I must get the fuckers to sort it out quickly. I need space, man." He took off his jacket and emptied out his keys and his change from the pockets. A slip of paper fell out and he took it up.

"What's that?" asked Lisa.

"It's that Barbara's number. She gave it to me."

"I bet she did, the little slut. Take some advice from a friend – stay well clear of that one. She's trouble."

"She's a friend of your brother's, isn't she?"

"Unfortunately, yes. I don't know what he's doing, hanging around with trash like her. I know Denise isn't exactly the life and soul of the party, but that's no reason for being with that whore."

"Whore?" Hugh's interest perked up.

"Well, she's as good as a whore in my book. She's a fixture on the social scene for years. She shags anything in sight. She's anyone's as long as he's paying. I don't know how she does it. I spotted her out having dinner with a minister last week. Here's me who can't get a date, and there's her lining them up quicker than she lines up her coke. Men! If a woman is beautiful and intelligent, nobody asks her out. You put the rumour out she's a slut and you have to pay for her and everyone wants her!"

"She wants to meet me," said Hugh.

"Of course, she does! As I said, you'd be advised to stay clear! A friend of mine said that Barbara went to a wedding recently that turned into one big coke fest.

Seemingly Barbara arrived looking like Ivana Trump and left looking like Patsy from that sitcom."

"Gotta take a piss," said Hugh, going into the bathroom.

"I'll bet you do."

"For fuck's sake!" came Hugh's scream from the bathroom.

"What is it?" Lisa shouted and went racing into the bathroom after him.

"I'm sorry – I just wanted to meet you," said a young girl of seventeen, who had been hiding there. "I snuck in when the chambermaid wasn't looking."

Hugh looked visibly shaken. "Get her out! Get her out!" he shouted.

"Get the fuck out before I call the police!" Lisa shouted at the girl, who fled from the suite in tears.

"She was hiding in the shower, and jumped out," said Hugh, stumbling out of the bathroom, white from the shock.

"I see what you mean about moving into Glenwood. You need to do it quick sharp. There's so much security around that place, nobody will get in to you."

Hugh started shaking as he sank to the floor and started to crawl.

"Hugh, are you okay? Hugh?" Lisa asked as he started to shake uncontrollably. "Hugh!" she shouted, getting down on the floor beside him and holding him.

But as he shook uncontrollably, he seemed to lose consciousness.

"Oh no! Oh no! What'll I do!" shouted Lisa, as she

began to shake from fear herself.

She went to the phone to tell Reception to call an ambulance. But then she remembered he had done some coke that evening – how would it look if it got out? It might destroy his career. It might destroy *her*, being found in a hotel room with a movie star having a freak attack.

There seemed to be no sign of his shaking stopping. She grabbed his mobile and went through the numbers looking for Gordon's. That was his agent from his management committee. He would know what to do.

"Hello, Gordon," Lisa voice was shaking as she got through him, "I'm a friend of Hugh Fitzroy's and he's having some kind of fit."

"Where are you?"

"We're in his hotel suite."

"Who else knows?"

"Nobody."

"Don't call anybody or tell anybody. I'll be over as soon as I can. Just look after him and make sure he doesn't move."

The phone went dead. Lisa stared down at Hugh in convulsions and thought about running from the hotel. Just running and leaving this awful scene. Tears were streaming down her face as she realised she couldn't.

"What are you doing to me?" she said, getting down on the floor beside Hugh and trying to cradle his head. "I'm not a rescuer. People look after me!"

*   *   *

Gordon let himself into the hotel room, accompanied by a nurse, and locked the door behind him.

"What happened?" demanded the nurse as she pushed Lisa out of the way.

"We were out for the night and came back for a nightcap." Lisa ran her fingers through her hair as she spoke between sobs. "He went into the bathroom and there was a fan hiding in there and she jumped out and gave him a fright and next thing he started shaking."

The nurse nodded at Gordon and started taking out a needle and preparing an injection.

"How much has he drunk?" asked the nurse.

"I don't know – quite a lot."

"Any drugs?"

Lisa wiped away her tears.

"I said – any drugs?" snapped the nurse.

"I think he did a line of coke earlier on in the evening."

Lisa looked at Gordon defensively. "I didn't have anything to do with it. He had it himself. I didn't take any."

"I'm not saying you did." Gordon took Lisa's hand, led her over to the sofa and sat down.

"What your name, hon?"

"Lisa."

"Lisa, it's fine. Nothing to worry about. You don't have to tell anybody about this." He reached into his pocket and took out a cheque book "I just want to give you a little present from Hugh to make sure this goes no further, okay?"

Lisa felt cheap at his suggestion and annoyed by it.

"I'm Lisa Cunningham, for fuck's sake. I'm selling you the house at Glenwood. I'm not a fucking groupie!"

"Oh!" Gordon put away the cheque book, embarrassed but relieved.

"Tell me what the fuck is wrong with him!" demanded Lisa.

"Hugh is an epileptic. Any shocks like he had this evening can send him into these convulsions. He'll be fine. It looks more frightening than it is. We have to keep it secret because it wouldn't be good for his image. And also would affect his insurance on film sets."

Lisa reached into her handbag and, shaking, lit herself a cigarette.

"I'm getting too old for this kind of shit," she said.

54

"Have you arranged a meeting for our architects in London on Monday?" Ryan asked Jodhi.

"Yes, they said they'll be around all day to go through what they've come up with for the Mill."

They were in the dining-room at Glenwood, seated at the table going through their paperwork and enjoying a bottle of Chilean wine at the same time.

"Denise is coming over for those three days we'll be in London."

"Oh?" Jodhi looked up from her paperwork.

"According to Denise, there has been a major falling-out in the Cunningham camp. Michael Farrell has left them."

"Really?" Jodhi sat back and smiled, folding her arms.

"His relationship with Ali O'Mara proved too much of a strain."

"That's a huge loss to Cunningham Homes."

"More than they realise or are prepared to admit to

themselves. As for Farrell's Auctioneers, I doubt it will even be in business in another year with the sister in charge."

Jodhi looked bemused. "Is that because it's a woman in charge?"

"No, it's because it's a drunk in charge."

"Farrell's departure has greatly improved our chances of getting the Mill."

"Sure has. There's been a bit of a development between me and Denise."

"Good."

"We're getting closer. Slowly but surely. But she doesn't want to live in Dublin if we are together."

"But your plan always was to live in Dublin!" Jodhi was seriously concerned.

"I know . . . but I have to take into account what she wants to do. She's not comfortable being here with her ex and his family all around."

"I see. Bang goes our whole marketing strategy for Heavey's Mill." Jodhi was irritated.

"This isn't just about a marketing strategy, Jodhi. I thought Denise valued her position so much in Dublin that she would need to continue here and so she would be delighted to be associated with Heavey's Mill. Now it seems that's not so important to her any more. Maybe she had enough of it with the Cunninghams. You know they've made out all these years that Cormac rescued her from a life of poverty and that she was lucky to be married into them. But, you know, it was they that were getting the benefit of having her with all the publicity she generated for them and their developments. I think she's tired of all that, tired of being a society queen . . . and I want whatever makes her happy."

"I see." Jodhi took up her pen and started to write notes again.

Ryan looked at her for a minute and then started to read his paperwork again.

* * *

Denise's eyes opened as she heard Cormac come into the bedroom. He undressed in the darkness and got into bed beside her. She kept her back to him and he turned his back to her.

"I have to go to London on Friday night," she said. "I have to meet a couple of charity heads over there for Forward. I'll be gone for three days."

"Whatever," he said.

55

Michael stared out of the window of Ali's apartment. Across the communal gardens and past the neighbouring building, he could see the construction activity of the final phase. He had just started devising a marketing plan for its launch. He wondered what Lisa would now come up with on her own. Free year's supply of vodka for every apartment bought?

He spotted Cormac walking through the construction site. He stopped at a couple of workers and started talking to them. Suddenly he started roaring at them, and the workers visibly cowered away from him. Michael shook his head. In a way he had always felt sorry for him. His parents were hard acts to follow, and they always let him know that. But why take it out on the rest of the world?

Ali came in and coming up to him put her arms around him.

"Just heading into the office," she said.

"We might head out to dinner tonight, if you feel like it?"

"I'd love that. What are you going to do today?"

"Meet a few contacts. But you know, nothing they can offer me is going to be right."

"What do you mean?"

"I don't want to work for just another estate agent. I want to get my teeth into something, like I did at Farrell's. I loved the whole lifestyle that we created at Glenwood. It's so much more than just selling houses. I was really looking forward to being part of creating something special at Heavey's Mill."

Ali nodded. She understood where he was coming from. Michael's brain was so active, it needed to be challenged and stimulated.

*   *   *

Ali was seething over the Cunninghams' treatment of Michael. She really admired the fact that, although he was hurt by his closest friends' betrayal, he was completely upbeat. She loved that about him. His strength and ability to always look on the bright side. In fact she was more angry at the Cunninghams than he was. And if they thought she had been an adversary of theirs in the past, they'd better watch out for the future. She would watch them like a hawk and take every opportunity to discredit and expose them for what she had known them to be all along.

She arrived at her office to be surprised by a display of flowers on her desk. Smiling, she took up the card, expecting it to be from Michael.

The card read: *"Ali – thanks for the write-up you gave me – much appreciated, Ryan Cantwell."*

Ali sat down and smelt the flowers. What a wonderful gesture, she thought.

She sat thinking for a while, slowly getting excited by her train of thought.

Then she picked up her phone and dialled Ryan's number.

"Ryan, Ali O'Mara here. Just ringing to say thanks for the lovely flowers – completely unnecessary."

"It's me who should be thanking you for that feature again. We're delighted with it."

"I meant every word I said. It's great to meet a man in your position who takes the job responsibly. Actually . . . there was another reason I was calling you. I was wondering if you would like to meet myself and my partner for dinner?"

Ryan thought for a second. "Yes – that would be great. I'm in London from Friday for the weekend though."

"Would you prefer to leave it till next week then?"

"How's about tonight?"

"Perfect. I'll make a booking at The Unicorn. See you then."

Ali hung up and sat back smiling.

Ryan closed his mobile shut and thought hard.

"Who was that?" enquired Jodhi. She was driving them in his car into town.

"Ali O'Mara. Wanting to meet up for dinner. A hack like her wouldn't phone me up to meet just because she had enjoyed my company. She wants something – and my guess is now that her boyfriend has parted company with the Cunninghams, information courtesy of Denise, she's angling for a position for him."

* * *

Ali rushed into the apartment.

"Sorry I'm late!" she said, running into the bedroom and rifling through her clothes to choose something to wear.

"You're all right. We've plenty of time."

"I've asked somebody to join us for dinner, if that's all right?"

"Eh, yeah – somebody from work?"

Ali threw off her clothes and changed into her one and only designer dress.

"In a way, yes, I did meet him through work. Ryan Cantwell – remember, who I interviewed?"

Michael came into the bedroom. "Ryan Cantwell? Of course, I remember the interview – it's the one that caused the war."

Ali sat down at the mirror and started putting on her make-up "I just thought he was a fascinating man, and it would be interesting to get to know him a bit better."

"You know, you'd be useless at poker."

"What do you mean?" She applied her lipstick.

"It's so obvious you're up to something. What exactly?"

"I just think it could do you no harm meeting someone who is about to become one of the biggest players in the construction industry in Ireland. And I think you'll like him a lot."

"And since when did you decide to become interested in business?"

She got up quickly and kissed him "Since I met you. Now come on." She grabbed his hand and rushed him out.

*   *   *

Ali waved over to Ryan as he came into The Unicorn. They were already seated by the window.

"Hello again," said Ryan, as he approached the table and shook Ali's hand.

"Hi, thanks for joining us. This is my partner, Michael Farrell."

Both men greeted each other and then sat down.

"The flowers were amazing. I couldn't stop looking at them all day."

Michael raised his eyes and laughed. "You send her flowers and she looks at them all day. I send her flowers and she sends them off to the kids' ward in a hospital and gives out to me for wasting money!"

Ali slapped him playfully on the shoulder. "Oh, be quiet. I never said I didn't appreciate them."

"Maybe Ali's become more indulgent to herself since she started seeing you," commented Ryan, enjoying their chemistry.

"Maybe I have," Ali looked at Michael, "but I think it's too late. He sent me diamonds when we started seeing each other, but I gave out to him for extravagance, and now I think I'll never get anything worth more than five euros from him again."

"Don't try and reinvent yourself at this stage in the relationship," chastised Michael. "It's hard to give someone anything when all they do when they get it is give you a lecture on the poverty that exists in the world."

"Well, if you try me again, I might just say thank you."

"I think she's angling for a present, Michael," commented Ryan, with a laugh.

"I'm damned if I do and damned if I don't," said Michael.

They ordered wine, then took their time studying the menu. Ali opted for the duckling, while Ryan and Michael went for the lamb.

While they discussed the menu, Ryan and Michael surreptitiously observed each other. Ryan knew that Denise was extremely fond of Michael, and he could see how she was drawn to his warm and open character.

"How are you settling into Glenwood?" Michael asked.

"Very well, thanks. Of course I bought the house through your agency, didn't I?"

"His old agency. He's left it now," said Ali.

"But you owned the agency, didn't you? Can you leave your own business?"

"Although it was my name over the door, I was a junior partner in the firm and I've decided to move on."

"Move on where?" asked Ryan.

"I'm just deciding that at the moment."

"He's had loads of offers already," Ali put in quickly, "but he wants to take his time to make the right move. I mean he's so well known in the Dublin property market that the world is his oyster."

"Ali!" said Michael, feeling embarrassed.

"No, she's right," said Ryan. "I might have been away from the Dublin property scene for a number of years, but you appear to be one of the leading lights here."

"It's Michael's marketing ability that's made him so well known. The ideas he comes up with to market developments are truly spectacular. He would do anything himself to attract a bit of publicity. I was always accusing him of prostituting himself to get publicity when we started seeing each other." She laughed.

"And have you prostituted yourself, Michael?" Ryan asked, bemused by the embarrassment Michael was obviously suffering.

"Not in the traditional sense of the word," said Michael. "But if I think a good idea might attract publicity for something we are selling, I don't mind doing something a little unconventional."

"You can say that again," said Ali.

* * *

Their starter finished, the main course arrived.

"You know, I don't know if we should even be sitting at the same table," said Ryan. "You're so heavily involved with the Cunninghams and we're both after Heavey's Mill."

"Oh, no, he's left that shower behind," said Ali.

"Ali!" said Michael, laughing. "I can speak for myself!"

"I know. I'm sorry!" Ali put her hands in the air.

"You've had a falling-out with them? Oh, has that something to do with why you've left Farrell's?" Ryan pretended to be innocent of all developments. It was so obvious what was happening. Ali was canvassing for a position for Michael. And Michael, although open to all offers, was wary of him.

"Yeah – I don't think it's a big secret," Michael said nonchalantly. "Most people in the Dublin property world know that we've had a parting of the ways and won't be working together again."

"Can I ask what the falling-out was about?"

Michael shook his head gently. "Don't really want to get into that here."

Ryan looked at Ali, who he suspected was dying to say exactly what had happened, but was under orders to say nothing.

The dinner passed by in entertaining conversation, and Ryan really warmed to Michael. He thought it would be hard not to like Michael. He seemed to be everyone's friend but nobody's fool.

Ryan finished his coffee. "Listen, I'd better be going. I really enjoyed the meal. Ali, thanks again for that feature. Michael, I'm sure our paths will cross again. Can I have your card?"

"Er – I've only got my old card," Michael was embarrassed, "and I've changed my mobile number since then. Here, I'll write my new number out for you."

Michael tore off a piece of paper and scribbled it down.

* * *

"He loved you!" said Ali, as they walked back to the apartment, arm in arm.

"He didn't love me. We got on – but big deal! I'm sure he gets on with loads of people."

"Look, if he gets Heavey's Mill, he'll be looking to open operations here, and who has more experience of the market than you? You'd be a huge asset to him. He's out of touch with the Dublin property market; he needs someone like you."

"And you were so obvious about it. You were really hustling him for a job for me."

"I'm a journalist – I'm used to hustling."

"Well, you embarrassed me."

"Did I?" she looked up at him, all concerned.

"But I loved that you were doing that for me."

He bent down and kissed her, and she rested her head on his shoulder as they continued walking home.

56

Denise stared out of the taxi window, deep in thought. It was Friday evening and she was on her way to the airport. The traffic was bad. She suddenly felt panicked that she would miss her flight.

"There's no quicker way we can go?" she asked the driver.

"Sorry, love!" he shrugged.

She sat back. If she missed the flight, then it just wasn't meant to be. She wasn't meant to go to London for the weekend and she would just go back to Glenwood. That gave her a sense of dread and she realised that she was really excited about going to London. She had briefly spoken to Ryan on his mobile that morning. He had been travelling out to the airport and he assured her he would be at Heathrow to pick her up that evening. She rubbed her temples.

*   *   *

She checked in and, as she was running late, went straight for Departures. She sat looking out at the huge windows at the Aer Lingus plane wondering what was in store for her. Wondering how her life had taken this turn of events. She took out her mobile and phoned Cormac.

"Just letting you know that I'm at the airport now," she informed him.

"Right. You're back . . .?

"Sunday night."

There was an awkwardness in the air. "Do you want me to collect you?"

"No, I'll just get a taxi. See you then." She turned off her phone.

"Calling all passengers on Aer Lingus EI346 from Dublin to Heathrow, we are now boarding. Please have your tickets and passports ready. Calling seats 1 to 45 first."

Denise remained seated. She hated queuing, and waited until everyone had boarded the plane before she got up and, taking off her sunglasses, strode over to the flight attendant.

* * *

Ryan stood expectantly in the Arrivals Hall in Heathrow. He looked up at the screen which informed him that Denise's flight had landed. He waited a little away from the rest of the people waiting to greet their loved ones. He was consumed with worry that she hadn't boarded the plane. What had their relationship been so far? Meeting furtively and discussing big plans. If Denise had got on that plane, then he knew she was serious about them. He held his breath as the double doors opened and passengers started pouring out. And there she was. Her hair tied back in a tight ponytail, her face hidden behind large dark glasses. Dressed in a black leather coat, tied tightly at the waist. He moved quickly through the crowd and waved, seeing she was scanning the people, looking for him. Seeing him, she cut through the crowd to him.

"Hiya, welcome to London," he said smiling, and taking her bag. He put his arm around her waist and directed her away from the chaos of the airport.

The smells and bustle of London were hitting her as they walked out to the pick-up area.

"How was the flight?" he asked, directing her to a blue Mercedes.

"Fine – quick," she said.

She noticed there was a driver at the wheel of the Mercedes. Ryan opened the boot and put her luggage in, before opening the back door for her. They both sat in.

"Where do you want to go?" he asked, an excited look on his face.

"I don't know." She shrugged and smiled, taking off her sunglasses.

"Are you tired, hungry, thirsty? Wherever you want to go we can go. If you want to go back to my apartment first and settle in, or have a drink first, that's fine. Or if you want to head straight into the West End, we can eat out or have a few drinks. Whatever you want!"

"I'd prefer to go straight out."

"That's fine." Leaning forward, Ryan said to the driver.

"Take us up to the South Bank. Drop us off at Waterloo."

The car speeded off towards the city.

Ryan talked a lot as they travelled. The conversation was light, mostly about the different meetings he had during the day. Denise didn't say too much, the whole thing felt so strange to her. And yet there was a thrill racing through her at the thought of all this being her new life. The car pulled over near Waterloo station.

"You can drop the bags back with the concierge of my apartment," said Ryan.

"Will you be needing me for the rest of the evening?" the driver asked.

"No, you can go home after that."

"He's your permanent driver?" Denise asked as the car took off.

"Yes. He's on the payroll of Aston."

Denise looked at all the people teeming in and out of Waterloo. He put his arm around her and directed her past the station and down the South Bank. The place was alive with workers out enjoying their Friday evening. She looked out across the river at the London skyline as Ryan busily pointed out different landmarks.

They came to The Oxo Tower.

"Have you been here before?" he enquired as they took the lift to the top floor.

"No. I only ever come to London for quick shopping trips," said Denise.

Walking out of the lift, she took in the all-glass walls of the restaurant that offered breathtaking views across the river.

"I'm sorry, we're all booked out," said the receptionist to a small party in front of them.

"Sorry, Jemina, I'm afraid I didn't get a chance to ring ahead for a booking," apologised Ryan as they approached the reception.

"Ah, Mr Cantwell, we'll see what we can do for you," said Jemina and beckoned over the head waiter.

"If you'll just follow me through, Mr Cantwell," smiled the head waiter, taking Denise's coat. She was wearing a satin beige dress and as they walked through the restaurant they attracted admiring looks.

They were seated at one of the best tables beside the balcony. The whole restaurant was flooded in the evening light through the massive windows.

"This is absolutely lovely," said Denise.

"I recommend the salmon," said Ryan.

"Okay," agreed Denise.

"And we'll start off with white wine?"

Denise nodded and Ryan gave the order to the waiter.

Denise suddenly put her hand up to her mouth and covered it.

"What's wrong?" asked Ryan.

"It's just that my husband thinks I'm at some stuffy charity conference."

Ryan reached over and took her hand. "Let's just forget about everything this weekend. Leave your life in Dublin behind and enjoy yourself here, okay?"

Denise nodded. "Okay."

After dinner, they moved into The Oxo Bar, sat up at the bar and ordered Manhattans.

The jazz band was playing "Take Five".

Denise had begun to relax and loved the ambiance of the place. She crossed her legs and flicked her hair back.

"So – tell me about Kate," she pushed.

"Kate – what's there to know?"

"Everything! You know everything about my life; I want to know about yours. So start talking."

"Kate . . . It didn't work out. I did care for her a lot. When I left Dublin, I was lost, absolutely lost. I didn't know where you had gone, why you had gone. I threw myself into my work, and then Kate came along and she helped me get on with my life. We were married for a long time. But she says she never really had me, so she left."

"And why didn't she have you?"

He looked at her. "Because I never got over you."

Denise took a sip of her Manhattan and licked her lips.

"You never contemplated having children with Kate?"

"We talked about it, but we never got around to it. I think we both knew deep down that our relationship wasn't as stable as it should have been. So we knew it would be wrong to bring kids into it."

"I don't want to have children, Ryan."

He looked at her, surprised.

"It's something that never appealed to me. I mean Cormac wanted them. He actually wanted them badly. But I've never felt the need. I've been thinking about it recently and maybe it's like you and Kate, maybe there are fundamental problems in my relationship with Cormac and so I didn't want to bring a kid into the equation. Maybe it's because having a child ruined my mother's life

. . . I don't know. But if you want kids, Ryan, I'm not the girl for you."

Ryan looked at her, trying to figure her out. He thought he had her down to a T. After her rejection all those years ago, he had been ruthless in his pursuit to become somebody she would want to be with. So that he could give her the life she needed. He was pursuing Heavey's Mill so as to impress her and give her the position in Dublin she needed. Only to be told she didn't want to be in Dublin. He always imagined them as a happy couple with a couple of kids. Only to be told this wasn't an option. Studying her face, he realised she wasn't lying when she said she had changed. He had so long put her on a pedestal, thinking he understood everything about her. Thinking he knew why she walked out on him all those years ago. But she was surprising him all the time. But as he looked at her, he knew it didn't matter. He wanted her more than ever. It was like a need in him to have her and possess her. A need that she would complete his life, and he would take her on any terms.

They left the Oxo Bar late, giddy from Manhattans, and strolled down the South Bank.

"So listen, what are we doing tomorrow?" she asked excitedly.

"I was thinking lunch up at Harvey Nichols, a shopping trip, a couple of museums. How does that sound?"

"Sounds okay. As long as you don't wake me before noon. I like my sleep-ins."

"Ah, well, you can forget about that when you come

and live with me. It'll be early rises. Sleeping on in the mornings is wasting your day."

She stopped and said sternly, "Ryan, I haven't said I'm coming to live with you, yet."

He felt stupid. "I know."

They continued walking in silence, before Ryan said, "Here's a cab, let's grab it."

The cab pulled up outside the apartment block and the concierge rushed out to open the car door.

"A warm night, Mr Cantwell,' said the concierge.

"Yes, did my driver leave a bag in to you?" asked Ryan.

"Yes, sir."

Denise looked up at the glass building. The concierge held the glass front doors open and they entered the marbled lobby. Ryan collected the bag from behind the concierge's desk and they headed to one of the elevators. Denise tried to imagine herself living there as the lift brought them up to the top floors.

"Well, what do you think?" asked Ryan as he opened the front door of his apartment and put on the lights.

Denise walked around the huge space which was ultra-modern with white furnishings on marbled floors. She opened one of the patio doors in the wall-to-ceiling glass and went out onto the large patio balcony with its views across the Thames.

"It's as I imagined it," she said, putting her hands on the railing and breathing in the night air. He came out of the kitchen with an ice bucket, champagne and two glasses and went out onto the balcony, putting them on the table out there. He disappeared inside and put on some music.

He put on Dire Straits' "Your Latest Trick," and she smiled to herself, remembering how he used to play it years ago. But as she listened she was overcome with sadness.

"I found one of your favourites –" He stopped when he saw there were soft tears coming down her face.

"Denise?"

She wiped away the tears.

"I'm just being stupid. Don't mind me. I'm just finding this all a bit emotional. Memories coming back and I just wonder where all the years have gone. I'm trying to remember me as this young girl and what kind of a life I'd have had if I'd been a bit stronger. Maybe if I'd given our relationship a try, where would we be now? I knew what I was about back then. I knew what I wanted and I knew I could achieve it. And I did. I got everything I wanted. And I was happy. So why am I standing here on your balcony in London?" He put his arms around here and stroked her back. "I wish I could erase the years and go back and make different decisions. Maybe stayed with you then," she said.

"It's not too late. We can fix it and be together now."

"I know Cormac has his failings. But if you knew him, there is a lot of good there – he just hides it well – too well. We did have a happy marriage once, but it just seems to all have gone now. And I can't take it any more."

He bent forward and they started to kiss.

* * *

"So where's the wife tonight?" asked Barbara as Cormac drove her out to Glenwood.

"Over in London at a charity conference."

"Sounds like fun." Barbara faked a yawn.

They were followed by two other cars filled with friends.

"Well, it's about time we christened your new house," she said.

"I'm warning you, Barbara, no red wine and no spillages. I would like to have my house in one piece tomorrow."

"You're such a bore!" She reached over and tickled his face.

"Will you stop, I'm trying to drive," he snapped, but laughed.

"I'll save it for later then." She winked at him.

He pulled into the gateway of Glenwood.

"Wow! This is amazing!" she said.

He opened his window and reached out to punch in the code.

"Don't you have a zapper?" she asked.

"No. The security firm in charge here advised against them as they can get lost or stolen. Every resident in Glenwood is given their own code unique to them to operate the main gates."

"Oh let me! Let me!" Barbara crawled across him and, sitting on his lap, reached out to the panel.

"You're such a fucking kid!" snapped Cormac.

"Go on, I want to do it. What's your code?"

"78787," said Cormac.

Barbara punched in the numbers and the gates opened.

"Will you move? I can't drive the car with you sitting on my lap," said Cormac.

"No, but you can do a lot of other things with me sitting on your lap."

"Move!" He pushed her back into her seat and drove into the driveway at No 1.

The other two cars followed.

Steve Foyle got out of one of the cars. "You sure she's not home?"

"She's at this moment fast asleep in some London hotel," Cormac assured him.

He went to the front door and opened it with his key and the alarm started bleeping.

"Oh, let me! Let me!" shouted Barbara as she raced to the panel.

"You're getting more childish by the day!" said Cormac. "18903."

She put in the code and the bleeping stopped.

Everyone piled into the house.

"Right, that's the bar over there, so everybody party!" said Cormac.

*　*　*

She had thought she would be consumed with guilt. But she wasn't. She thought it would feel wrong to be with somebody else after twelve years of marriage. But it didn't. It felt very right. They fitted each other perfectly. It was three in the morning and Denise looked out at the night sky through the huge windows close to the bed.

"Are you asleep?" she asked.

"No."

"Are you happy?"

"Very much so." He leaned forward and they started to kiss again.

*   *   *

Cormac swilled back his whiskey and looked at the several people drinking around his lounge. A couple were kissing passionately. Another couple were dancing. He wondered where Barbara had gone. And thought he'd better go looking for her in case she was passed out somewhere. Having looked all around downstairs, he went upstairs and saw a light on in their bedroom. He opened it up.

"Barbara!" he called.

The toilet in the en-suite flushed and Barbara came out rubbing her nose.

"I hope you didn't leave any signs of coke in there." He was annoyed she had gone into their en-suite.

"I cleared up after me." She sat on the bed. "I love this room. She's one lucky bitch."

"What's my one rule?"

"I know – we don't talk about her." Barbara patted the bed beside her. "Come on over and sit beside me, Cormac."

"Come on. Let's go back downstairs."

"Come on. Don't be prudish. It would be a real turn-on doing it here on your marital bed. Doesn't that turn you on, Cormac?"

He looked at her as she started to unbutton her blouse. She got up, walked to him and went to kiss him.

"Come on, the others will wonder where we are."

"Let them wonder." She went to feel his crotch.

"Seriously, let's go downstairs." He moved away from her to the door.

"All right!" She shrugged and put her hands into the air.

"Your loss, sweetie." She stopped as she went past him and tickled his chin. "One day, Cormac . . . one day."

She went to the top of the stairs and put her hand on the wall to steady herself.

"Mind the fucking panic button!" shouted Cormac.

It was too late as Barbara's hand landed on it and pressed it.

"Oh shit ! What have I done?" she asked.

"For fuck's sake. There are panic buttons all around the house." He took out his mobile quickly. "If you don't ring in with a password to the security company the place will be swarming with security guards in less than five minutes." He dialled the security number.

"Hi, Falstaff Security?"

"Yes, how can I help you, sir?" asked the woman.

"This is Cormac Cunningham of No 1 Glenwood. We're after pressing a panic button!"

"That's right, sir. We have security personnel on their way to you right now."

"It's a false alarm. We pressed it by mistake."

"And your code to confirm that, sir?"

"Honey."

"That's fine, sir. We'll call back our personnel. Enjoy the rest of your night."

Cormac put his mobile away.

"Sorry, Cormac," apologised Barbara.

"Will you be more fucking careful? Actually, I think it's time you all went home."

57

Ryan looked at the sleeping form of Denise beside him. The morning sunlight was streaming through the windows. As he looked at her he couldn't believe she was there with him. After all these years of wanting her and needing her and here she was in his bed.

He bent forward and kissed her cheek, and her eyes fluttered open. She turned and looked at him.

"Good morning," she said.

"Just think if you lived here we could wake up like this every morning. We could go and have breakfast at Fortnum & Mason, lunch at The Ritz. We could have such a good life here."

"A few less Manhattans might be advisable, though."

She rubbed her forehead.

* * *

Denise did spend the day picturing her life in London and

she liked what she imagined.

As they walked down the Kings Road in the afternoon sunshine arm in arm, her life in Dublin felt a million miles away. They went to the restaurant in Harvey Nichols for lunch.

"I met a friend of yours during the week,' said Ryan.

"Oh?"

"Michael Farrell."

"How?" She became concerned.

"Don't worry!" He laughed and put up his hand. "I didn't stalk him as part of my campaign to get you."

"Not so bizarre if you think of some of the stupid antics you did. Following me and joining Forward. There's part of me that still thinks you're touched, and I'm more touched to have anything to do with you."

"Moving swiftly on . . . his girlfriend, who interviewed me, invited me out for dinner with them."

"How is he?"

"Seemed in great form."

"Michael's great. Nothing gets him down."

"I felt they were angling for me to offer him a job." He studied her face for a reaction.

"I see . . . and is there a job for him?"

"If we got Heavey's Mill, then yes there would be. In fact I could imagine he would be a great asset."

"What's the problem then?"

"I don't want to do anything that upsets you. He worked with the Cunninghams, and if you preferred me to stay away, I would."

"Answer me truthfully: if you offered a position to

Michael, would that have anything to do with trying to get my favour?"

"No, absolutely not."

"Then offer him a job. Michael is a great guy and very loyal. Cormac and the others treated him terribly. I'd like to see him get back on his feet."

* * *

That evening they went to Claridges for dinner.

"You really don't have to bring me to all these beautiful places," objected Denise as she looked around the splendour of the dining-hall.

"Are you trying to tell me that your life isn't equal to this in Dublin?"

"No, I'm used to the good life." She shrugged.

"This is my life in London, Denise. You wanted to see it, and so here it is."

"I'm not saying I'm not impressed. And I'm not saying it's not what I want. I'm just saying it's not the only thing life is about for me . . . any more."

"And what is the most important thing to you?"

"To have a bit of peace. To just enjoy life."

"Then come and live with me." He reached out and held her hand.

"But can I trust you? Because if I leave Cormac, this must work."

"You know my career is important to me. Making Aston one of the most successful companies in this country is important to me. Getting Heavey's Mill is important to me. But there's other things more important to me . . . like you."

*　*　*

They sat in silence as Ryan drove Denise out to Heathrow on the Sunday.

"Do you have to go back?" he said.

"Yes, I've a lot of stuff to sort out, and some thinking to do."

She checked in and he walked her over to Departures.

"Why look so glum?" she said. "You're coming back to Dublin tomorrow."

"It's just the idea of you going back to him."

"Thanks for a lovely weekend. Talk to you during the week."

She turned and walked through into Departures.

*　*　*

Two hours later and Denise was letting herself into the front door at Glenwood.

Cormac was in the lounge watching television.

"Hi," she said, leaving her case in the hall. She avoided looking at him.

"How was your trip?"

"Fine. Nothing eventful. Anything been going on here?"

"No." He turned back and looked at the television.

Denise picked up her case and walked up the stairs, biting her lower lip.

58

Michael reached over and answered his phone. "Michael, Ryan Cantwell here. How are you?"

"Eh, fine." He had been lying in bed early on Monday morning and now sat up quickly.

"I was hoping to meet up with you. Wanted to go through a couple of things."

"Sure. Whenever suits you."

"I'm in London today. Perhaps tomorrow? Twelve o'clock, down at the Heavey's Mill site?"

*   *   *

Michael drove through the old Harbour district on the Tuesday, intrigued by what Ryan had wanted. Ali had been overly excited when he'd told her and insisted he was going to be offered a job. He had played it down, not wanting to get either her or his hopes up.

He arrived fifteen minutes early, but was surprised to

see Ryan's car already parked there. He was standing looking up at the old Mill, with a woman beside him.

"Ah, Michael, thanks for coming," Ryan said stretching out his hand and shaking Michael's. "This is my assistant, Jodhi."

Jodhi shook hands too.

"I suppose I don't need to tell you about this site since you're one of the leading lights of the Dublin property game," said Ryan.

"Yes, I'm very familiar with it."

"Then you know it's going for tender and the most innovative tender gets the deal?"

"I'm fully aware of all the conditions attached. I was working on the Cunningham tender."

"So, what do you think would be innovative to put on this site?"

Michael looked at him suspiciously. "I can come up with many innovative ideas, but I'm not just going to come out with them like that."

"But if I'm to offer you a job, how do I know that what I'm buying is worth anything?"

Michael was taken aback. Not just because he was being told he was offered a job, but because of the strange way it was being offered.

"What job exactly are you offering me?"

"Sales Director of Aston Construction, Irish division . . . that's when we get this Mill and have an actual Irish division. Don't worry. We'll match your salary to what you were getting before. And you'll have share options at Aston. What's more, you'll be getting one per cent commission on each unit sold here."

Michael couldn't hide his shock. "That's a very generous package."

"You'll have your work cut out for you. Firstly, we have to get this site, and after that the site is going to cost us ninety million. We're going to have to charge premium rates for apartments here, and although Dublin might be booming, look around here – it's wasteland for a couple of miles. Who the fuck will want to live here at the moment, particularly for the prices we are going to have to charge? Everyone is so anxious to get this site that they aren't looking to the difficulties that will occur after getting in. You'll be worth every penny because it will be your responsibility to make this site a success. I'll give you a day or two to think about it." Ryan and Jodhi got into their car and drove off.

Michael watched the car disappear and then he turned and looked up at the Mill that seemed to stretch forever.

He thought about the package he had just been offered and then he jumped into the air and punched the air shouting, *"Yes!"*

* * *

Ali rushed home after receiving Michael's good news. She found him at the table busily scribbling down notes with about twenty books opened around him.

"I'm delighted for you!" She kissed him.

"Couldn't have happened without you. You're a genius."

"I knew once he met you, he wouldn't let you go. And you know the great thing is that a company like Aston has such a great track record. They're the kind face of the corporate world."

"I thought there was no kind face of the corporate world," he teased.

"What are you working on?"

"I'm coming up with ideas for the Mill. What would make this a hive of activity. Something that will make people pay over the odds to live there."

"Over the odds?" Ali looked concerned.

"Well, for Aston to make their profit and still fulfil all the social commitments they have."

59

Michael didn't waste any time arranging to meet Ryan again and phoned him to arrange a meeting for Wednesday morning.

He drove up to Glenwood and pressed the bell on the panel for Ryan's house.

"Yes?" answered Jodhi.

"It's Michael Farrell here to see Ryan."

The CCTV camera turned around and focused on Michael and he casually waved up at it. A few seconds later and the gates opened. He drove down the road and pulled into the driveway of Ryan's house.

An hour later they were in Ryan's study with maps spread out all over the desk.

"Cunninghams' tender is going to be the very top end of the market. Luxury personified with a five-star hotel in the middle of it. Nobody does that kind of thing better than Cunninghams, so you need to offer Edel Garry something different. I like these plans your architects have drawn. You've a huge emphasis on quality of life rather than luxury, and that will appeal to Garry. But you're missing something. You don't have a USP, you know, a unique selling point. You need something to scream out to Edel Garry that yours is the only tender for the job. And you need something that will attract buyers in who will be willing to pay premium prices for what is, as you've pointed out, still an undeveloped area."

"But what?"

"I've been giving it serious thought and the answer is in what you were saying to me yesterday. It's a wasteland out there at the moment. It's going to be a number of years before it takes off. So why will people pay huge amounts of money to live there now? You need to give them something to attract them now . . . which is . . . jobs."

"I don't get you."

"The hotel idea we had for Cunninghams is going to provide a certain number of jobs, but the people who work in the hotel won't be able to afford to live in Heavey's Mill. But if we can get a top Information Technology firm to set up in Heavey's Mill, you're on to a winner."

Ryan was impressed. "If we got a computer firm to put their headquarters in the Mill, and got a thousand jobs out there or so, it would be a massive boost for the Harbour area."

"And those are well-paid jobs, so you can charge premium rates for the apartments which will either be bought by those working in the headquarters or investors guaranteed their rental income on their doorstep."

Ryan nodded. "It would mean that our proposal will

be mixed residential and industrial."

"So what? The Cunninghams' proposal is mixed residential and commercial. Only a hotel out there isn't going to work for a number of years until the whole area is developed. Our IT centre will work straight away. The only difficult part is now getting a firm ready to invest there. I'll get on to Enterprise Ireland and the IDA first thing tomorrow."

60

A large photo of Michael beamed from the front page of *The Independent*'s financial pages, under the heading "Farrell To Head Aston's Irish Division".

"*Well known estate agent and businessman, Michael Farrell, has been announced Sales Director of Aston Construction's Irish Division. Farrell, infamous for colourful marketing campaigns, has stepped down from running the company that bears his name, Farrell's Auctioneers to take up his new position. It is well known that Aston, one of the UK's leading construction firms, are very anxious to get into Dublin's booming property scene, and Farrell's appointment should ensure expert local knowledge. Aston's Irish ambitions are the latest in a series of expansions overseen by its MD, Irishman Ryan Cantwell. Over the past number of years his company has undertaken much construction activity in Eastern European countries and in London. Although Farrell remains a non-director shareholder at Farrell's, his loss will be firmly felt by the estate agents as he was the driving force behind the company. Farrell's MD chair has been filled by Lisa Cunningham."*

* * *

"Get me that fucking bastard on the phone now, or I'll come down and fucking drag him out of that meeting now!" Lisa screamed down the phone as she puffed nervously on her cigarette. Her mobile was constantly ringing which she was choosing to ignore.

She had been trying to get through to their accountant all morning, unsuccessfully. She felt the walls were caving in on her. People were ringing her looking for decisions to be made. Her staff kept putting things in front of her to sign that she hadn't time to read and so she kept scribbling her signature to anything. Somebody had forgotten to pay the phone bills and they had been cut off the previous day and she had spent two hours trying to get them reconnected. When she screamed at Reception asking who was responsible for paying the bills, the receptionist said Michael always took care of them, but he had some system going that he always left bills to the last minute to pay – but he never forgot to pay. She looked down at his smiling photo in *The Independent* and drew a big moustache across his face.

What a bastard! He just calmly went on with his life, without a second thought for the chaos he had left her to deal with. She needed to get the accountants more involved. They needed to take care of everything financial – she couldn't be dealing with it, and it didn't matter how much it cost.

The receptionist from the accountant's came back on the phone and apologised that she couldn't find him. Lisa slammed down the phone and lit herself another cigarette.

Then her office door opened and in waltzed Honey. Lisa groaned to herself. This was all she needed.

"I've been phoning you all morning and can't get through to you. What's your problem – out drinking with the movie star again?"

She looked down at her daughter, who looked wrecked.

"I'm trying to keep this fucking show on the road, with no help from anybody." Lisa dragged on her cigarette.

"I guess you can't make it for lunch then?"

"How can I – when this place is falling down around me?"

"Oh, pull yourself together and get on with it. It's hardly rocket science."

"Easy for you to say – have you seen this?" She flung the paper at Honey, who glanced at Michael's photo.

"Yes, I saw it – so what?" Honey assumed a bored air.

"So – he just waltzes on to great things and I'm left carrying this lot. Don't you care that's he's dumped all this shit on me?"

"I don't give a butcher's burger. I'm too busy today to hang around here listening to you moan. You know, that's why you're still single. Men hate to hear a woman moan. You never hear me moaning, do you? And listen, will you touch up that make-up. It looks terrible." Honey turned and walked out. Lisa looked at her watch. It was nearly twelve. She would give it another couple of hours and then sneak out to the pub.

* * *

Cormac slammed the door of the house behind him and flung his briefcase onto the sofa.

"What's wrong?" asked Denise, coming out of the kitchen.

"Have you seen this?" Cormac threw her *The Independent*.

Her stomach filled with butterflies when she read through the article about Michael.

"He's some operator, Farrell. Off joining the opposition at the first fucking opportunity!" He poured himself a large whiskey from the decanter. "Of course, he was always an opportunist. That's how he did so well over the years through us."

"You can't blame him after the way you treated him. He has to get on with his life any way he can."

"Whose fucking side are you on?" Cormac shouted.

"I warned you at the time that you should be working together."

"This is all O'Mara's fault. I knew she'd change him. I said she was dangerous. She's probably the one who's encouraged this move. She wrote the article praising Cantwell in the first place."

Denise knew from what Ryan had told her that it had been Ali who brought the two of them together. She felt guilty for knowing this information. She had always done whatever she could to help Cormac with his business, and now she felt so disloyal in every way.

Cormac went to the front window and arched his neck to try and see Ryan's house, but it was too protected by high walls.

"Now Michael will go and tell Cantwell all about our tender for the Mill and they'll have such an advantage over us. I got an email from Edel Garry today saying the tender has to be in next week and confirming the price of the site is sixty million."

"That's more that we thought, isn't it? Can we afford it?"

"Now most of Glenwood is sold we can just about get there. But we'll have to go to the banks to build the damned thing."

Denise saw the worry written across his face. Maybe it was always there and she just only noticed it now because Cormac took everything in his stride.

"Why didn't Cantwell stay in London or Eastern Europe or wherever the fuck else he was building. Why didn't he stay away from Dublin, from my patch and my life?"

Denise nodded and went back into the kitchen.

61

Ryan saw an email from *edelgarry@projectrum.com* on his laptop screen and opened it.

Dear Ryan,

I'm writing to you to confirm the last date for tenders for Heavey's Mill is next Friday, the 27th. I look forward to receiving your proposal. I also can confirm that the price for the site at Heavey's Mill is 60 million euros,

Kind regards,

Edel Garry

"Shit!" Ryan snapped his laptop shut after showing Jodhi the email.

"Does it give us enough time?" asked Jodhi.

"It gives us enough time to have the architects incorporate offices into our drawings, but it no way gives us enough time to secure an anchor tenant for those offices."

"If the worst comes to the worst, we'll just show the space designed for offices and say that we are working on securing a tenant."

"That sounds very lame. It's not even a half-baked promise – it's a prayer."

"You're right," Jodhi acknowledged.

Ryan picked up his mobile and phoned Michael.

"The tender has to be in next week, Michael. Any luck with Enterprise Ireland or the IDA?"

"I'm just out of meetings with them. And yes, they are very interested. They want to be part of the Harbour project and see it as an excellent location for foreign investment. But it's going to take time. It could take months to get an international firm interested in leasing those offices."

"Okay, talk to you later." Ryan hung up the phone. "I want to blow Edel Garry out of the water with our proposal which means going in there next week saying we have at least five hundred high-paid IT jobs ready to occupy offices at Heavey's Mill. Get me John Holden of Ski computers in Seattle on the phone."

* * *

Denise had arranged to be at Ryan's at eight and she slipped through the gap in the wall on time. All she had been thinking about was what her life in London would be like and it really excited her. No more arguments with Cormac. No more putting up with his family's snide comments. No more pressure of being a Society Princess –

she could relax and let her hair down unafraid that if she didn't watch herself all the time she would give away her background. And yet at the same time, because of Ryan's position, they would still have the life she always wanted – except this time it would be with the man she wanted. She got to Ryan's patio window and seeing the curtains were closed knocked on the glass. She got a start as Jodhi pulled back the curtains and stared at her.

She didn't know what to do, and almost turned to go away but Jodhi opened the doors.

"Hi, come on in. Ryan is running a little late."

"Oh!" Denise stepped into the house, feeling very uncomfortable.

She still wasn't clear on how much Jodhi knew. She seemed to be an intimate part of Ryan's life.

"Can I get you a drink? A coffee or a tea?" asked Jodhi.

"Just a coffee, if it's not too much trouble." Denise followed Jodhi out to the kitchen.

"He's been delayed over a meeting about Heavey's Mill," explained Jodhi, making the coffee.

"Heavey's Mill. It's all anyone seems to talk about these days." Denise attempted a smile.

Jodhi handed her the coffee.

"How long have you been working for Ryan?" Denise decided to use this time valuably.

"About six years."

"That long? He must trust you an awful lot."

"He does." Jodhi looked at her directly.

"Do you – enjoy the work?"

"Yes. I love it."

Denise was dying to bombard the girl with questions, but she felt it wouldn't be appropriate. Besides, by asking too many questions, she could be exposing herself.

The front door slammed and Ryan shouted, "Hello!"

"We're in here!" Jodhi called.

Ryan came in. "I'm so sorry I'm late. I got held up." He embraced Denise and kissed her, making her feel very uneasy as Jodhi was watching.

"I'm heading back to the hotel – I'll see you in the morning," said Jodhi.

"Sure – and thanks, Jodhi," said Ryan.

"I wish you hadn't done that in front of her," said Denise.

"Jodhi? She doesn't mind."

"Maybe not. But I do. I'm still a married woman."

Ryan put up his hands. "I'm sorry!"

"I'm just feeling so much pressure over this. Thinking someone is going to find out . . . listening to Cormac ranting about that fucking Mill all the time and furious that Michael has joined you. This has become so complicated . . ."

"You don't have to put up with it. You can come with me right now if you want."

She looked at him and sighed. "If only it was that simple."

"What's stopping you?"

She shrugged "Me. I don't know what I want any more. I could lose everything over you."

He went to her and held her. "You won't lose anything because we are going to be just fine together. Okay?"

She put her head against his chest.

"I have to go away for three days," he said then.

"Where?" She looked up at him.

"Seattle. There's a business meeting I have to attend."

62

Ryan had been in Seattle for two days and Denise had been putting off a visit, but decided she couldn't avoid it any more. She got a taxi from town.

"I don't usually travel out there," said the taxi driver, worried.

"I'll make it worth your while," she promised.

She dreaded these visits, but always made sure she went every couple of months. It was very painful but very necessary. As the taxi drove far out into the North Side, the familiar site of the flats came into view. Only there weren't as many now as there used to be as they had demolished some of them. There weren't as many people around either as the resettlement programme had started. She wondered if this resettlement would be more successful than the one that had brought them out to the flats in the first place. She hoped so.

"Just here on the right," she said.

He pulled over and she tipped him generously.

"Will you be all right here?" he asked, his face twisted in confusion and worry.

"Just fine," she smiled and got out.

She walked through the play area, now empty, and through the front door of the building. There was a lonely feeling about the place. There used to be loads of people around when she was growing up, but they must have been moved. The familiar smell hit as she entered the building: the mixture of detergent and chemicals, trying unsuccessfully to disguise other smells.

She pressed the lift button, and realised it was out of order.

"Some things never change," she said aloud as she began the climb up the steps.

She steadied herself as she reached her old home and then knocked loudly. After a few minutes it opened and her mother peered out through the chained door.

"I wasn't expecting you," said June. She said it every time her daughter visited.

She unlocked the door and as Denise stepped in the nostalgia swept over her, making her feel ill.

June reached forward and kissed her daughter on the cheek. Denise could smell the booze off her. She followed her into the small sitting-room. She had offered to get June a new home countless times over the years. Somewhere nice, down the country. June had always flatly said no. The only thing Denise could do was deposit money into her account every month.

She felt touched as she saw that, spread out on the coffee table, were photos of her posing in the social pages of different magazines.

"You look gorgeous in those photos," said June, sitting down.

"Thanks, Mum," Denise smiled.

"Of course I always hide these when anyone around here comes in. I say you're a receptionist in a swanky hotel if they ask. Not that there's many around here left asking questions. They're moving everyone out. They tell me I have a little ground-floor flat in a new development to go to."

"But that's great, Mum!"

"I don't want to go. I'm used to it here. I'll be the last one they manage to move. Why do you come back here, Denise? There's no need. You're in a different world now. You don't need bad reminders."

Denise forced herself not to cry as she saw examined her mother's once beautiful face, now all lined and sallow, her hair grey.

"I just want to see you. Nothing wrong with that, is there?"

"No. But it's enough for me to know you have a wonderful life. I hate to see you coming back here. I don't want to see you in this environment. I want to see you *here*." She lifted up the photo of her in *VIP*.

"Mum, I might be going away for a while."

June looked surprised. "Something to do with your husband's work?"

"Not exactly . . ." Denise trailed off.

June studied her daughter intently. "Oh, no, Denise... Don't tell me you've fallen for somebody else."

Denise bit her lip and nodded. "I think I have."

"Oh no!" June buried her face in her hands. "Don't make the same mistake I did! Don't put your life in the hands of somebody else. He'll only destroy you!"

"He won't, Mum. He came looking for me. You won't believe the extent he has gone to get me."

"After all I said to you when you were growing up! You have everything absolutely everything. Why throw it all away?"

"Ryan can offer me everything I want as well. But it's more than that, Mum; he makes me feel alive."

"Life has taught me bitterly to ignore feelings of being 'alive' as you put it – they'll only get you into trouble!"

Denise sighed "If I go with Ryan, do you wish me luck?"

June looked at her daughter. "Whatever decision you make in life, I'll support you."

"Thanks, Mum." Tearfully, Denise went over and hugged her.

* * *

They were tucked away in a corner in Ocean Bar.

"I'm listening to Cormac going on about that fucking Mill all the time . . . I'm usually completely behind him but not now . . . God, if he knew I was with you!"

"Then come to me."

"I mean, you've just been off in Seattle for three days. Is that what my life would be with you? You're going to have to be in Dublin for some time with this damned Mill.

Am I going to be alone in London all the time while you're out on business? Am I just going to be swapping a gilded cage for an ivory tower?"

"There's no point in lying to you. I will have to spend time in Dublin and I do have to travel. But I want you to come everywhere with me. Let me remind you. It's you who wants to leave Dublin. But if you want to stay in London, it's a quick commute. I'll fly back every night if I have to. And in a few months, Heavey's Mill will be up and running, and I won't need to come here as much."

"That's if you get Heavey's Mill."

"I'll get it all right. I've just put together a deal in Seattle —"

"Stop it, Ryan! I don't want to know. How can I go home to Cormac with him so stressed about this deal and have information that can help him?"

Ryan held up his hands. "Okay, I'll say nothing. It's usual for someone to share what's going on with the person in their life."

"And am I? The person in your life?"

"Well — yes, of course." Ryan looked down at the floor and put his hands together. "You are. I made my mind up a long time ago. But I don't think you'll ever be able to make up your mind."

Denise bit her lower lip, reached out and squeezed his hand. "I have made up my mind . . . it's you I want."

Ryan stared at her, a smile dawning on his face. "Really?"

She nodded. "Yeah. I just need to get things straight in my head and organise things."

Ryan smiled broadly. "I only ever want you to be with me because you want to, Denise. I don't want you ever to feel trapped in a relationship with me. I don't want you ever to feel you have to stay with me because of money or anything. That's why I haven't rushed you or tried to force the situation."

"I think I'm ready . . . but I'm terrified . . . I never thought I'd be able to make such a huge and brave move."

"Getting out of the flats all those years ago was a much braver move."

"No, it wasn't. When you have nothing to lose it's very easy to take risks. It's only when you've a lot to lose that risks become frightening. This had better work out between us, Ryan, because I could never go through something like this again."

"It will work out."

"I keep hearing you saying there are no certainties. But I can't go on living this deceit. I need to leave soon. As terrified as I am to do this, I need to do it soon."

"Name the day and I'll book us flights to London. Don't you need to tell your friends where you're going?"

"I'll contact them from London."

"And what about a divorce lawyer?"

"We can deal with that later. At the moment I just need to stop living this double life."

"I understand."

"Besides, the divorce should be straightforward enough. I'm the one ending the marriage, so I'll agree to anything Cormac wants."

Ryan was surprised. "That's putting yourself into a

very vulnerable position."

"I want to be fair. I'm not going to fleece Cormac. I went into that marriage with nothing, and I think it's only fair that I leave it the same way."

Ryan stared at her, still trying to figure her out after all these years. She had completely thrown him. A woman he had thought was driven by the need for financial security was willing – not just willing, but wanting – to walk away with nothing. He admired and respected her attitude. But the businessman in him found it infuriating.

"I'd better be getting home."

She reached for her coat and they walked out to her car.

"So when do you want go to London?" He could hardly believe it was actually happening.

"In a few days. Maybe Friday?"

She got in, he closed her door and she drove off.

The black Nissan waited until Ryan had got into his car and then pulled out and followed Denise.

63

Cormac looked up at the building Projectrum was in and felt himself begin to sweat.

Why was he sweating for? For fuck's sake, he was Cormac Cunningham. People got out of his way when they saw him coming. He held the portfolio under his arm tightly. Funnily when dealing with people he knew or when he was in charge, he was fine, but put him into a strange environment or in a position where he had to make an impression to get something, and he fell apart. If he had had Michael with him, he would have glided through this presentation. Michael would have done all the talking. He cursed the day that he had met O'Mara. He had phoned Lisa to see if she could accompany him, but she seemed to be falling apart under the pressure of running Farrell's. He sighed as he realised he would have to step in there before that company went down. But first thing was first and he pushed the door open and entered the building.

"Cormac, nice to see you again," said Edel as she shook his hand.

Her assistant closed the door as she left, leaving them alone.

Cormac found this cool woman completely intimidating.

"I've been looking forward to seeing your proposal," she said, crossing her legs, and giving him an eyeful of thigh.

"Eh, yes." He cleared his throat, and put the portfolio down on the desk.

Her blouse was already unbuttoned to her breasts and as she fiddled with the next button she asked, "Will I open it or will I leave it to you?"

"I'm sorry?" Cormac said, startled.

"The portfolio?"

"Oh!" Cormac went red, grabbed the portfolio and began to unzip it. "Allow me."

"Careful with that zipper, we don't want it to damage the goods," she said.

Cormac sat down and began to spread the plans across her desk.

She pulled her chair up beside him until she was sitting uncomfortably near.

"Em . . . this is what our guys have come up with. A top class apartment block with a five-star hotel right in the middle of it." He didn't waste any time – just came right out and summed up their whole proposal in one sentence. He wasn't one for marketing speak.

"Hmmm, exciting, Cormac. But will anyone want to stay in a five-star hotel in an area that is going to take five years to develop?"

"Well, we're planning for the future here. We're planning for when the area is fully developed."

She turned around and looked at him closely. "I suppose in the meantime it would be good for affairs. Hotels that are off the beaten track are always in demand for affairs, don't you think?" She licked her lips. "No witnesses."

"Sure . . . eh . . . whatever . . . everything that would be going into this apartment block would be top of the range. No expense spared to attract the very top end of the market."

"And what about your size, Cormac?"

"What ?"

"What size will the apartments be?"

"Oh, starting at 500 sq foot for the one bed, 700 sq foot for the two beds."

"Oh, that's a little small. I was hoping for something bigger. Now point out exactly where the hotel will be in the development."

He put his finger on the plan and traced the outline of the hotel. Edel moved her hand, placed it on his and gently guided it over the lines.

"I think I get the picture," she said. "And would you be hands on during the erection?"

"I look after the building of the site myself." He drew back his hand quickly.

She looked deep into his eyes. "You're exciting me, Cormac." She closed her eyes. "Your proposal here is very exciting."

Cormac tried to move away from her, but found himself sandwiched between her and the chair beside him.

"If you got the site . . . you and I would have to work very closely together. Late nights, weekends, making sure that both of us get the ultimate satisfaction out of this job. Would you be . . . okay with that?"

Cormac cleared his throat. "I guess it's a big job and that always needs extra attention."

"Oh, I insist on extra attention."

Cormac jumped up from his chair. "Listen, I'd better be heading. I've got another meeting soon."

She looked up at him surprised "Another meeting?"

"Yeah." He was still red and seemed very uncomfortable. "Look through the plans and any questions, give me a call." He turned and quickly left her office.

Edel was perplexed. Could it be that she had read the situation wrong? By the sounds of it Cormac Cunningham went with everyone and anyone. Maybe he didn't find her attractive. She took out her vanity mirror and studied her striking face. Nonsense, she thought.

Her mobile rang and she saw Des's number come up. She sighed and answered it.

"Yes, Des? And before you ask – no, I can't pick the kids up."

* * *

Michael put on his tie as he looked at himself in the bedroom mirror.

"I can't believe that guy. He's some operator. He heads off to Seattle for three days and comes back with a deal like this!"

Ali sat on the bed, almost as excited as him.

"How did he manage it?" she asked.

"Ski Computers were about to put their European Headquarters in Budapest and Aston had been commissioned to build the offices. Ryan somehow managed to convince them to put their European headquarters in Dublin instead, in Heavey's Mill. I don't know how he managed it. I'd say he offered huge discounts on construction costs. But it'll secure Heavey's Mill, that's for sure. Five hundred IT jobs!"

"And, excuse me, I get the exclusive on that one," demanded Ali.

"No surer thing," He turned and hugged her. "It's just amazing to be working for someone as bright and capable as Ryan Cantwell."

"If I can remind you, it was you who came up with the idea to put an IT firm into the development."

"Yeah, I know, but if that was the Cunninghams, they would have expected me to do all the work getting a firm in. Ryan clicks his fingers and has it done in three days. I've been wasting my time so much with the Cunninghams. I hear Farrell's Auctioneers is going down the toilet fast. Seemingly, Lisa, and her new best friend, the alco actor, have positioned themselves at the bar in The Shelbourne and never leave. I'm going to have a word with my solicitor tomorrow about trying to stop them using my surname for their company. And while I'm at it,

I'm going to try and pull out of Farrell's altogether. I don't care what it costs me."

"What time is your meeting with Edel Garry?"

"In about thirty minutes. Better run. Wish us luck."

She reached up and kissed him. "The very best of luck."

He grabbed his brief-case and raced off.

Her smile lingered. She felt happy – really happy – for the first time in a long time. Everything had worked out just fine for them, even though it had been a very bumpy ride. The only thing that was niggling in her mind was how Ryan Cantwell had been elevated onto a pedestal so quickly in Michael's mind. The man could do no wrong, according to Michael. She hoped Michael hadn't just swapped hero-worshipping the Cunninghams to hero-worshipping Ryan Cantwell.

64

Edel observed Ryan Cantwell, Michael and Jodhi sit down opposite her. She wished they had left the girl behind. Firstly, she appeared to be just a secretary – so why bother having her there? Secondly, Edel was a man's woman, and could never warm to women.

"Mr Farrell, you appear to have jumped ship midstream. Didn't I meet you before with the Cunningham tender?"

"That was very early on in the campaign. I've been with Aston Construction for the most part of this proposal being put together."

"So glad to hear it. Because if Aston are unsuccessful in their bid, everyone can just blame you!"

Michael chuckled and nodded his head. "Does that mean it works both ways? If we are successful, I can claim all the credit?"

"Ah, but if only life could work out as simply as that. Blame is a pie left uneaten, credit is a cake to be shared by all."

She was drawn to Michael's cockiness. He seemed bold and she imagined he would be game for anything. However, she was aware he was seeing Ali O'Mara, which was too dangerous a connection and put him firmly off limits. She turned her attention to Ryan.

"So, Ryan – what have you got for me?" She sat forward.

"Hope you're going to like this, Edel," said Ryan spreading the plans across her desk.

"So do I."

"We're going for quality living here. We are going middle of the market. Let's face it, anyone who can afford the luxury end of the market is going to be living in Donnybrook, and so there's no point in targeting luxury gaffs at them in an area that has to prove itself."

Edel nodded at the common sense of it.

"That doesn't mean we are cutting any corners. Quite the reverse. There is a high-standard finish throughout. I'm picturing the profile of the people who will be living here to be between twenty-five and thirty-five, young professionals. A lot of them will be buying their first home here."

Edel nodded. "And what have you earmarked for here?" She pointed to a large part of the site marked commercial. She made sure to brush her hand against Ryan's as she did.

"We're going to put in an office block here."

"An office block?" She looked surprised.

Jodhi spoke up. "Yes, we felt we needed to bring

employment into the area, which will in turn entice people to live here."

Edel looked at Jodhi coolly before addressing Ryan again. "An office block?"

"A mixed-use development," confirmed Ryan.

"I don't want to have a big office block with a *To Let* flag dangling from it for ages. It will be detrimental to the area."

"We've already secured an anchor tenant . . . Ski Computers are going to place their European Headquarters in the Heavey's Mill development."

Edel sat back. "Quite a coup."

"Ski is only interested in Heavey's Mill with us as the developers," Michael pointed out.

"Naturally . . . and how many jobs are we talking about?"

"Five hundred initially – who knows where it will lead in the future."

Edel cleared her throat "And you can show me confirmation from Ski that they have settled on Heavey's Mill?"

"I can have it emailed to you this afternoon."

"Thank you, gentlemen – and lady, for your presentation. It's been very informative, and I will be making a decision very shortly."

As she shook Ryan's hand, she decided his cool and in control manner was infinitely more attractive than Michael's cockiness. And as for Cormac Cunningham – well, he was out of the running – in every sense.

*   *   *

Cormac was in The Ice Bar and he didn't fancy a late night. He would have one more and head home. He felt unnerved after his experience with Edel Garry. Boy, but did she come across really different from how she really was. She had practically propositioned him there and then. He was annoyed with himself for not being able to handle the situation differently. Angry with himself for having done such a lousy presentation in the first place. He just was no good at stuff like that. Give him a building site and he knew exactly what he was doing. But he had felt like a fish out of water there today. And she had sensed it and probably gone in for the kill.

"Cormac, you wouldn't have a few quid, would you? I left my purse at home, and it's my round," said Barbara.

"Sure." He gave her two fifties.

"Thanks, doll."

She went to the bar and ordered a round.

"I forgot I have to make a call," she said to the barman. "Back in a second."

She flounced out of the bar and into her Mazda in the carpark. She punched in a number on her mobile.

"Hi, it's me. I checked my account and the money's gone through okay – about bloody time – Okay, have you got a pen and paper? The code for the front gate is 78787. The code for the alarm on the house is 18903 and if the panic alarm is set off, the security firm is Falstaff, the number he dialled was 01 8907234, and he gave the code name Honey."

65

"I'm not going to bed!" screamed Edel's oldest as he clung to the stair banisters for dear life. Edel stood over him with her arms folded, viewing him coolly.

"I think you might find you are," she informed him.

"Never!" he screamed.

"Please yourself." She turned and left him hugging the banister. "But I think you might find a warm bed is more comfortable than a cold stairs for the night." She entered the living-room and locked the door behind her. Des was sitting on the sofa, rocking the youngest in his arms who he had just managed to get off to sleep. Edel went to her desk and started studying Aston's proposal.

The eldest boy tried to come into the living-room and to his fury found the door locked.

"Let me in!" he screamed, hammering the door. "I want to watch television!"

His actions woke the baby and set him off crying.

"I can't fucking believe this!" shouted Des. "It took me

an hour to get him off to sleep!"

Baby still in his arms, Des stormed to the living-room door and unlocked it. The boy came storming in and switched on the television.

"You should have left him out there – he would have got bored eventually," admonished Edel, who didn't look up from her work.

Suddenly Cassandra appeared at the door in her nightdress.

"If he's allowed to stay up to watch television, then I'm staying up too!" she wailed.

Edel chose to ignore the ensuing row between Des and the children and concentrated on the proposals. There was no option really. Five hundred top jobs and Ski Computers European Headquarters going into Heavey's Mill secured the deal for Aston. It would kick the Harbour area project to a flying start. And be seen as quite a coup for her as well. She logged on to her computer and sent two emails.

* * *

Jodhi came into the lounge in Ryan's house. Denise was sitting on the sofa looking stressed, and Ryan had his arm around her.

"I've booked you two seats on an Aer Lingus flight departing at nine tomorrow night," informed Jodhi. "You can collect the tickets at the airport."

"Thanks, Jodhi." Ryan nodded his appreciation.

"I'd better hurry as I'll be late for my own flight," said Jodhi. She was due back in London for a meeting with the architects.

"You can handle the meeting all right tomorrow?" checked Ryan.

"Of course," she smiled her reassurance.

"Thanks, Jodhi."

Jodhi looked at Ryan as he put his arm around Denise, and tried to fathom the whole thing as she had countless times before. Why would a man as important and successful as Ryan want such a complicated situation? And the situation had become much more complicated as time went on. Gone was the initial plan of Ryan arriving back to Dublin triumphantly and living there with his ultimate trophy wife. Gone was the plan of how they, Ryan and Denise, would become the toast of the town and in turn through the huge publicity they would receive how Aston would quickly become the most prolific and biggest construction firm in Ireland. Now Denise wanted to have nothing more to do with Dublin, and was happy to retire from her social position. What was more, by the sound of it, she wasn't even going to bring a penny with her. Jodhi was so used to Ryan's mind and how it worked. He was calculating and shrewd and always looking at the bigger picture. When he had first told her about Denise, she had thought it a magnificent plan to conquer the Dublin property market. What better way than to marry the beautiful and connected wife of Dublin's leading construction firm owner?

Of course, he had talked about his genuine feelings for Denise. But as Jodhi closed the front door of the house after her, she wondered if she was the one who had been duped. By dressing up his love for Denise as beneficial to Aston, she had willingly gone along with all his plans to get her.

*   *   *

Denise heard the front door close.

"She's in love with you, you know," she said.

"What?" Ryan laughed.

"Jodhi's in love with you. It's quite obvious to me."

"Don't be ridiculous. She's my assistant, and a friend, and that's as far it goes."

"Oh, I know that. But she still can't help how she feels, can she?"

"You're being stupid." Ryan waved the subject away. "Think of it, this time tomorrow we'll be getting on the plane for our new life."

She sighed. "I've a lot to get through before that."

66

The next day Lisa was sitting at her desk smoking a cigarette, speaking on the phone.

"I'm afraid Michael has left the company, so I'll be taking over the sale of your house . . . well, I'm sorry , but if he's gone he's gone. There's nothing I can do . . . I know he was charming and inspired trust – who are you telling? But the man is no longer working here, comprendo? . . . What do you mean, you don't want me? I'm one of the best agents in town. You should be lucky that I'm even considering representing you . . . hello . . . hello?" Lisa put down the phone as she realised she had been hung up on. She looked at her watch. It was only two, but she'd had enough. Hugh had moved into his new house in Glenwood, and she decided to head over there for the rest of the day.

* * *

Cormac sat at his desk looking at his opened email from

Edel. The email very kindly but very firmly rejected their proposal. He was amazed at the speed with which Edel had made up her mind. Was it so obvious to her that they weren't right for the job?

There had been other construction firms tendering, but he knew that Aston were the other serious competition, and as such were the winners. He imagined Michael must be euphoric.

Strangely, he didn't hate him. Just wished he was still around.

Paul came into the office.

"Just been looking around the site. Shaping up pretty good. We'll be ready for a launch soon. Premium prices. Always save the best till last. Don't know who we're going to get to launch them though. Not sure if Lisa can handle it on her own."

"That's the least of our problems. I got an email from Edel Garry. We've been turned down for the Mill."

Paul was usually grumpy but even-tempered, but this time his blood pressure went though the roof.

"I always knew there was a reason why women should stay out of business! If one of the old school were in charge, we'd have got that fucking thing hands down!"

"Well, she is in charge."

"Giving it to the fucking Sassenach!"

"What can we do?" Cormac was resigned to the fact.

"Is that all you can say? We've about seven months of work left and then the company that I built up over forty years is going to grind to a halt because of your bad planning!"

"We'll get some more land."

"Where? You fucking tell me where, and I'll go get it today. You probably fucked up on the presentation. Easily known once Michael was gone, you wouldn't be able to pull it off. This is fucking great! Now I've not only one company going down the toilet, but two! Retirement is all very well and good, but I'm going to have to get back into the driving seat to get everything back in order."

Paul didn't bother closing the door after him as he stormed out.

* * *

Denise spent the day looking around Glenwood. She made some calls to friends and said she was going away for a while. She would let them know later exactly what was happening when she was settled in her new life. She would resign her post at Forward formally when she was in London. No doubt the news of her marriage break-up would be public knowledge by then. How shocked they would all be! Denise – who never put a foot wrong. She looked through her wardrobe and picked some clothes that were her favourites, chose a couple of items of jewellery from her collection and packed a suitcase. She wanted to time her meeting with Cormac perfectly. She wanted to get to his office as most of the staff were leaving, but obviously in time before he left. She went out to her car and drove towards town.

*   *   *

She sat parked in the workers' carpark at The Pavilions and waited as the workers poured out on the dot at five thirty. Then she got out of her car, walked past the security man and into the site and then made her way up to Cormac's office. She waited at the door of his office suite and clenched her stomach. This was the hardest thing she ever had to do. The door suddenly opened, making her jump. It was Cormac's secretary, Stella, heading home.

"Oh! Mrs Cunningham – you gave me a fright!" Stella laughed and put a hand to her chest.

"I'm sorry." Denise forced a laugh, but it helped alleviate her nerves.

"Have a nice evening!" Stella said breezily before disappearing into the lift.

Denise had always thought Stella was a nice friendly girl. Easy-going, filed her nails and chatted on the phone to her friends when she wasn't typing or answering the phone. Stella was well able for Cormac's rants because they went in one ear and out the other. You'd never find Stella handling an architect's meeting on behalf of her boss, like Jodhi did.

Denise steadied herself and entered the office, closing the door behind her.

The door of Cormac's office was open and she walked straight in. He was sitting, swivelling on his chair looking into space.

"What are you doing here?" he asked, seeing her.

While she thought of a reply he said, "We didn't get the Mill."

Say something, she shouted at herself! "When – when did you find out?"

"This afternoon – Edel Garry sent me an email."

"That's a shame."

She seemed not herself and he looked at her curiously.

"Cormac – I've come to say goodbye."

"Why? Where are you going?" There was a snigger in his voice.

"I've made a decision that I can't go on with our marriage, and so I'm leaving."

"I'm not really in the mood for this today. So can we play this game some other time?"

"There is no other time, because I'm leaving tonight."

"Leaving for where, for fuck's sake – back to the flats?" He laughed lightly.

"Thank you, Cormac. Thank you for just making this easier for me."

He studied her. "Are you being serious?"

"I've never been more serious."

"If this is some moneymaking scam of yours – try your best. I'll have the best solicitor. You don't even have a kid to support to claim maintenance – so you'll be getting nothing."

Denise shook her head. "You're unbelievable. And this is why I'm going – I can't deal with your attitudes and your vindictive and suspicious nature anymore. I'm going to take from this marriage what I brought into it – nothing."

"This isn't making sense. You're leaving and you don't want any money?" He nodded in realisation. "So who are you screwing?"

"His name doesn't matter."

Cormac slammed the table. "I knew it! I always knew I couldn't trust you."

"You know, the funny thing is you could trust me. All those times with your disparaging remarks about me having an affair and finding myself out on the streets if I did – the thought never crossed my mind once. I never dreamed of cheating on you. It was your attitude and your aggression and our arguments that made me realise when I met someone else that there is something else out there. Something soft and caring."

"And who is this soft and caring person?"

"It doesn't matter who he is. You don't know him."

"Try me."

She sighed. "Ryan Cantwell."

"As in Aston Construction?" Cormac whooped with laughter. "I would love to shake this man by the hand! First he takes Michael –"

"Who you pushed away."

"Then he takes the Mill –"

"Which you never had in the first place."

"And now he takes my wife! And as for you . . . he was on your stupid committee, wasn't he? The first rich guy who gives you the eye and you're off!"

"It wasn't like that. Me and Ryan knew each other a long time ago. We went out before I even met you. We just found each other again."

"Well, isn't that romantic! After all these years you find love with each other again. And what was I – the filler-inner?"

"You're in no position to judge me. Not with the amount of affairs you've had."

He slammed his hands on the table. "I've never been unfaithful to you! Not once!"

"What are you talking about – you've one of the worst reputations in town," she spat. "I hear them whispering in earshot of me. I've had to put up with the public humiliation for years."

"I have never slept with anybody else but you during the course of our marriage, and that I swear." He looked at her directly.

"But who are all those women you hang around with?" She was exasperated and confused.

"They're friends or acquaintances. But I never sleep with them."

She rubbed her forehead. "But if I'd known that all along – why did you never tell me?"

"You never brought it up – apart from making snide comments occasionally."

"But the whole city thinks –"

"The whole city thinks a lot of things about me. They want to believe a lot of things about big bad Cormac Cunningham. So – I have money. So – I like to go out and have a few drinks. Women like Barbara, they flock to men like me. But do you honestly think I would ever consider them? As if they could ever replace my feelings for you? You know, I always knew this day would come. Always knew you'd be telling me you had gone off with another man."

"Did your fear of it help it happen?"

"Don't try and blame me –"

"I'm not, Cormac. I take full responsibility for ending our marriage. But I only take half responsibility for our marriage. The arguments, the aggression –"

"They were fun in the beginning." He smiled as he shook his head. "I loved how you could stand up to me, but I resented you for it at the same time."

"The rows just started getting way out of hand."

"I just always feared you never really loved me, that you were just here for the money."

"And nothing I could do could ever convince you otherwise. Long after I didn't need it any more, you still thought that's what I stayed for." She sighed deeply. "Now I have to go. We're flying to London tonight. I am really sorry." She turned to walk out.

"You want to know something? In the first year of our marriage. Remember? When we could still be tender to each other without thinking we were showing weakness? I had a dream. I dreamt there was another guy, and I walked in and the two of you were together, holding hands, looking happy. And then you looked up and you saw me, but you were so consumed in your own happiness that you couldn't see it was breaking my heart. And I turned and walked out. And you got up and came running out after me and you said if I wanted, that you would leave this other guy and come back to me. But I could see you didn't really want to and I knew I could fight for you. I knew that in forty or fifty years' time we could look back on a life together. But I told you to go back to him and be happy. And you turned and went back to him. And I woke up crying. Because I knew it would happen to us someday, and I had to protect myself by building up a wall against you."

Denise was now close to tears. "Oh Cormac! If only we could have been more honest with each other. If only we could show our vulnerable and tender side to each other without being frightened of – I don't know what – losing face, losing control." She wiped away her tears. "I have to go, or I'll miss my plane."

She walked out quickly.

67

Lisa looked around Hugh's house at Glenwood, the interior expertly put together by Susan Haughey.

"Well?" he asked.

"It's fab. Very Hollywood."

"Which is what I am, baby!"

"True. And the great thing is you have total privacy and security here," said Lisa.

"No deranged fans jumping out of showers at me."

"Yeah, you can have as many epileptic fits here as you want and no one will give a shit."

"Cheers!" he said sarcastically.

"You know what I mean." Lisa sat down and took another gulp of her vodka. "I gotta pull myself together next week and concentrate on work. You're a bad influence on me," Lisa accused.

"Hey, my management says you're the bad influence on me."

"They weren't saying that when I pulled you out of the

gutter last week when you were having your fit."

"I guess I should say thanks for that. But now maybe you can see what I put up with. The fucking pressure I'm under . . . all the time." Hugh shook his head.

"You know, not one word from Michael. After all these years, he's just sailed on with his life without a backward look."

They both sighed and at the same time said: "Poor me!"

* * *

The black Nissan followed Denise as she pulled abruptly out of the carpark at The Pavilions and made her way back to Glenwood. Denise, usually a controlled and cool driver was breaking the speed limit in places, and the Nissan nearly lost her a couple of times. Then she pulled up to the gateway of Glenwood, punched in her code and drove into her driveway. She got out of her car and went into the house. The Nissan parked in its usual spot in a wooded lay-by across from the entrance of Glenwood where the driveway of No 1 Glenwood could just be seen.

68

Eamonn Ruan could see directly through the iron gates at the front of Glenwood into the Cunninghams' drive.

"She's been in there about fifteen minutes. Let's go," said Anthony beside him.

"Let's hope she's a quiet one," said Eamonn, as he started the car's engine and pulled out of the lay-by across the quiet country road and into the gateway. Opening his window he pressed '78787' into the control panel.

They drove down the main estate road and slid the car into the driveway, parking it by the garage hidden from view by the high walls around the house.

The curtains were drawn in the front of the house. They quickly put on balaclavas and, getting out of the car, rushed down the side of the house to the back and to the patio doors. Eamonn Ruan hoped she would be a quiet one. Like the one last year. An industrialist's daughter. They held her in a darkened room for two days and the family paid up pronto. No press, no guards involved. The secret was not to be greedy. Don't ask for millions, but a couple of hundred thousand that these families would be quite willing to pay for the return of their loved ones. The planning was what was important. Get to know their every move, so you knew their patterns and just when to strike. But as slow as the planning, the execution had to be as fast as lightning. They would have Denise Cunningham in the boot of the car before she even knew what was happening.

Looking through the patio doors, they couldn't see her. Anthony had the patio doors lifted in a few seconds, and they quickly entered the house. Crossing the room silently, the sound of the bleeping indicated to them that the alarm was on and Eamonn quickly went to the panel inside the patio and pressed in the code. Then they separated and Anthony went out one door into the hallway while Eamonn went through the double doors into the dining room and into the lounge. Seeing no sign of her as they silently searched the downstairs, they crept up the stairs and into the bedrooms.

A minute later they came out and silently looked at each other. Then downstairs again.

After a thorough search of the house Eamonn whispered, "Where is she?"

* * *

Denise sat in silence as Ryan pulled into the airport car-park. He reached over and held her hand.

"Are you all right?" he asked.

Her eyes lost their faraway look and she nodded and smiled at him. They got out of the car. Ryan took her case and his luggage and they walked towards the terminal.

She remembered an hour ago sitting on their bed in Glenwood staring at her packed suitcase, remembering the conversation with Cormac. Finally, Ryan had rung her mobile, jolting her into reality.

"We'd better hurry or we'll miss the plane," he urged. She had got up, lifted her suitcase, taken a final look around the house and then left through the patio doors. Then she had gone to Ryan through her familiar route through the gardens.

And now here she was at check-in about to embark on her new life.

Ryan quickly went through the procedures and then an air hostess met them and brought them through to the VIP lounge.

"I was thinking, tonight we'll just take it easy, all right? You've had a hard day. So I'll just open a bottle of wine and we'll drink it at the apartment. In the morning, we'll hit the West End. You're going to need lots of new clothes if that's all you've brought with you." He smiled and indicated her suitcase. "Then tomorrow, if you feel like it – dinner out. Anywhere you want – The Ivy, whatever. There's a couple of functions I'm invited to, but it's entirely up to you if you want us to attend." He reached over and took her hands. "I'm going to make it my mission that you enjoy every day of your new life."

* * *

Cormac sat in his office with the lights off looking out the window. He felt very empty. He didn't know what to do. She had left. Finally gone out the door. Finally done what he always feared she would do. He wanted to hate her. He wanted to go out with Barbara and all his friends and show the world he didn't need anybody. But the reality of her not being there when he got home. Of not being there tomorrow. He turned quickly and picked up his phone.

* * *

"I've searched everywhere – she's not here!" There was panic in Anthony's voice.

"She has to be. We saw her coming in the front door. Her car's still there. She hasn't gone back out."

"Maybe the house has a panic room?"

"They don't. I've checked all the plans," said Eamonn.

"I don't like this. Let's get the fuck out of here. It could be a set-up. Maybe Barbara has sold us out."

"She wouldn't dare. She knows her life wouldn't be worth living. And she relies on feeding information about her friends to feed her drug habit."

"What will we fucking do then?"

"Search the bleeding place again."

* * *

Cormac drove frantically out to the airport, praying that he wouldn't be stopped by the guards. Praying he would get there on time. He picked up his mobile again and rang his friend Tony who was a chief at Dublin Airport.

"I'm nearly there," Cormac said to his friend.

"I'm waiting for you at the main entrance. You know you owe me big-time on this, Cormac. Breaking procedures like this . . ."

"I will love you forever for doing this for me."

* * *

"This is fucking weird. I'm getting out of here," Anthony went to walk to the patio doors.

Eamonn pulled him back and grabbed him by the neck.

"You're not going anywhere. I've been setting this one up for a long time, and I'm not leaving here without a pay cheque. Now we've managed to get inside one of the poshest estates in Dublin, which means this place is full of millionaires. If we can't find the Cunningham bitch we'll keep going till we find somebody else!"

* * *

"Maybe I'll take a few days off work and I can properly show you around," said Ryan.

His words jolted her out of her near-trance and she turned to him and smiled.

"Sorry?"

He reached over and took her hand. "Are you all right?" She blinked a few times and nodded.

"Ladies and gentlemen, could all passengers for Aer Lingus flight EI 107 make their way immediately to Gate 14 for boarding," said the announcement over the loudspeaker.

"Come on. That's us," said Ryan smiling.

"Denise!" came a shout as the door of the VIP lounge swung open.

Denise looked around and her eyes widened as she saw Cormac standing there.

Cormac's first reaction was relief to see he hadn't missed her. His second reaction was a rage to see her holding another man's hand. He walked quickly over to them.

Denise's heart began to palpitate and she stood up. Ryan stood up alongside her, holding her hand tightly.

"Cormac! What are you doing here?" she asked.

"What the fuck do you think I'm doing here? I've come for you!"

"Denise? Do you want me to –" began Ryan, recognising who Cormac was.

"Just shut the fuck up, you!" snapped Cormac. "And let go of my wife's hand!"

"She's not your wife any more. She's left you," said Ryan.

"What kind of a fucking menace are you?" Cormac stared at Ryan. "Creeping around taking what doesn't belong to you. Do you know something? You're welcome to Michael Farrell, and you're welcome to the fucking Mill, but you're *not* welcome to my wife!"

"I think that's her decision and I think she's made it, don't you?"

Cormac looked at his wife. "Denise, I'm asking you to change your mind. I'm begging you to. I'm no good without you. You told me once that your life started the day you met me . . .well, my life started the day I met you too."

Ryan felt a wrench as Denise untangled her fingers from his. She started to massage her temples.

"I can't take this!" she said.

"You're upsetting her!" snapped Ryan. "Why don't you just go? We have everything planned. We've planned the rest of our lives together."

"You're very good at planning. I've never met you before but I can read you like a book. Planning and scheming. I might be many things, but at least what you get is what you see."

"Well, she doesn't like what she sees in you."

The loudspeaker came on: "Could all remaining passengers for Aer Lingus 107 make their immediate way to Gate 14 for final boarding."

Ryan bent down to pick up his brief-case and put his arm around Denise

"We'd better go quickly," he whispered softly.

Cormac stepped closer and the three could hear each other breathe.

"Was that true?" Denise asked as a tear fell down her cheek. "That you were never unfaithful to me?"

"I never could have been," answered Cormac.

Ryan turned her gently and they started walking to the exit.

"Denise! You can't go!" pleaded Cormac. "You belong to me!"

"Not any more," said Ryan. "She's mine now."

"I don't belong to anybody!" Denise said loudly, stopping abruptly. "I'm nobody's property! Nobody owns me!"

"You're wrong, Denise!" said Cormac. "You're my property and you belong to me! But do you know something? I belong to you just as much. That's what we're about. We belong to each other. Despite everything." She stared into his eyes. "Come home to me!" Cormac reached out his hand.

Denise turned slowly to Ryan. "I'm sorry, Ryan . . ."

Ryan tightened his arm around her, disbelief written all over his face. "Don't do this to me, Denise."

"I don't want to hurt you . . ." she said.

"In my experience people who say that are just about to do that," said Ryan.

"I understand him. And I don't think he understands me at all . . . but he loves me and he needs me. My life didn't make sense until I met him. No matter how bad our marriage has become, he's still my life. I didn't have a life before him . . ."

"Does that include when you went out with me?" asked Ryan.

"I can't go to London with you, Ryan. I'm sorry. I've no excuse. Will you be all right?"

Ryan shrugged. "Ah . . . yeah."

She leaned forward and kissed his forehead and then walked away from him to Cormac. Cormac and Denise put their arms around each other and Ryan watched them walk away.

Just before they left the lounge, Denise turned around and waved to him and he waved back and then they were gone.

69

"Will you turn off that shite!" pleaded Hugh. Lisa had been listening to "I'll Say Goodbye To Love," and "Love Don't Live Here Any more," repetitively on the CD all evening.

"Why did he do it to me?" said Lisa.

"Will you change the fucking record and I don't mean just that shite on the CD player. He's moved on with his life. He didn't want you. Get over it and find somebody else."

"Who? They aren't exactly queuing up for me. It's okay for you. You're famous – they hide in showers to jump out at you. They jump out of windows to get away from me."

"I think you're the one person in the world who's more self-obsessed than me." Hugh swigged on his beer.

"I'm not self-obsessed."

"Oh, yes, you fucking are. You never talk about anything but yourself. This bloke Michael you're always going on about – did you ever talk to him about him? Did you ever ask him about him or his life – or did you just moan on all the time about yourself?"

"I could take this from anyone, but I can't take it from you – Mr Vanity Personified!"

"I know what I am, but you haven't a clue what you are. Take a break from yourself and give everyone else a break as well. You might just find out you have a good life."

"What have I to be happy about?"

"Everything – if you could stop being so fucking negative about yourself."

"It's just – I suppose, I'm so used to my mother saying negative things about me, I just take up where she leaves off."

"Well stop it, because you're just giving yourself an excuse not to get on with your life. You're so blinded by this Michael guy, you can't see what's under your nose."

"Under my nose?"

"For fuck's sake! I'm not just hanging around you all the time because you can drink me under the table, you know!"

"You!" She started to laugh. "And me?"

"Why not?"

"Because we're as disastrous as each other. Anyway you live in a different world . . ."

He reached forward and kissed her.

"Just going up to the bathroom, won't be too long?" Hugh smiled and padded upstairs.

* * *

They knew No 2 Glenwood was a showhouse and so quickly moved on to No 3. There were no lights on and the curtains were open. Realising there was nobody there, they moved to the next house. The curtains were drawn and they scouted around the back. They observed the blonde woman through a chink in the curtains, on her own, deep in thought.

"We'll take her," said Eamonn.

"But who is she?"

"Who gives a fuck? Just another trophy wife of some rich bastard, who'll pay up a couple of hundred thousand to get her back. Let's get the car."

They went back for the car and, starting the engine and keeping the lights off, silently drove it into Hugh's spacious driveway.

"This is not what we usually do. We usually have it down to a T. We don't even know who she is!"

"She'll tell us once we have her and then we'll know!"

* * *

Lisa sat in thought. Why was Hugh Fitzroy coming on to her? He could have any woman in Dublin. He'd had every woman in Dublin. Maybe he saw her as just another groupie.

This was odd – the first man who was coming onto her in ages was a movie star. Maybe he genuinely liked her. She was so lost in thought that she didn't notice the two men come into the sitting-room until they were standing in front of her. Looking at their dark clothes and their balaclavas, she first thought it was Hugh playing a joke on her. But who was the other guy? Before she had time to think, she noticed one of them was holding a gun by his side.

"What is this?" she demanded.

"Get up!" demanded one of the men.

"Hugh?"

One of the men reached forward and grabbed her by the wrist, yanking her to her feet.

She screeched in terror.

He twisted her arm around her back, and she felt the gun in her back as she was propelled to the back door.

"Let me go!" she shouted. And then a hand was clasped over her mouth as they continued to move her on quickly.

At that moment, Hugh walked back into the lounge.

"Hey – time for another bottle of vodka, methinks," he said.

The he froze at the sight of the two men forcing Lisa through the kitchen.

"Shit!" said Eamonn, seeing the man enter the lounge.

He leapt forward to knock him out. And then recognised him as Hugh Fitzroy. A hundred thoughts went through his head. First of all there was panic that the kidnap was being witnessed by somebody of Fitzroy's fame. His presence would mean this would not be a low-profile kidnap without press involvement. Then his mind was working in a different direction.

"Get on the fucking floor!" he shouted at Hugh.

Hugh, looking at the gun, carefully got down on his knees. This was all his worst nightmares coming together.

"Who else is here?" demanded Eamonn.

"N-n-n-no one," said Hugh, starting to shake.

Eamonn went to the curtains, pulled off the ropes and tied Hugh's hands behind his back. Then he quickly scoured the house and saw there was nobody else there.

"We're taking him," Eamonn said.

"That's Hugh Fiztroy!" shouted Anthony.

"We're just about to go into a different league." He threw ropes at Anthony. "Tie her up and we'll lock her in the wardrobe upstairs."

Lisa was squirming and her heart was jumping so fast she thought she would have a heart attack. All she could do was start praying.

"Come on – you're coming with us." Eamonn hauled Hugh up on his feet.

Hugh's shaking started getting worse. Suddenly he was shaking violently. Eamonn stared at him, realising that this wasn't normal. Hugh fell fully to the ground and went into a full epileptic fit.

"What the fuck is wrong with him?" shouted Anthony.

Eamonn kicked him and shouted, "Get up!"

The action caused Hugh's shaking to get even worse.

"He's going to die!" said Anthony.

Taking advantage of his attention being drawn away, Lisa twisted free and raced to the kitchen. Anthony bounded after her, but she got to the panic button and pressed it hard, then collapsed in a huddle on the floor.

"You stupid bitch! What's the password?" demanded Anthony.

"Too late! Come on!" shouted Eamonn and the two of

them disappeared out of the patio doors. As Lisa heard a car start up in the front, she jumped up and pressed the panic button again and again.

* * *

The black Nisson tore up the gateway.

"Why won't it open?" shouted Anthony as they looked at the unmoving gates.

"There's a panel on the inside as well – put in the fucking code!"

Anthony opened his window and punched in '78787'.

They waited but the gates wouldn't move.

"Try it again!" screamed Eamonn.

But as Anthony pressed the digits again, they realised that there was a separate code to get out of Glenwood.

Then three security cars arrived at the gates at the same time.

* * *

Cormac and Denise got into his car in the airport car-park and, leaning forward, kissed.

"It's hard to get rid of a bad thing," said Denise.

"The way I've been behaving I could be accused of trying hard to get rid of you. Denise, I thought you were gone forever . . . I don't know what I would have done."

"Is this us being honest with each other?" she asked.

"At last. I think we need to start being kinder to each other."

She nodded. "I think we're both tired and need to start

being careful with ourselves and each other . . . let's go home."

As Cormac drove them out to Glenwood, a series of police cars with their sirens blaring overtook them, followed by an ambulance.

"Seems to be a bit of activity tonight," said Cormac.

"That's an understatement," Denise said. Her hand was resting on his leg as he drove.

They pulled into the gateway at Glenwood where a police car was parked.

"Can I help you?" asked the guard, shining his torch in at them.

"We live in No 1. What's going on?"

"There's been a disturbance at one of your neighbour's houses. Nothing for you to be worried about. There will be an officer calling to you tomorrow to see if you've noticed anything strange recently."

Cormac nodded and drove into their driveway.

"Maybe I should go down and check out what happened," said Cormac.

Denise reached over and kissed him. "No. Let's just go inside."

* * *

Honey came barging into the hospital, followed quickly by Paul.

They found Lisa sitting in the waiting area, a bandage around her wrist, a guard by her side.

"Are you all right?" Honey threw her arms around her.

The comfort of her mother's arms made her want to

burst out crying, but she fought the tears.

"I'm fine. Nothing serious."

"What happened?" demanded Paul.

"It looks like your daughter got mixed up in an attempted kidnap of Hugh Fitzroy," informed the guard.

"I knew hanging around that Hollywood trash would lead you into trouble!" said Honey.

"And this happened at Glenwood?" Paul was incredulous.

"Yes. Your daughter acted quickly and pressed the panic button, and then the kidnappers were trapped in the development as they didn't have the code to get out."

"I knew my smart genes would display themselves in you someday," said Honey. "Now, let's get out of here. I want to put seven hot whiskeys in you, and myself, and put you to bed."

"I want to stay and wait to see how Hugh is," said Lisa.

"Don't worry about him. He's got his own family and management and thousands of fans to worry about him. Come on, I hate hospitals."

Honey put an arm around Lisa and directed her to the door.

"No, Mum, I want to stay to see him and make sure he's okay."

"Darling, you just don't get away with this Florence Nightingale act. You've already had enough excitement for one night and we're parked on a double yellow line. Now, let's split!"

"Thanks for everything," said Lisa to the guard. "Will you tell Hugh to call me as soon as he comes round?"

"Of course," said the guard.

70

"It's after midnight – what are you doing here?" said Ryan, as he entered Jodhi's office at Aston in the London docklands.

She looked up from her paperwork, surprised. "I needed to have this finished for our meeting tomorrow."

"You know what they say." He put an opened bottle of wine and two glasses on her desk. "All work and no play . . ."

She took off her glasses. "I am dull anyway. Let's face it: I'm never going to win any awards for my partying skills. But why are *you* here? Where's Denise?"

"She's still in Dublin." He sat down.

Jodhi made a face, perplexed.

"She couldn't go through with it." He filled their glasses.

"Couldn't go through with it!" Jodhi was astounded. "But you had everything planned!"

"I know. We were at the airport, ready to board the

plane and next thing Cormac turns up and . . ." He didn't finish the sentence but looked down at the floor.

"I'm sorry, Ryan."

"Thats what she said, that she was sorry. She wouldn't be able to give an explanation. She never gave me one all those years ago."

Jodhi was incensed with anger. "But that's outrageous! She can't treat you like that!"

Jodhi rarely gave displays of emotion and he was touched by her outburst.

"It's my own fault. I knew what I was dealing with. She was someone else's wife, for God's sake! The whole thing was wrong. I just couldn't help myself. She just had this strange power over me over the years. It was like no matter what I achieved, I would only feel I had got to where I want to be when she agreed to be with me. Like I did things in my career just thinking that she would be impressed by what I did. I suppose when she walked out on me all those years ago, she made me feel so worthless and I've been trying to get that sense of worth back ever since."

"And now you have to go through it all again. How dare she! I'd like to slap her across the face!"

"It's really not her fault. She just couldn't feel she could leave her life in the end. No matter what I was offering her, I'm still not what she needs . . . Maybe that's it. Maybe what she needs is to be needed. And Cormac needs her."

"But *you* need her!"

"No – I *want* her – there's a big difference. I'd never be reliant on her though, not like Cormac is. You know, I prepared myself all along to be let down by her. All along, I thought to myself, she might not leave him – so prepare yourself for that. But it was just in the last couple of days I believed we were really going to be together – and that's the cruellest trick . . . I made such a fool of myself. Going to Dublin, joining Forward, buying in Glenwood. My rivals would have a good laugh if they knew."

"I think you've had a lucky escape, Ryan."

"Yeah . . . maybe . . . just, where to from here?"

"What do you mean? You've everything going for you."

"Yeah – I'd better just keep reminding myself of that."

71

10 weeks later.

The front page of *The Independent Property Supplement* read:

"The much anticipated launch of Heavey's Mill is taking place this weekend. Although building has not yet begun on the Mill, an extensive marketing suite has been built on the site, complete with two purpose-built show apartments. This is the first development being launched in the new Harbour District. Eyebrows have been raised at the high prices of the apartments which surpass even traditionally exclusive areas such as Ballsbridge. It is generally agreed that the high prices are a reflection of the fact that Ski Computers are basing their European Headquarters at the Mill. But Head of Sales at the site's developers Aston Construction, Michael Farrell, disagreed that the apartments are on the expensive side and believes they offer good value for money. 'There are few investments as sound as an apartment in Heavey's Mill at the moment. Buyers are being offered a chance to invest in an area at a very early stage of its development. In five years, when the Harbour district has

matured, it will be one of the most sought-after areas in the capital. Also the presence of Ski Computers at the Mill means this is a no-risk investment ensuring premium rents and excellent capital appreciation.' The marketing suite opens this Saturday at twelve o'clock and booking deposits are 10,000 euros."

Ali looked at the accompanying photos of the show apartments and had to admit the spread looked terrific. She was sitting at her computer at work. Barry had asked her to write a background feature on Ski Computers, as their announcement that they were setting up their European Headquarters in Dublin was causing much excitement in the business community and was another huge vote of confidence in the Irish economy. Ski Computers was an intriguing and inspiring story. Its founder, in true American IT folklore style, was a computer nerd who on graduating from university found he was rejected by one hundred and fifty computer firms. Finally despairing of ever getting employment, he started his own business in his parents' garage. Ten years later Ski Computers had taken the world by storm, being quoted as one of the top ten companies on the NASDAQ. But everyone knew that and Ali was trying to come up with different angles to actually make the feature interesting. Their PR department basically was dishing out success quotes and figures that were boring and predictable. Barry had given her the feature to write, thinking she could use Michael as an in. So far he hadn't been much help.

Her mobile rang.

"Hi, Michael. Well done for getting the front of the *Independent Property*. You must be delighted!"

"We're all thrilled. You can't buy exposure like that!"

"I'm sure buying a double-page advertisement for the Mill inside the supplement did help a little in getting you the front page!"

"How I love my cynical girlfriend. What would I do without you to keep me grounded?"

"Listen, now you promised me, no crazy stunts tomorrow at this launch, okay? I don't want to hear you landed on the roof of the Mill in a hot-air balloon dressed as a preacher or anything. Do you hear me?"

"I promise! It's going to be a straightforward launch. No gimmicks from me."

"And listen, you owe me, mate. You wouldn't be at Aston if it wasn't for me, remember?"

"I remember. How could I forget?"

"So how about doing me a favour back and helping me with this feature about Ski. I'm getting nowhere with them."

"Didn't you phone the number for their public relations department I gave you?"

"Sure I rang it, and nodded off to sleep while listening to her quoting me facts and figures. Come on, I need to give my readers something juicy here. You should at least be able to get me an interview with the nerd who owns the damned company. I could find out if he has ever done anything more exciting than sprinkle sugar on his cornflakes in the morning."

"I don't think I can manage that. The nerd, as you

kindly call him, never gives press interviews. I'm sorry, I know I haven't been much help, I've been distracted with this launch, but honestly I can't think of any exciting angle you can approach this from. I mean it's a Seattle computer firm with a nerd heading it – you ain't going to be able to sex that up. I doubt the fella has even had a car parking fine."

"Thanks a lot. Well, will you have a word with Ryan and see if he can come up with anything?"

"Will do. What time will you be home tonight?"

"Around seven."

"I'll be waiting for you with a smile in my face."

"Lovely! See you then."

She hung up and continued trawling through the internet looking for any information she could find.

"Ski Computers announces European Headquarters to be located in Dublin"

"Five hundred hi-tech computer jobs on way to Harbour Area"

"The Boom Goes on – Ski For Dublin"

She ran her mouse down the screen to read further headings.

"Ski expands into central Europe – acquires land outside Budapest for new European Headquarters."

Ali looked at the date of the heading. It was from eight months ago, before Ski decided to change its headquarters to Dublin. The Hungarians must have been furious, reasoned Ali. It was a big loss to their economy, in terms of jobs and prestige. She wondered what Ryan offered them to come to Dublin. It certainly must have been an offer they couldn't refuse.

She continued to trawl through the internet looking for inspiration for the feature.

Barry popped his head in around the door.

"We're going for a pint after work if you want to join us."

"I wish I could. But I'm stuck on this stupid feature on Ski Computers."

"Can't your lover boy help you?"

"He's too wrapped up in himself. Ski Computers seem clean as a whistle, Barry. Nothing to drag out of their closet. They're just one big happy family with a well-adjusted work force and an environmentally-friendly approach."

"Listen, don't worry about it. Just do a general story about what they're looking for in the Irish workforce, how hard is it to get a job there. What exact kind of jobs are going to be going there etc."

"Okay. I'll just get started and see you over in the pub in a little while."

Barry left and Ali rooted out one of the press releases she had got from Ski. She dialled the main switchboard number in America.

"Can you put me through to Personnel, please?"

"Hi, my name is Lauren. How may I help you?" came the friendly American voice.

"I was just looking for a couple of jobs specs for the new European offices."

"What area are you working in?" asked Lauren.

"I'm a computer programmer." Ali knew if they got a

hint she was a journalist she would be quickly transferred to PR and she wouldn't get what she was looking for.

"You've got good English, so that's an advantage," complimented Lauren.

What did the silly cow think they spoke in Ireland, Ali wondered.

"Okay, we're not recruiting just now for that, but interviews will begin in two months. So it would be good if you could register with us now and then we can contact you for an interview."

Great, thought Ali – no joy here.

"I'm actually looking for a job spec and a little more information. Salary scales, that kind of thing."

"Uh huh. That's no problem. But I'm not taking details directly. We've appointed a recruitment agency in Europe you can register with and get further information from, okay?"

"All right." More red tape – thought Ali.

"Okay. Got a pen? The address of our agency is Worldwide Recruitment, Budaski Ut, Budapest and their number is –"

"Budapest?"

"Sure, and their number is –"

"But why are you using a recruitment agency in Budapest to recruit in Dublin?"

"Dublin?" Lauren sounded confused for a moment and then spoke quickly. "Oh, I'm afraid we're not recruiting for Dublin just now," and she hung up the phone.

72

After the Hugh Fitzroy kidnap, eight houses in Glenwood went up for sale immediately, amid security fears. This was regardless of the fact that it was the security system of the development that had trapped the kidnappers as they were unable to get out. Among the eight houses that went on the market, one belonged to Hugh Fitzroy, one to Ryan Cantwell and another to Cormac and Denise Cunningham.

* * *

Lisa put down the phone in her office at Farrell's or as it had recently been renamed Cunningham Auctioneers. After lengthy and tricky legal negotiations, the Cunningham family had bought Michael completely out of the firm. And his house on Adelaide Road had also been sold and so that was the end of all connection between them and Michael. Between her and Michael. It was hard to believe that after all these years he was completely out of her life.

After the kidnap attempt on Hugh, Lisa had taken a while off from work to recover. During that time her father had taken the opportunity to quickly sweep into the offices at Farrell's and fire half the staff who he perceived as loyal to Michael. He then proceeded to appoint a new chief executive who happened to be a married man in his forties, with four children, a teetotaller who seemed to be very religious as well. The man seemed to have no sense of humour. In fact, Lisa suspected Paul had searched high and low for a person who would have the least in common with Lisa for fear she might make a new drinking buddy. Still he seemed good at his job and made sure everything was paid on time and ran smoothly. In other words Lisa could get back to her old life.

In fact she was expecting Honey at any minute to collect her to go to lunch. After that night at Glenwood, all the papers had been full of how there had been an attempted kidnap on Hugh Fitzroy. But as Lisa had constantly re-run the night's events in her head she knew the kidnappers had no idea Hugh was there until he appeared. The kidnappers were shocked when they saw Hugh. She had been desperately worried about Hugh and had tried to get in contact with him countless times. But after the kidnap attempt, his management wouldn't let anybody make contact with him and he was whisked out of the country back to California. They weren't going to take any more risks with their investment. According to the papers he was under virtual house arrest in his Beverly

Hills mansion. She knew he would hate that and felt really sorry for him. She really missed Hugh and in fact thought about him much more than she did about Michael. She remembered their conversation before the kidnappers had broken in. She remembered how he had kissed her. And now she'd never know if they could have had something.

Honey barging into her office interrupted her thoughts.

"You're going to have to tell that new girl on Reception to put on a bit of lippy. It's not a great image when the first thing customers see is a pasty face," she said. "Come on, I've booked The Shelbourne for two."

Lisa reached over for her handbag

"Have you put on weight?" asked Honey, casting a critical eye over Lisa as she stood up. Lisa stopped and looked at her mother and she thought back to the last conversation she had with Hugh and how he told her to stop being negative about herself.

"Mum – why did you say that?" Lisa asked.

"Because I think it's true!" Honey said back.

"But did you ever stop to think that what you say might hurt me? Do you ever stop to think before you speak that you might be saying something hurtful to me?" Lisa looked earnestly at her mother.

Honey stood still and looked deeply in to her daughter's face for a while, thinking hard.

"Oh, will you stop being so melodramatic and get a move on!" she said loudly, turning briskly and walking out the door. "There's a lovely new Manager at the Hotel and I want you to meet him. He's from good stock and if you play your cards right he might even ask you out. Of course, not that you will play your cards right."

As Honey continued talking loudly, Lisa shook her head and smiled before following her out.

73

Edel Garry drove up the road leading to Heavey's Mill the afternoon of the launch. She had classical music blaring from the radio, but it wasn't enough to drown out the screaming of her four children in the back seat, or the shouting of Des beside her as he tried to chastise them. The first thing she noticed was the gigantic flag hanging down the full length of the Mill with the words: *'Welcome To The Future – Your Future.'* Yep, Michael Farrell sure was unbeatable when it came to the wow factor. The second thing she noticed was the number of cars parked around the Mill. There must have been three or four hundred cars there. She parked the car.

"Now this is Mummy's work, so if you could all be on your best behaviour," Edel requested and she got out of the car and herded them towards the marketing suite.

The marketing suite had been built in the courtyard of the Mill. It was a dramatic glass structure that had models of the future development on glass tables inside. On the walls were plasma televisions everywhere offering virtual reality tours of the apartments and the developments. Logos for Ski Computers were everywhere, and the place was thronged with buyers. The sales reps from Aston were run off their feet taking orders and answering questions. Cheques for 10,000 were being handed over to agents as if they were confetti. Edel was impressed. She saw Michael in the midst of several potential buyers answering their questions.

"I'm sorry, ground, first and second and third floors are all gone. Only fourth and fifth floor left, I'm afraid," she could hear him saying.

Her children were running amok and she realised it was a losing battle to try and control them in such a hectic environment. She made her way into the show apartments. They had constructed a replica one-bedroom and two-bedroom apartment at the marketing suite and as she entered the two-bedroom unit classical music was blaring. Again the show apartments were crowded with people viewing. They were truly stunning, with every attention to detail.

She came back into the marketing suite. It was like the gold rush, she thought.

"*And sold!*" she could hear Michael shout. "That's two hundred apartments sold. I'm sorry, ladies and gentlemen, there are no more available. It's cancellation only from now on."

She walked over to him. He was gulping down a glass of water.

"Two hundred apartments sold in two hours. Not bad

going!" she said to him.

"Not bad! It's fucking fantastic!" His adrenaline was high.

"Where's Ryan?"

"He couldn't make it over. He's in Budapest."

"Oh!"

She was disappointed. She had expected to be dealing a lot with Ryan Cantwell. But he seemed to never come to Dublin any more having appointed a series of project managers to get on with the job. Still, there was always Michael. She had been working quite close to him on the launch. He was so damned sure of himself, he was almost irresistible. But that girlfriend of his made him far too dangerous, she reminded herself.

She was distracted by a thundering crash and turning around she saw that two of her children had pulled one of the glass models of the Mill to the floor causing it to smash apart. The two children were subsequently crying uncontrollably.

"Looks like your kids are having a smashing time," commented Michael.

"Hmmm . . . where's Des gone to? Ah, there he is." Des had arrived over at the scene and was berating the two children.

Edel smiled at Michael. "We must do lunch next week," she said.

"Sure. Give me a call."

* * *

607

Michael came bounding into the apartment with a huge bunch of flowers.

Ali came out of the kitchen.

"We sold out in a couple of hours! Two hundred apartments snapped up like that!" He clicked his fingers. He kissed her, handed her the flowers and then threw himself on the sofa, his hands behind his head. "It was fucking magic! Even Edel Garry was impressed." He was talking fast and excitedly. "Although she coolly walked out after her kids had pulled the place apart. I was speaking to Ryan and he's over the moon. Really delighted. It's one massive fucking success! Do you know how much money I earned today? And now the house in Adelaide Road is sold and I'm getting the money from the auctioneers from those Cunningham bastards. We're rich! I think we should move on to something a bit bigger. What do you think?"

"I suppose. I kind of love my little apartment though."

"Ah, I know, darling. We'll just keep it and rent it out, so you'll still own it. How's that? You should have seen it there today. I had classical music blaring through the show apartments. I had models giving out free cocktails. The atmosphere was amazing. They were throwing booking deposits at us! We're in the money!" He punched the air. "And I owe it all to you. Showing me I was wasting my time with the Cunninghams, introducing me to Ryan. I know I haven't been much help with the feature about Ski you're writing. But now his launch is over, I'll get on to it for you. Even if I have to set up an interview for you with the nerd!"

"Ah, yes, my feature. I've been working away quietly on it myself. They're a bit of a strange company. I don't think they know what they're up to. I got through to the personnel department in the States and they seem to think that the European Headquarters are actually going to Budapest and not Dublin."

Michael's smile dropped and then he was smiling again. "Idiots! What were you ringing the personnel department for anyway?"

"Oh, I was grasping at straws and was going to find out their working conditions."

"Never mind all that, love, I'll sort out a great angle for you next week. I'll get Ryan to sort something for you."

"But then the woman in personnel I was speaking to got me wondering about what they had planned in Budapest. So I got messing on the internet and, do you know, Ski bought a considerable site in Budapest in 2004 for their headquarters."

"Well, everyone knows they were going to go to Budapest, but they scrapped that idea and decided to base themselves at Heavey's Mill."

"Sure – sure. But they are just going to lease the offices at Heavey's Mill – right. But they actually *bought* the site in Budapest. So I wondered what they were doing with the site there, after spending so much money on it. So I rang a contact we have at a Hungarian paper and asked him to check out for me what was happening at the site. And according to him the plant that started being built in 2005 is still being built and by the looks of it will be completed soon. And also there are signs all around the site saying that Aston Construction is building it."

Michael shrugged. "They must be going to lease it or something."

"But it doesn't make sense , does it?"

"Makes perfect sense to me. They bought a site, Ryan made them a great offer to come to Heavey's Mill, but they had half-built the plant in Budapest so they are finishing the construction and then they are selling it off."

"Which is all very well. Apart from when I rang Worldwide Recruitment in Budapest, the company that Ski told me to phone, they told me that officially they couldn't say anything but yes they were actively recruiting and they expected the Ski European offices in Budapest to be opened in four months. They even invited me in for an interview!"

Michael was beginning to look concerned. "I don't know what you're getting at."

"I'm wondering . . . supposing Ski European Headquarters are going to Budapest . . . then what the hell is going into the offices at Heavey's Mill?"

"You're making something out of nothing!. Why don't you relax and chill out and we'll have a nice bottle of wine?"

"No, Michael, something smells rotten here."

"You're Ali O'Mara – everything smells rotten to you!"

"If you can't tell me, then I'll ask Ryan. I've still got his number in my mobile." She picked up her phone and started looking through her numbers.

"Wait! Don't ring Ryan!"

"Why not? There's a mix-up and I want to get to the

bottom of it." She dialled his number and put her hand on her hip. "Ryan, hi, it's Ali O'Mara here."

Michael jumped up, grabbed the phone off her and turned it off.

"What is wrong with you?" he demanded.

"What's wrong with *you*? Give me back my phone!"

Michael ran his fingers through his hair "Look, you'll never understand how business works. So why don't you just stay out it?"

"Michael, I will not let this go till I find out exactly what is going on."

They stared at each other.

He eventually spoke. "Ski Computers are putting their European headquarters in Budapest."

"Go on," Ali demanded.

"Ryan tried everything he could to get Ski to come to Heavey's Mill when he went to Seattle. But they wouldn't agree to it. They had put too much planning into Budapest to change. More importantly they said Dublin would be too expensive to set up shop here. Wages are too high. They could do it for much cheaper in Budapest. We desperately needed to win the tender. Ryan came to an agreement with Ski that they would say they were relocating to Dublin, and we would keep this going for a period of a few months in return for a discount on the cost of building the offices in Budapest. By Ski saying they were coming to Heavey's Mill, we could win the tender, and then after a few months they would just make a quick announcement that they had decided to go to Budapest after all and we would have a new firm to go into

Heavey's Mill by then. It was no skin off Ski's nose as the building of their plant in Budapest won't be ready for a long while and they get their discount."

"So you all used deceit to get the Mill?" Ali was horrified.

"We pulled a bit of a scam to stop the Cunninghams getting the Mill, big fucking deal."

"Michael, it's deceitful beyond compare."

"Are you trying to tell me the Cunninghams wouldn't do the same?"

"I despise the way the Cunninghams do business. But I asked you once have you ever done anything illegal and you said no!"

"And I haven't. This isn't illegal."

"I'm ashamed of you." She shot her hand to her mouth and went to sit down. "All those people who have bought apartments today! They're buying there in the belief that Ski Computers are setting up shop there. They're paying over the odds because of that belief."

"It's no big deal. We'll have another firm in there before the apartments are taken over. It will be another two years before the first of the apartments are ready to be taken over anyway."

"When are you thinking of letting the world know that Ski isn't going into Heavey's Mill?"

"In about three months. When the Budapest offices are completed and they are ready to start work there."

"By then the two hundred people who put deposits down today will be tied into contracts and it will be too late for them to get out. Isn't that right?"

Michael said nothing.

"Isn't that right?" Ali shouted.

Michael nodded.

"This makes me sick. Who thought this up?" Not getting a response from him, she shouted again, *"Who thought this up?"*

"Ryan."

"And all that bullshit he fed me about a caring corporation! And you . . . oh, Michael you've just gone from being the Cunningham's henchman to Cantwell's."

"Listen, you really need to calm down on this, Ali. We'll get another firm in there – better than Ski, and all those people who bought today will be over the moon. They will be coming back in a couple of years with huge equity on their apartments, thanking their lucky stars they managed to get one today."

"That doesn't matter, Michael. You're duping those people into paying more for those apartments than they're worth."

"Who says they are being duped? Who says they are paying more? The market dictates what something is worth and the market decided today that apartments in Heavey's Mill were worth what people paid for them."

"The market was fed wrong information that inflated those prices." Ali ran her fingers through her hair in frustration.

He went over to her, went down on his knees and took her hands. "Think logically. Nothing exists at Heavey's Mill except a derelict Mill, yeah? Those people today are buying a dream, that's all – nothing more. Buying a dream that one day that will be a luxurious development. When they went into those show apartments which cost thousands to kit out, I can guarantee you the apartments they end up living in won't be a tenth as nice as them. Those people who bought today know that deep inside. But they still bought into the dream. In the same way they bought into the dream that a top international firm would be part of the development – and it will be. It just won't be Ski."

Ali listened intently and then pulled back her hands. "You're fucking good, Michael. You really are. But this is fraud. I've spent my whole life fighting against this and I can't allow it to happen."

"Why, oh fucking why are you so worked up? Do you honestly think those two hundred people who put their deposits down today give a shit about you? Do you honestly think those people would raise a hand to help you if you were in any kind of trouble? They are out for themselves, just like everyone else. They are buying those apartments because they think they can make money there. And they will, so just leave it, eh?"

"I can't, Michael."

Michael jumped up and started pacing the room. "And what do you want me to do then?"

"I want you to announce tomorrow that Ski Computers are not putting their European Headquarters at Heavey's Mill. And then allow those people who put deposits down to decide, knowing the truth, if they want to proceed with the purchase."

"Are you fucking mad?" Michael almost shouted. "I

can't do that."

"Because you would have two hundred deposits returned to you tomorrow."

"You're impossible. Do you know that? I would lose my position at Aston immediately."

"So, you can get another job."

"What do you want from me? I've already lost my company because of you. Farrell's Auctioneers is now Cunninghams' Auctioneers because I put my love for you first, didn't I? Didn't I?"

"I'm not disputing the fact." She got up quickly and took her mobile off the coffee table. "As I said, this is my life's work, exposing fraud. And if that includes you, then I've no choice. I really thought you were different. I really believed that you were really good, just kept the wrong company. If you won't tell the truth, then I have no choice but to." She began to dial a number.

"What are you doing?"

"I'm calling the paper – I'm going tell them about this swindle."

"And you accuse *me* of doing anything for my career! What about *you*? You're ready to throw our relationship away so you can get an exclusive? So you can get another journalism award? Oh, they'll love that! She cared so much to expose corruption she shopped her own partner. They'll throw awards at you."

"Hi, Vanessa, Ali here. Can you put me through to Barry, please?" Ali rubbed her nose and wiped her eyes.

Michael sat down on the couch and stared at her with pleading eyes.

"I did it for us, Ali. I've sacrificed everything for you – my company and my house. I'd do it all again."

Vanessa came back on the phone. "Ali, Barry says he's really busy. Can he call you back?"

"No, I need to speak to him. It's urgent."

Michael stood up and walked towards her. "What have you done to show me you care for me? Because you doing this means you're throwing away our relationship – putting your career and two hundred strangers before us."

She started crying as Michael enveloped her in a hug and started stoking her back.

"I did it for us. I love you. Trust me and I'll make it all right."

Barry's voice came on the mobile. "Yeah, Ali what is it? Ali?"

She turned the mobile off and allowed herself to continue to be hugged and rocked gently by Michael.

"I hate you for what you've done," she said between sobs. "Not just to those people today, but showing me how weak I am." She allowed the crying to flow freely as he continued to soothe her.

74

Cormac and Denise looked at the sprawling field that swept down to the sea on the outskirts of Galway.

"What do you think?" asked Cormac.

"It's a beautiful site. Fantastic views."

"I know all that!" snapped Cormac. "But what do you think of it as a vehicle for our company?"

"Well, excuse me! I'm still getting used to being consulted on decisions as opposed to just been told to turn up and smile for a photo for a property supplement."

"Seriously – yes or no?"

In the absence of being able to find building land in Dublin, Cormac and Denise had spent a month touring around the country looking at what was available outside the capital. The winner so far was this site with full planning permission for a housing estate.

"I think it's a wonderful property and I think we'd be mad to let it go. I think you could build an exclusive estate here of luxury houses. I think with those views and its

617

closeness to Galway city it would be a runaway success."

"Honey and Paul aren't too impressed. They said the idea of us moving out of Dublin is a step backwards and the Cunningham name will lose its status in Dublin." Honey had shouted the old catchphrase: *'To hell or to Connaught!*

"Honey and Paul are no longer in charge at Cunningham Homes – you are. And you're trying to make a forward decision that will ensure the company's survival, which is needing a lot of lateral thinking."

"And how would you feel about spending a good bit of time down here? We've already had a couple of moves in a short period of time," he said.

They had made a decision pretty quickly, when they had salvaged their marriage, to leave Glenwood and move back into the penthouse at The Pavilions.

"I'd like it. We could rent a house somewhere near the sea. And besides we can go back up to the penthouse any time we want."

"It would mean you wouldn't be able to attend all the meetings with your charity."

"I'll just tell them I'm winding down my workload for a little while. I'm sure they can survive without me. It would mean you won't be able to go to the Ice Bar as much." She was smirking.

"As if I've been there much recently anyway. And we'd be missing all the socialite functions."

Denise adopted a very serious look. "And worst of all, we wouldn't be able to make it to Honey and Paul's every Sunday."

Cormac pretended to be very serious as well. "In that

case – we've no option – we definitely have to buy it!"

They walked through the field.

"You know this would be a nice place to bring up a family," Denise mused.

Cormac stopped abruptly and stared at her in excitement. "You're not . . ..?"

"No, I'm not!" Denise snapped and, grabbing his arm, linked him as they continued to walk. "I'm just making an observation that one day it might be nice to raise kids in an area like this."

"One day? Well, even that is a major step forward."

"Look, are you going to make the call and put in a bid?"

Cormac slipped his phone out of his pocket and rang the estate agent.

"Hi there, Cormac Cunningham here. Just getting back to you about the property. I'm putting in an offer of the guide price."

Denise held her husband's arm tighter with excitement as they continued to walk.

Cormac stopped abruptly "What? When? How much? I'll have to talk to my accountant and get back to you . . . and my wife." Cormac snapped his mobile shut, put it back in his pocket and then kept walking. "Can you credit that?" he said, shaking his head in disbelief.

"What is it, Cormac?" Denise asked anxiously.

"They received another offer this morning. Half a million over the guide price."

"Oh no! What will we do now?"

"I was hoping you'd have the answer."

"Me?" Denise asked perplexed.

"After all – when we first started dating – you did promise that with my looks and your brains we'd go far."

THE END

Direct to your home!

If you enjoyed this book why not
visit our website:

www.poolbeg.com

and get another book delivered straight to
your home or to a friend's home!

POOLBEG

All orders are despatched within 24 hours.

Published by Poolbeg.com

This

MODEL LIFE

A. O'Connor

Top Irish model Audrey Driver is a well-known face around Dublin's social circles. And her connected solicitor boyfriend, Aran Murphy, is the perfect catch. Set to land a big American contract, Audrey wonders can life get any better than this?

PR guru, Peter Murphy, is at the peak of his game and the Childwatch Fashion Show will cement his reputation. His prestige-obsessed wife Lynn is pushing him to succeed and there is no room for mistakes.

Takeover Queen Chloe Gallagher has climbed to the top of Macken PR, thanks to an appetite for destruction and underhand tactics. She will stop at nothing to get what she wants and hates it when someone else is in the limelight.

As their paths cross, sparks fly, mettles are tested and they are forced to face up to their real strengths and weaknesses.

When things go pear-shaped there's nothing worse than reading about it in the newspapers.

ISBN 978-1-84223-197-5

Published by Poolbeg.com

Exclusive

A. O'Connor

Celebrity – glamorous, addictive, destructive

As manager of an exclusive nightclub, Kathryn Foy knows what celebrities want and makes sure they get it. Now it is her turn to take centre stage – but she is desperate to keep her personal life in the dark.

Party-animal Lana Curtis suddenly finds herself in the limelight when her tycoon father runs for election – not a good thing when you have an addictive personality and a dangerous lifestyle.

Rock-star Cathal Fitzgerald is well used to the glare of publicity. When he meets Lana, they become the latest golden couple. But he lives in fear of a shady past resurfacing.

Nicole Donnelly, psychotherapist, is delighted when her partner, Tony O'Brien, lands a job in celebrity magazine *Hi Life* – until he is seduced by the glitzy lifestyle. How far will she go to hold on to him? And how far will he go to succeed?

**THEIR LIVES ARE RULED BY CELEBRITY
– BUT THEN, ISN'T THAT TRUE OF US ALL?**

ISBN 978-1-84223-239-2